DEVOTIO: THE HOUSE OF MUS

By: William Kelso

Visit the author's website http://www.williamkelso.co.uk/

William Kelso is the author of:

The Shield of Rome

The Fortune of Carthage

Devotio: The House of Mus

Caledonia – Book One of the Veteran of Rome series

Hibernia – Book Two of the Veteran of Rome series

Britannia – Book Three of the Veteran of Rome series

Hyperborea – Book Four of the Veteran of Rome series

Germania – Book Five of the Veteran of Rome series

The Dacian War – Book Six of the Veteran of Rome series

Armenia Capta – Book Seven of the Veteran of Rome series

Devotio: The House of Mus

Published in 2013 by FeedARead.com Publishing – Arts Council funded

A CIP catalogue record for this title is available from the British Library.

To: Winston Churchill, saviour of his country

Chapter One - Honouring the Dead

PART ONE – Spring 298 BC - The Roman Colony of Sora

Gaius and his father strode along the path that ran alongside the Liris river. Out in the water a few children were playing and splashing about and laughing at an old fisherman who was berating them for disturbing his peace. Gaius was maturely built for an eighteen-year-old and on his chin, were the first wisps of a beard. A purple birthmark ran along his neck. His black hair was cut short and he was clad in a simple white woollen tunic with short sleeves. Cautiously he glanced at his father. The old man looked somber. Was he angry, upset? His father had not said a word since they had left Sora. Normally Gaius could judge his mood quite well but not today. The old man had said nothing when Gaius had jumped onto the speakers' platform in the forum, the market square of Sora. He had remained silent as Gaius had made his announcement to the large crowd and he had looked on stoically as Gaius's offer had been accepted with respectful clapping by the townsfolk. Gaius stirred uneasily and shifted his gaze to the river and the forest beyond. Surely the old man would not say no. If his father forbade the match then he, Gaius, was going to look like an idiot. But his family were in trouble and as eldest son it was his duty to prepare for the day when his father died. Then he would take over as head of the family. Gaius shrugged off the unease. His family needed to survive. They needed him. That was all that mattered and there was no going back. By now the whole colony would have heard about his challenge.

Gaius looked up at the snowcapped mountains to the north and east. His father's farm was a couple of miles away from the walled city of Sora. Their land came right up to the banks of the Liris. From the very beginning when, five years ago, the Roman and Latin colonists had first arrived in Sora and his father had taken over the abandoned farm, Gaius had loved the place. The farm with its generous land, clean air and the gentle fascinating river beside it, had offered so much space and potential for

3

adventure. It had been a world away from the cramped, dangerous and dirty home they'd had in Rome. The original Volscian owners had been killed during the last war and the land had been allocated to Gaius's father as part of the contract between the Roman colonists and the Roman State. Through the trees along the riverbank Gaius caught a glimpse of his home. Smoke was curling up from the chimney and as it rose his heart sank. His mother was not going to like his news.

As they approached the main gate a girl of around ten came racing towards them from the river. She shouted their names in delight. 'Gaius, father, you are back, come see what I have made,' the girl cried. She readied herself to jump up around her father's neck.

'Cassia, go inside and tell everyone to come to the dining room,' her father interrupted sharply. The girl hesitated and blushed in confusion. She glanced quickly at Gaius.

'Do as father says,' Gaius said.

'Afterwards, will you come and see what I have made?' Cassia said stalling.

'Cassia fetch the others, do it now,' her father snapped. There was something in his tone that brooked no argument and the girl turned quickly and silently on her heels and ran away towards the farmhouse.

The handsome home with its white washed walls and neat red roof tiles stood on a small rise a hundred paces from the river bank. Inland from the house was a cattle pen and a pig enclosure. Both were empty save for a solitary fat swine that was rooting around in the straw. Once there had been six cows, a horse, two oxen and a dozen pigs but one night, a year ago, the farm had been raided by cattle thieves. The family had barricaded themselves inside their home and had survived the raid but the loss of the valuable life stock had plunged Gaius's father deep into debt. Further out two fields, which had just been

4

planted with wheat, stretched away to the edge of a forest. It was Gaius's father's final desperate attempt to make the farm profitable. If the crops failed, the family would not only be ruined but they would starve for the money lenders in Sora had refused any further credit and were insisting that the existing debts be paid on time. The date for repayment was in ten day's time. If the money was not produced by then, Gaius's father would either have to sell the farm or become the slave and property of the money lenders. Both were too terrible to contemplate.

As Gaius and his father approached the house a woman appeared in the doorway. Her face was creased and weary looking. She folded her arms across her chest as they came up to her.

'What is going on?' Gaius's mother asked. She was dressed in an old white Stola dress, which bulged outwards around her stomach. She looked tense and nervous. The baby would be born before the summer solstice the doctor had said.

Gaius's father strode past his wife without saying a word and vanished into the house. His mother raised her eyebrows and fixed Gaius with a sharp penetrating look.

'Well?' She demanded.

Gaius met his mother's gaze and held it. Then he too pushed past her without saying a word. As he stepped inside the house he heard his mother's sharp intake of breath behind him.

The dining room was the largest room in the house. It was the place where the family would take their meals and spend their time playing, talking and enjoying each other's company. The wood in the hearth was already burning when Gaius stepped into the room. A metal pot filled with stew was bubbling away over the fire. On a shelf above the hearth, the small statues of the Lares, the household gods, stared down at him in curious silence. His father had sat down in his favourite chair beside the window. Cassia was kneeling beside the cooking pot stirring the food with a wooden spoon. On the other side of the room Gaius's younger brother Marcus leaned against the wall and smirked at him. Gaius ignored Marcus. His younger brother always enjoyed it when Gaius got into trouble. Behind him he heard his mother enter the room and with it he felt her angry disapproval at his behaviour. But he was a man, Gaius thought, and it was men who decided the fate of their family. The last to join them was his older sister, Atia. She came in behind her mother and cast a quick concerned look at Gaius, which he ignored.

When the whole family had gathered together, Gaius's father rose to his feet and turned to look out of the window.

'You have all heard that Lucius died a few days ago,' his father said in his deep, powerful voice. 'Lucius was our leader, he led all of us through the gates of Sora when we first came here five years ago, all four thousand colonists. He was a great man. In Sora our kinsmen are preparing to honour him. There will be a funeral.'

'What has this to do with us?' Gaius's mother interrupted.

Gaius's father turned round and looked at her. Then he turned to Gaius.

'The funeral will take place in two day's time. Afterwards there will be a feast. The whole colony is invited, not only Romans and Latins but the Volscians too.' Gaius's father paused and glanced out of the window. 'Lucius was a great man and to honour him in death there is going to be a gladiatorial combat between two fighters. In his will Lucius stipulated that one of the fighters should be a Roman colonist and that the other should be from the original Volscian population of Sora. When we were in the market this morning, Gaius volunteered to represent Rome.'

'No,' Gaius's mother gasped raising her hand to her mouth in shock.

6

'Was his nomination accepted?' Marcus said with bulging eyes.

'It was,' Gaius's father nodded solemnly. 'Lucius's family and the city elders have agreed to it.'

'Ha,' Marcus exclaimed turning to stare at Gaius with wild, excited eyes.

'The gladiatorial combat will be to the death. Only one man will be left alive. That is Lucius's will.' Gaius's father said looking Gaius straight in the eye.

The room fell silent. Then a sob escaped from Gaius's mother's mouth. Atia touched her shoulder to steady her mother.

'No, you cannot allow this to happen,' Gaius's mother suddenly blurted out. 'He is only eighteen. He is still a boy. He doesn't know what he is doing. He is going to get himself killed, for what? Let someone else volunteer. Not my son.'

Gaius was studying his father tensely. The old man's face was an unreadable stoic mask. His father shook his head.

'The boy has made his choice,' he replied sternly. 'He made it freely. He must do what he has said he will do. He has my permission.'

'Forbid him to fight,' Gaius's mother cried out. A tear rolled down her cheek. 'You have the authority to forbid it. Go to the elders and explain that it was all a mistake. No one will look differently at him for it.'

'I will not,' Gaius' father replied. 'That is my final decision.'

'But why? Why does he have to fight?' Atia interjected coming to her mother's aid.

'I chose to fight,' Gaius interrupted, 'because the winner will receive a prize. The winner will get a great amount of money. It says so in Lucius's will. The sum is large enough to pay off all

7

our debts and buy new life stock. I have to do this. I have to do this for all of us. Don't you see?'

'I think he should fight,' Marcus exclaimed with a silly grin.

'You fool,' Gaius's mother shouted at him, 'You think you are going to win. But what if you lose? Who is going to help out in the fields? Who is going to help protect our home? You selfish little boy. What have you done?'

Calmly Gaius turned to face his mother. 'I will not lose,' he said with a quick shake of his head. 'I am eighteen, mother, and one day I will be head of this family. I am doing the right thing. I cannot stand by whilst those moneylenders take everything away from us. Believe me, if there was another way out I would take it, but the lenders want their money in ten day's time and we don't have it. We do not have any choice. I do not have any choice.'

The dining room fell silent but the fury on Gaius's mother's face did not fade. Then Gaius's father stirred.

'The matter is settled,' he said gravely, 'Gaius will fight and if the gods favour him he shall win and we shall have our debts settled.' He paused and suddenly his stoic mask slipped and he looked troubled. 'There is something else,' he muttered turning to look once more out of the window. 'There was a Fetial priest in the forum today.'

Gaius's mother sobbed and wiped the tears from her face. Then she shook her head in despair, turned and fled from the room followed by Atia.

'A Fetial, are you sure?' Gaius said.

Gaius's father nodded grimly and sat back down in his chair. 'When I have the time I will speak with the elders to find out what it means,' he replied.

8

Chapter Two - The Samnite Forest

Gaius sat alone beside the river staring up at the mountains to the east. It was late in the afternoon. He'd had to get out of the house after his father had told everyone about the gladiatorial fight. The tension inside had become too much. Everyone had stopped talking and the silence had become stifling and oppressive. It was like the end of a hot, humid week when everyone knew that the thunder and lightning storms were close at hand. On the opposite river bank the forest came right up to the water's edge. The forest was Samnite territory and the Liris was the official frontier between Rome and Samnium but Gaius had often crossed the river. The best hunting was done in the Samnite forest and he didn't fear the fierce mountain people. The Samnites didn't mind him either. Often they had invited him along on one of their hunts and although the wounds from the long war between Rome and Samnium were still fresh with the older men, Gaius had always felt he was in the company of friends. The current peace between Rome and Samnium had lasted for six years and there was no reason, at least to Gaius, why it should not continue.

He turned as he heard a noise behind him and his shoulders slumped. It was Cassia, his little sister. She came towards him twirling a stick in her hands. For a moment she was silent. Then he felt her small fingers run across the birthmark on his neck.

'Do you believe the prophecy?' Cassia asked

Gaius shook his head but said nothing.

'It does look like a wolf,' Cassia said as her fingers traced the outline of the birthmark. 'The prophecy could be true you know. Maybe you are the boy who will one day save Rome?'

Gaius sighed wearily. Was she trying to annoy him? Over the years the two of them had had this conversation a thousand times. Cassia was fascinated by the story and never seemed to tire of talking about it. Since he could remember the birthmark on his neck had come with a prophecy that one day he would save Rome. The birthmark could represent many different shapes or animals depending on one's imagination, but to the midwife who had helped deliver him and to Cassia, it was a Wolf. The mark of Rome. When he'd still been a baby, a priest had told his mother that her son had been touched by the gods. He'd told her that her son had a destiny, a great destiny. The story may have thrilled his little sister but after hearing it for a few years, Gaius had become thoroughly bored with it. How could he save Rome? He was just an ordinary farmer's son. It was a ludicrous suggestion and he would have forgotten about it long ago if Cassia had not kept reminding him.

'What do you want Cassia?' Gaius said annoyed at the intrusion.

The little girl refused to look him in the eye. She twirled her stick nervously.

'Will you come and see what I have made?' she said.

Gaius rolled his eyes. It would have to be done or else Cassia would go on and on about it. She could be very annoying when she wanted to be. It was her way of getting what she wanted. He got to his feet and stretched out his hand to his little sister. She took it quickly and led him towards the farmhouse. When they reached the eastern wall of the house she stopped. A heap of wooden tree trunks lay piled up against the wall waiting to be used for cooking fuel. Cassia crouched down and rolled a few of the trunks away to reveal a dark hole in the ground. She stood up and pointed proudly at the hole.

'See I have built myself my own house,' she exclaimed. 'Now I can live like the rabbits do.'

Exasperated Gaius stared at the hole. 'You are a strange girl,' he said.

'Why am I strange?' Cassia   frowned.

'Well, you don't do the normal things that girls of your age like to do. You should be inside helping mother and Atia. At least then you would learn something useful.'

'I don't like the things they do,' Cassia replied. 'They are so boring. When I am older I want to see the world. I want to go as far as Hispania.'

Gaius laughed. His laughter however was abruptly cut short as he caught sight of his father coming towards him.

'I will see you later Gaius,' Cassia said as she skipped away.

Gaius nodded and then turned to face his father. The old man looked stern. He came up to Gaius.

'Walk with me,' he said.

The two of them strode out into the fields behind the farm and his father stooped now and then to inspect the newly planted wheat.

'I will win the fight, father,' Gaius said.

His father didn't look up from where he was crouching on the ground. 'I know you will,' he replied quietly, 'I know you will.'

'Is mother still angry with me?'

The old man straightened up and laid a hand on Gaius's shoulder. His grip was firm and for a moment Gaius felt his father's strength flood into his body.

'She is but she will accept it before the end. She is praying for you.' His father turned to Gaius with a sudden sadness in his eyes. 'Do not quarrel with her Gaius. She is a fine woman and she is only saying what she believes is true. Respect her for that. Men may rule a family but without our women we are nothing. Remember that.'

Gaius nodded solemnly.

His father released his grip on his son's shoulder and bent down to pluck a weed from the soil.

'So have you considered what weapons and armour you will use,' his father's tone was abrupt.

Gaius nodded. 'I will fight in the Samnite style. I will use their weapons.'

'The Samnite style,' his father raised his eyebrows, 'That's good,' he muttered. 'I don't yet know who your opponent is going to be. The Volscians have not yet announced it.' The old man glanced at Gaius. 'We can do some more training later, I can get out the wooden swords that we used to use?'

But Gaius shook his head, 'You have taught me everything you know and you have taught me well, I know how to handle a sword and shield.'

'The gods do not like an over confident man,' his father growled, 'You must earn the respect of Fortuna. You must work to earn her favour, always. Let that guide you. We have talked about this many times. You cannot expect her to be on your side. Nothing is written. The gods will never reward those who are cowards. Whatever you do during that fight, do not be a coward. Honour yourself and you will honour us and the spirits of the departed.'

Gaius nodded solemnly. 'I know father, I know.'

The old man grunted something beneath his breath and turned to look towards the Liris. His face suddenly looked troubled.

'What is it?' Gaius asked turning to look in the same direction.

'I don't know,' the old man murmured, 'That Fetial priest that I saw in the forum. Something has changed. It troubles me.'

***

Gaius waded across the river. The water level was high for the winter snows in the mountains had started to melt but even so the water only came up to his waist. He made the opposite bank and scrambled over the stony shore towards the Samnite forest beyond. It had been a fine spring day and the Samnites would have been out hunting today. He knew where they liked to make their camp. He vanished into the forest, picking his path with ease. The forest was vibrant and as he headed deeper into the woods he saw and heard the cheerful singing of birds, the rustle of animals in the undergrowth and the playful fluttering butterflies. The forest knew that the summer was coming and was looking forward to it.

The smell of roasting deer gave the Samnite camp away. Gaius's nostrils twitched as he caught the delicious scent. He strode towards it and a few moments later heard the sound of voices. From amongst the trees he caught a glimpse of the Samnite camp, a small clearing in the forest beside a rock face. He grinned. He'd been right. They had been hunting. Five men were sitting around a fire over which they were roasting a chunk of meat. A deer carcass, complete with its head and antlers lay to one side.

Gaius stepped out from the trees and raised his hand in greeting.

'Friends, may I join you?' he called out in the Oscan language of the Samnites.

The five hunters jumped to their feet. Their conversation ceased abruptly as they grabbed their weapons. Gaius hesitated. He had gone into the forest unarmed for he knew all the hunters by sight and they knew him but their strange hostility had taken him by surprise. He frowned and took a tentative step towards them.

'What's the matter? You know who I am?' he said.

13

For a moment, no one replied. The Samnites were rugged and powerfully built men in their prime, a few years older than Gaius. They looked fearsome in their rough animal cloaks and coarse black beards and strange long haircuts. Gaius suddenly sensed movement behind him. He spun around, just as a voice spoke.

'Ofcourse we recognise you Gaius. You are always welcome to share our hunt,' a man said in accented Latin.

Gaius grinned in relief as he recognised the newcomer. It was Egnatius, his friend. The man he had come to see. Egnatius handed the dead rabbit he'd been holding to one of the hunters and gestured for Gaius to take a place around the fire. He was a tall man with a grey beard and like the other hunters he was rugged and strong but he was older, much older. Gaius studied him respectfully. Egnatius was a living legend. Every time he had hunted with the Samnites, Gaius had seen the respect with which the Samnites treated Egnatius. He was their leader. The hunters had told Gaius that Egnatius had fought against the Persians when he had joined Alexander's army on its invasion of the Persian Empire. That had been thirty-six years ago. Egnatius had made it all the way to the mythical land of India. He had even spoken with the great Macedonian conqueror.

'Give our friend something to eat,' Egnatius growled at the hunters. The five men looked reluctant but then at last one of them tossed Gaius a piece of meat. Gaius nodded his gratitude. When he was finished eating he looked up. Egnatius had sat down across from him on the other side of the fire and was studying Gaius with bemused interest.

'Forgive my friends here,' Egnatius said in his accented Latin, 'they are tired from the hunt and long for their wives. They have forgotten the rules of hospitality.'

One of the hunters spat into the fire.

'So what brings you here into our forest, Gaius?' Egnatius said with a tired smile.

Gaius glanced cautiously at the hunters around the fire. They looked sullen and none wanted to meet his gaze.

'I am to fight in a gladiatorial combat at the funeral of Lucius,' he said at last. 'I have chosen to fight in the Samnite style. I need weapons and armour. I was wondering whether I could borrow some of yours, Egnatius?'

One of the hunters farted loudly. Gaius ignored him. For a moment, the Samnite leader seemed to consider the request. Then he looked up.

'Yes I have heard about the funeral and the death fight,' Egnatius murmured. Then he fixed his eyes upon Gaius and there was something in his look that sent a sudden shiver of unease right down Gaius's spine. 'I was your age when I first faced the Persians across the Granicus river,' Egnatius said quietly. 'I know what you are thinking. I know what you are about to experience and I know how you are going to react. I am glad that you have chosen to fight with our weapons and in our style. You honour us by doing this.' Egnatius looked away searching for the Latin words. 'I will give you some of my weapons and my armour for the fight. The Volscians are a good people but I hope that you will win.'

'Thank you,' Gaius dipped his head in gratitude.

'Don't thank me boy,' Egnatius muttered, 'tomorrow at dawn come back here to our camp and I will give you the weapons and armour. At dawn! Do you hear me? Don't be late Gaius. I am a busy man.'

One of the hunters laughed.

Chapter Three - Alone

It was still dark when Gaius crossed the Liris. To the east however the sky was turning dark blue. Dawn was not far away. He would have to hurry. Egnatius had specifically told him not to be late. He cursed as he slipped on a stone in the river and nearly fell in but steadied himself just in time. Then he was across. He paused at the edge of the forest to listen. The forest was quiet. What had happened to the cheerful singing birds he'd heard yesterday? He began to make his way through the trees. He knew this forest inside out and even in the dark he had no problem finding his way. Then at last, as the darkness began to give way, he spotted the small clearing and the jagged rock face. He strode towards it and halted at the edge of the trees. The clearing was empty. There was no one there. Puzzled Gaius stepped out of the trees. The blackened remains of yesterday's campfire were still visible and so were some of the animal bones but there was no sign of Egnatius or his weapons and armour. Slowly Gaius turned in a full circle. Where was Egnatius? He glanced up at the sky. The sun was about to rise above the mountains. He wasn't late. Confused he kicked at one of the stones that circled the dead fire. What had happened to the Samnite?

Wearily he leaned against the rock face. Egnatius was late. Maybe something was holding him up. He would have to wait for the man. The sun rose majestically above the mountains and began its journey across the sky. For a while Gaius watched it as it rose higher and higher. Then at last he sighed in frustration and turned to look at the forest. Where was Egnatius? Had the man lied to him or had he forgotten? Baffled Gaius shook his head. Egnatius was not the sort of man who would forget such a thing. Then he froze.

To the west smoke was rising up into the sky. It was coming from the direction of his farm. Gaius stared at the smoke and as he did so his eyes suddenly widened in alarm.

'Oh no,' he whispered. Then he was running, dashing through the trees, back towards the river and his father's farm. As he tore through the woods his alarm grew and added speed to his legs. Something was wrong. Something was terribly wrong. The trees flashed by, he tripped and tumbled to the ground but he was up on his feet in an instant. Then through the trees he caught sight of the river glinting in the early morning sunlight. He burst out of the forest and came to a skidding halt beside the water. He gasped in shock. Then a strangled cry of panic escaped from his lips.

Across the Liris he could see his farm. The farmhouse was on fire. The flames were tearing away at the roof with a furious crackling, roaring noise. With a shout Gaius plunged into the river. Furiously he propelled himself through the water. Then he was across and storming towards his home. Where were his family? The heat from the flames forced him back. He raised his arm above his head to shield himself. The fire was too intense, too strong. Again he shouted, calling out to his father and mother but there was no reply. The roar and crackle of the fire seemed to grow in volume and intensity. Gaius rushed around to the front of the farmhouse. Maybe they had managed to get out. Maybe they were safe. Then he groaned. His father's body lay in front of the main door. A blood-smeared sword lay beside the corpse. A few paces away from his father, Gaius caught sight of Marcus. His brother lay spread eagled on the ground. Someone had stabbed him in the head. Marcus had not even had time to dress himself. For a moment Gaius stared at the corpses unable to believe what he was seeing. Then he turned towards the doorway of the house. It was open but the flames were licking all around it. Without thinking he ran forwards and flung himself through the flames and into the house. He rolled onto the paving stones in the hallway and smashed his shoulder into the far wall. Pain surged through his body but he hardly felt it. He opened his mouth and screamed but there was no reply from anyone inside the burning house.

Shielding himself with his arm over his face he forced his way into the kitchen. It was empty. The heat from the flames was terrible and he started to cough as the black smoke filled the room. Wheezing and coughing, he stumbled into the dining room. The smoke was becoming unbearable. He would not be able to last much longer. He would have to get out. Then he moaned in horror. His mother lay on the floor of the room. She'd been stripped naked and her throat had been slit. A large pool of blood had gathered beside the corpse. Atia lay slumped over the wooden table. She too was naked and her throat had been cut. Gaius stumbled back against the wall. Tears welled up in his eyes. He stretched out a hand towards the dead women. They were all dead. His family had perished. They were all gone.

The smoke was becoming unbearable. He bent forwards and wretched onto the floor. He had to get out but part of him did not want to leave. Part of him wanted to stay here and die and follow his family into the afterlife. Then they would all be together again. He crumpled to the ground as the tears rolled down his cheeks and buried his head in his hands. He would stay here until the smoke and flames took him. Then from what felt like faraway he suddenly heard a voice screaming. He lifted his head and opened his eyes. The voice was screaming his name. His eyes burned and his throat stung. Then he heard it again. A child's voice screaming out his name.

'Cassia,' he whispered. He had forgotten about Cassia. His little sister was still alive. She needed him. He stumbled to his feet and threw up again. Where was she? The screams came again, more urgent this time. The little girl sounded terrified. Where was she? He turned and stumbled back into the hall. As he did so a roof beam crashed down into the dining room behind him. The little girl screamed again and this time she sounded closer. Then Gaius knew where she was. He stared at the space where the doorway had used to be. The flames were all over it and he couldn't see the daylight through the thick black smoke. With a savage cry he flung himself at the flames and swirling black smoke. His momentum sent him crashing out of the burning house. He rolled over the ground. His clothes and skin were singed and his face was covered in black soot. He coughed, spluttered and threw up again. Then he was on his feet and racing around the house. The flames were licking at the heap of tree trunks. In a minute or so they would devour the lot. Cassia screamed again. She had hidden herself in her rabbit hole. The clever little girl had managed to save herself. Wildly Gaius flung the tree trunks aside. The hole in the ground appeared and in it he saw a little terrified face looking up at him. Gaius bent down and dragged Cassia roughly from her den. The little girl was crying and screaming. Her fingers clawed at his face and her nails scratched him as he dragged her free from the burning house.

'Cassia it's me,' Gaius shouted as they made it to a safe distance.

The girl's face was soot covered and she looked terrified. Tears streamed down her cheeks. Then she flung herself around Gaius's neck and held on to him with surprising strength.

Slowly Gaius sank to his knees with Cassia still clinging onto him. He stared at the burning house as part of the wall collapsed inwards. Then he turned to look at his little sister. Cassia was sobbing quietly and Gaius wiped his own tears from his face before he gently loosened her grip.

'It's all right, it's all right, you are safe now,' he whispered hoarsely. 'What happened Cassia, who did this to us? Who murdered our family? Was it those cattle thieves?'

The little girl took her time before she was capable of answering. Then at last her faint little voice spoke.

'They came at dawn,' she whispered. 'I heard them coming. Father went outside to talk to them. Then they came into the house. They took mother and Atia into the dining room. I heard them screaming so I ran to my rabbit house. I hid there. Then the fire started. Gaius, I am scared, I am really scared.'

19

Gaius stifled a gasp of pain as new tears sprang up in his eyes. He reached out and pressed Cassia to his chest.

'Don't be scared anymore little sister,' he said hoarsely. 'Father and mother would not want you to be scared.'

'I won't be scared when you are with me,' Cassia whispered.

Gaius nodded and stared at the burning house.

'Your friend, Egnatius, I saw him,' Cassia said suddenly. 'He is the one who took mother and Atia into the dining room.'

Gaius froze and turned to stare at Cassia in horror. 'Egnatius,' he exclaimed, 'Are you sure it was him?'

Cassia nodded and sniffed. 'It was him,' she whispered.

Gaius turned to stare at the burning farm. He looked confused and horrified. Had Egnatius really led the attack on his farm? Had he really raped and murdered his mother and sister. But how could this be? The man had been his friend. Then as he stared at the raging fire everything seemed to become clear - his father's unease about seeing the Fetial priest in Sora and the strange hostility of the Samnite hunters.

'Oh no,' he said as the truth finally dawned on him.

'War,' he muttered. 'We are at war with the Samnites,' he said turning to Cassia.

She looked up at him without comprehending and Gaius was suddenly conscious that she was waiting for him to make a decision. The realisation came as a shock. He was responsible for her now. He turned to stare at the raging inferno.

'We can't stay here,' he muttered. 'We must go somewhere where we will be safe.'

'But   where?'   Cassia   whispered.

Gaius rose unsteadily to his feet and turned to look at the Liris. Then he turned to look south.

'We will go to Sora,' he said firmly. 'The walls of the town should protect us. Let's hope the Samnites haven't yet attacked the town. We must hurry.'

The little girl nodded and wiped her cheeks with her hand. Gaius was about to set off down the track that led to the Latin colony when he hesitated. Then he sprinted back towards the burning farm. A minute later he returned holding his father's blood smeared sword in his hand. Cassia gave him with a frightened look. Then she took his hand.

'You have father's ring,' she exclaimed as she looked at his fingers.

'It belongs to me now,' he replied.

The two of them started off down the track at a brisk pace. Now and then Gaius cast a nervous glance at the forests and fields around him but he saw no one. Then as they plodded on along the river he started to notice the plumes of black smoke rising from the countryside around him. So, war had broken out he thought grimly and the Samnites had managed to land the first blow. It would be the same story all along the frontier. He groaned as he remembered what his father had said about the Fetial priest. One of the duties of a Fetial was to officially declare war on a foreign power. Maybe that was what had brought the priest to Sora? Fetial priests were rarely seen in public. His father had been right to be troubled.

'Where were you this morning?' Cassia asked suddenly.

Gaius looked away with sudden embarrassment and did not reply. Cassia's question however made him focus on something that had been bothering him. If Egnatius had not told him to come to the forest at dawn both he and Cassia would be dead by now. Gaius frowned. But if Egnatius had known that war was

21

coming then why had he asked Gaius to come to the forest clearing? Why had he not just killed him there and then? A little colour suddenly shot into his cheeks. There was only one explanation. Egnatius had summoned Gaius into the forest in order to get him out of the house before the attack began. Egnatius for some reason had decided to spare him.

Chapter Four - Priests and Priestesses

As they fled towards Sora Gaius noticed more and more plumes of black smoke rising across the valley. The Samnites were ravaging the countryside far and wide. But had they attacked Sora? The town was a major Roman colony. There were four thousand colonists living there plus the Volscians. The town had walls. Surely it would not be so easily overcome. He gripped Cassia's hand tightly and nearly dragged her along as they sped on down the track. About a mile away from the town Gaius suddenly caught sight of people. They were farmers and they too were fleeing towards the town. Some were pushing carts laden with belongings. Others had managed to bring their cattle and horses. All looked frightened and there was urgency in everything they did. The noise of crying babies and bellowing cattle mingled with cursing, anxious voices. No one spoke to Gaius and Cassia but a few of the refugees stared nervously at Gaius's blood smeared sword.

At the gate into the town all was chaos. A crowd of people were clamouring to get into the town but the guards on the walls had closed the wooden gates. People were screaming and banging their fists on the wood. Some of the refugees had started to throw stones at the armed men on the walls. Others turned to look nervously at the Liris, which was only a hundred paces away. How long would it be before the Samnites came? Gaius pushed his way through the crowd towards the gates. The armed men on the walls were silent as they looked down at the refugees with helpless embarrassment.

'Why won't they let us in?' Cassia cried.

'They have been ordered to close the gates,' Gaius growled, 'No one has ordered them to open them.'

He stopped beside the gate and kicked at it. The solid wood did not yield. Behind him the angry, frightened colonists yelled and shouted. Gaius took a step back and looked up at the men on the walls, five yards above him. Then he raised his bloodied sword above his head.

'See this,' he roared at the top of his voice, 'This is my father's sword. It has the blood of my enemy upon it. Open the gates. We are you kin.'

The armed men did not reply but stared stoically down at the refugees. Then a moment later a man dressed in a white toga appeared pushing his way up onto the parapet. He rubbed his hand over his head in dismay as he caught sight of the multitude below him. Then he turned to the guards and spoke to them urgently and a moment later, to a loud roar of approval from the refugees, the gates began to creak open. Gaius and Cassia and the rest streamed into the town.

Sora was a small town. Its walls had a length of barely two miles and its streets were narrow and twisting. The stone houses were built up against each other and there was no running water or sewage system. The pressure of the crowd behind them pushed Gaius and Cassia up the street that led to the forum, the market-square and heart of the colony. People were everywhere. They stood in the doorways to their houses staring at the refugees in alarm. Some had climbed up onto the roof of their homes and the city walls were lined with anxious armed men. The whole town seemed to have been plunged into chaos.

The refugees came streaming into the forum. Down a side street a fight had broken out and two men rolled over the ground wrestling with each other. Further along a woman was screaming hysterically. Gaius tightened his grip on Cassia's hand. The two of them managed to stop in the centre of the forum.

'Will the Samnites come here?' Cassia said looked up at him anxiously.

'They will,' Gaius nodded, 'But they won't get past those walls. We are safe here. Come let's see if we can get something to eat.'

Gaius looked around him and spotted the shrine of Diana. It was just a statue of the huntress on a plinth but already a group of women and children had gathered around the deity. They were kneeling around the statue as if in prayer. A young priestess clad in her formal robes was doing her best to calm the people. Gaius strode towards her half dragging Cassia along behind him.

'Kneel,' Gaius said sharply to Cassia as they reached the statue. The little girl looked up at him, surprised by the tone in his voice.

'You don't have to talk to me like that,' she said hotly.

But Gaius shook his head. There was a stern glint in his eye. 'I will look after you Cassia but you must do what I tell you, as if I was father,' he said.

Cassia blushed. Then without another word she knelt before the statue of Diana.

Gaius dipped his head respectfully at the young priestess as she turned to him. There was a calm dignity and grace about the woman. She gave Cassia a gentle smile.

'Lady, I will be needed on the walls,' Gaius said, 'Can I entrust you with the care of my little sister. I have nothing to give the huntress in return except my respect but when this is over, I promise on my father's good name, that I will come back and present our huntress with a gift for her protection.'

The young priestess nodded solemnly. 'Leave your child with me. The huntress will protect all her children.'

Gaius nodded gratefully and took a step towards the priestess. He bent down so that his head was close to hers.

'But if I return,' he whispered in her ear, 'to find that you have sold her or abused her, there will be a reckoning and I will piss all over you and your goddess. Got that?'

The young priestess took a step back in surprise and alarm and as she did so she caught sight of the blood on Gaius's sword. With an effort she managed a little polite smile.

'Do not have such fears,' she murmured.

Gaius nodded and crouched beside Cassia and ruffled her hair. The little girl looked nervous and refused to look him in the eye.

'Everything will be all right,' Gaius muttered. 'You must stay here now with the Huntress. She will look after you.'

'Where are you going?' Cassia said still refusing to make eye contact.

'They will need me on the walls. I will come back when it is over.'

Cassia was silent and Gaius stood up. Then without another word he turned and strode away. Maybe he should not have been so harsh on the priestess but right now he didn't care. He should have been there to defend his family. In their moment of need he had let them down. He had abandoned them. He had let himself be tricked. He felt shame burn fiercely on his cheeks.

A crowd of anxious colonists had gathered around the speakers' platform in the forum. It was the same platform onto which he'd jumped to volunteer to represent Rome at the funeral games. Today however three toga-clad men had taken the stand. The anxious colonists pressed around them crying and shouting at their city elders.

'What news? Where are the Samnites? Why were we not warned?' The questions and demands poured in from all sides swamping the huddle of elders like an angry sea. Gaius struggled towards the front of the crowd. When he reached the edge of the stone platform a distinguished looking man with white hair was speaking. He was reading from a prepared parchment, which he was holding up with trembling hands. Some in the crowd had started to jeer and boo. Gaius looked around. The crowd was close to breaking into a riot. Then another man climbed onto the platform and pushed the speaker aside. At the sight of the newcomer a hush descended on the anxious colonists. The newcomer was clad in a dusty travelling cloak and was hooded. He raised a spear high in the air and showed it to the people and the crowd fell silent.

'Behold the spear of Mars,' the Fetial priest cried, 'Hear the will of immortal Jupiter.' The priest paused glaring at the crowd from beneath his hood. There was an authority about him that brooked no challenge.

'Men of Sora, Romans, countrymen, allies and friends of Rome. I, Pater Patratus, chief amongst all Fetials declare that Rome is now at war with the Samnite nation. Our war is just. It is the will of Jupiter that we destroy the Samnites. Rome has been called upon to enforce the judgement of the gods. Let no man be in any doubt. Jupiter has spoken. It is your duty, men of Sora, your sacred oath to the King of Gods and to Rome his people, to hold and protect your town.'

The Fetial priest paused and half turned to receive something given to him by a younger colleague. Then he turned back to the crowd and held something up in his other hand. It was a small flint stone. The Fetial was silent as he turned to show the stone to the crowd. The colonists stared at it eagerly. Then with a sharp movement of his hand the Fetial flung the stone onto the platform and a brief solitary spark glowed and died as the stone bounced off the stone paving.

'Let any man who disobeys Jupiter's will, fall like this stone,' the Fetial roared. The priest flung back his hood and glared at the populace. He was an old man Gaius saw but behind the grey beard a pair of sharp intelligent eyes stared down at the crowd. For a moment no one in the   crowd dared to speak.

Then a solitary voice cried out. 'The town is not prepared. How much food and water do we have? How long can we hold out if the Samnite army besieges us?'

The Fetial took a step forwards and scowled. 'Do you think that Jupiter worries about such matters?' he thundered. 'We will make do with what we have got. We will hold this colony until the Consuls come to our aid. And they will come citizens, Rome will not abandon her own. Jupiter will not forget his people. Have patience, have pride in yourself and your settlement and in each other and all will be well.'

'Will the Consuls come?' two voices cried out at the same time.

'They will come,' the Fetial said with a self-assured nod.

Chapter Five - The Games the Gods Play

It was dark. Along the walls of Sora the Roman and Latin colonists crouched waiting for the morning light. The night was silent and in the heaven's a multitude of stars gleamed and twinkled. Gaius sat on the wall close to the main gate. His back leaned against the ramparts and his hastae, his thrusting spear, and a battered old oval shield lay across his lap. He couldn't sleep. Every time he dozed off a restlessness woke him, urging him to do something, anything, but there was nothing he could do but wait. There had been no sign of the Samnites but all day Roman and Latin refugees from the countryside had come pouring into the city. The tales they had brought with them had formed a pattern. Samnite raiding parties had appeared everywhere. The Samnites had killed, raped, burnt and pillaged without mercy. The whole frontier along the Liris had gone up in flames. Hundreds had been killed and countless others taken as captives together with their cattle and horses. It was said that Fregellae further south was being besieged and that one of the Consuls had met with disaster. But these were just rumours, passed on to the refugees by others. Only the firm authority and conviction of the Fetial had rallied the people of Sora and prevented them from fleeing in panic out of the nearest city gate.

Gaius closed his eyes. The image of his burning home and the corpses would not go away however hard he tried. He had not even had time to give them a proper burial. Now the wild animals of the forest would be feasting on their flesh. Would his family's spirits manage to find their way to the afterlife without a proper burial? He sighed and looked away in lonely despair. There was nothing he could do for them right now.

A sudden noise beyond the wall brought him back to reality. The colonists around him had heard it too. A faint muttering passed down the line. Something had moved beyond the wall. Gaius gripped his spear and shield, turned and crouched against the ramparts and peered into the darkness. He could see nothing. Then he heard it again. It sounded like the soft footfall of

29

running feet. Then from the walls of the town two burning arrows arched gracefully into the sky and as they descended to the ground, in their glow, Gaius suddenly caught a glimpse of men storming towards the walls.

'We're under attack!' a voice along the wall screamed. The shout was taken up by more defenders. Abruptly the silence of the night was rent with yells, screams and hurried, shouted orders. Gaius's eyes widened in shock as he heard the whine of an arrow shoot past his head. He staggered backwards and nearly fell off the narrow walkway behind the parapet. Then with a thud a wooden ladder slammed into the battlement right in front of him. In the darkness below the wall he heard men grunting and cursing. A moment later the shape of a man appeared at the top of the ladder. He had a knife clasped between his teeth. Gaius stared at the Samnite in horror. Then he rammed his spear into the man's chest. The force of the blow sent the Samnite tumbling silently back into the darkness from whence he'd come. The blow seemed to release Gaius as if from a spell. Suddenly he felt raw energy flowing through his veins. A mad blood lust filled him. He screamed and pulled his father's short italic sword from his belt. Another Samnite appeared at the top of the ladder. Gaius lunged forwards, ducked under the man's wild, clumsy sword sweep and stabbed him in the head. His father's sword crunched sickeningly into flesh and bone. A spear flew past Gaius missing him by inches. He ripped his sword from the man's skull and the corpse flopped back into the darkness. Below him he heard the Samnites cursing and yelling. To his right and left the whole wall seemed to be filled with struggling, fighting, desperate men. Shrieks and cries of panic, terror and pain erupted all along the ramparts.

Gaius snatched a glance to his left and right. The defenders to his right seemed to be holding their own. He could hear their voices but to his left, towards the gatehouse, things were ominously quiet. What had happened to the men defending the gate? Gaius dropped his sword and grabbed hold of the top of the assault ladder and with a mighty roar pushed it away from the wall. The ladder felt heavy, as if loaded with bodies and as it became vertical he heard men's shouts of alarm before the ladder fell back into the darkness. Gaius stooped and wildly felt around for his sword. Where was it? Then his fingers were gripping the pommel but before he could rise, a figure rushed up from his left, tripped over Gaius's crouched body and with a startled cry tumbled from the wall and into the town. Gaius rolled onto his back and emitted a strangled cry of pain. The man's knee had caught him in his stomach. For a moment, he was winded. But there was no time. He forced himself up to his feet. The Samnite ladder had not returned. Gaius winced and glanced to his left. He could see nothing in the darkness. Something had gone wrong beside the gatehouse. He could sense it. Holding his large oval shield before him he started to advance cautiously into the darkness. The walkway along the walls was narrow and was just wide enough to let a single man pass on down it. Dead and wounded men lay sprawled all over the parapet and he had to be careful not to trip over them.

Suddenly without warning a man charged at him. Gaius felt's the man's sword thrust slide off his shield. The force of the sword blow travelled right up his arm. Gaius stabbed at the figure and felt his sword penetrate soft flesh. Someone moaned and his attacker dropped to his knees. Gaius was about to push his opponent from the walkway when he heard the man's desperate pleas for mercy. Gaius cursed. The man he'd stabbed was one of the Roman colonists. In the faint moonlight, he caught sight of him. He was on his knees and had dropped his sword and his hands were pressed to a wound in his abdomen.

'Where are the men defending the gate?' Gaius hissed in Latin.

The man he'd stabbed groaned in pain.

'Dead, they are dead,' he whispered hoarsely, 'The walls are lost,' he gasped. 'The Samnites are into the city, all is lost, save yourself.'

Gaius shook his head and stepped over the wounded colonist and continued onwards down the wall holding his shield out in front of him. Up ahead he could hear the sound of a fierce desperate struggle. He must be close to the gate by now. Suddenly out of the darkness he came face to face with a fierce looking mountain of a man. The Samnite cried out in alarm at exactly the same time as Gaius but Gaius was a fraction quicker and stabbed him. Then with a cry born of panic and rage he smashed his shield boss into the warrior and the force of his attack sent the attacker tumbling from the wall and into the town. Something sharp sliced across Gaius shoulder and a searing pain cut through his body. He screamed. From the darkness ahead something was moving towards him. Gaius screamed again. Blood was trickling down his arm but somehow he knew that the wound was not serious. Without thinking he charged forwards using his shield as a battering ram. He collided into a body and heard someone panting and straining. For a moment the force of the collision knocked the wind out of him. Then Gaius kicked into the darkness and struck the man's shinbone with his heavy hobnailed army boot. His opponent screamed and Gaius thrust past him sending the man tumbling off the wall. A sword scraped against his shield. Gaius punched the boss of his shield into the darkness and was rewarded with a yell. Then he was clear and was stumbling up to the entrance to the gatehouse. As he reached the doorway a sword punched into his shield and slid away. Close by someone was breathing heavily. Gaius cried out in Latin and the shape in the darkness hesitated.

'This is my city,' an accented voice shouted.

'It is mine also,' Gaius cried.

From the direction he'd just come Gaius sensed movement. He turned and managed to raise his shield just in time. A heavy blow landed squarely on the shield boss and Gaius cried out in pain as the force of the blow swept right through his body. Beyond his shield a voice snarled in Oscan. Then he heard more Oscan voices. They seemed to be everywhere. Panic threatened to engulf him. He was surrounded by Samnites.

'Roman,' the accented voice close by hissed, 'We need to fight back to back, there are too many of them. Take the wall from which you came. Use the corpses to protect yourself. Do it now.'

Gaius had no time to reply. A dark shape loomed up before him, snarling and spitting like a wild cat and another blow landed against his shield. Wildly Gaius stabbed into the dark but his sword cut missed. Then his attacker grunted and collapsed onto the walkway with a spear sticking out of his back. Gaius cried out in savage delight. The Samnite had been killed by his own side. In the darkness both sides were as confused as each other. From behind him he heard the other man's laboured breathing as he too fended off an attack. Suddenly a shrill nearly hysterical cry pierced the darkness and Gaius heard a body collapse to the ground. He didn't dare to look around. If his friend had just been killed, he too would be dead.

'I am still here,' the accented voice gasped.

Gaius cried out in pain and relief. Then another blow smashed into his shield and a spear scraped against his calf. The enemy were trying to get around his shield in any way they could. Gaius could hear their heavy laboured breathing as they sought to force their way along the narrow walls and into the gatehouse. The narrowness of the walkway meant however that only one man could attack him at a time. If they got into the gatehouse they would be able to open the gates and when that happened all would be lost. Whatever happened Gaius thought grimly, the Samnites must not get into the gatehouse.

Behind him his friend had started to sing to himself and in that instance Gaius knew who he was. The man defending the gatehouse with him was a Volscian, one of the original inhabitants of Sora. From out of the darkness a Samnite roared and charged at Gaius. At the last moment Gaius screamed, raised his shield and punched his sword forwards. The sword sank deep into exposed flesh yet the momentum of the attack sent Gaius staggering backwards with the weight of his attacker bearing down on him. Gaius ripped his sword free. His attacker gurgled and a spray of fine blood splattered across Gaius's face. Then the man died and Gaius flung him backwards onto the walkway. The corpses in front of him had begun to pile up.

'Are you still there Roman,' the Volscian cried from the darkness.

'Keep singing,' Gaius gasped. Then he glanced at the town. The sound of fighting was still going on. Gaius had no idea whether the colonists were winning or losing. He opened his mouth.

'To the northern gate, to the northern gate. Help us! Help us!'

His yells were answered by Oscan curses. A man came towards him but his attacker had to clamber over the corpses to get at him and as he did so Gaius stabbed him in the shoulder. With a cry the man slithered away.

'To the northern gate! To the northern gate,' the Volscian behind him cried as he copied Gaius.

From the darkness there was no immediate answer. Gaius readied himself for the next attack but whether it was his cries or the pile of corpses in front of him, protecting him, none came. Suddenly a trumpet blared out. Behind him the Volscian cried out in delight.

'I know that signal. That's the Samnite signal for retreat.'

Gaius did not reply. He peered into the darkness from behind his shield. There was movement there in the darkness but no one came at him. Were the enemy really retreating? For a whole minute, nothing happened. Then a voice cried out in Latin from the darkness close by.

'Who is there? Who are you?'

Gaius stared into the darkness. 'We hold the gatehouse,' he shouted back. 'Where are the Samnites?'

'They are gone, they have fled,' the voice cried joyously. 'Don't attack, we are coming towards you.'

Gaius raised his sword in the air and screamed for joy and relief. Behind him he heard the Volscian slump to the ground with an exhausted sigh. Then a moment later the darkness was rent by a chuckle.

'Do you know that I was supposed to be fighting in a gladiatorial combat today at Lucius's funeral,' the Volscian said. 'I was going to fight your people's champion. Instead I end up nearly dying defending the gatehouse. What tricks the gods play on us eh Roman?'

Gaius lowered his shield and turned to stare into the darkness where he could just about see the figure of the Volscian. Then he dropped his shield and flung back his head and roared with laughter.

Chapter Six - To Forget

Gaius leaned against the wall in the forum and stared at the statue of Diana. It was noon. In his hand he held a jug of wine. Ten days had passed since the Samnite night assault. The enemy had withdrawn to lick their wounds and had not attempted to attack the city again but from the walls the defenders had seen the Samnites preparing for a siege. Nothing had come in or out of Sora since then and supplies were already beginning to run low. The city elders had instituted rationing but the one commodity that there seemed to be plenty of was wine. Gaius raised the jug to his lips and burped. In the noon heat he was slowly getting drunk and it felt good. He deserved a drink.

At the base of the statue the usual crowd of women and children had gathered to prey to the Huntress for deliverance. They were sitting and kneeling, muttering their prayers with the young priestess leading them. Ever since the siege had started the town's people had been on edge and it wouldn't take much for panic to break out. Everyone knew what would happen if the Samnites broke into the city. A general massacre would ensue, no one would be spared, not even the children. The city would be given up to the soldiers and wiped out. The Samnites had tried to exploit this fear. Every day their heralds had ridden up to the walls and conveyed news and rumours about what was going on in the outside world. The news had always been bad. Roman arms had met with disaster everywhere. But each time that the heralds had appeared the Fetial had come up onto the walls and had raised his holy spear high above his head in reply.

Amongst the crowd of worshippers, he noticed Cassia. Gaius raised the jug to his lips again and took another long swig of wine. Then he wiped his mouth with his hand. The gods and their games he thought contemptuously. The gods were laughing at him. They were mocking him, letting him think that he was the master of his own destiny. All his life he had expected and had prepared himself to take over from his father and follow in the old man's footsteps but the farm was gone and so were his family. He had believed that Egnatius was his friend but the man had raped and murdered his family and now he had become friends with the Volscian whom he had been scheduled to meet in a fight to the death. Gaius chuckled and took another sip of wine. What was he supposed to do now? He hadn't got a fucking clue. If he survived this siege he could go anywhere and do anything he wanted. He was a free man. Across from him a young prostitute gave him a coy little smile and a subtle glimpse of her breasts. He grinned at her and the girl smiled again and twirled her fingers in her long black hair. She glanced pointedly at the dark open doorway of her brothel. Gaius was about to move towards the prostitute when a voice stopped him.

'Why do you drink so much wine?' Cassia said indignantly. The little girl stood before him with her arms folded across her chest.

'That is none of your business,' Gaius replied. Then as to make a point he raised the jug to his lips again.

'You are drunk,' Cassia said with disgust, 'Father would have called you a disgrace.'

'Go back to your prayers little sister and leave me alone,' Gaius growled glancing at the prostitute. The whore smiled at him and inclined her head towards the doorway.

'You drink because you want to forget,' Cassia said stubbornly. 'You drink because you feel guilty that you were not there when they died. I too want to forget what happened but I can't. I dream about it every night.'

Gaius turned to look at his sister in surprise at the sudden wisdom in her voice.

'Mother doesn't want you to drink,' Cassia went on, 'She doesn't want you to feel guilty. She understands. She really does. She just wants us to survive. She told me herself when you were down by the river. She wants you to become the man that you were always meant to be.'

Gaius grunted in surprise and stared at his little sister. The wine was clogging his mind.

'So who am I supposed to be?' he snapped angrily.

'The boy who was born to save Rome,' Cassia replied without hesitation.

Gaius staggered backwards in despair. Not this nonsense again. From the corner of his eye he noticed the prostitute approaching. The whore ran her fingers lightly across his chest and circled him letting him have a whiff of her cheap perfume. 'Come on, what are you waiting for?' she purred.

'Leave him alone,' Cassia snapped, 'He is not interested in you.'

The prostitute turned sharply towards Cassia. 'Run along to your mother little girl,' she exclaimed,' this is between him and me. Now go away.'

But Cassia did not move. 'My mother is dead,' she cried, 'She was murdered by our enemy. They raped her and cut her throat and that of my sister too and that is what is going to happen to you to if the Samnites get into the town. Now you leave my brother alone. Now you leave us alone.'

The prostitute raised her hand to her mouth and stared at Cassia in disgust. Then with a shake of her head she strode away.

'Cassia,' Gaius said raising both his hands in dismay. 'What are you doing?'

Cassia took a step forwards and kicked over the jug of wine that stood on the ground. The red liquid spilled out onto the paving stones.

'Stop drinking,' she cried fiercely. 'They don't like it when you are like this. They are watching us, father and mother, Atia and Marcus, they will always be watching us.'

***

Gaius ran towards the ladder that led up to the walkway behind the walls. On the ramparts he again heard the cries of alarm. All around him the defenders were rushing to their positions. Slinging his shield over his back Gaius clambered up onto the walkway and stood up. It was late in the afternoon. Beyond the walls he could see the Samnite pickets.

'Are we being attacked?' a man beside him called out.

'The Samnites are leaving,' a voice replied joyously, 'Look, they are crossing the river. They are heading back to their own territory.'

Gaius craned his neck to get a better glimpse. Men pushed past him down the narrow walkway. Then he caught sight of the enemy. The Samnites were indeed retreating across the Liris. A multitude of warriors were wading through the water in a great, disorganised mass but the Samnites didn't seem to be in a hurry. Their pickets were still in place watching the town. Gaius turned and began to make his way along the wall towards the eastern gate. The walls were crammed with defenders all eagerly staring at the retreating enemy.

'It could be a trap, they could be feigning retreat to hit us when we think they have gone,' a voice called out.

No one replied. When he reached the eastern gatehouse, Gaius paused and grinned as he caught sight of his friend. Taking a step forwards, he stretched out his arm towards a big, brawny youth with black hair and a deep suntan. The young man was the same age as Gaius. The youth smiled and clasped the outstretched arm in greeting. The Volscian with whom Gaius had defended the gatehouse gestured at the Samnites with his spear.

'Look Gaius, they are leaving. Things are looking up.'

Gaius nodded. Tullus was the son of a dentist and he had been born a hopeless optimist. Nothing seemed to get him down. The young man managed to see a positive side to everything. Gaius had immediately liked him for his infective cheerfulness. Gaius peered at the enemy. 'I wonder why,' he muttered. 'What has changed? It wasn't one of your bad jokes was it?'

Tullus, the Volscian youth smiled and shook his head. 'I don't do bad jokes,' he replied. 'But never question our good fortune Gaius, just accept it. Whatever has made those arseholes leave, I don't care, as long as they don't come back.'

Tullus glanced at Gaius and he suddenly became serious.

'Now that the enemy is leaving,' Tullus muttered, 'do you think they will still want us to fight each other in gladiatorial combat at Lucius's funeral?'

Gaius stiffened. He hadn't thought about that. The death fight and the funeral seemed like ancient history. He stared out across the walls. For a moment the two friends were silent.

'I will not fight you,' Gaius said at last. 'You are my friend now Tullus. I have already lost enough friends. Things have changed.'

The Volscian was studying Gaius carefully. Then he raised his eyebrows, sighed and turned to look back at the retreating enemy.

'Nor will I fight you,' Tullus muttered. 'Together we saved this town. Lucius may have been a great man but I didn't see him with us on the walls that night. They will have to find someone else to honour him.' Tullus paused and a cheeky smile

40

appeared on his face. 'I bet his spirit must be well pissed off that his funeral was so rudely interrupted.'

Gaius nodded solemnly, 'But if we had fought,' he said calmly, 'I would have kicked your arse all over the arena.'

'Ha!' Tullus exclaimed, 'They would have had to scrape you from the floor. Don't get cocky with me Roman.'

Gaius smiled. Their banter was interrupted by a sudden hush amongst the men on the wall. Gaius turned. The Fetial priest had appeared a dozen paces away. The priest was staring at the Samnites. The defenders on the wall moved aside in silent reverence to give him some space. The Fetial was clad in his long robe and his head was hooded so that none could see his face. In his hand he clasped his holy spear.

'Fetial, what does this mean?' a voice suddenly cried out. 'Why are the Samnites retreating? Are we safe?' a few more voices called out. The defenders had turned to stare at the priest in eager anticipation.

The Fetial did not reply right away. Then as the silence on the wall lengthened he slowly raised his spear high in the air.

'Rejoice men of Sora,' the Fetial cried out, 'Jupiter smiles upon you. The Samnites are leaving. They will not come back. There is only one reason for this. The Consul is approaching. Rome is coming to her children's aid.'

There was a moment of stunned silence. Then the wall erupted in joyous shouts and cries. The noise seemed to spread along the walls and into the town. Gaius raised his spear and yelled with pure delight. In the town, the citizens, Roman, Latin and Volscian rose to their feet or appeared in doorways. The news spread. The Consul was approaching. The siege of the town was about to be lifted. Around him the defenders were crying out praise to the gods. Gaius caught sight of Tullus and raised

41

his hand. The Volscian clasped it in a firm embrace like an arm wrestler and a broad emotional grin appeared on his face.

'With our backs to each other, till the end, so we stood Gaius,' the Volscian cried out. 'I will not forget it.'

'Nor will I, Tullus, nor will I,' Gaius said feeling his cheeks burn.

***

It was early evening when a shout from the walls informed the town that the final Samnite pickets were leaving. Gaius was still up on the wall. He rubbed his tired eyes. The Samnite rearguard was across the Liris when to the south he suddenly spotted horsemen. The riders had appeared on the track from the direction of Fregellae. They paused as they caught sight of the town. One of the horsemen was carrying a standard but they were too far away to see any details.

'They are here, they are here!' the excited cries spread along the walls. Men rose to their feet and turned to look out beyond the parapet.

'Which Consul will have come?' Scipio or Fulvius?' Tullus said excitedly. 'They say Scipio is the better general. Fulvius has never fought a battle before.'

'As long as they come, I don't care,' Gaius said tiredly. 'I could sleep for a week. I will sleep for a week after this.'

Tullus poked him playfully in the ribs. 'When this is over my friend, I will steal my father's money and we will spend a whole week in the whorehouse. That will revive you. I know the girls. They are brilliant.'

Gaius smiled ruefully. 'I am not sure my little sister will let me,' he muttered, 'But your father's money will be well spent.'

Beyond the wall the group of horsemen had started to move towards the town. As they drew nearer Gaius saw that they were clad in proper bronze breastplates and were holding hastae thrusting spears and small round cavalry shields. The riders were proper soldiers unlike the armed colonists who had defended the walls clad mainly in just their linen civilian tunics. The defenders stared down eagerly as the riders approached. Amongst the horsemen Gaius suddenly caught sight of a man wearing a fine red mantle and sash over his armour. The officer had an attic helmet on his head from which protruded a black horsehair plume. At his side a signifer, wearing the head of a wolf, clutched the military standard of the Fifth Legion. The circular discs and crescents gleamed in the fading light and on top of the standard Gaius saw the letters SPQR. The officer raised his arm and the cavalry troop pulled up before the gate. The officer with the attic helmet looked up at the men crowding the walls.

'Citizens, men of Sora,' he cried, 'Open your gates for the army of Consul Gnaeus Fulvius Maximus Centumalus.'

Chapter Seven - The Consul of Rome

The Consul sat in his chair in the middle of the forum. It was late in the morning. Around him the city elders and towns people had gathered and were eagerly trying to speak with him. Some had stretched out their hands towards him and were calling him by name, begging him to notice them. The crowd however was held back from approaching the Consul by a line of stony faced Roman soldiers armed with shields and spears. Fulvius with one elbow on the side of the chair was resting his head against his hand and was staring into space. He looked bored. Behind him, like a statue, stood the Fetial quietly holding his spear. Two aristocratic ladies clad in fine colourful clothes and bedecked with jewellery sat close by sunning themselves and chatting quietly to each other.

Gaius stood in the crowd close to the line of soldiers. A full Consular army, four legions plus a strong contingent of allied Campanian cavalry had arrived at Sora shortly after the first group of scouts had announced Fulvius's approach. The 20,000 or so men had made their camp outside the walls on the Consul's orders. Sora was too small to house so many men.

A commotion in the crowd made Fulvius look up. Gaius could see that the Consul was a tall man with white hair and dark shrunken, hollow cheeks that made him look like he was a victim of famine. There was a stern, authoritative look on his face. He was clad in splendid armour over which he wore a red cloak. In his left hand he was holding the bundled rods with an axe head sticking out, the Fasces, symbol of his office and power.

The crowd parted and one of the Consul's lictor's pushed past the soldiers, strode towards Fulvius and bent down to speak to him. Gaius was too far away to hear what was said. The Consul nodded and raised his hand and beckoned for someone to step forwards. The soldiers parted to let an armoured and dust covered soldier in and the messenger rushed forwards, knelt before the Consul and with his head bowed stretched out a

44

leather satchel. The Consul took the despatch, opened the satchel and unrolled the parchment message. The crowd fell silent.

When he had finished reading Fulvius handed the despatch to the lictor and rose to his feet. The Consul turned to the Fetial. Gaius was close enough to hear their conversation.

'Egnatius is retreating towards Bovianum. He's gathering all his forces to defend the Samnite capital.' the Consul growled.

'Then to Bovianum you should go,' the Fetial said calmly, 'Confront Egnatius, defeat him and take their capital. Teach these Samnites that any attack on Roman land will come at a high price.'

Fulvius grunted and seemed to consider the advice. He was about to say something when Gaius cried out.

'I know Egnatius, Sir.'

Fulvius and the Fetial turned to stare in his direction. Gaius tried to push his way forwards but a soldier's spear blocked his path.

'Who said that?' the Fetial demanded glaring at the crowd.

'I did Sir,' Gaius cried. 'I know Egnatius. I have unfinished business with that man.'

Both Fulvius and the Fetial priest were staring straight at Gaius now.

'Let him through,' the Consul snapped and the soldier blocking his path withdrew his hastae spear and Gaius slipped into the open space beside the Consul. The town's folk and refugees fell silent. Fulvius was examining Gaius critically.

'What do you know about Egnatius, boy?' the Consul snapped.

Gaius knelt on the ground and bowed respectfully before the supreme Roman war leader. 'I used to hunt with Egnatius, in the forests just north of here. I believed him to be my friend but he was not.'

'And you bother me with this?' the Consul growled in disappointment. 'I have more important things to do than listen to your sorry story.'

Gaius refused to move. He was suddenly conscious of the Fetial's sharp intelligent eyes upon him. He took a deep breath.

'Consul,' Gaius said calmly, 'under the Lex Talionis it is my right to claim compensation from Egnatius for what he did to my family. When you beat him Sir. When you capture him, I should have the first right to be compensated for my loss.'

Fulvius stared at Gaius with an incredulous look. The Consul looked genuinely taken aback. But it was the Fetial who replied first.

'You dare tell the Consul what he should do?' the priest said.

Gaius stood his ground. 'It is the law,' he replied. 'Egnatius raped and killed my family without provocation. I have a witness. I am entitled to compensation.'

Fulvius was glaring at Gaius. The crowd around him seemed to have grown tense with expectation as to the outcome of the unexpected confrontation. No doubt many of the refugees were thinking about their burnt and destroyed homes.

'What compensation do you demand from Egnatius?' Fulvius growled. The Consul had started to look uncomfortable and seemed to be regretting letting Gaius have an audience.

'I seek his death, his life for those I have lost,' Gaius said without hesitation.

'Don't we all boy,' Fulvius snapped. The Consul glanced irritably at the eager crowds. Then he turned on Gaius. 'There are many who have similar claims. But I do not have the time to sit in judgement. I have a war to win boy. Now give your name to the Fetial priest and be gone.'

The crowd around him had started to mutter. Gaius nodded gratefully and dipped his head before rising to his feet. The chances that he would ever catch up with Egnatius seemed slim but if he did manage to, and was able to, he would kill him. Gaius did not want to know why the Samnite had spared him. It was not important. He just wanted to know how a man who had pretended to be his friend could have turned on him so viciously.

Gaius approached the Fetial just as the crowd broke out in a loud clamour. The people all had their grievances and claims. The Fetial was studying him with sudden interest. Gaius gave the priest his name and was about to turn away when the Fetial's hand restrained him. Gaius felt the man's fingers brush lightly over the purple birthmark across his neck.

'Many years ago,' the Fetial said in a quiet yet clear voice,' I heard about a boy who had been born in Rome and who carried the mark of a Wolf on his neck. The story goes that this boy has a destiny, a great destiny. He is the boy who will one day save Rome.'

Again Gaius felt the soft fingers tracing the outline of his birthmark. Annoyed, he shook his head and pulled himself free from the Fetial's grip and turned away. 'It's all bollocks, Holy Father, I don't know what you are talking about,' Gaius replied as he walked away.

'You cannot escape from it,' he heard the priest mutter. 'You should embrace who you are Gaius, son of Marcus.' The priest's quiet laughter was lost in the noisy shouts and cries of the people as Gaius slipped away into the crowd.

He hadn't gone far when a hand suddenly grabbed his shoulder forcing him to a halt. Gaius looked up in surprise as a second man appeared and took hold of his arm. What did the Fetial think he was doing? The two big men who had grabbed him looked unfriendly. Gaius was about to protest when his words were choked off before he could speak. A third man, older than the others and clad in expensive looking clothes and accompanied by a slave was coming towards him. There was a little smile on the man's face.

'Oh fuck,' Gaius groaned as he recognised who it was.

'Yes, oh fuck,' the moneylender said as he stopped before Gaius. 'Did you really believe that war would release your family from the debt it owes me?'

Gaius felt his heart thumping in his chest. He had completely forgotten about the family's debts.

'The time for repayment has passed,' the moneylender snapped, 'I have been looking for your father everywhere but he doesn't seem keen to show his face. I want my money back plus interest and I want it now.'

Gaius did not reply. Then as the silence lengthened he stared at the moneylender with growing contempt.

'What kind of man thinks about money and profit when the town is in such danger? Gaius said.

The moneylender shrugged. 'I do, that is my business. I did not force your father to take out a loan and it is my right to make a profit. Now where is your father? Where is my money?'

'My father is dead and my farm is burnt and destroyed. My crops are ruined and I have no money to give you,' Gaius replied.

The moneylender sighed and turned to the slave who was hovering close to his master's   shoulder.

48

'A pity,' the banker muttered as he fondled the colourful rings on his fingers, 'But as I suspected. What can we salvage?'

The slave was examining Gaius as if he were a cow about to be sold in a cattle market. The slave turned to his master.

'The land should cover about a third of the debt,' the slave explained. 'It could be more if the house and farm buildings have survived in a repairable condition. I can't judge that though until I have seen them. If you take him as a slave and providing there are no other creditors,' the slave paused to do the mental calculation, 'I suspect that we could get half our money back but without interest.'

'Damn, damn,' the banker growled glaring at Gaius. 'Your father was a fucking bad loan. What a mess. Now I must incur a loss.'

The slave raised his hand, 'I forgot,' he muttered, 'he has a little sister. She is uneducated but unmarked and fairly good looking. If you sold her, on a good day, we may be able to get six out of ten Denarii back from our investment. There is also the chance that he is lying and that the family have some hidden wealth stashed away somewhere.'

'Yes,' the banker's eyes gleamed and he stroked his chin thoughtfully. 'Well Gaius, are you lying to me? Did your father stash away anything that belongs to me?'

Gaius was staring at the slave. Then slowly he turned to look at the moneylender. At his side the two big men who were holding him seemed to tense as if they knew from experience how clients were likely to react.

'I will make a deal with you,' Gaius said calmly. 'But not here. Let's go somewhere we can talk in private.'

'Good,' the banker said looking pleased.

Gaius led the small party away from the noisy and crowded forum and into a maze of alleys that formed the heart of the old

Volscian town and where most of the Volscian inhabitants of
Sora lived. The alleys were dirty, narrow and stank of shit, urine
and vomit. When they had arrived five years ago the Roman
and Latin colonists had taken over all the best houses in the city
and the Volscians had been restricted and contained to the old
and poorer part of town. But it had not stopped the Volscians
from maintaining a deep and fierce pride in their beloved city.

There were few people about and those that they did see
withdrew hurriedly as they caught sight of the moneylender and
his two thugs. At a junction of four alleys Gaius halted and
turned to the banker.

'Let's talk,' he said calmly.

The moneylender nodded and waited.

Gaius glanced at the two thugs who were still holding him in a
firm grip.

'If you wouldn't mind letting go, then I can discuss my proposal
with your employer,' he said in an irritated voice.

The two men turned to the moneylender. The banker nodded
and the thugs released their grip and Gaius rubbed his
shoulder. He gave the thugs an annoyed glance and then
turned to peer down an alley before taking a step towards the
moneylender.

'So I propose we do this,' Gaius muttered. Without hesitating he
lifted his leg and kicked the money lender in his groin. The blow
caught the banker completely by surprise and the man went
down with a deep agonising groan. The slave's eyes bulged in
horror. Gaius grabbed the slave by his throat and sent him
flailing into the two thugs behind him. Then he was off down the
alley. Behind him he heard a wild confused shout and the noise
of running feet as the two men set off after him in pursuit. There
was no time to look behind him. Gaius raced down the alley. He
came to another junction, skidded to a halt and darted to his

right. A woman squealed in alarm as he thrust past her. Where was the damned place? Had he taken the wrong turn? Behind him he heard another shout and the noise of running feet. Up ahead the alley split at a T-junction. Gaius turned left and nearly slipped on a pile of shit that had been thrown out of a window. He regained his balance and sprinted along the alley. Then suddenly he recognised where he was. At the end of the alley a dentists sign hung above the door of a house. He snatched a glance over his shoulder. The two thugs had not yet come round the corner but he could hear them. They were close. Gaius vanished through the open doorway into the dentist's shop. Tullus looked up in surprise from the table where he was cleaning his father's metal instruments. Then seeing the expression on Gaius's face, he rose quickly to his feet.

'Into the back room,' Tullus snapped hastily, 'There is a trap door in the floor. Get into the cellar.'

Gaius had no time to reply. Outside he could hear the sound of running feet approaching rapidly. He darted into the backroom and looked around wildly. Then he saw it. A small trap door set in the floor. He stooped, lifted it up and slithered down into the darkness below. The trapdoor closed above his head just as he heard a man's angry voice cry out.

The cellar was cool and damp and cramped. There was just enough space for him to crouch without hitting his head on the ceiling. Gaius strained to hear what was going on above him. Tullus seemed to talking to someone but he could not catch what he was saying. Suddenly he froze as above him he heard footsteps. Someone had stepped into the backroom. If they lifted the trap door he would have no chance to defend himself. He bit his lip and tried to control his breathing. Time seemed to pass with agonising slowness. Then to his relief he heard footsteps moving away from him. The house fell quiet. Gaius waited. He could feel his heart thumping in his chest. Then after what seemed an age the trap door was suddenly lifted up and Gaius blinked in the daylight. Tullus stood looking down at him with a grin. The Volscian stretched out his arm and Gaius grasped it and clambered out of the cellar.

'They have gone,' Tullus said.

Gaius breathed a sigh of relief. 'Thank you,' he muttered. Then he gripped his friend's arm.

'I will explain later,' Gaius said quickly, 'Tullus, find my sister and bring her here as soon as you can. Those men will be looking for her. Cassia is down in the forum. Don't let them get hold of her, please.'

**

'So what you are going to do now?' Tullus asked as the three of them sat around the table in Tullus's house eating their hot soup. It was late in the evening and outside the stars twinkled in the black sky. Tullus lived alone with his father but his father, the dentist, was out visiting a patient. Gaius glanced at Cassia. His sister was eating her food as if she hadn't eaten in days. She seemed oblivious to the big decision he had just made.

Gaius turned to Tullus. 'That banker will be out looking for me,' he muttered. 'We can't stay in Sora. I wish I could settle the debts but I cannot, at least not yet.' Gaius gave Tullus a sad smile. 'There is only one thing for it. Tomorrow I shall enlist in the Consul's army. I am young and I know how to fight. If fortune favours me then I may be able to get my hands on some loot when we take Bovianum.' Gaius paused to rub his cheeks. 'Well at least I should be able to pay my debts and start again.'

'You want to go and fight against the Samnites,' Tullus said thoughtfully. 'That is a dangerous job. These Samnites are tough. They won't give in so easily. Surely there are other things that you can do to repay the money?'

'Can you think of any?' Gaius said with a shake of his head. 'The sum that I owe is quite large. It's not something that I can earn. Such a sum can only be won by fighting in a war.' Gaius sighed. 'If I don't repay it I shall never be able to return to Sora. This is my home Tullus. I am not going to be driven from my home.'

'I am going with you,' Cassia interrupted suddenly. She had finished her soup and was staring down at the empty wooden bowl.

Gaius picked nervously at his fingernails. Then he glanced at his sister with sudden relief. He was glad. He was glad she had made her own decision and he'd not had to force her. However much he hated to admit it she was right. The girl could not stay here in Sora whilst the moneylender and his thugs were out looking for them. The army would be a dangerous place for a woman and Gaius would have very little time to see her but at least they would be together. Some instinct had warned him that if he left Cassia behind he would likely never see her again.

'That's a difficult decision,' Tullus said as if reading Gaius's mind.

Gaius nodded. 'It is,' he murmured, 'but Cassia is right, we will go together. She must find herself a place amongst the camp followers. It's going to be an education.'

The room fell silent, as the three of them seemed lost amongst their own thoughts. Then Tullus suddenly brightened up.

'Well at least you got to kick that banker in the balls,' he exclaimed. 'I know a lot of people around here who will applaud you for that.'

Gaius however did not look amused. He turned to Cassia and gave his sister a little nudge with his elbow.

'There is something we need to do before we leave,' he said quietly.

She looked up at him. 'What?'   she inquired.

53

Gaius blew the air from cheeks. 'You must be strong Cassia. You are not going to like it,' he replied.

***

It was mid morning. Gaius and Cassia stood beside the four newly dug and covered graves. An old army pickaxe lay at Gaius's feet. The graves were covered with broken paving stones to stop the scavengers from digging them up. It was the best that he could do for his family. Beyond the graves the broken, blackened and burnt out ruin of their farmhouse stained the earth. The smell of rotting pig flesh filled the air. Gaius sighed and looked up at the abandoned wheat fields. At his side Cassia had gone very quiet. Then slowly she slipped her hand into Gaius's hand. The two of them stood staring down at the graves.

'You need to say something,' Cassia whispered at last.

Gaius nodded and glanced at the ruined farmhouse. Then he looked towards the Liris and finally he raised his eyes towards the sky. He cleared his throat.

'Today we bury our father and mother, our brother and sister,' he murmured. 'Their lives were cruelly taken from them.' Gaius paused. 'But we Gaius and Cassia survive them and will honour and remember them. Let the gods hear us and know that it will be so.'

Gaius nodded solemnly and fell silent.

'Let's go,' Cassia said turning away from the graves.

***

The twenty Soran volunteers who had decided to join the Consular army stood in a straight line awaiting the inspection by their new centurion. They were all young men like Gaius. It was noon and the heat from the sun blazed down on the new recruits. Close by the Roman army camp was a hive of activity

54

as the rows upon rows of neat white army tents were being dismantled. Beyond the camp the walls of Sora gleamed and basked in the sunlight. Gaius could hear the officers shouted commands. Soldiers passed by in a continuous coming and going but no one paid the new recruits any attention. Everyone seemed far too busy for that. Gaius licked his cracked lips and examined himself once more. Despite his protests Tullus had taken his father's money and had gone to the local blacksmith to buy Gaius proper military equipment. As he examined himself Gaius ran his fingers lightly over his Roman pectoral body armour. On his head he was wearing a bronze Montefortino helmet with a black horsehair plume and large cheek guards and in his hand he clutched a long hastae thrusting spear. The helmet felt heavy and unfamiliar. On his feet he was wearing brand new heavy hobnailed marching sandals and leaning against his knees was a Scutum, a large oval shield. The weapons would qualify him for a position within the Roman heavy infantry companies but due to his age he would most likely end up in the Hastati, the first line of the Roman armies newly adopted battle formation, the Triplex Acies. It was the Hastati who would be the first men into battle, the first men to make contact with the enemy battle line.

Cassia had hardly recognised him when he had first appeared fully dressed. He'd told her to find and stay with the camp followers, slaves, merchants, servants and women who followed an army whether it went. Cassia had been in a bad mood when she had left him. The girl was being asked to grow up very fast but such was the way of things. She would be all right he had told himself. She was strong, smart and healthy. She would be all right. Tullus had not forgotten about her. From a merchant, he'd purchased a new woollen cloak and leather sandals. The little girl would need them in the cold, harsh mountains. Gaius had solemnly sworn that he would repay Tullus the expense he had incurred but the jovial Volscian had waved him away saying he could repay him when he had the means. Tullus it seemed had made it a habit of taking his father's money without permission but the old man would not mind, he'd explained. He would tell him that he'd spent it on whores.

Gaius sighed as his fingers touched his father's short italic stabbing sword. It was the only piece of equipment that he could truly call his own. Earn the respect of the gods. Never be a coward, his father had said. From the corner of his eye Gaius caught a glimpse of a centurion coming towards him. The officer was big and solid like an oak tree and he looked annoyed and in a hurry.

'You volunteers,' the centurion growled in a rough provincial voice as he reached the line of new recruits. 'My name is Verrens. You are being assigned to the Tenth Maniple of Hastati of the Fifth Legion. That's my unit. Now I will make this brief as I have got a list of things to do as long as Jupiter's cock. Have any of you served in the army before. Take a step forwards if you have.'

Gaius and a few others took a step forwards and the centurion grunted in approval. Slowly he went down the line and when he came to Gaius he paused.

'Where and with whom did you serve?' Verrens said looking Gaius straight in the eye.

'I have never been on campaign Sir,' Gaius replied. 'But I defended the walls of Sora during a Samnite night assault.'

The centurion frowned. 'So you have seen some action,' he grunted. 'That's good. I served in the last Samnite war and I can tell you that defending a wall and meeting the Samnites in open battle are two very different things. This is not going to be a pleasant outing into the mountains. The Samnites are tough. They are better warriors than us. They will be defending their homes. When you meet them face-to- face in the field you are going to shit yourself. So, do you still wish to join my company?'

'Yes Sir,' Gaius replied.

'Good,' Verrens muttered as he moved on down the line. When he had completed his inspection, he turned to face his men.

'I took a lot of casualties on the march here so my company is under strength. That's why they have given you to me. Now get moving and follow me. You are in the army now, so boys, don't give me an excuse to use my vine rod on your backs.'

'What happened to the Tenth Maniple?' One of the Soran volunteers called out.

'Shut the fuck up,' the centurion bellowed.

Chapter Eight - A Republican Army on the March

Gaius turned to look behind him. The long column of heavily armed soldiers extended as far as he could see. The rhythmic tramp of thousands of hob-nailed boots shook the earth. The jangle of equipment mingled with curses, bellowing oxen and shouted orders. The sun glinted and reflected off the soldiers plumed bronze helmets, breastplates and large oval shields. Maniple after Maniple came on marching behind each other, eight men abreast in a long rectangular formation preceded by their centurion, with his signifer holding up the unit standard and a single trumpeter carrying his long straight tuba. At the rear of the companies an optio, the second in command was there to deal with the men who dropped out of formation. It was early in the afternoon and a cloud of dust hung over the marching men. To their left the branch tributary to the Liris river sparkled and gurgled as it made its way towards the sea. The tributary was wider here than the Liris at Sora. Gaius licked his lips and stared longingly at the water. Then he wiped the sweat from his brow. He strode along in the middle of his Maniple of Hastati. He was parched but Verrens his centurion had not allowed them to refill their water skins from the river. The shock at coming face to face with army discipline had been hard for the Soran volunteers. One man had already felt Verrens's vine stick on his back for breaking ranks without permission.

Gaius blew the air from his cheeks and marched on. Six days had passed since they had left Sora. Fulvius had not crossed the Liris as Gaius had expected but had marched back the way he'd come, back down the Liris valley towards the old Roman colony of Fregellae. At Fregellae, an important and strategic town, they had been joined by reinforcements. After a day's pause the army had swung east and south and had started to follow the Liris valley in the direction of the Samnite town of Casinum. On reaching the town they had hardly paused. The Samnite population had already fled into the wild-forested mountains that towered above their home. The town had been empty and abandoned. Nevertheless, Fulvius had ordered it burned and ransacked. That had been yesterday. Now the army was following the tributary of the Liris south once more. The Tenth Maniple of Hastati had been marching since dawn.

Gaius turned to look ahead. Empty fields bordered the river and there was no sign of any local inhabitants but some fields showed signs of recent human activity. Here and there a clump of trees provided a welcome diversion from the flat valley. On all sides, however the snow crested mountains closed in and to Gaius they seemed to be growing higher and more rugged the further he marched. Through the dust clouds up ahead he suddenly saw a troop of cavalrymen riding back down the long column of infantry. They were preceded by a young tribune. The young man looked the same age as Gaius. Gaius glanced at the riders as they swept past the marching men.

'Sir,' a soldier, one of the Soran recruits, cried out, 'Will the Samnites stand and fight or will they run for the hills like they did at Casinum?'

'How the fuck should I know,' Verrens replied.

The centurion was a huge hulk of a man from the Roman coastal town of Lavinum. The remaining original soldiers of the Tenth Maniple had told the Soran newcomers that he was a ship builder by trade. He was thirty, which made him much older than the average age of the soldiers in the company, who were mostly barely out of their teens. Gaius stared at the long white scar that ran down the centurion's arm. Verrens was by far the most experienced soldier in the company having already served for eleven campaigning seasons including four in the last Samnite war. The officer was a strict disciplinarian and Gaius and his comrades had quickly learned that they could not cut corners in anything that their commanding officer demanded from them. But at least Verrens only punished his men when they deserved it and not because he enjoyed exercising his power like some of the other centurions Gaius had heard about. His fairness had gained him his soldiers' respect, and amongst themselves, the men had muttered that they were lucky to have him as their commander.

Verrens's sharp command brought the company to an abrupt halt. The Maniple in front of them, the Ninth of Hastati had come to stop. In the distance Gaius heard shouted commands. He glanced at Verrens but the officer looked unconcerned. A moment later a tuba rang out.

Then the Ninth, ahead of them, started marching again. A few moments later they halted again. Gaius glanced at his comrades. No one had a clue as to what was going on. Verrens muttered something and strode forwards to confer with the centurion in command of the Ninth. A few moments later he was back.

'Soldiers,' he cried, 'We're turning east and crossing the river. The engineers up ahead have built a bridge. We must wait our turn to cross. If you want to fill your water skins now is the time.'

Gaius and his companions needed no urging. They ran towards the riverbank. Groups of Roman soldiers were already there. Taking his helmet from his head Gaius scooped it into the river and drank. Then he splashed the water across his face. He had only just finished filling his water skin when he heard Verrens cry out ordering his men back into formation. The Ninth had already moved off along the river. Hastily the Tenth hurried to catch up. Gaius glanced at the river. It was wider and deeper than at Sora but still, he thought; a man could have waded across if he had to. Why the need to build a bridge?

'Make your water last,' Verrens shouted, 'Were going up into the mountains boys.'

It was only when the Tenth Maniple crossed the river that Gaius understood the need for the bridge. You fool he thought. A man may be able to cross the river but the heavily loaded baggage train and supply carts with their lumbering oxen and mules could not. Without their supplies the army would be lost. The bridge was there to ensure that their supply lines stayed open. A cavalry troop stood watching the heavy infantry companies crossing the bridge and further along the river the combat engineers who had built it sat resting in the grass. Their pick axes had been stuck into the ground like stakes in a palisade.

All that afternoon Gaius marched. The direction was east, away from the Liris. As they progressed Gaius noticed that they had started to climb. The country was becoming wilder and more rugged. Their speed began to slow. Wearily Gaius looked up and peered ahead. How long before they would stop to build their camp? He couldn't see the front of the column but he could see that they were climbing up into a mountain pass. The gentle, cultivated fields and meadows of the valley began to give way to great rock boulders and jagged rock faces and trees, endless green trees that covered the lower slopes of the mountains. Here and there a small white, mountain stream cascaded and twisted its way down the slopes. Higher and higher they went. It was late in the afternoon when Verrens suddenly cried out.

'Look lively boys, we are being watched!'

Gaius blinked and turned to look in the direction in which the centurion was staring. For a moment, he saw nothing amongst the rugged terrain. Then high up on a cliff top he caught sight of men standing along the tree line. There had to be at least a hundred of them and they were armed with shields and spears. The men were watching the Roman progress.

'Yes boys,' Verrens cried gleefully, 'They are Samnites. There is your enemy. Get used to how he looks and smells for he may be the last man you will ever see.'

'What are they doing Sir?' one of the Soran recruits in the rank behind the centurion shouted.

'Oh nothing much,' Verrens exclaimed, 'They are just seeing how many of us there are and where we are going. They won't attack. They will wait till tonight when you are asleep in your tent.'

The Soran volunteer who had spoken suddenly looked anxious. The man didn't see the grin, which had appeared on Verrens's face.

'Remember this boys,' the centurion cried, 'The Samnite is a formidable warrior. He is tough and resourceful. He has the same weapons as we do, in fact the Samnites have such good weapons and tactics that we have copied them. He is the master of the ambush and he knows these mountains better than you know your own mothers. But there is one thing he doesn't have.'

'What's that Sir,' another Soran asked falling into the trap.

'My bloody vine rod on your back, if you dare run away from the battle line,' Verrens thundered. 'If any of you takes one step back during a fight I will personally beat you to death for cowardice. There will be no shame in the Tenth.'

The company had no more questions after that. As they climbed higher up into the mountain pass Gaius caught more Samnite pickets watching them from the surrounding ridges and forests. At one point a Roman cavalry troop turned their horses towards a group of Samnites who had got to close but before the cavalrymen could reach their enemy the Samnites had melted away into the forest.

It was dusk when the companies ahead of them halted and a trumpet blast announced the end of that day's march. Gaius turned wearily to look back down the way they had come. They were high up in the middle of the mountain pass. In the distance he could just about see the green valley through which they had marched that morning. It seemed far below them. Suddenly he shivered. The air up here was cooler. Startled he looked up as Verrens was suddenly standing before him. The veteran commander jerked his head   down the mountain pass.

'You,' he growled at Gaius, 'go and see if you can find our tents amongst the baggage train. Bring them here when you have found them.'

Gaius nodded, remembered to salute and turned away. Around him the mountain side had come alive with the shouts and orders of the officers as the men were set to work building their marching camp.

***

The night was a restless one. Gaius had drawn guard duty and now he stood on top of the earthen rampart with its crude wooden palisade made from felled tree trunks. A full moon hung in the sky. Below him a deep V shaped ditch gave the camp some additional protection. Beyond the earthen rampart and ditch the night was quiet. Gaius rubbed his tired eyes and blinked as he stared into the darkness. Drawing guard duty was just bad luck but there were worse jobs. Beyond the camp a number of Roman pickets had been placed to give advance warning of a Samnite attack. If the Samnites were truly determined, the few men out there wouldn't stand much of a chance.

He slapped his face to waken himself up. Verrens had made it perfectly clear that any soldier found sleeping on duty would be executed. Such was army discipline. None of the men in the company had doubted him. Gaius sighed and lifted his leg and tried to balance himself on one leg. Anything to keep himself awake and relieve the boredom. Despite all his tasks he'd still found time to go and find Cassia like he'd done every night. He'd found her with the baggage train. The girl was doing what he had told her to do. That was good. She had greeted him sullenly and had spoken little but there were no marks on her body and she didn't seem to be upset or agitated. Someone was giving her food. He hadn't asked who it was and she hadn't told him.

A sudden movement in the darkness brought him back onto two feet. He grabbed his spear and swung it and his shield in the direction from which the movement had come.

'Password,' Gaius shouted.

For a moment, the darkness was silent. Then a rough Latin voice answered.

'Garum.'

A figure appeared and in the pale moonlight Gaius saw that it was Verrens. The centurion was on his inspection round of the guards. Gaius relaxed at the sight of the centurion's plumed helmet. Verrens gave him a brief nod and turned to stare out beyond the ramparts. He was silent for a while.

'Tomorrow we shall fight,' the centurion muttered, 'Prepare yourself soldier. The Samnites will not let us enter the mountain passes into the heart of Samnium without a fight. You can count on it.'

Then without another word Verrens passed on down the ramparts and into the darkness.

***

When the trumpets woke the camp at dawn Gaius felt that he'd hardly had any sleep. Grumpily he helped pack away the army tent in which he had spent the night. Then after a quick breakfast of cold porridge, Verrens deep voice boomed out and the 10th Maniple of Hastati rushed to form up into a square. The optio strode down the ranks counting the men and checking to see that all had the right equipment.

'All present and correct Sir,' the optio bellowed turning smartly towards Verrens. The centurion nodded and turned to his signifer who was holding the unit standard in his hand.

'Tenth company. Forward. March,' Verrens roared and behind him Gaius and his comrades started forwards.

All that morning they marched. The army camp had been built in the middle of the mountain pass and that morning they descended into a narrow green fertile valley beyond which Gaius could see a new range of mountains. The mountains looked bigger, more rugged and higher than the ones they were leaving behind. As they went down into the valley he caught sight of men flitting in and out of the trees parallel to their marching route. The Samnites were keeping a careful eye on them. But the Roman army ignored the enemy.

Mid-morning found the army in the valley and Verrens allowed them a brief respite to fill their water skins from a small stream. Then they were on the move again. At noon the army started to climb once more. The mountain pass they were heading into, was obscured by mist and a dark forest. As they climbed higher the land seemed to grow more desolate and rugged. Huge boulders littered the mountainside and soon it became impossible for the company to keep its formation. Some of the men started to fall behind and the optio had to shout and threaten the men to keep going. The track they were following grew steeper and narrower and they started to pass ravines, gullies, cascading mountain streams and strange rock formations. To Gaius it felt as if the mountains themselves were trying to force the Romans back. The pace of the army began to slow. It was late in the day, with the column hopelessly strung out along the mountain pass, when the Ninth Company in front of them came to a complete halt. Verrens raised his hand and the Tenth too came to a halt. The men cast nervous glances towards the mountainsides on their flank. The forest could hide a whole army of Samnites. Then from far away Gaius heard a trumpet. His heart started to beat faster. That had not been a Roman army signal. The others too had heard the noise. Gaius glanced towards Verrens. The centurion looked tense. The officer said something to his signifer. Then he was stomping off up the track towards the front of the Roman column.

He was gone for a full ten minutes. Then suddenly he reappeared hurrying down the track towards them. Every man in the 10th Maniple was staring at him in anxious anticipation. The centurion looked grim.

'We are going to retreat,' he exclaimed.

Chapter Nine - Retreat

The Maniple milled about in confusion. From further up the mountain pass Gaius heard urgent shouted orders. Again, the alien trumpet noise echoed off the mountain walls. A horde of Velites came descending past him in a disorganised stream. A signifer was valiantly trying to restore order. The Ninth Company in front of them had not moved. Gaius looked up at the sky. It was evening. It would be dark soon. Were they really going to retreat down the pass during the hours of darkness? Why had Fulvius not decided to build a camp and fortify his position?

'Tenth Company, form up, marching order,' Verrens screamed and the authority in his voice brought the men back into line. The centurion was just about to issue the order to turn and start moving back down the pass when a horseman galloped up to him. The cavalryman was wearing a red cloak and an Attic helmet. He looked a couple of years older than Gaius. The man's face was flushed.

'Centurion,' the young tribune cried, 'You and your men will stay here. Hastati companies Three through to Ten will form a line and hold their positions. You are to let the army through and protect their rear. When we have passed through you are to retreat in good order and keep the enemy at a distance.'

Verrens had turned at the officer's approach. He saluted smartly and nodded.

'Yes Sir, the Tenth will do as ordered, Sir.'

'Good man,' the tribune nodded.

'How long do we have?' Verrens said looking up at the young officer. The tribune shook his head.

'Not long, the main Samnite army is encamped on the top of the pass. Hold the line centurion and watch out for their cavalry.'

Then the tribune was urging his horse on down the pass. For a moment Verrens watched him go in silence. Then he turned to his men.

'Well you heard the officer, we're to form a rearguard boys - so that the rest of the army can retreat. Now form a battle line. Three deep. Form a line!'

Gaius and the Tenth Company rushed to form up across the mountain track. The ground was steep and broken but they managed to form a somewhat irregular and thin front, forty men wide and three deep. The men placed their shields on the ground, resting them against their legs and held their hastae spears upright. All were staring up the pass from which Maniple after Maniple were pouring down. The optio strode along behind his men inspecting the line. Up ahead the Ninth was moving off to their right, extending the line towards the forest. Gaius glanced to his left; another company was doing the same in that direction. A rock formation blocked his view of what was happening further out. Then a movement close by made him look round. The signifer, holding the unit standard had taken up position close by. The boar's head he was wearing seemed to be snarling and growling. There was stoic expression on the man's face. Then to his right in the gathering gloom Gaius caught sight of horsemen. They had appeared at the edge of the forest.

'Samnite cavalry on our flanks Sir,' the optio screamed at Verrens. The centurion had seen the riders too. He gave a little shake of his head. There was nothing he could do about that. The flank companies would have seen the danger. Gaius stared at the horsemen. Their numbers were increasing rapidly. Would they attack? The Ninth's line was already wheeling round to deal with the threat.

'Why is Fulvius not building a camp, Sir?' Gaius exclaimed. 'It will be dark soon. The Samnites would never attack a fortified camp.'

The signifer glanced quickly at the massing Samnite cavalry. 'We can't build a camp,' the soldier muttered, 'Those horsemen will prevent us from gathering wood. The Consul has no option but to retreat.'

***

It was dark when the last army formation passed through the thin rear-guard screen. As the final Triarii Company disappeared down the track and into the gloom, Verrens turned to look up the pass. The night was quiet. Nothing could be seen. The Tenth had not moved from their positions. The Samnite cavalry had not launched a full-on attack but the riders had started to harass the Romans. Horsemen had ridden up towards the Roman line and had started to hurl spears and javelins at them. On the flanks the Samnite horsemen had whirled around like flies, darting forwards and then retreating and for the legionaries there had been no rest. The mental strain was slowly and steadily exhausting them. Along the battle line Gaius could see a number of burning torches, one for each company of Hastati.

Then from the darkness Gaius heard the noise of a galloping horse. Quickly he grasped his shield, raised it and lowered his spear in the direction from which the sound had come. The men on either side of him did the same.

'Friendly, I am friendly,' a Latin voice screamed. A moment later a figure on horseback appeared. In the light of the burning torch Gaius saw that it was the young tribune who had given them their orders earlier in the evening. Gaius lowered his spear as behind him he heard a man running towards him.

The tribune tightened his grip on his horses' bridle.

'Centurion,' he growled, 'We're done. Order your men back down the pass and rejoin the army.'

'How far behind us are they Sir?' Verrens grunted.

'Not far, not far at all,' the young officer snapped. 'Keep your men in formation centurion. Their cavalry will not attack you if your men stick together.'

'I know, I know, I wasn't born yesterday, boy,' Verrens growled irritably. The officer didn't seem to have noticed the remark.

Verrens turned round sharply, 'Tenth company, follow me, stay together. We are going to walk down the pass. Now move, move!'

Grasping the flaming torch from his signifer, Verrens turned and started down the track. Around him Gaius heard the men lift up their shields. In the star light silent figures started to leave their positions and follow their centurion. On the flanks the other torches too had started to descend the mountain slope. It was an eerie sight as hundreds of troops began to descend the slopes. Soon Gaius could hardly see anything in the dark and the broken and rough terrain started to cause problems. As the darkness grew the night began to be filled with curses and bad-tempered muttering as the men strove to find their way.

'We will walk down this mountain,' Gaius heard Verrens's shout. 'Follow my torch. We will walk, we will not run!'

Behind him Gaius suddenly heard the noise of horses' hooves. The noise was rapidly drawing closer.

'Cavalry,' he screamed whirling round to face the darkness behind him. Around him the darkness exploded with cries, curses and shouts. Gaius stared wildly into the night. He could see nothing. Then with a whooshing sound a javelin came flying out of the darkness. The projectile slammed harmlessly into a boulder but the second one struck a man. There was a shriek of pain followed by a horrible gurgle and close by a shield and spear clattered onto the ground.

'Leave him,' Verrens cried out. 'Stay together boys.'

Gaius was staring wildly into the darkness but there was no sign of the Samnite cavalry. They had vanished as quickly as they had come. Hurriedly he scampered on down the slope after the burning torch.

All night the Roman rearguard stumbled on down the mountain pass. The rough terrain slowed them down and it was impossible to see what lay ahead. The men followed the burning torches praying that their officers knew where they were going. The Samnite cavalry harassed them all the way. In the darkness behind him Gaius could hear their blood curdling yells and screams and now then a volley of spears was launched at the retreating Romans but the enemy drew back from a full out attack. Maybe the rough, broken ground made the Samnites reluctant or maybe they feared a Roman ambush, Gaius thought as he clambered over a boulder and struggled on behind Verrens's torch.

By the time dawn came Gaius was exhausted. As the light grew he saw they were still in the mountain pass. His companions were strung out in a disorganised column and some had lost their shields. Some of the Hastati companies had got mixed up with each other and their men now stumbled on down the mountain in groups. All of them looked utterly exhausted; but the fear of the Samnites behind them kept them going.

'Here they come,' a soldier suddenly screamed.

Gaius whirled round. In the growing light, he could see the Samnite cavalry spread out in a long line a couple of hundred paces behind them. For a while now the riders had been walking their horses, happy to drive the Romans before them like a sheep dog would do to a flock of sheep, but now the horsemen were picking up the pace. Gaius's eyes grew in alarm. The Samnite cavalry were coming in to attack. Now that it was light enough, the enemy must have decided to finish off the Roman rearguard.

'Tenth company, form up, prepare to receive cavalry,' Verrens's deep urgent voice boomed. The centurion too had seen the Samnite movement. Gaius had no idea what to do. He had never received any training. There had been no time. Some of the more experienced soldiers had however formed a tight circle around the signifer. Gaius ran to join them. His companions had placed their shields next to each other so that they overlapped and were kneeling on one knee. Their spears pointed outwards forming a dense line of spear points aimed at the enemy. Gaius sprinted into the circle and copying his companions took up a position within the formation.

'Hold your position boys, those horses will not charge your spears. Don't let them frighten you,' Verrens roared. 'We stand together or we die together.'

More men joined the circle around the unit standard. Gaius felt his heart hammering in his chest. The Samnite cavalry were charging down the slope towards them. The few Roman stragglers didn't have a chance. As the Romans desperately tried to join their comrades the Samnite cavalry thundered through them and the stragglers were cut down with contemptible ease. Terrified panic-stricken shrieks echoed off the mountains. To his right one of the Hastati companies had failed to form a circle and the men were running wildly down the mountainside. A line of Samnite cavalry swept through the fleeing men cutting them down with their swords and spearing them in their backs. The morning was suddenly rent with the screams and shrieks of terrified and dying men. Gaius's attention was suddenly fixed on another line of horsemen galloping straight for him and his comrades. The Samnites were practically standing up on their horses. Gaius's gasped in horror at the sight. From where he knelt the horses looked huge and unstoppable.

'Hold,' Verrens roared, 'Hold your position!'

Gaius felt his spear shaking in his hands. Then at the last moment the horses shied away and the Samnite line divided in two and swept around the tight circle of Roman infantrymen. As they flashed past the Samnites released a volley of javelins at the Roman defenders. A spear hammered into Gaius's neighbours shield and behind him he heard a shriek as a man was hit. Then the cavalry were past them.

'Hold,' Verrens screamed. Not a man moved. Not a man said a word. All eyes were fixed on the Samnite cavalry whirling around the mountain slopes. More cries and shrieks echoed off the mountain walls. Whoever was not in formation was a dead man. The Samnites were taking no prisoners. Gaius felt his arm shaking with nervous exhaustion. How long could they maintain this position? How long before the men just gave up through utter exhaustion. How long before they were overrun by these wild mountain men? It didn't take a genius to understand that their position was desperate.

He raised his head a little and glanced up the mountain pass. There was no sign yet of the main Samnite infantry force. But they would not be far behind. Was that what the Samnite cavalry were doing? Preventing the Romans from moving until the main Samnite army caught up with them? When that happened, Gaius knew, he and his comrades would die. They were far too few to withstand a determined infantry assault. The Samnites had them trapped. Gaius turned to look at Verrens. The centurion stood in the centre of the circle beside his signifer. There was a grim resigned expression on his face. Verrens knew it too. They were trapped, unable to move. Gaius closed his eyes. He was going to die here on this bleak mountain slope. His desire for vengeance on the man who had murdered his family had just been another game that the gods had allowed him to play.

Verrens said something to his Trumpeter and a moment later a long hideous sounding trumpet blast echoed across the mountain valley. The blast was followed by another and then another. Gaius stared at the Trumpeter and blushed, as he understood. Verrens was calling for help. But who would come? Who would be able to drive the Samnite cavalry from the field?

Across the mountain pass other trumpet blasts could suddenly be heard and their noise filled Gaius with sudden hope. Some of the other companies had survived. They were not completely alone.

'Here they come again,' a soldier screamed. Gaius twisted his neck to look behind him. A line of Samnite cavalry were charging towards the Roman position. He wrenched his head to look ahead. His back felt horribly exposed but there was nothing he could do.

'Hold boys,' Verrens screamed. Then the Samnite riders were upon them and sweeping around the circle of desperate Roman defenders. A volley of spears hammered into shields, flesh and earth. With a cry the signifer collapsed with a spear protruding from his back. As he hit the ground a Roman bounded forwards, snatched the unit standard from where it had fallen and raised it. Shrieks and shouts rose from amongst the defenders. Then the Samnite riders were past them and reforming a hundred paces away. Gaius could not stop his hands from trembling. His spear point moved from side to side. Two more men had collapsed within the circle.

Gaius stared at the line of horsemen ahead of him. The Samnites were preparing for another charge. Then they seemed to hesitate.

'Come on you bastards,' a Roman had suddenly stood up and was yelling at the Samnite riders, 'What are you waiting for? I am here, I am here.' The man sounded like he was close to breaking point. Verrens struck the soldier across the head with his vine rod and the man fell to the ground with blood streaming down his face. The soldier looked up at his centurion in terror.

'I said, hold,' Verrens thundered, his face dark with rage. 'I will kill the first man who leaves his post.' And as he said the words the centurion drew his sword from its scabbard. Gaius didn't dare move. His eyes were fixed on the Samnite cavalry. What were they waiting for?

Then behind him he heard one of the men cry out.

'Our cavalry, our cavalry are here. Look, look, look!'

Every pair of eyes in the company turned to look in the direction in which the soldier was pointing and sure enough coming towards them and up the valley was an extended line of Roman cavalrymen. The morning light glinted and reflected from the cavalrymen's armour and shields. They came on at a brisk trot led by their officers and standard bearers.

'Campanians,' Verrens hissed with sudden delight. 'We're going to be all right boy's, the Campanian horse are here.'

Chapter Ten - The Battle for the Mountain Pass

The Roman army stood drawn up for battle. Its rear companies pushed up against the steep boulder strewn mountainside. The Maniple formations straddled the mountain valley like a chequer board with empty spaces separating the individual Maniples. The broken and uneven ground made it difficult to form a straight front but the Tribunes seemed to have done the best they could under the circumstances. Their efforts to organise the troops could however not conceal the blatant truth that Fulvius was being forced into battle. The Roman army was still not out of the mountain pass. The rough, broken terrain would favour the hardy Samnites who had grown up in the mountains. Fulvius must have decided that the risk of being ambushed whilst retreating was too great. Behind the front line Hastati companies were two more lines of soldiers. The soldiers' shields rested against their legs and each man was armed with a hastae spear and his short italic stabbing sword. On the flanks Gaius could see cavalry squadrons drawn up to protect the flank of the army. The men's armour and weapons glinted in the morning sunlight and beside each unit, the signifers, their heads covered with animal skins, stood motionless, holding up their proud standards and banners. So Fulvius had decided to stand and fight Gaius thought wearily, as he and the survivors of the Tenth Maniple of Hastati limped towards their comrades. Gaius's legs felt heavy and he barely had the strength to lift up his shield. His spear rested over his shoulder.

As the tattered remnants of the Roman rearguard approached their comrades the escorting Campanian cavalry turned and trotted away down the pass towards the right flank. The presence of the Campanian cavalry had stopped the Samnites from attacking the exhausted infantry companies but now their job was done and they were needed on the flanks. As Verrens led his men back towards the Roman army a screen of Velites, agile but lightly armoured young men with slings and throwing spears advanced to cover Gaius and his comrades. Verrens led the way. He was holding the unit standard. The centurion was muttering to himself. Ever since the Campanian cavalry had come to their rescue the centurion had looked annoyed. Why had they not left the cavalry to cover their retreat in the first place he had snarled after the first joy at their relief had passed? No one had dared answer him.

Amongst the survivors Gaius suddenly spotted the young tribune who had given them their orders. The officer must have remained with the rearguard all that time. The tribune had lost his horse and was striding along on foot. His face was streaked with dust and sweat and in his hand he was carrying the standard of the Third company of Hastati. Blood was smeared across the banner.

The Tenth were guided to their place in the line by another tribune. The Hastati normally made up the front line but as they were in no fit state to fight the rearguard companies were allotted a place in the second line. Their front was being covered by Maniples from the Principes - men in their prime. As soon as they had taken their place in the line Gaius and his comrades collapsed to the ground too exhausted to care what happened to them. Verrens and the other officers said nothing and did not intervene as the men dropped where they stood. Gaius closed his eyes and was asleep within seconds. He was woken by a gentle hand shaking him. A slave, a camp servant thrust a loaf of stale bread into his hand and moved on without saying a word. Gaius raised himself up onto his elbows. Some of the men were wolfing the bread down. Others still lay on the ground where they had collapsed. Three slaves were pulling along a cart loaded with bread. Gaius rubbed his eyes and blinked. At least the Roman supply system was still working. He glanced up at the sky. The sun was already high. It must be near noon. He glanced round and saw Verrens sitting on a rock. The centurion had his eyes closed.

As Gaius watched his commanding officer, a messenger on horseback came galloping up to Verrens. The centurion opened his eyes as the rider halted before him.

'Take your company into the front-line centurion. You are to replace the Principes and await the signal to advance on the enemy. Legate's orders.'

Verrens nodded that he had understood and the messenger galloped on towards the next company.

The centurion rose to his feet, took a deep breath. 'Tenth company, stand to attention. Form up, three deep.' he roared.

Gaius rose, stuffed as much bread as he could into his mouth, picked up his shield and spear and hurried to take his position in the rectangular formation that was forming in front of Verrens.

'Seventeen men missing and unaccounted for Sir,' the optio reported as he saluted in front of his commanding officer. Verrens nodded. It was impossible to know what had happened to the missing men. Some undoubtedly had been killed whilst others must have simply got lost in the darkness.

Verrens took a step forwards and addressed his men. 'Boys,' Verrens said in an uncharacteristically mellow voice. 'We're going to be in the front line. I know many of you have never been in a battle before. Stand your ground and trust in the man beside you. The Samnites may be valiant soldiers but they are no better than you. There will be no retreat from where we plant our standard. No retreat.'

The company turned to follow their centurion, filtering through the line of Principes who had been guarding their front. The older men glanced tensely at the young Hastati troopers. If the Hastati were unable to force a decision on the battlefield, it would be the task of the Principes to do so and if they failed, then the battle would go to the Triarii, the men in their mid and late thirties. As the Tenth Company took up their position in the line Gaius caught his breath at the sight that met his eyes. Holding the higher ground, a few hundred paces away, stood thousands upon thousands of Samnite infantrymen. The enemy line extended across the mountain valley. The Samnites were drawn up in similar Maniple formations as the Roman army. Gaius could see the enemy standards arrayed along their lines. Apart from the tramp of his comrades boots Gaius could hear nothing. The mountain pass was eerily silent as the two armies stared at each other waiting to see what would happen. Gaius rubbed his eyes. His tiredness however had vanished. Both armies must have used the morning lull to gain some rest and prepare for what was coming.

'Company, halt,' Verrens roared as the company took up its position. Gaius could see that the Tenth formed the extreme right of the Fifth Legion's front. The Fifth, the Boar Head Legion and the Third, the Wolf Head Legion, held the centre of the Roman line with the infantry from the two allied legions on their flanks. Further out the Roman and Campanian cavalry squadrons would be covering the army's flanks. Gaius looked up the slope towards the Samnites. The enemy facing him were clad in white, even their shields had been whitened and here and there he caught a flash of silver. Gaius felt a tremor of unease as he recognised the enemy troops. He was facing the best of the best of the Samnite heavy infantry, the Linen Legion. There was no one between him and the enemy. He stood in the front row. The Tenth Hastati had formed up in the standard forty men wide, three deep formation, but the third line was weak due to the casualties they had taken. The empty spaces on either side of his Maniple made the unit flanks look horribly exposed but the gaps were covered by the Principes companies who stood drawn up further back in the second line. Gaius glanced at the man to his right, some six feet away. The young warrior had a soldier's scarf, a Focale tied around his neck to stop his armour chafing his skin. Trust in the man beside you, Verrens had said. Gaius glanced to his left. A small wiry man, a full head shorter than Gaius stood staring at the enemy. As Gaius looked at the man he noticed a wet patch on the ground below the man. The soldier had pissed himself.

A Roman trumpet suddenly rang out. A few moments later Gaius sensed movement around him. Groups of Velites came hurrying through the gaps between the stationary heavy infantry companies. The Velites ran forwards, straight at the enemy, readying their throwing javelins and whirling their slings above their heads. From the Samnite position's similarly armed men advanced to meet the Roman attack. Then the air was filled with projectiles. Spears went hurtling through the air and stones zipped up and down the mountain slopes. Here and there men cried out as they were hit and collapsed to the ground. Gaius reached down to raise his shield from where it rested against his legs. The men beside him seemed to have the same thought but Verrens had anticipated their thoughts.

'Wait,' he screamed, 'Wait for my order.'

The Roman Velites were at a disadvantage as the Samnites held the higher ground and slowly the skirmishers were driven back.

Then as Gaius stared nervously at the advancing enemy light infantry two Roman trumpets rang out nearly instantaneously. The mountain valley was suddenly filled with noise and movement. Above the din Gaius heard Verrens voice.

'Tenth company will advance. Hold your line. We walk.'

Gaius grasped his shield and lifted it off the ground. His hands were damp with sweat. Then he was advancing up the slope. Along the entire Roman line the Hastati companies of four legions were doing the same. Gaius suddenly became aware of a new noise. The Romans were beating their spears on their shields as they advanced.

'Samnium must die. The Samnites must die!', the Romans had started to chant their battle cries. As the heavy infantry companies advanced the Samnite skirmishers hurled a final volley of stones and spears at the Roman line and then briskly retreated. Gaius raised his shield to cover himself as close by a stone smacked into a soldier's shield. As he did so he caught a quick glimpse of Verrens. The centurion was striding out ahead of his men followed closely by the new signifer holding up the company standard. From the Samnite lines Gaius heard jeering. Then the front line of Samnite heavy infantry were advancing down the slope to meet the Roman advance. The enemy were clad entirely in white. Their extremely short tunics barely covered their genitals and across their chests they wore bright shining bronze pectoral armour. Their left legs were protected by greaves and on their heads they wore the same plumed Montefortino helmets as the Romans. When the two lines were thirty paces from each other they halted. Gaius could hear the deep throated Samnite battle cries. The noise sounded like a pack of wild dogs baying for blood.

For a moment the two armies stared at each other. Then the Samnite soldiers seemed to collectively draw back their arms and a volley of heavy javelins hurled down at Gaius and his comrades. With a mighty roar the Samnites charged forwards down the slope. Gaius raised his shield. A spear slammed into it and the force of the blow made him stagger backwards. As the tip of the projectile buried itself in his shield the long wooden shaft broke off leaving just the embedded metal point. Around him Gaius heard men's cries and screams. There was no time to wait for orders. The battle had gone beyond that point. With a cry he lowered his shield so that he could see what was happening in front of him. A line of wild Samnite infantrymen were charging straight for him. Then with great splintering crash the Samnites slammed into the Roman line. A Samnite impaled himself on Gaius's spear. There was a shriek. Then with a groan the man slid to the ground taking Gaius's spear with him. Before Gaius could react a huge snarling man came slamming into Gaius using his shield like a battering ram. Gaius staggered backwards under the man's weight but just as it looked like he was going to be pushed to the ground, his attacker tripped over a rock. Gaius ripped his sword from its scabbard and plunged the weapon into the Samnites exposed back. Blood welled up from the wound. With a cry Gaius stabbed his attacker again. Around him the Roman line had descended into a snarling, shrieking mob as desperate, vicious men lunged and parried and tried to stab, maim and kill each other. Then as soon as it had begun the two front lines recoiled from each other and the Samnites were retreating back up the slope. The same seemed to be happening all along the battlefront.

'Reform, reform,' Gaius heard a Roman voice screaming. Dimly he was aware that the voice belonged to Verrens. He took a step forwards and yanked his spear from the chest of the Samnite he'd killed. The metal came away with a sucking noise. The man with the Focale and the soldier who had pissed himself were still on either side of him. Blood was smeared across the face of the man to his left. Gaius stared up the slope. The Samnites had not gone far and were already reforming for another charge. Along the Roman line the bodies of the slain had formed gaps, which were quickly filled by men from the second row. A Roman, trailing his intestines, was desperately trying to crawl back towards the rear. His pathetic groans for help went unanswered. Gaius stared up the slope. The Samnites were charging towards them once more. Their shrieks and cries were terrifying. Then as the Samnites stormed towards the Roman line Gaius saw that the angle of the Samnite attack had changed. The enemy was going for the company Standard. They intended to capture it. Gaius did not move. As the Samnites closed he steadied himself. Then with a cry he thrust his spear at a man who was leaping towards him. The Samnite was old but still agile enough to evade the spear thrust. His attacker was an experienced man for he smashed his shield boss into Gaius's shield knocking him back and in the same movement plunged his knife into the exposed side of the Roman who'd pissed himself. The knife slid into the man, just under his ribs. With a scream Gaius's neighbour staggered backwards his hands pressed to his side. Then he collapsed. All along the line the Samnites crashed into the Romans and the battle line rippled along the valley as thousands upon thousands of men clashed, stabbing, battering and shoving at each other. The afternoon was filled with shrieks, cries and screams. Gaius caught a glimpse of Verrens. The centurion was straining to hold back the Samnite attack. His shield was pressed up against the Samnites and the two sides were pushing and shoving at each other trying to make the other fall back. Behind Verrens the company standard was held up high so that all could see it. Then after the shock of clashing shields and swords, the two battle lines once more recoiled from each other. The Samnites however did not retreat far and once again they began to prepare for the next charge.

Gaius was panting. He glanced to his left. A big strong-looking man had taken the place of his fallen comrade. There was no one behind the man on his left. On either side of the Tenth, two Principes companies had moved up and had closed with the enemy so that the Roman line had become a continuous front. Gaius blinked. He had not noticed the Princeps moving forwards. There was no time to ponder on the development. The Samnites were once more rushing towards him. Gaius picked up an enemy javelin and hurled it at the Samnites. The spear slammed into a shield. Then the enemy were upon him. A sword hit his shield and slid away. He nearly tripped over a corpse as the shock and weight of the enemy assault pushed him back. A Samnite was pushing against his shield. Gaius shoved him back. All along the line, men were doing the same. The Roman line was holding. The Samnites had failed to break through. Blindly Gaius jabbed his sword around the edge of his shield. It struck an enemy shield. Nearby someone was shrieking in a high-pitched voice. It was a horrible noise. Then the Samnite line recoiled once more. Gaius leaned wearily on his spear as the Samnite line stumbled backwards. The enemy too, seemed to be tiring. How long had they been fighting? Gaius had completely lost track of time. He snatched a glance down the mountain valley but all was confusion further out on the Roman flank. It was impossible to see what had happened to the Roman cavalry.

The Samnites took their time before they launched their next assault. For a while the bloodied, bruised and battered lines of men stared at each other. Then led by their Standard bearers the Samnites came on down the slope. Their pace slowed however and grew more cautious as they closed with the Romans. The two sides sparred and jabbed at each other with their spears but failed to close with each other. The enemy were tiring but so too were the Romans. Gaius noticed that the line held by the Tenth was becoming thinner and thinner. The young man with the Focale around his neck was still beside him. Gaius parried a Samnite spear thrust and lunged with his own spear. A man cried out close by. From behind his shield Gaius stared at the enemy. He could see them clearly. The Samnites were staring straight back at him. Their eyes glinted dangerously as they searched for any opening, any weakness in the Roman line. The fighting rippled along the battlefront but it was becoming clear to both sides that a breakthrough was not going to come soon. Neither side seemed prepared to give way.

Once more the Samnite heavy infantry tried to break through the Roman line and once more they were repulsed and once more they recoiled from the shock of battle. The afternoon wore on with neither side giving in. The Roman standards had not moved an inch backwards and neither had the Samnite ones. Gaius stood his ground wearily but the fear he'd felt at the start of the battle was being replaced by a stubborn resolve not to give in. He was not going to run away from the enemy. Not now that he and his comrades had fought the Samnite assault to a standstill. Not after having repulsed four enemy charges. The stubborn resolve seemed to have spread amongst the soldiers. The officers didn't need to tell them what to do. Every man knew what he had to do. Every man knew what was expected of them. Raw recruits had become veterans.

It was growing dark when, with the two battle lines still pushing, shoving and stabbing at each other, Gaius heard a distant trumpet. Then starting from the Roman right flank a great victorious roar rose from the Roman ranks. Gaius and the Samnites directly before him turned at the noise. Then the roar swept through the ranks of Roman soldiers around Gaius.

'The Campanians have defeated the Samnite horse,' a voice cried out. 'They have fallen on the Samnite rear. The battle is ours!'

Another Roman trumpet, closer by, suddenly rang out. Gaius raised his spear and cried out in delight. The Samnites in front of him had suddenly fallen silent. Then behind him Gaius sensed movement. He risked a quick look behind him. Pushing towards him were the grim but fresh looking faces of the Triarii, the third and final Roman line. Fulvius was sending in his reserves. Gaius felt pure elation pumping through his body. The Triarii, the most experienced soldiers were being sent in to finish off the Samnites. They were going to win.

The Triarii came on in close formation, six men wide and ten deep, their shields overlapping and their front bristling with spear points. As they came on Gaius heard them singing their battle song.

'Samnium will die, Samnium will die. Hear us immortal Mars, God of War. Samnium will perish on our spear points.'

In front of Gaius the Samnites milled around in confusion. Some of their men charged alone at the Roman line but were cut down. Then in an instant the Samnites turned and began to flee up the mountain pass into the gathering darkness. The speed of the enemy collapse took Gaius by surprise. Then from the gloom he heard Verrens's voice booming out.

'After them, kill them, kill them all!'

With a roar Gaius and the Roman front line set off in pursuit up the mountain slope. The Samnites were running for their lives now. Across the whole mountain valley, the entire Samnite army seemed to be in flight. Thousands of tiny figures were running and scrambling back up the mountain pass. After a hundred paces, however Gaius stumbled to a halt. He was exhausted. The broken ground around him was littered with bodies and discarded weapons. He stared at the fleeing enemy. They were going to get away. The onset of darkness was going to save them.

A Roman voice close by cried out in triumph. To his right a soldier stabbed a wounded Samnite in the head. Gaius took a step forwards, bent down and picked up a discarded Samnite Standard from where it had fallen. Then he raised the captured banner above his head and as he did so the Romans around him raised their swords in the air and cheered.

Chapter Eleven - Bovianum

It was dawn when Gaius and his comrades finally learned how the Consul Fulvius had managed to turn a desperate situation into a great victory. Gaius sat beside a small campfire, his shoulders covered with a woollen army blanket. The night had been cold. The small group of men around the fire were silent, some had their eyes closed and one man was poking at the fire with his sword. All of them looked exhausted. The battlefield around them was strewn with corpses, discarded weapons and dead horses. A few Roman soldiers were wandering about looting the dead of anything valuable and in the sky, vultures, hungry for meat, had started to circle in anticipation of a feast. Gaius examined the silver armband he'd taken from a dead Samnite. The silver was engraved with the image of a two-horned god. The armband would fetch a good price if he lived long enough to be able to sell it. He slid the band across his arm. It fitted perfectly. Maybe he would keep it he thought, as a reminder of this battle.

He looked up and stared at Verrens who was sitting across from the fire. The centurion had his eyes closed. Verrens had said little after the battle had ended. The Tenth Company of Hastati had lost half its men and from the volunteers who had joined the army at Sora only Gaius and two others remained alive. The men who'd had no training seemed to have suffered the highest casualties. Across the mountain valley Gaius could see more campfires. Closer by a tribune was holding up a captured Samnite heavy throwing spear, a pilum. A small group of staff officers were examining the weapon with interest. Further up the mountain slope a line of weary cavalrymen on horseback were walking their horses up the mountain pass. The enemy, it seemed, had fled into the mountains leaving it's wounded behind. Fulvius had ordered that no prisoners be taken and all night Gaius and his comrades had listened to the screams and shrieks of desperate pleading men. The men around the fire looked up as a newcomer joined them. It was the optio. The officer had a nasty looking knife wound across his arm. Dark circles had formed under his eyes. He sat down beside the fire and warmed his hands.

'I met a decurion down near the baggage train,' the officer murmured. 'He told me that the battle was decided when the Samnite horse decided to go for our baggage. The Consul had left it undefended.' The officer chuckled. 'The Samnites thought they were going to get away with all our valuables. Then in comes the Campanian horse and catches the enemy with their pants down. The decurion said that it was a massacre. So Fulvius orders the Campanians around the enemy flank. Samnite infantry didn't stand a chance after that.' The optio flicked a piece of wood into the fire. 'They were lucky that it was growing dark or else we would have had them all,' he growled.

Gaius seemed to jerk awake. He turned to stare sharply at the officer. 'The Samnites attacked our baggage train?' he gasped in sudden alarm.

'That's what I said,' the optio snapped.

Gaius swallowed. Then he was up on his feet. 'Where are they? Where is the baggage train?' he cried.

The soldiers around the fire stirred and looked up at him.

'Down the mountain pass, that way,' the optio said gesturing with his arm. 'Why? Left something behind that you can't do without?' the officer added.

Gaius didn't reply. He was already running in the direction in which the optio had pointed.

'His little sister was with the baggage train,' Verrens muttered.

**

Gaius came to an abrupt halt as he caught sight of the Roman baggage train. In the growing light the carnage was worse than he had imagined. Small groups of exhausted and sullen looking

88

slaves and camp servants huddled around small fires or were rummaging through overturned wagons and piles of discarded belongings. An ox was bellowing loudly and a woman was weeping as she searched for something amongst the dead. The optio had been right. Dead Samnite cavalrymen and horses lay everywhere. In some places the dead lay piled on top of each other. The fighting around here had been a massacre. The Campanian horse must have caught the Samnites after they had dismounted and had their arms full of loot. Gaius brought his hand to his nose. The stench was revolting.

Anxiously he peered at the Roman carts and wagons and at the faces of the slaves huddled around their cooking fires. There was no sign of Cassia. What had happened to her? He strode amongst the groups of weary camp servants but no one had seen her. The slaves looked like they'd had a rough time. Then just as he was about to give up all hope he heard a squeal. Then he saw her. Cassia came running towards him and flung her arms around him. He lifted her up and she buried her head in his neck. She clung to him for a long time without saying a word and as she did so Gaius sensed that his sister must have experienced something terrible for her body was taught with tension. When he released her she wiped the tears from her cheeks and smiled up at him bravely.

'You made it,' she whispered.

'So did you,' Gaius replied.

'I hid under one of the wagons,' she whispered her face blushing. 'The enemy cavalry were stupid. They died because they were stupid. They deserved to die. They were stupid and greedy.'

Gaius nodded. There was a sudden maturity about his little sister that he'd never seen before, as if the girl had aged during the battle. Her dark eyes studied him. She must have seen things and heard things that no girl her age should have, Gaius thought, but if she had, she

89

seemed reluctant to talk about it.

'I am sorry Cassia,' Gaius murmured, 'I should not have brought you with me. Maybe it would have been better to have left you with Tullus in Sora.'

For a moment Gaius thought he saw contempt in Cassia's eyes. His little sister turned to look at the enemy dead.

'Now you are being stupid,' she snapped. 'I am fine. I am alive and so are you. That is all that matters.'

***

The city of Bovianum, capital of Samnium and of its largest tribe, the Pentri, did not look much bigger than Sora, Gaius thought as he finished hammering another nail into the crude wooden ladder that he and his comrades were making. He straightened up and rubbed his aching back and stared at the town walls. It was morning. Four days had passed since the battle in the mountain pass and after cremating their dead and sending their wounded back to Fregellae with the supply columns, Fulvius had led his army over the mountain pass without meeting any resistance. The Samnite army had been scattered and from prisoners the Romans had learned that a Samnite general had been killed in the rout. Gaius had made inquiries but the dead general had not been Egnatius. The remnants of the Samnite army seemed to have fled into the mountains but Verrens had told him that a large number of the enemy had retreated into Bovianum. Upon arrival Fulvius had ordered the town to be besieged. Gaius and his comrades had been posted to the eastern section of the town where Verrens and the Tribunes had put them to work building siege equipment and assault ladders.

Gaius hammered another nail into the ladder and paused again to examine the enemy walls. The fortifications had been cleverly built into the natural rock to give them added height and strength. On top of the walls he could see figures staring at the

Romans. Whatever one's opinion about the Samnite defenders he thought, no one could argue that they lacked balls. Just that morning the Consul's demand that the city surrender had been rebuffed with a show of naked arses from those manning the walls. The Samnites it seemed were prepared to fight to the death. The Roman assault was scheduled to start shortly.

'Worried that the ladders are not going to be long enough?' a dust-covered soldier beside him said with a mocking grin.

Gaius did not reply. His attention was suddenly drawn to a smartly dressed young tribune. The officer looked about the same age as himself. The young man was wearing a fine attic helmet and from the cleanliness of his armour the officer looked like he had just arrived in the camp. He was being escorted by the optio, the second in command of the Tenth company. Gaius paused to stare at the newcomer and as the tribune passed by he saw Gaius staring at him and gave him a shy smile. Gaius did not return the smile.

'Now that's a sight you don't see very often,' the dust-covered soldier beside Gaius exclaimed as he saw Gaius staring at the tribune. 'That's a man with a lot of wealth. He will be a patrician out hunting for some glory.'

It was half an hour later when the work on the assault ladders had been completed that Verrens called his men together. Gaius and his comrades ran to form up before their centurion. A few new recruits had arrived with one of the supply convoys and the new men had brought the strength of the 10th Company of Hastati back up to 80 men, still only two thirds its authorised strength. The new recruits were all young men of eighteen and nineteen and to Gaius and the other survivors from the mountain battle, the new recruits looked like babies.

'10th Company, stand to attention,' Verrens cried as he inspected the new men. When he seemed satisfied the centurion took a step back and folded his arms behind his back. Then he nodded to his optio and the deputy commander beckoned to someone, who Gaius could not see, to step forward. A moment later the young, fresh looking tribune, wearing his attic helmet and fine armour strode into view. It was the youth Gaius had spotted earlier. The young officer halted beside Verrens and the centurion saluted smartly. The tribune looked about eighteen. The boy cast a nervous shy glance at the stone-faced soldiers standing before him.

'Due to our proven valour in battle,' Verrens cried in a loud voice, 'Our general has decided that the 10th Company will be leading the assault on the section of the enemy wall behind me.'

Verrens glared at his men daring them to speak but no one did. 'This is Bovianum boys, the enemy capital,' Verrens roared. 'One more hard fight and we will take it and once we hold it, we will never, I repeat, never give it back to these mountain men.' The centurion paused to examine his men. Then at last he gestured at the young tribune.

'Our assault will be led by myself and the tribune here.' Verrens glanced at the young officer, 'Sir, have you something you wish to say to the men?'

The boy turned to face the soldiers and as he did so a furious blush of embarrassment appeared on his face.

'Men, I am Quintus Decius Mus,' he cried. 'I know that the 10th Company is a fine unit of proven valour and courage. I shall lead you into battle today. When we take the enemy walls, the town will be yours and everything inside will belong to you. Honour Rome and honour yourself!'

The tribune turned to Verrens and once more the centurion saluted smartly. The officers clustered closely around the young tribune as if their presence would somehow lift the young man's stature. From the ranks Gaius looked on with silent contempt. The tribune seemed to have rehearsed his little speech for it sounded like he'd been reading from a script. Every man in the company knew what was going on. A young, fresh, inexperienced youth from a wealthy patrician family was being given his first taste of battle. The tribune may think he would be leading the assault on the walls but in reality he would be kept well back in the rear. The public display Gaius had just witnessed was there purely to build up the young man's reputation. Once the battle would be over the tribune would be able to boast of his great deeds in the field. Such boasting would be necessary if the young man wanted to start a public career.

'What are we now, babysitters,' the soldier standing beside Gaius muttered under his breath. The man's mouth had hardly moved but at the tribune's side, Gaius saw Verrens sharp eyes turn in his direction. The centurion peered at him suspiciously and his vine stick tapped gently against his thigh. Gaius turned to examine the young tribune. The boy looked nervous and frightened. He didn't look like a soldier; the boy seemed ill at ease in his uniform and in the company of the men. The tribune looked soft. The man looked like he would run at the first sight of the enemy. Gaius's contempt grew. Then he straightened up as he caught Verrens glaring at him.

Chapter Twelve - The Standard of the Tenth

The Roman assault on Bovianum started with a single trumpet blast. It was noon. As the trumpet died away the Roman assault companies stormed towards the walls carrying their ladders. They were met with a barrage of missiles hurled at them by the defenders manning the walls. Gaius was the fourth man on his ladder. A stone smacked into his shield and nearby a soldier was hit and went down. There was no time to drag the man to safety. Javelins, stones and arrows were coming at them from everywhere.

'Move, move,' Verrens's urgent voice cried. Another stone slammed into Gaius's shield and the soldier in front of him shrieked as a stone hit his helmet and bounced off. Gaius nearly tripped over a corpse. The hail of missiles lessened as they reached the relative safety of the Samnite wall. Gaius grunted as the ladder was raised and placed against the wall. He snatched a quick look up. The ladder reached all the way to the parapet. Thank the gods that they had got the length right. All along the wall the Roman assault companies were raising their ladders. On the walls the defenders were howling and shouting and flinging everything they had at the attackers.

The first man on the ladder clambered up holding his shield above his head. Then the second man followed. A few moments later Gaius too was climbing up the ladder. Above him he heard a shriek. The first soldier plummeted to the ground with a Samnite spear sticking in his chest. He was followed moments later by the second man, felled by an arrow. Along the wall to his right the Samnites had managed to push one of the Roman ladders off the ramparts and it fell back to earth taking her screaming men with her. Further out a ladder collapsed under the weight of the men climbing up it. Gaius held his shield above his head. He could see very little of what was happening. Then the feet of the man above him vanished. The soldier must have made it over the parapet. With a cry Gaius thrust himself upwards. His companion was standing on the parapet desperately trying to protect himself from the furious Samnites.

Gaius scrambled over the wall and landed on the walkway. An old bearded Samnite warrior swung an axe at him and Gaius took the blow on his shield. Then he stabbed the man and smashed his shield boss into the defender's face. The Samnite staggered backwards and tumbled off the wall and into the town without a sound. Another defender thrust his spear at him but Gaius knocked it aside with his sword. Then he was bracing himself as a Samnite tried to shove him back over the walls. Gaius grunted and strained as the Samnite shield pushed up against his own. For a moment, the two men seemed evenly balanced as they strained and pushed at each other. Then behind Gaius another Roman clambered over the wall and stabbed Gaius's attacker in the arm. The pressure on Gaius's shield fell away. An arrow hammered into his shield and Gaius staggered backwards in shock.

'Clear these walls,' he heard Verrens's booming voice behind him. More Romans had managed to get over the parapet. The Samnite defenders yelled and shrieked in growing desperation as they were driven back. Gaius snatched a quick look into the town. A crowd of men, women and children had gathered just inside the walls. They were throwing stones at the Roman soldiers.

A Samnite thrust his sword at Gaius but the man's attack was half hearted and the blade missed him completely. Gaius took a step towards the man sensing the reassuring presence of a comrade to his right. The Samnite retreated. Behind Gaius more Romans were clambering over the parapet. It was the same all along the wall. The assault on Bovianum was turning out to be easier than he had expected. Gaius and his comrade, sheltering behind their large shields took another step forwards and again the Samnites retreated. The enemy were scared of him Gaius suddenly realised. The realisation brought on a surge of contempt. The men defending the walls were ordinary townsfolk. They weren't like the Samnite soldiers he'd fought in the mountain pass.

95

Gaius snatched a glance behind him and saw that the signifer carrying the Standard of the Tenth Maniple of Hastati had made it up onto the walls. The signifer, clad in his boar's head cloak was closely followed by the young tribune who had addressed the troops earlier that day. The boy looked horrified as he caught sight of the bloody mess up on the walls. The officer took an uncertain step forwards. Then as Gaius stared at him for a moment longer, a Roman soldier standing beside the officer, by accident or design, suddenly barged into the young officer's back sending the boy staggering forwards. The tribune tripped over a corpse and with a terrified yell tumbled off the walls and into the city below. Gaius eyes bulged. Then he thrust himself past the growing numbers of Roman soldiers on the wall and snatched the Standard of the Tenth from the signifer's surprised fingers.

'No, no,' Gaius heard Verrens's cry of alarm as the centurion guessed what he was about to do. Gaius ignored him and with a hoarse cry flung the Standard of the Tenth into the city where it vanished into the Samnite crowds milling about below the walls. Gaius didn't pause but leapt after it. The distance from the walkway to the ground was not as high as that of the outer wall and his fall was broken by a body in the crowd. Someone cried out as he landed. Then he scrambled onto his feet. The town folk around him had moved back in sudden fear. He could see that they were armed with little more than stones and knives. The Samnites were staring at him in horror and fear. Gaius crouched low and snatched a quick glance at the body of the tribune. The boy was lying on the ground groaning softly. Blood from where he'd hit his head was oozing out onto the paving stones. Then a Samnite came at Gaius wielding a stout stick. At the last moment Gaius smashed his shield boss into the man's face and stabbed him. His sword cut into the man's flesh and his attacker stumbled backwards with a groan, his hands pressed to the wound in his side from which blood was welling up.

A moment later Gaius heard harsh cries above him. Then his frantic comrades came jumping down onto the ground around him. The Samnite crowd howled and shrieked. Then the mob turned and fled into the surrounding streets. Gaius took a deep breath and bent down over the wounded tribune. Quickly he cut a strip from his tunic, lifted up the boy's head and bound the linen strip tightly around the wound. The thud and crash of more Roman soldiers jumping down around him continued as the Romans frantically sought to reclaim their Standard. The tribune opened his eyes and stared at up Gaius. A trickle of blood was oozing from the corners of his mouth.

'Thank you,' the young officer murmured before his eyes closed once more.

On the wall above him Gaius could hear shrieks and desperate pleas for mercy as the Roman soldiers finished off the last of the defenders. In the street where he crouched, his comrades had set off in pursuit of the town's people. The assault on Bovianum was about to descend into a massacre. A pair of boots suddenly landed beside him. Gaius turned to look up. A fist came smashing into his face. The force of the blow sent him crashing against the city wall. Pain exploded in his head. Verrens's furious face hovered over him. The centurion hit him again. Then a sword point was touching Gaius's throat.

'Go on, just say one word and I will spit you like a fish,' Verrens roared. The centurion's face was dark with rage.

Gaius remained motionless and averted his eyes from the centurion. Pain hammered in his head and he grimaced but he didn't dare move. Behind Verrens, a Roman soldier kicked down a door and disappeared into a house. A moment later Gaius heard a shrill female scream.

'You had better pray that they find my Standard,' Verrens hissed, 'for if they don't your life is going to end here.'

***

Gaius sat with his back against the wall. There was a sullen expression on his face as he stared vacantly into the space ahead of him. A soldier stood guard over him. The man's spear point rested on Gaius's shoulder. In the city of Bovianum the terrified screams of the civilian population had not ceased for three hours. The Romans had broken into the town and like the young tribune had promised, the town had been turned over to the soldiers. Gaius's comrades had fanned out into the narrow streets and had started to massacre the male civilian population. The soldiers would be out looting and stealing as much as they could but Fulvius had issued strict orders that women were not to be harmed or raped. All women and children under twelve were to be sold into slavery. Whether the soldiers would obey the Consul's orders was however uncertain.

Gaius looked on tight-lipped. Had he blown his chance? He had taken a huge gamble by saving the tribune's life. Would the boy be worth it? He damn well hoped so. How much easier it would have been to do nothing. He could have been out there now with his comrades looting the town. Was that not why he had joined the army? Did he not have debts that needed settling? He could have been a rich man by now. If he was wrong about the boy he was going to regret it for a very long time. He turned his head as he heard a man approaching. It was Verrens. The centurion was holding the Standard of the Tenth in his hand. He stopped in front of Gaius. There was a hard, angry look on the officer's face and his right arm was stained with dried blood. Gaius smiled sadly as he stared up at the Standard.

'Don't think your life is spared,' Verrens growled, 'You disobeyed a direct order. I can still have you executed for that.'

Gaius looked up at his commanding officer. 'Permission to speak Sir?' he muttered.

Verrens nodded.

'Sir, our tribune had fallen off the wall,' Gaius exclaimed. 'I flung the Standard into the enemy crowd because I believed his life was in danger. I believe it was my duty to try and save him.'

Verrens's angry face darkened. He took a step forwards and grabbed Gaius around the throat. The centurion's grip was terrifyingly powerful. Verrens's face was suddenly close to his.

'Do you take me for a fool. Don't think I don't know what you are doing,' he hissed. 'If you think kissing the arse hole of a superior officer is going to get you noticed and rewarded you are wrong. I will make sure any rewards you get will not remain yours for long. That was an incredibly stupid thing you did. You are not the Standard bearer in my company. I will not tolerate men who disobey me. Do you know the shame that I would have had to endure if I had to report that I had lost my Standard? I haven't made centurion to lose it all to a little glory hound like you.'

'Centurion,' a voice suddenly called out behind them. 'A word if I may.'

Verrens turned sharply. Then he stood up and saluted. The young tribune lay on a makeshift stretcher that was being carried by four slaves. A white bandage had been wrapped around his head. Standing behind the wounded officer was a big, well built man in his mid-thirties, dressed in an immaculate grey woollen tunic. A sword hung from his belt but it was clear from the man's clothing that he was a civilian. The man's short black spiky hair was carefully groomed.

The tribune raised himself up onto his elbows. 'Centurion, why is this man under arrest? He saved my life. I want you to release him at once.'

'He disobeyed a direct order Sir,' Verrens replied clearing his throat.

'So shall you, if you don't release him,' the young tribune said sharply.

Verrens looked uncomfortable. He turned towards the soldier who was guarding Gaius and managed to kick Gaius in his ribs as he did so.

99

'Release him,' Verrens muttered as Gaius grimaced in pain.

'Stand up soldier,' the young tribune said as he peered at Gaius curiously. Gaius did as he was ordered pressing one hand painfully to his ribs. Quintus, the tribune sniggered and grinned.

'I am returning to Rome to allow my wounds to heal,' he announced grandly. 'The Legate has given me permission to take a small escort with me. I would like this man to accompany me to Rome. You will release him to me at once, centurion, without hurting him again please. Is that clear?'

Verrens raised his eyebrows. 'Yes Sir,' he said smoothly.

Gaius was staring at the tribune. They were the same age but the difference in social class was huge.

'I know you probably feel nothing but contempt for me,' the tribune muttered suddenly, 'I was not born to be a soldier like you. But if you come with me now I will make it worth your time. Isn't that's the reason why you saved my life?'

Gaius blinked in surprise. Then unable to think of any other response he grinned. From his stretcher the tribune's eyes twinkled mischievously.

Gaius turned to Verrens and saluted smartly. Then Verrens beckoned Gaius to him and as Gaius stepped forwards the centurion grasped him by his shoulder and turned him away from the young officer.

'He comes from a wealthy and powerful family,' Verrens muttered under his breath. His father was a Consul a few years ago. You will profit from the association.' Verrens paused and Gaius felt the centurion's grip on his shoulder tighten. 'And when you do,' Verrens hissed, 'don't forget about your friends. I will see you one day Gaius.'

Gaius blinked and then to his surprise Verrens stretched out his arm. After a moment's hesitation Gaius clasped it in the soldier's way. Then he turned to the tribune.

'Sir, I have a sister, she is with the baggage train. I will not leave her behind.'

Quintus turned to the big, spiky haired civilian who standing behind him.

'Crispus,' the boy yawned, 'find his sister and bring her to my tent. I want to be on my way by dawn and make sure you get two additional horses.'

Chapter Thirteen - A New Role

Gaius stood outside the tent waiting to be called inside. It was late in the evening and the town of Bovianum was on fire. The raging flames lit up the night sky with an eerie demonic glow and the smell of smoke was everywhere. The Romans had thoroughly looted the town and Gaius had seen his comrades returning laden with spoils, Greek gold and silver coins, fine jewellery, clothes, statues of Samnite gods and coloured stones. The soldiers had been in an ecstatic mood for all the hardships and pain they'd had to endure had paid off in the end. After the initial massacre a long line of bedraggled and terrified people had shuffled out of the city gates. The men, women and children who had escaped the soldiers' murderous intent had been placed in neck chains by the slavers who had accompanied the army. It had been a sorry sight. Bovianum had been the capital of the Samnite nation. Now it was being reduced to a blackened smouldering ruin.

The tent flap was drawn back and Crispus, Quintus's servant beckoned for Gaius to come inside. A few oil lamps lit up the interior of the tent and in their light Gaius saw Quintus, the tribune lying on a comfortable looking couch. The young man was eating an apple. He gestured for Gaius to approach. Crispus took up a position a respectful distance from his master and folded his arms across his chest. His eyes were fixed on Gaius.

'Are you hungry?' Quintus said gesturing to a basket of fruit that stood on the table beside the couch.

Gaius took a step forwards and saluted.

'No Sir, I have already eaten, thank you Sir,' he replied.

'There is no need to call me Sir,' Quintus said quietly. He finished his apple and the tent fell silent as Quintus took his time studying Gaius. Then a faint smile appeared on the young tribune's face.

'Yes, I think I am going to like you Gaius,' Quintus said at last, 'Tell me, have you had any education, has anyone ever bothered to teach you beyond basic reading and writing? Do you know anything about geography, philosophy, poetry, medicine, rhetoric?'

Gaius swallowed nervously. Where was this conversation going? The tribune was taking him into an unfamiliar world.

'I am a farmer,' Gaius replied lifting his chin proudly, 'My skill is with animals and in the fields. That's what I know.'

The tent fell silent. Quintus glanced across at Crispus and Gaius wondered whether he had said the wrong thing.

'You are also a soldier,' Quintus said quietly, 'The men in your unit respect you.' Suddenly Quintus looked away. 'I must ask you whether you already have a patron to whom you are bound and contracted? Please do not lie for I can find out the truth if I want to.'

Gaius shook his head. Quintus looked pleased and rose from his couch and poured some wine from a jug into two cups before offering one of them to Gaius. Gaius took it, sniffed at the liquid and then downed it in one go. Quintus laughed.

'I am glad to see that you like a drink,' he said.

Gaius wiped his mouth and nodded. The wine had tasted good. It must have been expensive.

'What is it that you want from me?' Gaius said turning to look Quintus straight in the eye.

For a moment Quintus looked surprised. Then he rose to his feet and placed his hands on the table. He looked down at the wood.

'I am not much of a soldier,' he said, 'But I am no fool. You saved my life today for a reason and I suspect that reason has to do with money or some other reward. I meet men like you all the time. They hear that I am the son of Publius Decius Mus and they think that I am an easy target for their moneymaking schemes. Yes I have seen it all before.' Quintus looked up at Gaius. 'But I have never come across someone who was prepared to put his actual life in danger for me. That took guts. You are exactly the sort of man that I am looking for. I would like to help you.'

'Help me?' Gaius inquired.

'I want to give you a job,' Quintus replied. 'I want you to be my client. You understand the obligations of a client to his patron don't you?'

Gaius remained silent for a few moments. He looked thoughtful. 'I have debts,' he said at last.

Quintus raised his hand. 'Consider them paid,' he replied.

Gaius nodded in appreciation. 'My sister, I would like her to have an education. I would like her to have a proper tutor and regular lessons.'

Quintus frowned, 'An education for a girl, what does she need that for?' Then seeing Gaius's face, he sighed. 'Very well then, I will see what I can do. Was that it?'

Gaius nodded again and Quintus grinned in delight.

'I am glad that you have agreed,' the young tribune said stretching out his arm, 'You will not regret your decision or find my friendship lacking. Do this for a year and if you wish to leave after that you will be free to go. In the meantime, you shall refrain from suing me, you shall vote for my father and accompany me to war when necessary and you shall take no other patron whilst you are in my service.'

Gaius grasped Quintus's outstretched arm in the soldiers' way and the two young men   grinned at each other.

104

'Come and have a look at this,' Quintus said as he reached for a large parchment scroll that was lying on the table. He unrolled it and beckoned for Gaius to come and have a closer look. Gaius peered at the document. It was filled with boxes, lines and names. Right at the top he noticed the name of Ajax.

'It took me two years to create,' Quintus said proudly.

'What is it?' Gaius muttered looking puzzled.

'My family are not patrician,' Quintus said quickly, 'We're plebeian nobility, we're New men. The patricians hate us because we are competing for the privileges, which they have traditionally enjoyed. In Rome, the older and more venerable your family ancestry and identity is, the more power, respect and influence you will have. So, I have created a family tree which shows that we are descended from Ajax, the Greek hero who fought in the Trojan wars.'

'Is that true?' Gaius frowned.

'Of course not, how could I know this,' Quintus exclaimed, 'Everyone fabricates their family identity, that's not the point. The importance of this document and the reason why it has taken me two years to create is that no one can disprove it. It has been designed to withstand the scrutiny and cross examination of the best lawyers.'

Gaius raised his eyebrows. 'So if it's all fabricated, why not choose your families descent from Hercules or Venus?'

'They were already taken,' Quintus muttered, 'The Fabii have Hercules, the Julii have taken Venus.'

Gaius wanted to laugh but the serious expression on Quintus's face restrained him.

Quintus was staring at the family tree.

'Power in Rome is closely associated with ancestry,' Quintus said. 'It's no joke. So now that I have created our family ancestry I need to advertise my family origins. I need people to know where we come from and who we are.' Quintus looked up. 'I am building a network of clients and my clients are promoting my family name and origins. When my time comes to lead the House of Mus I shall have friends in all the right places. That's why I need you Gaius. You are a soldier, you are a farmer, ordinary people will respect you when you tell them about me.'

Gaius looked perplexed.

'One final matter,' Quintus said glancing at Crispus. 'My father and I do not get on. The less you tell him the better.'

***

The four wheeled Arcera, carriage, pulled along by a team of horses, swayed and rumbled over the paving stones of the newly built Appian Way. It was morning and the small party rode on in silence. Seven days had passed since Gaius had been ordered to escort Quintus to Rome. Their journey from Bovianum had taken them south west to the Campanian capital of Capua from where they had picked up the Appian way and headed north to Rome. Gaius rode a black horse. He glanced at the Arcera. The carriage was covered with wooden planks over which hung loose red drapery. The vehicle was normally used to transport the sick and the elderly but Quintus had chosen to use it for his journey back home. The young tribune reclined in the back of the Arcera. The white bandage was still wrapped around his head. Gaius allowed himself a brief smile. He still couldn't make up his mind whether to like or despise the young officer. Quintus's head wound, had in the end, turned out to be not very serious, yet he had made a great deal of fuss about his wound. To Gaius it seemed as if Quintus was happy to have been wounded because it meant that he had an excuse to go home. It was clear that his new friend and patron hated being on campaign and hated being a soldier.

Gaius glanced over his shoulder at Crispus and the four mounted soldiers who were bringing up the rear. Cassia was riding just ahead of them. Her woollen cloak, the one Tullus had bought for her in Sora, looked soiled and dirty. She looked tired. The war had left its mark on her. His little sister had not spoken much since they had left Bovianum. Her experiences during the battle had knocked the cheeky adventurous spirit out of her. Now she seemed burdened by something, something that made her silent, resentful and sullen. One day, Gaius thought with a sigh, he would need to sit down with her and get her to talk about what she had seen and witnessed. No man would want to marry her in her present condition.

'Gaius,' Quintus said suddenly, beckoning to him. Gaius urged his horse up to the side of the swaying carriage. Quintus Decius Mus looked cheerful.

'Another half a day's ride and we will be in Rome,' he exclaimed. 'Have you ever been to Rome Gaius?'

'I was born in the city,' Gaius replied.

'Do you still have family living in Rome?'

Gaius shook his head.

'Then you and your sister will come and stay at my house. We have plenty of space,' Quintus beamed. He turned to look at the fields that bordered the road. 'My father has already been a Consul twice and my grandfather was also a Consul in his day,' Quintus said. 'He fought at the battle of Veseris in the Latin war. Maybe you have heard of him?'

Gaius nodded. 'I heard your grandfather died during that battle,' he replied.

Quintus turned to examine Gaius carefully. Then he nodded. 'Yes, so you see I am descended from a line of soldiers, brave heroic men, all of them. It was my father's idea that I should join the Consul Fulvius on campaign,' Quintus continued. 'My father is a magnificent soldier. He is one of the most respected leaders that we have got. He wants me to follow in his footsteps.' A painful expression crept onto Quintus's face. 'But I think I am going to disappoint him. I don't think I have got the same qualities as my father and grandfather.' Quintus smiled. 'He doesn't see it though. My father doesn't realise that I am not like him. I have other talents, other qualities, but they mean nothing to him.'

Gaius looked thoughtful but before he could reply Quintus was pointing at the birthmark along his neck.

'I bet the priests told you it meant something special,' Quintus grinned.

Gaius touched his neck. 'They say that I am the boy who will save Rome one day,' he muttered. 'The birthmark is supposed to look like a Wolf.'

Quintus peered at him and for a moment he didn't reply. 'Yes,' he exclaimed at last, 'You are right it does look like a Wolf.' The grin on his face broadened. 'I hope that you will not be offended Gaius, but I will let you into a little secret.' Quintus raised his hands to the sky in mock reverence. 'The gods don't exist,' he exclaimed. 'Religion is just superstition. I believe in science. I believe in philosophy. The patricians use religion to control the ordinary people. Prophesies, fortune-tellers, the're all bollocks, rubbish, just another scam. I don't believe a word of it. So, if you think that crap the priests have told you is true, then I am afraid that you are going to be disappointed my friend and I will argue that with anyone.'

A little smile had appeared on Gaius's face. He turned to study Quintus and as the young tribune beamed in conviction, Gaius suddenly knew that he was going to enjoy his patron's company.

Chapter Fourteen - Rome

Rome's walls gleamed in the sunlight barely a mile away. The Arcera and her small escort had just reached the crest of a hill. It was late in the day. Gaius slowed his horse to a halt as he caught sight of the city. It had been more than five years since he'd been in Rome. Before his father had volunteered to become a colonist in Sora, he, Gaius and his family had lived in a cramped house on the Quirinal. Gaius sniffed as he remembered the smell of the city, the buckets of shit emptied out onto the streets, the smell of unwashed bodies, the stale sweat of the craftsmen in their workshops and the disgusting, putrid smell of garum, rotting fish soup. No he had not missed Rome. Life in the countryside was incomparably better and healthier, yet here he was returning to the city where he had been born, like a runaway child returning to an abusive mother.

At the sight of Rome, Quintus however cried out excitedly. 'When we get to my father's house I will have the cooks prepare us a great feast. Do you like door mouse, Gaius?'

Gaius nodded and urged his horse on down the Appian Way. On both sides of the road the tombstones and vaults of the dead had began to appear and as the party approached the city walls, the number and density of the tombs increased. The traffic on the road had also grown and they passed carts and wagons, pulled by oxen and horses and heading in the opposite direction. Their drivers, clad in their rustic grey tunics and wide brimmed hats, stared curiously at Quintus and the soldiers in his escort. Just as they were approaching the Capena gate Quintus cried out and the small party came to a halt along the road. Quintus jumped down from the Arcera and snapped his fingers at his servant.

'Swap places Crispus,' Quintus grinned. 'It's your turn to ride in the carriage.'

Crispus bowed his head gracefully and dismounted smoothly from his horse and Quintus heaved himself onto the horse and carefully adjusted the large white bandage that was wrapped around his head wound. Then Quintus urged his horse to the very front of the party. Gaius raised his eyebrows. The young tribune looked like he was about to enter Rome like a conquering hero. He shook his head. It was, he supposed, all part of the act that Quintus was performing. A smile began to grow on Gaius's face as he watched Quintus raise his hand and order the party on up the road towards the city gates. Quintus was going to make it a good act. He seemed to have a flair for such work.

They entered Rome and to Gaius the sight of the narrow twisting streets and alleys instantly brought back a thousand memories. People were everywhere and the noise was tremendous. Ox drawn carts creaked and groaned and horses' hooves clattered on the cobblestones. Vendors were calling out to the multitude in the streets, advertising their wares in loud voices. From the back rooms of the tiny shops that lined the streets, Gaius could hear and smell tradesmen, blacksmiths, bakers, butchers, shoe repairmen and fishmongers at work. He craned his head to get a glimpse of a bar in a side street. He grinned as he saw it. The bar was still there, it's front with its large circular holes containing barrels of wine pushed right up to the edge of the street. He caught a glimpse of a fat lady handing out cups of wine. Was that his old boss? He'd had his first job in that place, rolling the barrels of wine from the back room into the front and preventing children from stealing the purses of the customers.

Quintus led them up the streets in the direction of the forum and the Sacred Way. He was sitting bolt upright on his horse and taking his time. People moved out of the way as the party clattered up the street and Gaius caught many a person staring at the young tribune in his fine clothes and armour. Quintus seemed to be enjoying the attention. His face looked composed, serious and stern – a young conqueror, wounded in battle, and now returning home from the Samnite war. Gaius shook his head in disbelief. As they penetrated deeper into the city however, he forgot about Quintus as childhood memories came flooding back. He peered down an alley and sighed. It was down there that he'd often been beaten up by a local bully. The bully however, had not enjoyed his reign of terror for long, for he'd fallen foul of one of the criminal gangs that ruled the different neighbourhoods of Rome and one day his body had been found dumped in the street. Life was hard and short for the vast majority of the people in Rome.

Finally they emerged onto the Sacred Way, the street that led to the forum and the heart of the city. Quintus however turned in the direction that led towards the Palatine hill. The Palatine hill was the grandest of all addresses in Rome. It was on the Palatine, overlooking the valley in which the forum was located, that the original settlement of Rome had started. It was here, the priests had told Gaius, that the She Wolf had suckled Romulus and Remus. It was the hill where the rich and powerful had their homes. If you were anyone in Rome, you would have a town house on the Palatine.

Quintus's town house was a modest building in the heart of the Palatine district. As the young tribune approached, a slave came running towards him and took the bridle of his horse. News of their arrival must have preceded them. Quintus slid from his horse and snapped his fingers.

'Crispus, you may dismiss the soldiers,' he ordered. 'Give them some money so that they can get pissed.' Then the tribune beckoned for Gaius and Cassia to follow him. Gaius dismounted and glanced at his sister. Cassia looked nervous. She looked up at her brother and Gaius gave her a reassuring nod. Then he laid his hand on her shoulder.

The town house was fronted by a small colonnaded vestibule and stone busts of men's heads stood on either side of the double wooden door. Gaius glanced at the busts. The men looked strong and dignified. The door was opened by a slave who bowed silently as Quintus, without acknowledging him, strode into the house with confident steps. Gaius and Cassia followed him into the house. They passed through a hallway with a decorated mosaic depicting a battle scene set into the floor. From further in the house Gaius could hear the sound of running water. Then they were through the hall and into a surprisingly spacious atrium, the open central courtyard around which the rooms of the house were arrayed. A rectangular basin filled with water had been sunk into the centre of the atrium and above it the roof opened up to let in the day light. A stone stairway to one side led up to a balustrade and a landing, around which Gaius could see doorways leading to more rooms. A lady of around forty, beautifully dressed, was coming down the stairway. Her light blue Stola slid across the stone steps and her fingers and neck were bedecked with jewellery and sparkling gold rings. Her hair was fixed with an elegant silver fibula.

'Mother, I am back from the wars,' Quintus cried as he opened his arms wide. 'Your son has returned home.'

'So you have my dear, so you have,' the lady said with a posh accent. There was a little smile on her face as she offered Quintus her cheek. Then she glanced at Gaius who still had his arm wrapped around Cassia's shoulders.

'And who may this be?' she said raising her head and examining Gaius and Cassia with a cold, superior look. She was a tall lady and would have been beautiful too, if it wasn't for her large nose which ruined her appearance. To Gaius it suddenly felt as if the lady was looking down at him. He tried not to look at her nose. It made him want to laugh.

'These are my friends, Gaius and his little sister Cassia,' Quintus said with a broad smile. 'Gaius and I fought together when we took the walls of Bovianum. I have invited him to stay with us.'

Quintus's mother regarded Gaius and Cassia a little longer. Then she turned to her son and nodded her head ever so slightly.

'You are wounded,' she exclaimed, 'Is it bad. Should I send for the Greek doctor?'

Quintus touched the large white bandage around his head.

'It will heal given time,' he muttered. 'Come I will show my guests to their rooms. We can talk later, mother.'

Quintus's mother nodded. 'Your timing is perfect, Quintus,' she said in her posh voice, 'the whole family is arriving tomorrow. I have instructed the slaves to prepare us a feast. Your father and sister will be delighted to see you. There is much to discuss and Decia is bringing her husband. Fabius is coming too so make sure you wear your finest clothes.'

Quintus frowned, 'What feast, what's the occasion?' he muttered.

His mother folded her arms across her chest. 'Don't tell me that you have forgotten. Our family has a feast every year on this day - the feast that honours your grandfather. We have done it every year for the past forty-two years.'

Quintus's eyes suddenly lit up as he remembered. 'Of course,' he said blushing, 'Has that day come already? My apologies mother, so much has happened. I have forgotten. I will make amends and pray to my grandfather's spirit tonight after supper.' Quintus grinned, 'It will be great to see everyone in the same house. I know how little time we all get to spend with each other.'

His mother acknowledged him with a little dip of the head. Then without giving Gaius or Cassia a further glance she glided away into one of the rooms.

Chapter Fifteen - The House of Mus

It was night and the town house was asleep. Gaius lay on his bed staring up at the dark ceiling. The stone bed was covered by a woollen mattress. It was comfortable enough but Gaius could not sleep. Outside he could vaguely here the noises of the night, the laughter and shrieks of late night revellers returning home and the rattle of a cart in the street below his window. Cassia lay in a bed across from him. In the dim oil lamp-light he could just about see her dark shape. Quintus had been as friendly and affable as ever but his mother, Quirinia, had not said a word to either him or Cassia. The lady had gone about her business as if the two of them did not exist. Quintus had explained, whilst the three of them had taken a late meal in the kitchen surrounded by the household slaves, that his mother was always like this with guests that she didn't know. Quirinia was from a respectable patrician family, from old money, from a family that could trace its ancestry back to the founding of the city, but she had married into a plebeian family. Quintus's father, Publius Decius Mus, was a plebeian, an ordinary citizen whose family had made their fortune from banking. The family were New men with self made money and his fortune had allowed Quintus's father to take on a patrician's wife with connections into the elite circles of Roman society. Quintus had however been quick to point out that having a patrician's wife had not meant that the House of Mus had been accepted as an equal by the old patrician families, who dominated the Senate and political power in Rome. Quintus had been very knowledgeable about the politics of the Republic and had spoken about it with some passion. The patricians, he'd added, hated and feared the New men and any plebeian who tried to rise above his place in society. In the Senate, the law may state that one Consul should be a patrician and one a plebeian but in private the old patrician families continued to despise the New men and plot their downfall in any way they could.

'Gaius,' Cassia suddenly whispered, 'Are you awake?'

Gaius turned to look at the dark shape across the room. 'Yes,' he whispered.

'Why do we have to stay here?' Cassia whispered. 'I don't like this house. That woman, she is awful, she doesn't like me and I don't like that slave, Crispus. There is something odd about him. Have you noticed how obsessed he is with tidiness and cleanliness?'

Gaius sighed and folded his hands behind his head.

'Quintus has promised me that he is going to hire a teacher to educate you. I have arranged for you to get lessons. You know how difficult and expensive it is to get an education, especially for a girl? We must take this opportunity, Cassia.'

Cassia was silent for a while. 'What about Egnatius? What about avenging our family? Have you given up?' she whispered.

Gaius's eyes glinted in the dim light. 'I have not forgotten,' he whispered. 'One day I will avenge our family; I swear it. The opportunity will come but for now Cassia, for now we must look after ourselves.'

Cassia was silent for a long time and Gaius turned to listen to the nocturnal noises in the streets outside.

'She has a big nose, hasn't she?' Cassia whispered suddenly.

In his bed Gaius burst out in a shriek of laughter. Then Cassia too was giggling.

***

The house rose at dawn. The slaves looked stressed as they started to prepare for the banquet and feast that would be held later that evening. After breakfast, with Quintus preoccupied, Gaius found a little time to explore the house. The family it seemed slept in the rooms on the first floor, closest to the atrium whilst he and Cassia and the slaves seemed to have their

115

quarters upstairs. Beyond the atrium at the back of the house there was a small rose garden. The garden was enclosed by high walls. In a corner stood a marble statue of a stern looking Roman Consul, dressed in a toga and holding up his Fasces. The statue stared down at Gaius as he placed his hand on the cool marble foot.

When he returned to the atrium Gaius found Quintus talking to a tall stranger. The stranger was old and clad in black cloak and had a leather satchel slung over his shoulder. He looked to be in his late forties and on his chin, he'd grown a grey goatee beard. The two men turned as Gaius approached.

'Gaius, this is the teacher that I was telling you about,' Quintus exclaimed. 'His name is Pytheas of Marsillia. He's a Greek. Maybe you have heard of him? He is a famous man.'

Gaius nodded respectfully at Pytheas. 'I am afraid I have not,' he replied. 'Let me go and fetch Cassia.'

When a few moments later he returned with his little sister, Pytheas's mouth fell open in surprise. The teacher turned to Quintus.

'A girl,' he exclaimed, 'You want me to teach a girl, it's unheard of Sir,' Pytheas said in accented Latin.

'You are being paid for your time, are you not?' Quintus replied.

'Well yes, but a girl?' Pytheas looked perplexed.

'Do you agree to teach her or not?' Quintus said sharply.

The tall Greek turned to examine Cassia. For a long moment, he said nothing as he examined her.

'All right,' Pytheas muttered nodding his head, 'I suppose that I can teach her what I know about music, sewing and running a household.'

'You will teach her reading, writing, arithmetic, rhetoric and geography, just as if she were a boy,' Quintus said firmly.

Pytheas raised his eyebrows and turned to look at Quintus as if he were mad. The young tribune smiled. For a moment, no one spoke. Then Pytheas turned and stared at Cassia.

'Very well then,' he muttered, 'Come along girl, your first lesson starts today.'

Cassia's eyes widened in shock. Quickly and silently she took a couple of steps forwards, grasped Quintus's hand and kissed it. Then without saying a word she turned and followed her teacher into one of the rooms.

Quintus looked pleased. He winked at Gaius. 'Pytheas was a famous explorer once,' Quintus said, 'But recently he's fallen on hard times and must make his living from teaching. Your sister is a lucky girl. She will be taught by one of the most learned, well travelled and accomplished men of our age.'

Gaius bowed and there was genuine gratitude on his face. 'I don't know how I can thank you,' he murmured as a blush appeared on his cheeks.

'Yes you do,' Quintus replied. 'Come Gaius, you can entertain me whilst we wait for my father and sister to arrive. I have a little spectacle planned for tonight and I want to do a rehearsal. It involves you and Crispus.'

***

Gaius stood in one corner of the atrium holding a small round wooden shield. He was bare-chested. In his other hand he gripped a wooden sword. Diagonally across from him, with the rectangular rainwater basin separating them, stood Crispus. The older man too was bare-chested and armed with a wooden shield and sword. Quintus stood in between them. He turned to Gaius and then back to Crispus grinning as he did so.

'Tonight during the feast,' Quintus said, 'I want you to perform a fight for me, my family and our guests. It will be a re-enactment of the storming of the walls of Bovianum. You Gaius, will be the Romans and you Crispus, I'm afraid, will have to be the Samnite defenders. You will fight here in the atrium. The first man to strike his opponents body three times will be the winner. Now let's practice.'

Quintus stepped quickly out of the way and clapped his hands. Gaius glanced warily at his opponent. Crispus looked like he could handle himself. The slave looked like a dangerous man, an experienced swordsman. Quintus had told him that Crispus was a Paeligni from Corfinium, a mountain man, closely related to the Samnites and that Publius, Quintus's father had purchased him ten years ago from an old lady who no longer required him. Cautiously the two men began to move around the water basin. Crispus looked his usual quiet, stoic self but Gaius was not fooled. Someone had taught the slave how to fight. He could sense it. Gaius could feel his heart thumping in his chest. Then Crispus came at Gaius with astonishing speed. Gaius took the sword blow on his shield and stumbled backwards. Crispus kept up a flurry of blows and then with a superb faint he lured Gaius's shield arm in the wrong direction. A split second later Gaius felt the wooden sword tap his shoulder. Quintus clapped and raised his hand. The fight had been decided in seconds.

'Great, well done Crispus,' Quintus said as he strode in between the two fighters. From the doorway of one of the rooms Gaius was suddenly aware that Quirinia was watching the fight. Quintus too caught sight of his mother.

'What do you think?' he exclaimed, 'Won't our guests love it?'

Quirinia did not look amused. 'I suppose so,' she said in her posh voice, 'But only if the Roman manages to win the fight.'

Quintus laughed and turned to Gaius. 'She has a point, my friend,' he said.

118

Gaius was panting lightly. His torso was covered in sweat. He wiped his forehead. Crispus was smirking at him from across the atrium.

'I will do my best,' Gaius muttered.

Gaius was beaten twice more and when he felt the wooden word strike him for a third time a wave of crushing humiliation washed over him. He had been beaten by a slave, a slave. He lowered his weapons as Quintus strode in between them. Quintus raised Crispus's arm in the air.

'Samnium wins,' Quintus cried with a mischievous twinkle in his eyes. Gaius was panting from his exertions. He stared at the older man. Crispus was without doubt the finest swordsman he'd ever seen. The man was so damned fast and agile. His feet had hardly stopped moving.

'Good, that will do,' Quintus said, 'Now go and rest and prepare for tonight, both of you. I will have some new clothes brought to your rooms.'

Crispus gave Gaius a proud look as the two of them moved off towards their rooms.

***

The sound of loud voices in the hall brought Gaius out of his room. It was late in the afternoon and he'd been dozing on his bed. He paused at the balustrade and looked down at the commotion in the hallway. A young woman dressed in a fine white stola and still wearing her travelling cloak came striding confidently into the atrium. A slave girl was hurrying after her, holding out her hands as the lady handed over her gloves, neck scarf and parasol. The lady was talking in a loud, self-assured voice. Quirinia followed behind her at a somewhat slower pace.

'Has father arrived yet?' the young lady said as she plumped herself down on a couch. Quirinia paused beside the

119

rectangular rainwater basin. 'He is expected shortly,' she said with a slight look of concern. 'My dearest Decia, daughter, you look tired. We have heard that the most horrible things are happening in the north. Is Arretium still safe? How was your journey? '

Decia sighed and looked around her. 'Arretium remains loyal, just about, but things are not good in Etruria,' she murmured. 'Most of the Etruscan league have declared war on Rome but Valerius and his legions have them bottled up in their cities. The Etruscans are hiding behind their walls. They don't dare venture out and there has been little actual fighting.' Decia shook her head wearily. 'They can be such cowards these Etruscans.' She looked up at her mother. 'The latest news is that the people are talking openly about siding with the Samnites, now that we are at war with them again. I do what I can to persuade them that Rome is not their enemy.' Decia shrugged. 'But I don't think many people in Arretium want to listen to me. I was spat at in the street the other day and called a Roman whore.'

'Barbarians,' Quirinia said wrinkling her nose distastefully, 'Still I am glad that Arretium remains loyal to Rome. Your husband's family does after all owe their position to our intervention.' She paused. 'And where is your husband by the way? I was expecting to see him.' Quirinia inquired lightly.

'Ah,' Decia rolled her eyes, 'He couldn't come I'm afraid. The situation in Arretium is delicate, mother. There are many amongst the poorer citizens who would like to join the war against Rome. I told Proculus that it would be best if he remained behind to keep an eye on matters.' Decia looked up at her mother and smiled sweetly. 'It's just me I'm afraid.'

Quirinia looked away. The expression on her face was disapproving. 'So your husband now takes orders from his wife?' Quirinia snapped. 'I know he may be only an Etruscan but still, this is not right Decia, you are a woman and women do not offer men their opinions on matters that do not concern them. Even for an Etruscan I am surprised that your husband allows you to treat him like you do.' Quirinia looked annoyed. 'A woman's role in the household is clear. You have a duty as a wife and a mother and at all times you serve and support your husband. Politics and war are not your concern.' Quirinia's eyes flashed angrily. 'When are you going to learn to behave like a proper lady, like a proper wife?'

'It's good to see you too, mother,' Decia replied sharply. Annoyed she got up and made to walk away but Quirinia moved to block her path.

The patrician matron folded her arms across her chest. To Gaius standing beside the balustrade, Quirinia suddenly looked a formidable matriarch. 'You spend far too much time enjoying yourself and meddling in the affairs of men,' Quirinia said. 'Decia, listen to me, men will grow bored of such behaviour. Men expect you to do your duty. Men expect you to give them children, sons.' She paused, 'Talking about that particular matter, what progress have you made, may I ask?'

Decia shook her head in bewilderment. 'Maybe I will give my husband a son, but that is now my business, not yours,' Decia retorted. She paused and sighed in frustration. 'You don't understand. The women in Etruria are different to us, mother. They have much more freedom. Men allow them to speak their minds; they treat us like equals and sometimes they even seek our advice. An Etruscan woman could have a dozen lovers if she chose and her husband would think nothing of it.' Decia shrugged. 'You know the sort of things that the Etruscans believe, that their fate has already been written and cannot be changed. So, they like to enjoy themselves whilst they can.'

'Decia,' Quirinia cried out raising her hand to her mouth, 'I will not have such talk in my house.'

Decia shrugged, 'I am who I am, mother. There is much more of my father in me than there is of you. You may not like it but there it is. Do we have to quarrel about this every time we meet?'

Decia froze as she caught sight of Gaius looking down at her from the landing.

'Who are you?' she inquired frowning. 'What are you staring at?'

'He is one of Quintus's guests,' Quirinia interrupted with a tired sounding voice, 'he is staying with us. Him and his little sister.'

Decia turned towards her mother and as she turned Gaius was suddenly struck by how beautiful she was.

'Quintus is here, he is back from campaign?' Decia cried in delight.

'Yes,' Quirinia muttered, 'he was wounded.'

***

An hour later Gaius heard another commotion in the hallway. He strode out onto the landing. Excited voices were coming from the hallway. Then Quintus and his sister Decia appeared and came into the atrium. They looked excited. Quintus still had the white bandage wrapped around his head. Gaius shook his head in disbelief. His friend was turning the presentation of his wound into an art form. Gaius glanced again at Decia. He guessed that she was in her early twenties. Without her travelling cloak he could get a good look at her long pitch-black hair and large dark eyes. She had a good figure and dimples when she smiled. He blushed and looked away. The girl was attractive, damn attractive.

The household slaves suddenly emerged from another door and quickly and silently formed a single line across the atrium. Crispus appeared. The big slave, immaculately dressed and turned out, strode quickly down the line inspecting them. Then he turned to face the hallway. For a moment no one spoke or moved. Then from the doorway leading from the hall, a man appeared. His grey white hair was cut short and he had a handsome tanned face and quick, calculating eyes. Publius

Devotio: The House of Mus

Decius Mus, ex Consul, Senator, hero of the Second Samnite War and head of the House of Mus, strode into the atrium with a warm grin on his face. He was followed closely by Quirinia. His wife surveyed the assembled slaves with a cold and strict expression. Publius was clad in a long white toga with a thin purple border running down the side. His eyes gleamed as he nodded to his son and daughter. Then he swept past the line of motionless slaves, each of whom lowered their head as he passed by. As he approached Quintus, the boy took a step forwards and embraced his father. Then it was Decia's turn. She smiled sweetly at him and her hug was both warm and genuine. Publius acknowledged Crispus and turned to look around the atrium. Gaius could see that he was a short, stocky man with well-developed shoulders and arms. He looked to be in his early fifties.

Publius clapped his hands together and the slaves turned and started to file out of the atrium. The clapping noise seemed to release everyone as if from a spell.

'There is no need for such a welcome,' Publius said gently chiding his family. 'I have only been gone for a week.'

'But you know we will do it for you anyway,' Decia said with a broad, warm smile.

'Father,' Quintus said respectfully, 'it is good to see you again Sir. Tonight for our feast in honour of grandfather, I have organised a little entertainment for us.'

Publius turned to look at his son and Gaius noticed a hint of disappointment in the older man's posture.

'I am surprised to see you here in Rome, Quintus' Publius said, 'I was under the impression that you were serving with Fulvius and on campaign. Was that not what I asked you to do?'

Quintus swallowed nervously and touched the white bandage around his head.

'I was on campaign,' he murmured, 'I took part in storming the walls of Bovianum and I was wounded, father.'

Publius examined his son carefully. Then he smiled and looked away.

'Wounded,' he muttered.

Quirinia leaned back carefully on her couch as the rest of her family did the same. Her cold eyes flickered from her husband to Decia and then to Quintus. Then she saw Gaius standing on the landing and as she saw him, Gaius turned and slipped quickly back into his room.

Chapter Sixteen - The Feast to Honour Publius Decius Mus

It was late in the evening when Quintus came to fetch Gaius from his room. The dinner party in the atrium had been in full swing for a couple of hours. The mellow notes of a harp drifted through the house, mingling with laughter and the delicious scent of food. Gaius and Cassia had not been invited to the party. Quintus had a cup of wine in his hand and he was dressed in a fine white toga. He grinned apologetically at Gaius who was standing, clad in just a loincloth and his sandals. On his bed lay Gaius's wooden sword and small shield.

'You look good my friend,' Quintus said as he circled and inspected Gaius. 'Crispus is my friend too, but tonight I want you to win the fight.'

Quintus took a step towards Gaius so that his face was close to Gaius.

'This is how it will be,' Quintus whispered, 'Crispus will win the first round. Then he will let you win the second. Then he will let you win the third.'

Gaius took a step back and gazed at Quintus.

'Why?' he said. 'Crispus is a better swordsman than me. Why must he lose?'

Quintus nodded and shrugged. 'Fabius is our guest tonight. I cannot have a Samnite defeat a Roman. He won't like it.'

'Then make me the Samnite and Crispus the Roman,' Gaius replied.

Quintus shook his head. 'That won't work. You are a Roman and everyone knows where Crispus comes from. No, it will be like I said it will be.'

Gaius stared at Quintus. Then he nodded. Quintus was his patron. He had to obey when his patron demanded it.

'But you must make it look realistic,' Quintus whispered. 'Afterwards my father may have some questions for you. You know what to say.'

Gaius nodded and in return Quintus stretched out his arm and Gaius grasped it in the soldier's way.

Gaius turned to pick up his wooden sword and shield and as he did so he caught Cassia looking at him. His little sister gave him a bemused smile.

As Gaius came down the stone stairway the delicious smell of some kind of food grew stronger. He paused at the bottom of the steps as Quintus strode into the centre of the atrium and raised his hand. The dinner guests were reclining on their couches around a table upon which lay all kinds of exotic looking food dishes. A couple of slaves stood motionless against the far wall. In a corner a slave girl was playing on a harp. Gaius glanced at the guests. There were four of them, Publius, Decia, Quirinia and a fourth, a man of around sixty who Gaius didn't recognise. The newcomer must be the Fabius that Quintus had spoken about. Gaius felt a sudden tug of nerves. He was in the company of two of Rome's leading men. The guests fell silent as they caught sight of Quintus.

'As promised,' Quintus announced with a bow to his audience, 'I have organised some entertainment for you tonight, in honour of my grandfather, who I was never destined to meet but to whose spirit I offer these games. May his name never be forgotten and his deeds, in life and death, honoured for all eternity.'

'What have you got for us Quintus?' Publius said with a gentle smile.

Quintus nodded, encouraged. 'I took part in the storming of Bovianum recently,' he declared. 'The Consul Fulvius took the

126

enemy city in one single attack. Tonight, we re-enact that fight with two men.' Quintus turned and beckoned to someone standing in a darkened doorway. A moment later Crispus appeared, clad in a similar loincloth to Gaius but instead of a sword the slave was carrying a wooden spear. Gaius's groaned in silent dismay. The slave didn't even have a shield. This was becoming humiliating.

'I give you the ferocious, formidable and cunning Samnite mountain warrior,' Quintus exclaimed grandly.

The four guests reclining on their couches clapped approvingly. Quintus turned in Gaius's direction, grinned and beckoned for him to step forwards.

'And here,' Quintus said with a short bow, 'I present you with the fine, indomitable and victorious Roman Hastati. Long may their glory echo in eternity.'

Gaius stepped into the middle of the atrium and turned to show himself to the diners. His appearance was met with more clapping and a little female cheer. Quintus gestured for Crispus and Gaius to prepare themselves for the fight.

'Does anyone wish to place a bet on the outcome of this fight,' Quintus said with a grin.

'That would be a little unwise, don't you think,' Fabius exclaimed, 'As we already know the outcome of the battle?'

Quintus blushed and quickly stepped away from the centre of the atrium.

'You may start,' he said gesturing at Gaius and Crispus.

The contest ended exactly as Quintus had arranged it. When Crispus clumsily exposed himself, Gaius dutifully slapped his wooden sword against the man's thigh. Quintus beamed as he raised Gaius's arm

127

'Rome is victorious!' he cried. The dinner guests clapped politely. Then Publius rose to his feet. He looked annoyed. The atrium fell silent. Quickly Quirinia gestured for the slave girl on the harp to stop playing.

'Quintus,' Publius boomed angrily, 'Is this your way of honouring my father? You have made a mockery of all of us with this charade. You would have done better if you had remained at your post in the Consul Fulvius's army like I instructed you to. I sent you to Fulvius and the army because I hoped that they would make a man out of you. What are you doing here? You don't look wounded to me? Take that ridiculous bandage from your head. You are disgrace.'

Quintus blushed with embarrassment. 'But I was wounded father,' he muttered.

'You,' Publius turned and pointed at Gaius, 'My son tells me that you were with him during the storming of Bovianum. He tells me that you saved his life. Is this another lie? Are you just another of his useless friends pretending to be a soldier, here to tell me what I want to hear? Is he paying you to stay in my house?'

Gaius was suddenly conscious that everyone had turned to look at him. Publius's eyes smouldered as he waited for an answer. There was something in the man's expression that suddenly reminded Gaius of Verrens.

Without thinking Gaius snapped out a salute. 'No Sir, I didn't know your son until ten days ago. I was assigned to the 10th Company of Hastati of the Fifth Legion. I was there when we took the walls of Bovianum. I saw your son in action. He fought bravely, he is no coward Sir.' Gaius swallowed. 'It is true, I did save your son's life. He was knocked off the walls and I jumped down to protect him from the Samnites.'

Publius's face lost some of its fury as he glared at Gaius.

Publius raised his eyebrows. 'You jumped into a crowd of hostile town's people?'

'Actually, he flung the Standard of his Maniple into the hostile crowd before jumping after it,' Quintus interrupted.

Publius stared at Gaius with growing interest. From the corner of his eye Gaius could see Quintus watching him intently. Behind the imposing figure of Publius, Gaius caught a glimpse of Decia. She was staring at him with a fascinated expression.

'Who was your commanding officer?' Publius said sharply.

'Centurion Verrens, Sir, he came from Lavinum. He is a ship builder. That's all that I know about him. There wasn't much time, Sir.'

Publius was studying Gaius intently. Then abruptly he turned away. For a moment the atrium was silent.

'Ah yes the Fifth Legion, the mighty boars,' Publius said with a faint smile. His earlier anger seemed to have completely vanished. He paused. Then he turned to look at Gaius. 'You sound like an honest man. Forgive my earlier outburst. I would like to thank you, on behalf of my family, for the service that you have rendered me and my son.' Publius's eyes glinted. 'Now I suppose that you have agreed to come here with my son because you are seeking some kind of reward. Well?'

'Father,' Quintus protested but Publius silenced him with a single movement of his hand.

Gaius stared straight back at Publius. 'Yes Sir, that was on my mind,' Gaius murmured.

Publius studied Gaius. Then he smiled. 'Good, now I know that you are an honest man. Honesty is a virtue beloved of the gods.' Publius returned to his couch and as he did so, Quirinia gestured for the slave girl to start playing the harp again. 'Come tell us about the battle,' Publius said, 'tell us how Fulvius really took Bovianum.'

Gaius glanced quickly at Quintus. 'Has your son not already told you everything?' he said.

'I want to hear it from you,' Publius said.

Gaius told them then. He told the diners everything from the very beginning. He told them about his farm on the Liris, the hunts with Egnatius, his family's murder, the siege of Sora and the subsequent march towards Bovianum, the mountain battle and the final storming of the city. It was as if a damn had burst. The words came tumbling out of him and as he spoke he felt a great sense of relief. He had not realised how much he'd longed to speak to someone, to tell them about his experiences and share what he and Cassia had been through. When at last he fell silent he blushed as he realised who he was talking to. The diners, reclining on their couches, were staring at him in silence.

Then at last, Publius stirred.

'I think it is time that we honoured my father,' he said.

***

Two slaves appeared carrying a marble statue. It was the statue that Gaius had seen in the small rose garden. They placed it on a table against the wall. The smell of incense suddenly wafted across the atrium. The slave girl had stopped playing the harp. Publius rose from his couch and as he did so, the others rose with him. There was a sombre expression on his face. Gaius turned to leave.

'No, you will stay,' Publius said sharply.

Gaius hesitated and glanced at Quintus who nodded. The room seemed to have suddenly grown heavy with expectation.

Crispus, still only clad in his loincloth appeared and placed four scented candles around the statue. Silently he lit them. Then he bowed to the statue and took a few steps back. Quintus gestured for Gaius to come and stand next to him. The atrium fell silent as the flames swayed and flickered in the gentle draft. Gaius stared at the shadows as they moved across the smooth white marble statue. Publius took a step forwards and slowly got down on his knees before the statue.

'Honoured father, honoured ancestors, spirits of the departed' Publius murmured, 'tonight, your son remembers you and your deeds in life and death. You gave us life, you gave us glory and purpose and you gave us strength and courage and wisdom. I thank you father and ask that your spirit keep watch over his kin.' Publius paused and there was a quiet dignity about the way he knelt before the statue. 'There is news father,' he murmured, 'We are once more at war with your old enemy, the Samnites, but Fulvius has taken Bovianum and all seems well. With Jupiter's aid we shall once more be victorious. I have yet to decide whether to run for the Consulship again. I shall await a sign from you father as to what I should do. May your eternal rest be pleasant and filled with joy.'

Abruptly Publius rose to his feet and turned away from the statue. Gaius blinked. The ceremony it seemed was over.

'I am going to bed,' Decia announced with a yawn. She turned and kissed her mother and father lightly on their cheeks. Then she turned to Fabius. The older man bowed to her respectfully.

'You are worth a whole legion, Decia,' Fabius said with a warm smile, 'Hold Arretium for Rome and make your father proud.'

Decia smiled and pecked the old man on his cheek. 'I shall do my best Fabius,' she replied, 'It is such a shame that my husband is not here to meet you.'

'Oh I don't know,' Fabius said, 'I believe I have spoken with the right person tonight. May your beauty match the strength of your heart Decia. I shall see you again soon I hope.'

Decia smiled at the compliment. 'You will,' she purred as she slipped away towards her room. Just as she disappeared however, she looked up and caught Gaius's eye. It was only for a fraction of a second. Then she was gone.

'I too, should be going, the hour is late,' Fabius said, turning to his hosts. Quirinia offered him her cheek. Then it was Publius's turn. He stepped forwards and embraced the older man in a warm embrace. The two men grinned at each other.

'It is good to see you old friend,' Publius muttered, 'It is always good to see you. I shall have Crispus and my slaves escort you home.'

Fabius nodded. 'Your father was a great man, Publius' he said. 'The service he gave to Rome equals that of the greatest deeds of the greatest men that the Republic has known. You may be a New man, but your family have more honour and integrity than many of the patrician houses I know. I am honoured that you always invite me to your feast.' Fabius dipped his head. 'I shall see you in the Senate House my young friend. There is much that needs to be debated.'

When Fabius had gone and the slaves had removed the statue, only Quintus and Gaius remained behind in the atrium. Quintus was picking nervously at his fingernails. Publius appeared in the doorway to the hall. For a moment the father of the House of Mus examined the two young men. Then he pointed his finger at Gaius.

'You,' he said quietly, 'Come and find me at noon tomorrow. I want to talk with you.'

***

Gaius was tired when he got back to his room. The night was already well advanced. A single small oil lamp lit up his room. Cassia seemed to be fast asleep in her bed. He'd had no time to ask her how her lessons with Pytheas had gone. He was thinking about the look Decia had given him when a silent figure suddenly slipped through the doorway into his room. Startled he took a step back. It was Crispus. The slave glanced at Cassia and then back at Gaius. His face was a mask of stoicism. Then he took a step towards Gaius and abruptly the mask dissolved into a broad grin and the warm smile was so infectious that it made Gaius smile in reply.

'It was not fair that you were forced to lose the contest,' Gaius whispered.

Crispus shrugged. 'It doesn't matter. I serve the House of Mus. I do what Quintus tells me to do.' Crispus paused. 'I have come to tell you something about him. Something you must understand.' The slave paused again and again glanced at Cassia but she seemed fast asleep. 'Quintus has a good heart,' he whispered. 'He treats me well but he is never going to be like his father. As you witnessed this evening, he and my master do not get on, but one day Quintus will be the new head of this family and when that day comes he will need friends, friends upon whom he can rely.'

'I know this,' Gaius murmured, 'Why are you telling me this?'

Crispus grinned, 'Because if you betray Quintus, I am going to ram my wooden sword right up your arse,' he whispered.

Gaius stared at the slave. Then he nodded solemnly. 'I believe you would,' Gaius whispered, 'But you should not have such fears.'

'Good,' Crispus muttered still smiling. The slave turned to leave.

'Wait,' Gaius whispered, 'Crispus, what happened to Quintus's grandfather? I know he died in battle but why the feast to honour him each year?'

Crispus hesitated. Then he frowned. 'You don't know?' he muttered.

Gaius shook his head.

'Forty-two years ago, today,' Crispus whispered, 'Publius Decius Mus, Quintus's grandfather was a Consul at the battle of Veseris during the Latin war. During the battle, he purposefully sacrificed his life so that Rome would win the battle. Rome did indeed win that day and because of this the city became the undisputed leader of Latium.'

'The Consul sacrificed himself? I heard that he died but I didn't know that he sacrificed himself,' Gaius whispered. How had he not heard about this story?

Crispus nodded. 'He devoted himself and the enemy army to the gods of the underworld,' Crispus whispered hoarsely. 'He and his enemy will languish in hell for all eternity because of what he did. Quintus's grandfather is the last man known to have performed the Devotio.'

Chapter Seventeen - The Interview

It was noon and Gaius stood waiting to be shown into Publius's study. He had no idea what the man wanted with him. Quintus had been out all morning and had been unable to enlighten him and Cassia had been no support for she had been closeted with Pytheas since dawn. Gaius had hardly slept. So much had happened in such a short space of time. When he had finally fallen asleep he'd dreamed of Decia. He'd dreamed that she was naked and sitting on his bed.

'He says you may enter,' a slave said quietly.

Gaius turned and stepped through the doorway and into the study. The room was long and narrow. At the far end stood a wooden table across which lay scattered a heap of parchments. A map of Rome and Italy hung on the wall. Publius Decius Mus was sitting in a chair reading a scroll, which he was holding up with two hands. He laid it down on the desk as Gaius approached.

'Please sit,' Publius said gesturing to an empty chair. He was clad in his white Senators toga.

Gaius sat down and Publius regarded him sternly for a long moment.

'Last night you told me that you had a farm near the colony of Sora and that your family were murdered by a Samnite raiding party,' Publius said quietly. 'Do you have no other family except your sister?'

'No Sir,' Gaius shook his head. 'I had an uncle but the plague took him a few years ago and I never got to know my mother's family. My sister is the only family I have Sir.'

Publius nodded. 'Your commanding officer, this Centurion Verrens you spoke about. If I was to make enquiries would he back up your story about the   storming of Bovianum?'

Gaius swallowed. 'I believe he would Sir.'

Publius nodded again. 'What about your morality?' he said sharply. 'Do you steal, Gaius? Have you ever robbed a man, have you ever engaged in homosexual activity, have you raped a woman, murdered a child?'

Gaius shook his head. 'I have not Sir,' he paused, 'although after the battle in the mountains I did look for loot amongst the Samnite dead. I took this silver arm band from them.'

Publius glanced at the silver band and grunted.

'What about debts? Have you or your father ever failed to settle any debts?'

Gaius paused. 'I do have debts Sir,' he replied. 'Your son has agreed to pay them off. It is part of the agreement I made with him.'

Publius grunted again and looked down at his parchments. 'I see. He has recruited you as one of his clients,' he murmured. 'Very well. I trust these debts were not gambling related?'

'No Sir,' Gaius said shaking his head.

Publius looked up and studied him carefully for a moment. 'You are a full Roman citizen? You are freeborn? You love your country and have never betrayed her?' he asked.

'Yes Sir,' Gaius replied with growing confidence. 'Our family have been citizens as far back as my father could remember. My great grandfather was one of the men who defended the Capitoline hill when the Gaul's sacked the city Sir.'

'Good, that is good,' Publius muttered. He rose and turned his back on Gaius. For a moment the study remained quiet.

'My son, Quintus,' Publius said with a sudden sigh, 'is not the man I hoped he would be. He is weak and effeminate. He loves

136

his books, prostitutes and taverns too much. If he is to become a Consul one day, he will need to change. He will need to become a soldier, a man like you, a proper man.'

Gaius looked down at his feet and said nothing.

'I do what I can,' Publius sighed wearily, 'for one day he will be the head of this family and it is my duty to prepare him for that day. But the boy does not listen. He spends all his time compiling that useless family tree. Deeds and action are what impress people, not names on a parchment.'

Publius turned to fix his eyes on Gaius. 'You however seem to have some influence over my son. So, I want you to help me make a man out of him. I want you to help me convince Quintus to become the man he should be. The old patrician families are always watching us, waiting for us to make a mistake and when we do they will pounce and destroy us. They will be watching my son like starving wolves. They will be looking for ways in which to attack him. He cannot be seen to be weak. He must be a man and face up to his responsibilities. Trust me, politics can be as dangerous as the battlefield, I should know.'

Gaius remained silent and a faint sad smile appeared on Publius's face.

'I like you Gaius,' Publius said quietly, 'You have some of the old Roman virtues in you which have made our city and our people great and feared by our enemies. Quintus will need a friend, a companion and I am glad that he has recruited you as one of his clients. My son has a reputation to uphold. My father and I have worked hard to get where we are and I will not let my House slip into oblivion.' Publius paused. 'Quintus will need a friend for he is of that age now where he will start to make enemies amongst the young patricians. He will need a man who has stood in the front line and looked the enemy in the eye. Wherever you go defend him, tell people what my son did at Bovianum,' Publius looked away, 'even if it isn't true. In Rome, Gaius,   reputation   is   everything.'

Publius gestured that the interview was over and Gaius turned away smartly.

Outside the door to the study Quintus was waiting for Gaius. The young tribune gave Gaius a questioning look.

'Everything all right?' he ventured cautiously.

Gaius nodded and grinned and as he did so Quintus too broke out into a smile. Then Quintus caught Gaius by the arm and was dragging him through the hall towards the doorway.

'Come,' Quintus cried, 'Were going to find ourselves a good tavern and get gloriously pissed and after that we will go to a brothel. Or we can visit the brothel first if you like,' Quintus said with a mischievous look. 'Then,' Quintus added without waiting for Gaius to answer, 'When we can take no more sex and wine, you can tell me all about what you and my father discussed just now.'

Chapter Eighteen - The Lord of the Mountains

PART TWO - Spring 298 BC

Egnatius stood on the ridge staring down into the green mountain valley that stretched away below him. A group of men in single file were climbing up the steep rocky path towards him. The group vanished into the trees and Egnatius shifted his gaze northwards and eastwards to where plumes of black smoke were rising on the horizon. For a moment, he allowed his bitterness to show. The Romans had taken Bovianum and had sacked the town. He raised his hand and touched the fresh wound that grazed his cheek. He and his Samnite heavy infantry had fought like demons to protect their home. They had held Fulvius in the mountain pass. They had stopped the Consul's advance dead in its tracks. Then the Samnite cavalry led by that fool Statius had abandoned their position and opened up his flank. Egnatius closed his eyes as he remembered the disaster, the sheer gut wrenching humiliation of running for one's life, the waste of so many good men. But he had survived and so had most of his men. Some had fled to Bovianum but most had followed him into the trackless mountains and forests where he was regrouping the Samnite army.

He sighed and turned away from the plumes of black smoke on the horizon. The mountains crowded around him, fierce, rugged, huge and indomitable just like the people who lived amongst them. His men had made their camp amongst the high forest close to where the trees stopped growing. The bleak and bare, pointed peak of Mount Miletto, over six thousand feet high, towered above them, its summit covered in snow. Egnatius was clad in his loose fitting woollen clothes. The clothes were held together by metal claps, which gave his body maximum freedom of movement. For a moment he stared at his men. The Samnite warriors had built their shelters from anything they could find, branches, sticks and stones. Despite their defeat and the sacking of Bovianum the men seemed to be in robust spirits and as he watched them going about their business, Egnatius felt a surge of pride. These hardy men of the mountains, simple shepherds, goat herders, small farmers and hunters were the equal of Alexander's Macedonian phalanx. The war was not lost. Bovianum may be burning but his men were still willing to fight.

As he strode through the camp he caught sight of the sybil. The witch, an old woman with pure white hair and gnarled bony fingers was staring intently at a chicken's liver, which she had placed on a rock. Beside her on the ground lay the carcass of the unfortunate animal. Egnatius paused and came up to the sybil's side.

'What do the omens say?' he growled in his native Oscan language. The witch did not look up, nor did she answer him. Carefully she plucked and picked at the liver with her bony fingers. Then at last she looked away.

'You must climb the mountain,' the witch rasped in a gravelly voice, 'You will find the answer that you seek on the very top of the mountain.'

The old woman chuckled as Egnatius frowned.

'Which mountain?' Egnatius snapped.

The witch turned to glance up at the peak of Mount Miletto behind them. Egnatius grunted in surprise and gave the chicken's liver a suspicious look.

'The Romans are planning to establish a new colony at Carseoli,' the sybil murmured, 'to keep an eye on the Aequi. They are trying to surround your mountains with an unbreakable ring of iron.'

Egnatius frowned and took a step towards her. 'How come you know so much about the plans of the Romans? Do they come to you and tell you what they are about to do?'

The sybil chuckled again. 'You are not my only servant,' she said. 'There is another, one who hides deep within Rome itself. When the time comes I shall reveal him to you, for he is your friend and ally.'

'Servant?' Egnatius said in an annoyed voice. He spat on the ground and turned away in disgust.

'There is one more thing,' the sybil cried and Egnatius paused, 'The omens say that there can only be one Lord of the Mountains. They will have to choose and they will choose badly.' Again the old woman chuckled and for a split second her laughter reminded Egnatius of the noise that a chicken made.

***

Egnatius was waiting for the party of men he'd seen earlier climbing up the mountain. They appeared suddenly from amongst the trees, wearily climbing towards him up the steep path through the forest. The men were armed with their pilum's, their throwing spears, shields and swords. Some of them were wearing the white and silver tunics of the Linen Legion. Their leader was a tall, powerfully built man with a short black beard and a clean-shaven head. The man looked around fifty. He came towards Egnatius and the two men embraced briefly.

'We heard that you had fled to the sacred mountains,' Statius said as he glanced around him at the men in the camp.

Egnatius snorted. 'We did not flee. It was our cavalry that abandoned us. You left my flank wide open.'

Statius blew the air from his cheeks. He looked tired and his face was covered in sweat. He turned to look at Egnatius and nodded.

'I made a mistake, it is true,' he growled, 'Many of my men died but I will not hide myself away and let shame kill me. We have not lost this war and I intend to make the Romans pay a heavy

141

price for what they have done. I am not giving up. I am here to fight. I am here to win.'

'So am I,' Egnatius snapped, 'So am I.'

Statius nodded again. 'How many survivors have you managed to gather?' he said.

'Four or five thousand so far,' Egnatius muttered turning to look at his men. 'More are coming in everyday as the news spreads. It is an encouraging sign. Our people have not given up hope.'

'That's good, that's good,' Statius muttered.

'What about Bovianum? What news is there?' Egnatius asked.

Statius shook his head. 'It's all gone. The Romans have burned the place to the ground. The women and children have been sold into slavery. The men and boys have been butchered. There is nothing left except a pile of burnt out ruins.'

Egnatius sighed and looked away.

'I am sorry about Bovianum,' he muttered. 'I know that it was your tribe's capital. Did most of the inhabitants flee to the mountains?'

'Some did,' Statius said with a tight voice. 'My father decided to stay. He refused to abandon his house. I shall meet him again in the afterlife.'

Statius turned to look at Egnatius and there was a sudden purpose in his eyes.

'Tomorrow evening we will slaughter a goat and gather the Meddix Council,' Statius said quietly. 'We are facing a military emergency; our people are being threatened like never before. It is time that the Council elected a supreme war leader. One man who can coordinate our war effort; one man who can

142

organise every warrior in our land; one man who can lead us to victory against Rome.'

'One Lord of the Mountains,' Egnatius muttered.

Statius nodded, slapped Egnatius on the back and strode on into the camp.

***

It was dawn when Egnatius rose from his sleeping place around the fire. The forest floor was covered with sleeping bodies. Through the trees he could see smouldering campfires and now and then he heard a man's cough and snoring. A couple of horses, tethered to a tree, stood watching him. He glanced up at the peak of Mount Miletto, which was just visible in the light. The witch had never been wrong. He'd known her since he'd been a ten-year old boy, forced to flee from his home. She had been old even then he thought. The witch had helped him get out of Italy. She had been his only friend when everyone else had abandoned him. He stared up at the mountain peak. The sybil could see the future and the past, she could read the will of the gods but she never revealed more than she had to and she liked to speak in riddles like all sybils. Once when he had tried to force her to reveal what she knew she had disappeared and he had not seen her for nearly a year. The woman liked to keep her secrets to herself.

He strode on through the trees and soon he'd left the camp behind him. As he picked his way towards the edge of the tree line he suddenly came face to face with a man and a boy of around thirteen. The two of them had travelling packs on their backs and each was holding a pilum. The older man blushed in surprise as he caught sight of Egnatius. The man had recognised him. Then he muttered something to the boy. Egnatius ignored the newcomers and continued on his way.

'Meddix, Egnatius,' the older man called out pushing the boy forwards. 'My son wishes to know whether he is old enough to fight. What say you Meddix?'

Egnatius glanced at the boy but didn't pause.

'If he is old enough to die, then he is old enough to fight,' he muttered.

'That's him?' he heard the boy say behind him.

'He is the leader of our tribe. He is the first man of the Caraceni,' the older man replied proudly. 'He has seen the edge of the world with Alexander, King of the Macedonians.'

**

Egnatius emerged from the trees and started the steep climb up the rocky, boulder-strewn slope. He could feel the sun on his back but its warmth gave him no encouragement. The mountain peaks soared into the sky all around him but their beauty was lost on him. Now that he was alone again Egnatius allowed his bitterness to show. Fortune was not his friend. The gods hated him and he hated them in return. The gods could go suck his cock. Nothing in his life had been successful in the long run. His ventures had started out promising enough but in the long run they had always turned sour and his repeated failures had turned him into a disappointed and bitter man. It had all started over forty-four years ago with a monstrous injustice. As a ten-year old boy he'd watched his father being murdered in the streets of Aufidena. It had been about an unpaid debt. His father's killers would have taken him and his mother as slaves for the unpaid debt if the sybil hadn't helped them escape. They had travelled to Pella in Macedonia where his mother had found a position at the court of King Philip of Macedonia. She had eventually died trying to please a husband who was not worth a copper coin and Egnatius, still only eighteen, had joined the young King Alexander's army and had crossed the Hellespont with him.

144

East they had marched as if Alexander had wanted to conquer the very place where the sun rose from its bed. Egnatius had belonged to a mercenary unit that had accompanied Alexander's army. He'd been a peltast, a skirmisher. On the plains of Gaugemela he had witnessed the awesome power of the Macedonian phalanx and had seen Alexander and his Companion cavalry rout the Persian King of kings. What a day that had been. Fifty thousand Macedonians outnumbered five to one and far from home. Alexander had triumphed. It had been Alexander's day and Egnatius, already a battle-hardened veteran at twenty-one, had loved him for it. Those days marching with Alexander had been the happiest in his life. So he had followed the young conqueror east into snow-capped mountain ranges and later into the land that men called India. He should have died out there in vast tracks of the east he thought bitterly, just like his hero Alexander, whose death at a young age had immortalised him before he could suffer any reverses, for then he would not have had to endure what came afterwards. He had seen the glory and beauty that was Persepolis. He'd met a beautiful Persian woman and had married her. But fortune had intervened once more. His King, his beloved Alexander had died at the age of thirty-three and with his death his Empire, for which Egnatius had toiled so hard, had started to crumble. Within a year his new bride was dead too, dying in childbirth. Life in Persepolis began to dim.

He was paid off and tried his hand at various careers but none were a success. Eventually he drifted back to Pella where he married a Macedonian woman. The girl gave him two sons but within a year his youngest had been carried off by the plague. As a veteran of Alexander's campaign's, he received a lot of respect from the locals but as his money started to run short, so it seemed did the respect. He'd started to drink, gamble and sleep around. His wife had started to hate him and his son had not turned out to be man he'd hoped he would be. Then with his life heading towards a sad end the sybil had found him. He was needed at home she had told him. His people were desperate. So, one night he had left his wife and son and taken a ship and

145

crossed the sea and returned to Aufidena. He had been away for thirty-eight years. His first act had been to seek out his father's murderers but they had all died long before and there was no one on which to take revenge. The Caraceni, his tribe had begged him to stay. The war with Rome was going badly. Egnatius had urged his countrymen to make peace and after much debate the Samnite league had agreed to peace terms with Rome. That had been six years ago.

Egnatius paused to catch his breath. The summit of Mount Miletto loomed above him. He stared up at it. What would he find on its summit? He turned and started up the mountain again. As he climbed higher he suddenly became conscious of a large bird soaring in graceful circles high above him in the sky. It was an eagle. He paused to stare at the hunter and as he did so his shoulder slumped. Was this a sign from the gods that this, his latest endeavour, was also going to meet with disappointment? The eagle was a bird sacred to the Romans, his enemy. He shook his head wearily and kept on climbing.

When at last he emerged onto the summit he was panting and his face was covered in sweat. He strode up to the highest point and looked around him. The rocky summit was deserted. There was nothing here apart from the ageless rocks and the gentle breeze. He sat down and allowed his breathing to return to normal. The sybil had known what was on his mind. The war with the Romans was not going well. It was not because his countrymen were bad soldiers, far from it, but they lacked a plan, a comprehensive and bold plan with which to defeat Rome. He sighed, stood up and glanced about. There was nothing here. But the sybil was never wrong. She may speak in riddles but there was always a core of truth in what she said. What was it that she had wanted him to see? He clambered up onto a rock and glanced eastwards. It was nearly noon and the sky was blue and cloudless. Far to the east he suddenly caught sight of the sea that separated Greece from Italy. For a moment he stared at it. Then he turned to look to the west and there on the distant horizon he caught sight of the Tyrrhenian Sea. He blinked. He could see both seas. He blinked again. Was this

146

what the old woman had wanted him to see? The two seas of Italy. Then as he turned to look eastwards and westwards again his cheeks coloured. Suddenly he knew why the sybil had told him to climb the mountain. He felt a tug of excitement, it was the same feeling he'd felt when crossing the Hellespont for the first time. Suddenly everything was clear and he knew what the old woman had meant. The colour on his cheeks grew. Why hadn't he thought of it before? Hastily he jumped down from the rock and hurried off down the mountain slope. There was urgency in his step as he stumbled on down the mountain. His pace sent a few stones rattling off down the mountainside and above him he heard the savage high- pitched cry of a bird. The cry seemed to echo off the mountain walls. He looked up. It was the eagle. The bird was still soaring high above him.

'Are you afraid, eagle?' Egnatius shouted, 'Have I frightened you? For you should be. You should be terrified, eagle of Rome.'

***

Egnatius strode purposefully into the Samnite camp. The men were lounging about, cleaning and sharpening their weapons, cooking and chatting. They fell silent and glanced up at him curiously as he passed by. When he reached the spot where the Standard of the Linen Legion had been placed he paused, stooped and splashed some water from a bucket onto his face. He was wiping the sweat from his forehead when Titus, the young commander of the Linen Legion approached. Titus was wearing a blood soaked bandage around his shoulder. The man saluted with a painful expression.

'Does it still hurt?' Egnatius said gesturing at the wound.

Titus nodded grimly. 'Yes Meddix, but it will heal.' The young commander cleared his throat. 'There is news Egnatius,' he said quietly. 'It came in whilst you were away.'

'Well what is it?' Egnatius growled.

'A thousand or so new men have joined us since yesterday,' Titus replied but the Samnite commander didn't look pleased. He coughed. 'And Fulvius has taken Aufidena. Our scouts report seeing black smoke rising above the town. We must assume that the population has suffered the same fate as Bovianum. I am sorry, Meddix, I know Aufidena was your home town.'

Egnatius turned to look at the ground. For a moment, he was silent.

'Was there anything else?' he muttered.

'Many of the Caraceni want to return home,' Titus replied stiffly, 'They want to go home to protect their homes and families. I think it would be wise if you spoke with the men.'

Egnatius nodded, 'I will Titus, I will.'

Titus grimaced as he saluted and turned away. Egnatius ran his hand wearily across his face. Then behind him he sensed movement. He turned and saw that it was the sybil. The old woman was sitting on an improvised litter made up of two wooden poles and animal skins. The four litter bearers slowly lowered her to the ground. The woman's pure white hair fluttered in the breeze. She gave Egnatius a sharp penetrating look with her pale blue eyes but Egnatius refused to meet her gaze. There was something about the woman's eyes that always made him turn away as if he was afraid of what he would see if he did.

'You saw it?' she said wheezing as she did so.

Egnatius nodded.

'Good, good,' the sybil muttered, 'Then carry out your plan Egnatius. The Meddix Council meets tonight.'

'Will we succeed, will my plan work?' Egnatius snapped.

The witch slowly shook her head and chuckled. 'I do not know. The omens are silent but they do tell me that you made a mistake when you let that boy live.'

'What boy?' Egnatius frowned.

'The Roman boy who hunted with you in the Samnite forest. You should not have allowed him to live. That boy has a destiny. It is written on his neck. You should have killed him.'

Egnatius blinked as he remembered. Gaius, the eighteen-year old Roman who liked to hunt with his Samnite neighbours from across the river. He sighed and for a brief moment the heavy blanket of disappointment and bitterness that had wrapped itself around him lifted and he was reminded of that brighter happier man he had once been.

'I know, I know,' the sybil murmured.

Egnatius looked down at the ground. Maybe the witch was right and he had been a fool to have allowed the boy to live but Gaius had somehow reminded him of that young man who had crossed the Hellespont with Alexander. Abruptly he turned away without saying word. He had spared the Roman because deep down, he'd wished to give the boy a chance to survive and succeed, for despite all his disappointments in life, there was still a part of him that did not want to die a bitter old man.

Chapter Nineteen - The Meddix Council

The smell of roasting meat wafted through the camp. It was dusk and the forest was alight with hundreds of small campfires. The Meddix Council of the Samnite League had gathered in a circle around a fire over which a goat was roasting on a spit. A young boy stood to one side turning the spit handle. Egnatius glanced around the circle. Not every member of the Council was present but no one had expected that everyone would be able to make the meeting. The Roman invasion had made travelling difficult but he was glad to see that most of the members were present including the priests of Mars and Hercules and the four Meddix Tuticus's of the Samnite tribes that formed the Samnite League. Statius, the Meddix Tuticus, leader of the Pentri tribe, the most powerful and populous Samnite tribe, was speaking. He was criticising the conduct of the war to date.

'How were we expected to beat the might of Rome,' he growled, 'With an army that was raised to fight against Lucanians?' Statius looked around the circle of assembled men. 'What we need to do is rethink our entire war strategy. This war with Rome is not like the last one. The Romans will not just restore our former lands, captives and treaties to us if we make peace. They intend to destroy us completely.' Statius paused. 'We are fighting for our very lives, for our very existence as an independent nation.'

'Statius is right,' Egnatius interrupted, 'This war is not like the last one or the one before that. We need a new strategy, a new plan.'

'What would you know about the last war or the one before that?' an old grizzled warrior cried from across the fire. 'I don't recall seeing you with us then. No, you were far too busy helping the Macedonian King conquer the world.' The old warrior with long sideburns spat into the fire. 'Well if Alexander had come west instead of going east he wouldn't have been called 'The Great,' I can tell you.'

The old warrior's words were met with an outburst of laughter. Egnatius smiled too and glanced around the Council.

'Old Pontius speaks plainly,' Egnatius replied as the laughter subsided, 'But maybe he forgets that Alexander beat armies that were several times larger than his. That he took cities which had never been taken before.'

'He and you fought against a bunch of eastern pussies, women, slave soldiers, conscripts,' Pontius interrupted with a roar. 'If he had come up against real men, real soldiers he would have not been so lucky and besides it was his father Philip who created the Macedonian army. His son inherited everything. I know because I was there, sixty years ago now, boy.'

Egnatius shook his head. 'Yes,' he growled with sudden anger, 'You may have been there old Pontius but you were also at the Caudine Forks were you not? Was it not you who allowed the trapped Roman legions to go home untouched with their hearts filled only with hatred for us? Did you not ignore your father, Herennius's advice and allow an enemy who should have been destroyed to escape and return to ravage our lands? Why are you still talking to us when your shame dishonours us all?'

Pontius spat once more into the fire but he seemed to have lost some of his edge and aggression.

'Those Roman legions returned under the yolk,' Pontius cried. 'It is they who carry lasting shame for they gave up the right to be called warriors.'

'You do not understand our enemy,' Egnatius thundered, 'Rome does not care about such matters. They are interested in one thing and one thing alone and that is to win and conquer. They will never rest until they have won. The only way to deal with such an enemy is to obliterate them, exterminate them to the last man. Only then can we live in peace and security.'

Egnatius turned and stared at Pontius from across the fire. The old man stared back at him defiantly.

'So what happened,' Egnatius cried, 'When the Roman Senate refused to ratify the terms of your Caudine peace and went to war with us again?'

'I asked the Romans to return to us the legions which I had captured and to respect the promises that they had made to me,' Pontius growled.

'And did they?'

'No they did not,' Pontius said glaring at Egnatius.

Egnatius fixed Pontius with a withering look, 'You are an old fool. Do never again interrupt us or lecture us on what we should do.'

The Council fell silent. For a moment, all that could be heard was the crackle of the fire and the distant murmuring voices of the Samnite army.

'Our Samnite League was formed to fight against Rome,' Statius said breaking the silence. He glanced around the fire at the solemn faces of the Council. 'Let us not fight amongst ourselves. We are one people bound together by common worship, language and customs and we have one enemy, one enemy against whom, all of us, have sworn to fight to the death. You all remember your sacred oath. We will stand united and we will win this war.' Statius's eyes gleamed in the firelight. 'But we are facing a military emergency so I propose that we vote to elect a single supreme war leader, one man who will lead our war strategy.'

Statius glanced around the circle and saw that most of the Council were nodding in agreement.

'Who will stand as candidates?' one of the priests of Hercules called out.

The Council remained silent as the Council members glanced at each other.

'I shall stand,' Statius said abruptly.

'So shall I,' Egnatius replied in a loud voice.

The priests glanced around the circle but there were no more candidates. The Council was silent as the priests turned to consult amongst themselves.

'So be it,' one of the priests cried at last. 'The Meddix Council shall vote. All those in favour of Gellius Egnatius, raise your hands.'

Egnatius turned to look around the circle and his heart sank as he saw only two hands. He had lost the election.

'All those in favour of Statius as supreme war leader,' the priest cried.

Egnatius closed his eyes as he saw the vast majority of the Council had voted for Statius. He opened his eyes and caught Pontius smirking at him. His harsh verbal treatment of the Council elder must have cost him the election. Had Statius and Pontius colluded to set this up? The decision had gone overwhelmingly in Statius's favour.

'Thank you,' Statius said with stern and proud expression, 'As elected war leader of the Samnite League I have two matters for which I request your immediate advice. Firstly, considering our desperate situation, I intend to ask the gods to give us victory. When the next spring comes, we will once more have a holy spring, a Ver Sacrum. One tenth of all babies and animals born during spring time shall be sacrificed to the gods.' Statius paused and his eyes gleamed red in the firelight. 'The babies shall be killed by their mother's hands and, not like in the past, allowed to leave their homes when they are adults. This is no time for weakness, we need the gods to be pleased, our very existence is at stake.'

Egnatius glanced around the fire. No one seemed opposed to the measure.

'What is your second point?' one of the priests asked.

'It concerns our war strategy,' Statius said rising to his feet. 'Like I said earlier we fought Fulvius with an army that was raised to meet a Lucanian enemy. We need some time for our forces to regroup and new recruits to be trained. I do not want to face the Romans until we are properly prepared this time.'

'So we are to do nothing?' the Meddix of the Hirpini tribe cried out.

'No,' Statius replied holding up his hand, 'We will disperse into the mountains and forests and in small groups we will start to attack the Roman supply lines, we will attack their foraging parties and isolated garrisons. We will make them bleed from a thousand tiny cuts. Then when we are ready we shall face them in battle, defeat them and drive them from our land. This is my strategy.'

The Council was silent as its members considered what had been said. Then Egnatius raised his hand.

'I have a different plan,' he announced.

All eyes turned to look at him. Statius coughed and cleared his throat.

'I climbed to the summit of Mount Miletto this morning,' Egnatius said in a clear and calm voice. 'When I stood on the peak I saw the western and eastern seas. I saw both seas by just turning my head.'

'What's your point?' the Meddix of the Caudini called out.

154

Egnatius got to his feet. 'Don't you see it,' he exclaimed. 'The gods wanted me to see both seas. It is a sign. We must envelop the Romans from coast to coast. We must surround them with enemies.' Egnatius paused and his eyes shone with sudden excitement. 'We must destroy the Romans once and for all. We must build a grand alliance, a grand alliance with just one purpose, the destruction of Rome and her eradication from history. We must ally ourselves with the Etruscans to the north and with the Umbrians to the east. We must build a grand alliance from coast to coast and surround Rome with enemies. Then when we are united we will attack Rome and march on her walls and make the proud Senators of that young Republic shit in their pants with fear. Together with the Etruscans and Umbrians we will have the numbers to overwhelm Rome and her allies.'

The Council was staring at Egnatius in stunned silence. Then at last Pontius spoke.

'Such an alliance has never been achieved before. We have tried it in the past but it never worked. It was impossible to get all the different armies to concentrate in the same place at the same time. The Etruscans and Umbrians have proved themselves fickle allies, easily swayed by bribes of gold and silver and such pretty things. They lack the stomach for hard fighting.'

Egnatius shook his head. 'Maybe that is so, but we must try, we must try before it is too late, before Rome crushes us one at a time. The Etruscans and Umbrians are no friends of Rome. They have fought each other since as long as all of us can remember.' Egnatius's eyes glinted with sudden passion. 'We must try, we have to try for we will have only one chance at this. If we do not seize this moment we will, all of us, fall into the power of Rome and our long and valiant fight for independence will come to an end. Do you want it said by future generations, that you councillors, when offered the chance, our last real chance to defeat Rome, declined it in favour of a strategy that will buy us time but which will   lead us nowhere?'

'I think old Pontius is right,' Statius exclaimed. 'We have tried such an alliance in the past and it didn't work. The Etruscans are weak like children. They would make fickle allies.' He paused and fixed Egnatius with a stern look. 'I have made a decision. We will carry out my plan. There will be no more talk about a grand alliance.' Statius turned to the assembled councillors. 'Tell your men this. Tell them that they are to return home and start to attack the Roman supply lines. Tell them to prepare and train their young men for war. Tell them that the Samnite army will gather on the first day of summer. Tell them that next year we will confront the Romans and drive them from our land. Tell them to keep their faith for we are Samnite warriors, lords of the mountains and we will win and we will be victorious.'

The men around the fire growled in agreement and nodded solemnly.

Chapter Twenty - The Banquet of Temptation

Autumn 298 BC - The Etruscan City State of Arretium

Decia raised her cup and pretended to drink her wine. She could not afford to let wine cloud her senses, not in this place, not whilst she was sitting in the very heart of her arch enemy's house. She smiled politely at the couple across from her. The man and woman had to be the most boring couple she had ever met. Was that why Vela, the wife of her host had placed her opposite them? That lady was capable of anything. Her eyes wandered down the long banquet table. The table was covered with dozens and dozens of delicious and expensive food dishes and there was no shortage of wine. The guests were in a boisterous mood, even though the banquet was being held in honour of a dead man. But now that the funeral rites for Lars Larna, Vela's father in law, had been completed the guests were in the mood for some fun. The table had been placed in a splendid Etruscan garden and men and women sat mixed up together in the Etruscan way. On the sides motionless slave boys stood like statues waiting to spring into action when a guest needed something. From inside the villa music drifted out into the garden. It was late afternoon and there was a slight chill in the air.

Decia turned as she searched for her husband but she couldn't see him anywhere. He must have gone into the house. Her husband was the Zilach, the chief magistrate of Arretium and his family the Cilnii were the de facto rulers of Arretium, although as everyone knew, the Cilnii were being propped up by the real power in the city, which was the small Roman city garrison and the Roman legions that were campaigning across the Etruscan countryside. Decia suddenly looked troubled. Surely he wouldn't have business to attend to at a funeral she thought. She glanced idly at the doorway into the villa. What was he doing inside? A great roar of laughter made her turn and look round. Marce Larna, Vela's husband and the banquet host had fallen off his chair. He was helped to his feet by a slave. Decia smiled. Marce was around fifty and his family, the Larna, owned the great metal smelting works on the coast near Populonia. The metal industry had been in the Larna family's possession for generations and had made them into one of the wealthiest and most influential families in all Etruria. They were also staunchly anti-Roman and a long-standing rival to the Cilnii.

Marce's nose had turned red and he was drunk. He was an exceedingly ugly man Decia thought. As he regained his chair he belched. Decia closed her eyes. Marce may be one of the wealthiest men in Etruria but he had the manners of a goat herder she thought. The other guests, all thirty-five of them and representing the richest and most powerful families in Arretium, however didn't seem to mind. They roared with laughter and raised their cups in the air. All of them seemed well on their way to becoming drunk. Decia smiled again and stole a quick glance at her two widowed friends, Ramtha and Arnthi. The two women had both recently lost their husbands to disease but the loss of their husbands did not seem to have bothered them much. The two women, both slightly older than Decia were smiling and laughing happily. Decia lips formed into a bemused little smile. Ramtha she knew, had a taste for slave boys and Arnthi liked to get out of her mind on Nepenthe, the drug of forgetfulness.

'Now I wonder where that husband of yours has got to?' a quiet, sober female voice suddenly said behind her.

Decia turned sharply and looked up. It was Vela. The woman was around forty. A little cruel smile played across her lips. Her hair was done up in the Etruscan style and she was wearing a beautiful red dress.

'I am sure he will be back soon,' Decia replied coolly.

Vela studied Decia and whilst her lips were smiling there was a coldness in her eyes that seemed to drive a chill straight into Decia's bones.

'I would keep an eye on such a handsome husband if I were you,' Vela said, 'There are many ambitious women in this town who would dearly like to steal him from you.'

Decia smiled, 'Are you one of them?' she inquired.

Vela smiled and bent down so that her mouth was close to Decia's ear. 'I hear that your husband likes it both ways,' she whispered, 'Poor you. When I saw him go into my house just now he was following one of my male slaves. That slave has a penis the size of a sword. Maybe you should go and check if your husband is all right, my pretty little Roman whore.'

Vela glided away before Decia had a chance to reply. Decia turned to watch her hostess move down the banquet table. A little blush had appeared on her cheeks. Vela was the cruellest woman she had ever met. Vela was her arch enemy. The two of them had hated each other from the first moment they had met. It had all started three years ago. A Roman army had just restored her husband's family, the Cilnii to their position in Arretium following an uprising by the poorer sections of the city. The uprising against the Cilnii had been motivated purely by jealousy of the family's wealth and a longing to have some of it but the anti-Roman party in the city had been quick to take advantage of the situation and they had turned the uprising into an anti- Roman rampage.

After order had been restored and to strengthen the bonds between Rome and the grateful Cilnii, a marriage had been arranged and Decia had married a man whom she had never met. He wasn't a bad husband she thought. Proculus was just rather weak and ineffective. Decia had quickly realised that her husband could be easily persuaded and pushed around. It had been an eye-opening discovery but one that brought risks for there were many people in Arretium who sought and sensed a chance to use her husband to promote their own interests and chief amongst them was Vela, Vela the bitch, Decia thought scornfully. Vela had resented the fact that a leading Etruscan noble had married a Roman woman. She had bitterly resented

Decia's influence for deep down both women had recognised in each other the same desire, the fierce, driven and ruthless ambition to have their men, their husbands retain and occupy the most powerful political position in the city. When war had broken out between Rome and the majority of the City States of the Etruscan league, Arretium, through the influence of the Cilnii family and the Roman garrison, had chosen to stay neutral. Decia had suddenly found herself leading the pro-Roman party within the city whilst Vela had become the force behind those who wanted war with Rome.

Decia glanced at the entrance to the house. Should she go and investigate? But that was exactly what Vela wanted her to do. With a mighty effort, she resisted the temptation to get up. No, she would not be a pawn in that woman's games. If her husband was indeed engaged in sex in that house it couldn't be helped. She touched her wine cup and twirled it nervously around in her fingers and as she did so she suddenly wished that her father was here. She loved her father. Publius Decius Mus was like a man ought to be. Handsome, calm, competent, strong and wise. Ever since she had been a little girl she had admired her father. Well she reminded herself with a sudden ruthlessness; she was his daughter. She may not be able to fight in battle like a man but she would show these Etruscans that Roman women were not to be mocked and ridiculed.

She was just about to get up when a wave of perfume came wafting towards her. The perfume was sweet and fine, one of the best. She hesitated and glanced round. A handsome, well-built youth of around eighteen had sat down beside her. He gave her a brilliant smile showing off a line of fine white teeth. Despite the interruption Decia found herself smiling back at the young man.

'My name is Larth,' the youth said, 'And I must say that of all the beautiful women in this city, you are the finest and most beautiful. Why have we not met before?'

Decia blushed at the compliment and it took her a moment to collect herself. From the corner of her eye she caught sight of Vela glancing in her direction.

'That is very sweet of you Larth,' she replied, 'but I was just about to leave. Will you excuse me?'

Decia was just about to rise to her feet when Larth placed his hand on her leg. Suddenly his face was close to hers. 'Listen,' he whispered, 'I know that was a rather rude way in which to introduce myself but I do mean what I say.' Larth glanced quickly at the guests around the table. 'They will be going inside soon, ' he whispered, 'Look I will do anything you want. Straight fuck, threesome, anal, cunnilingus, just tell me what you like and I will do it. But believe me, I am the best in town at what I do.' He grinned, 'I guarantee triple satisfaction. What do you say?'

Decia raised her eyebrows and smiled.

'Did Vela pay for you to come and seduce me?' she whispered.

Larth tried to kiss her but Decia deftly evaded his lunge. The male prostitute suddenly looked embarrassed.

'She did,' he muttered.

'Triple satisfaction,' Decia murmured. Then she looked up. 'Are you really as good as you say you are?'

Larth nodded confidently. Decia leaned forwards and covertly slipped several gold coins into Larth's willing hand.

'I will remember you,' she whispered, 'But from now on you will be my exclusive friend and you will serve me when I need help. Now go away and if Vela asks you what went wrong, you are to tell her that I have arranged for us to meet at another time and place.'

Larth's eyes lit up. 'And are we?' he whispered.

'No,' Decia said firmly as she rose to her feet and headed for the doorway into the villa.

***

The villa was empty apart from a few slaves milling about near the kitchen. Decia stepped inside and poked her head into the rooms around the atrium. They were all empty. She turned and glanced at the stairs leading to the second floor. The stone steps weren't steep as she climbed up them. She emerged onto a landing. There was nobody about. Close by she suddenly heard a noise. Boldly she strode into the room. A male slave was kneeling on the bed covering his hands in massage oil. Her husband was standing beside the window looking out over the garden. He turned as he heard her come in and blushed. Without a word Decia strode across the room, took her husband's hand and led him out of the room and down the stairs. Then she guided him out into the garden. As they emerged into the sunlight he tried to let go of her hand but she tightened her grip and refused to let go.

'No husband,' she whispered, 'this is the time to show our unity. I did not marry you so that I could become a laughing stock.'

'It was just a massage,' he muttered.

Decia did not reply. She made straight for where Vela and her husband were sitting entertaining their guests. Vela saw her coming and the smile on her face faded. Decia stopped and ignoring Vela addressed herself instead to Marce, Vela's husband.

'My husband and I must return home,' she said with a graceful bow. 'I would like to thank you for your great hospitality. I will honour your father in my prayers for he was a great man, a great patriot of this city.'

Decia bowed once more and as she did so she heard someone snigger at her grave and polite manners. Marce was staring at

162

her drunkenly. He looked like a fool. Then he opened his mouth and belched and the smell of bad breath filled Decia's nose. The belch sent some of his guests off into fits of laughter. Decia looked un-amused. She took a deep breath.

'There is one other matter,' she said in a quiet, dignified voice, 'I have heard that the Roman Consul Scipio Barbatus and his legions have made it difficult for you to operate your metal works at Populonia. Maybe there is something that I can do to help you. My father is good friends with the Consul.' Decia paused to let her words sink in. 'Maybe we can arrange a meeting in a few day's time where we can discuss the matter? I shall send my slave to bring me your answer.'

The banquet host was staring at her with a crazy grin. Then he suddenly reached out and before she could stop him he ran his hand over Decia's breasts. There was a sudden lustful look in his eyes.

Decia grasped his arm and quickly removed his hand. At her side her husband remained silent. A few of the drunken guests giggled. With an effort Decia forced herself to smile.

'Good day to you lady Larna,' Decia said dipping her head. Then she turned and half dragging her husband with her she strode away. Her departure was met with more sniggering and giggling but as they left the garden Decia did not see the dark calculating scowl that had appeared on Vela's face.

'What's this about the Consul? Should we not first discuss such matters together?' Proculus hissed. 'I am after all the chief magistrate of this city.'

'We just did,' Decia snapped.

163

Chapter Twenty-One - The Haruspex

Decia sat perfectly still as the slave girl rubbed the oil into her skin. Another slave girl stood behind her doing up her mistress's hair. Decia was sitting in her dressing room, the room where men were forbidden from entering. She was staring at her own reflection in the mirror. Two weeks had passed since the banquet in the garden of Vela's house and still she had not received an answer to her proposal. Arretium was full of Roman diplomats but the men, commissioned and paid for by the Roman state, were only interested in enriching themselves and having a good time. None of the Roman diplomats had made any progress at changing Etruscan hearts and minds. Each and every Roman attempt to open peace negotiations with the Etruscan League had been firmly rebuffed. No one it seemed could persuade the Etruscan League to change its mind. Decia's scorn deepened. Those diplomats who claimed to be serving Rome were utterly useless. The slave girl suddenly trembled in alarm and stopped what she was doing. The girls face grew pale and Decia realised that she had been scowling into the mirror.

'Have I done it wrong, mistress,' the slave girl muttered.

'No, it is just fine,' Decia murmured with a little smile.

The slave girl did not reply. She finished applying the oil and took out the tray containing the pots and vials of perfume.

Decia stared at her own reflection. She was lonely she thought, for she had no one to confide in and the sense of isolation hurt. There was not a single person in the whole of Arretium who she trusted. It was a sad state of affairs but one that she had tried to ignore over the years. The proposal she had made to Marce Larna had been a gamble, a high stakes gamble. She had no authority to make any such commitments on behalf of Rome. No one in Rome knew what she was doing. She had acted purely on her own initiative. The Consul would likely not even consent to meet her, let alone hear what she had to say. She sighed.

She had made Marce Larna a proposal, which she would in all likelihood, not be able to fulfil and when he learned of this, her reputation would be gone. But something had to be done. Someone had to try and change Etruscan hearts and minds. Someone had to knock the Etruscans out of this war for her country was dangerously overstretched by all her commitments. Rome needed peace in the north. It had been the last thing that her father had muttered to her before she had set out to meet her future husband.

Decia closed her eyes as the slave girl straightened her eyelashes. Her marriage to Proculus had been arranged by her father. Proculus was not a bad man and he did his best to satisfy her both emotionally and physically but she did not love him. How could she? He had not been her choice. He had been her father's and Rome's choice. But she was not angry with her father. She understood his reasons. Rome was asking her to sacrifice her body, mind and happiness so that Arretium may not stray from its alliance and loyalty to Rome. Many women might have found that a hard burden to bear but Decia had embraced it wholeheartedly for her marriage allowed her to do the one thing she cared deeply about - to serve her country. For that was what she really wanted to do. Ever since she had been a little girl she had longed to serve her country like the men did every year when they went off to war. She remembered the day when her father had told her she had to stay at home and be a girl. She had cried her eyes out.

There was something noble and touching about the way, every year, the stoic, grave and dutiful Roman farmers, young and the old, had streamed into Rome from the countryside to enlist in the legions and follow their leaders into battle. No one demanded that they come and yet they did. They came to fight for their land, for their families and friends and for the glory of Rome and Decia had loved them. She had loved them all for they were her people.

The slave girl who was doing up her hair took a step back and dipped her head indicating that she had finished. Decia twisted her head to get a better look.

'Thank you, perfect,' she said.

The slave girl behind her lifted a tray upon which lay an assortment of jewellery. Decia pointed at her favourites.

As the slave girl placed a sparkling necklace around her neck Decia's thoughts turned to home. It had been nearly six months since she had last seen her father and her family at the feast to honour her grandfather. She missed them, especially her father. She missed his strength. His wise warm smile. Her father would know how to handle the Larna family. He would know how to outmanoeuvre Vela but he was not here. She was alone. It was up to her to do what she could. She sighed. The turmoil and war in the Etruscan countryside had made travelling increasingly difficult but when spring came, she had decided, she would make the attempt to travel to Rome. The Consul Scipio Barbatus and his army were ravaging the countryside of those Etruscan City States that had declared war on Rome. The roads were dangerous even with an escort but when spring came she would go. The thought of going back to Rome always cheered her up but there was one thing that troubled her. Crispus. She didn't like her father's slave. The man was obsessed with cleanliness and orderliness and was always worried about illnesses. His room was never untidy and he himself was always spotless but that wasn't the worst. Ever since she had become a woman she had, now and then, caught him watching her and there was something in his look that had made her feel dirty and uncomfortable. Once it had got so bad that she had tried to convince her father to sell Crispus but he had just laughed it off.

Her thoughts turned to Quintus and she wondered where he was. No doubt her father would have sent her brother to join one of the Consuls. She wondered whether he was safe. There had been no news from Rome, no news at all in nearly six months. The only news she'd heard had come from her husband. Proculus had told her that an Etruscan army had finally had the courage to come out from behind their fortifications and face Scipio in battle. That had been two days ago but there had been nothing since then. Nobody knew whether a battle had indeed been fought let alone who had won.

The slave girls finished applying her perfume and jewellery. Then respectfully they each took a step backwards. Decia rose and examined herself in the mirror. Then she turned to her girls and nodded.

'You may go, thank you,' she said.

***

Luca, her slave boy was waiting for her outside the door to her dressing room. He was sixteen. Decia had found him one day lying half dead in the gutter outside her house. Someone had bashed him over the head and when he'd regained consciousness she had discovered that he'd lost the ability to speak. She had guessed that he'd been a member of one of the gangs that roamed Arretium and that he'd fallen out with someone but it was impossible to know. Unable to leave him in the street she had taken Luca into her house as her servant and the boy had repaid her kindness with a fierce loyalty. As she emerged from her room she saw that he was holding a letter. He handed it to her and she glanced at the wax seal. It was from the House of Larna. Quickly she broke the seal and read the letter. When she was finished, she handed the parchment back to him and strode away down the corridor with Luca following on close behind.

The Larna villa was in one of the smartest neighbourhoods of Arretium and only a few hundred paces from her own home. Decia climbed the steep stone steps that led to the villa on the hill. It was mid-morning and she had not been planning to go out, but the letter from Marce Larna had changed matters. She could have had her slaves carry her to the Larna house but she liked to walk, especially when she was nervous or excited. The

167

exercise seemed to calm her down. Behind her she heard Luca's light reassuring footsteps.

A slave opened the door to the villa and Decia strode past the man, through the hallway and into the Roman style atrium. She paused as she reached the centre of the house. Squeals of laughter were coming from a room upstairs. The slave who had opened the door had followed them into the atrium.

'I shall fetch my master,' he said quietly.

When Marce Larna appeared from the garden he was dressed in a white Roman style toga. Decia sighed with relief. At least the man was not drunk this time she thought. Marce had a serious expression on his face, which did not change as he caught sight of her. He strode into the atrium and gestured for Decia to take a seat. Luca remained standing beside the doorway to the hall.

'So you got my message,' Marce grunted as he too sat down and flipped a single grape into his mouth.

'I did,' Decia replied, 'I have come to speak with you. To see if I can arrange something that will benefit you and Rome.'

Marce nodded and swallowed. 'You have heard the news?' he exclaimed looking her straight in the eye. 'Our Etruscan brothers have gathered an army and have confronted Scipio near Volaterrae. I expect we shall know the outcome of the battle shortly.'

'Scipio will win,' Decia replied, 'He has a better army.'

'Maybe, maybe not,' Marce snapped tensely, 'But were your people to lose then I expect our conversation today is meaningless. If Scipio is beaten the Roman legions will be forced to retreat southwards to defend Falerii and Tarquinii and I shall encounter no more interference with my business affairs.'

'If that is your judgement then why did you ask me to come and see you?' Decia replied.

'Because,' Marce said reaching for another grape, 'I like to be prepared for each and every eventuality. I don't like risks. If Scipio is victorious I expect the Roman stranglehold on Etruria will get worse. I am a businessman; men depend on me and my industry for their livelihood. So, I shall make an agreement with the consul. If Scipio wins I want him and his Roman troops off my back. The Populonia metal works are to remain free from Roman interference.'

Decia nodded and glanced down at her toes.

'So what does Scipio want in return? Money, slaves, land?' Marce snapped.

Decia looked up. 'He wants you to use your influence and your family's influence to convince the magistrates of the Etruscan League that Rome is not their enemy,' she said calmly. 'He wants you to go before the Council of the League and tell them that it is time to start peace talks with Rome.'

Marce eyes widened in surprise. Then he howled with laughter. He reached for another grape, chuckled and flipped it into his mouth.

'And why should the Etruscan League make peace with Rome?' Vela's sharp voice said suddenly. 'The people want war. The ruling classes want war. There are many here in Arretium who don't like your family and who want war with Rome. The League is united and strong in its purpose. Everyone knows that Rome intends to conquer all the Etruscan citystates and extinguish our independence. Peace will just encourage the spread of Roman influence.'

Vela glided across the smooth paving stones of the atrium and calmly sat down beside her husband. She placed her hands in her lap and then looked up and stared straight at Decia with a cold, calculating expression.

Decia held her gaze and stared straight back at Vela. The atrium fell silent as both women refused to back down and blink first.

Marce cleared his throat as the silence lengthened. 'I could go before the Council of the League I suppose,' he grunted. 'It would take time but I can guarantee nothing. Support for this war is strong. The Etruscan League believes that it is the will of the gods that they fight. Like my wife has just mentioned, amongst the poorer sections of our own city, there are many people who want war with Rome. It could be dangerous to go against their wishes. I am sure that you don't want to provoke another rebellion like the one we had three years ago.'

'Nevertheless that is the price that Scipio demands,' Decia said turning to Marce.

'He demands?' Vela raised her eyebrows, 'No dear, you do not make demands whilst you are in my house. This is the great Etruscan city of Arretium not a colony of Rome.'

'My husband is the chief magistrate of this city and it is his will that Arretium upholds the treaty that we have concluded with Rome,' Decia retorted.

Vela rolled her eyes in disgust and turned to her husband. 'Dear,' she said touching him on his arm, 'Why don't you ask her why Scipio has decided to use a woman to communicate with us instead of using the proper diplomatic channels. None of the Roman diplomats know anything about these communications. Maybe,' Vela said turning to look at Decia, 'She is just bluffing and making it all up, maybe she has no authority to make these promises. Maybe she is lying to you, husband. Then what a fine fool she will have made of you.'

Decia ignored Vela and turned to look at Marce.

Marce leaned forwards. 'Well is my wife right? Why is Scipio using you and not the other Roman diplomats? It does sound rather odd.'

Decia stared at Marce for a long moment and as she did so a triumphant smile began to grow on Vela's face.

'I have no idea,' Decia replied at last in a calm voice, 'Maybe you should go and find the Consul and ask him yourself but like I said my father is good friends with Scipio.' Decia paused. 'So shall I tell Scipio that you are not interested and have rejected his offer?'

The triumphant smile on Vela's face faded. Then she shook her head.

'Maybe we should,' she said defiantly. Decia turned to Marce. He was studying her intently. Then he leaned back on his couch with a gentle smile.

'I shall make no decision whilst the outcome of the battle at Volaterrae is still uncertain,' he exclaimed. 'And my wife is right. I would need proof from Scipio himself that he intends to honour our agreement before I can go before the Etruscan League Council and advocate peace talks with Rome.'

Decia nodded in agreement. 'I can get you that. Give me some time,' she said.

'Really,' Vela interrupted, 'Will the great Scipio come here in person or will he send a message bearing his own personal seal? For nothing else will do, dear. There are so many skilled forgers around these days.'

'I said that I would get you the Consul's reply.'

'I still don't believe her,' Vela said sharply turning to her husband. 'We should ask the gods whether they want Etruria to make peace with Rome. I think that we should consult the

171

Haruspex in the Temple of Saturn. The Haruspex will be able to tell us what the gods want us to do.'

Marce nodded in agreement. 'Yes you are right. Nothing should be done without consulting the gods. I will summon the Haruspex.'

***

The Temple of Saturn looked a foreboding place. It stood on the crest of a hill dominating the hilly slope upon which Arretium had been built. Decia paused to catch her breath. The climb up in the noon heat had been tiring. She glanced up at the tall white columns that held up the temple roof. Broad stone steps led up to the temple entrance and on its roof, she could see a sculpture of Saturn. Beside the entrance a couple of priests were talking to each other and at the base of the steps a beggar was holding up a wooden bowl.

Decia hesitated as she stared up at the temple. Suddenly she was reluctant to enter the house of the gods. The temple made her feel nervous as if she feared that the gods would somehow intervene to expose her gigantic bluff. Her whole body felt like a compressed coil ready to explode. It had not surprised her when Marce had mentioned the Haruspex. The Etruscans made no decisions of any importance without consulting the gods and the way to talk to the gods was through a Haruspex. But she had promised Marce proof that Scipio would honour the terms she had negotiated and yet there was no way of knowing whether the Consul would. She had never met Scipio. He had no idea who she was. She didn't know where he was. Her father and Scipio had never been friends as far as she knew. The Consul had absolutely no idea about what was being done in his name. No one did. She was gambling that she would be able to communicate with Scipio and convince him to agree to her plan. Her chances seemed slim but she had to try, her father had said that Rome needed peace in the north. It had to be important. She had to try. She sighed as she looked up at the magnificent temple. Her father and grandfather were gamblers too; it came

172

with the family blood and once long ago gambling had made the family a fortune but it had also led to her grandfather's self sacrifice and death. She groaned. If she failed to deliver on her promise her life in Arretium would be over and no one would ever trust her again. Her groan ended in a faint whimper. If she failed she would have brought everlasting shame to her family.

'Luca, give the beggar a coin,' she said as she started up the steps holding up her Stola with one hand so as not to trip over it. At the top of the steps she turned. From the temple entrance, she had a fine view of the city and the wide fertile plain beyond. She understood why Rome had been so interested in Arretium for the city occupied a strategic position because it controlled communications between southern Etruria and the Appenine mountain-passes to the north. She turned to stare at the horizon to the north. Had it only been a few months ago since this very same plain had been filled with thousands upon thousands of wild, half savage Gallic tribesmen all heading south and westwards? That summer the Senonian Gaul's had crossed the Appenines in huge numbers and had descended upon the City States of Etruria. The Etruscan magistrates had tried to turn this misfortune to their advantage by bribing the Gaul's into joining forces with them against Rome. Only Arretium with its Roman military garrison and Proculus, on Decia's urging, had refused to go along with this strategy and time had proved her right. For the Gaul's had taken their bribe but when the moment had come for them to march against Rome the Gaul's had claimed that the bribe was not for making war on Rome. The cunning barbarians had argued that if the Etruscans really wanted them to fight against Rome then the Etruscans would have to give them land in exchange. Decia smiled as she remembered listening to the long and anxious debates amongst the city elders. In the end, though, no Etruscan had been willing to have a barbarian Gaul as his neighbour so the City States, in order to send the Gaul's away, had been forced to pay the barbarians a second massive bribe. The Gaul's had subsequently returned home weighed down with treasure for which they had had to do very little. The whole episode had been a farce Decia thought. It had revealed how pathetic Etruscan power and courage had become.

She took a deep breath, steeled herself and entered the temple followed by Luca. Three days had passed since Marce had demanded that the Haruspex should be involved. The priest had said that it took three days to prepare himself for the inspection of the chicken's liver. As she strode into the inner chamber of the temple and made for the doorway that led into the central room a young woman passed her going in the opposite direction. The young woman glanced at her with a little secret smile. Decia frowned and turned sharply to see the woman slip quickly out of the temple and into the sunlight beyond.

The inner chamber of the temple of Saturn was the most sacred part of the temple complex. It was small, dimly lit and stank of incense. A couple of oil lamps were fixed to the walls. The Haruspex was sitting in a chair. He was the only person in the room. He looked around forty with thick black hair. He was blushing and he looked flustered. Decia paused in the doorway and dipped her head respectfully. As she did so she noticed that the priest had soiled his clothes. She frowned and turned to look at the stone altar that stood beneath a huge statue of the god Saturn. A chicken's liver lay upon the altar. She felt the nervous coil inside her tighten. The divination had taken place.

The Haruspex ignored her and remained in his seat. As she waited Decia could hear the priest was panting. She turned to look at him but the priest refused to meet her gaze. The minutes passed by in silence. Then at last she heard footsteps and Marce and Vela, escorted by some of their slaves, came towards her. Vela shot Decia a withering look as she swept past to take up her seat on the opposite side of the room. The Haruspex nodded at Marce, stood up and walked round to stand behind the stone altar. As he did so Decia caught Vela staring at her tensely.

'You will understand that this is a private divination,' Marce said breaking the silence as he turned towards the Haruspex. 'We are not here on state business.'

The Haruspex cleared his throat and glanced quickly at Vela. Suddenly he looked uncomfortable. 'I understand,' he muttered.

'Did you inspect the chicken's liver?' Marce asked in a loud voice.

'I did,' the Haruspex's voice was barely audible. A bead of sweat had appeared on his forehead. He cleared his throat again.

Marce raised his hand in the air. 'So what do the gods say? Do they favour peace talks with Rome or not?'

The room fell silent with sudden tension. Decia stood rooted to the ground. Her fingers were playing gently with the gold necklace around her neck. Across from her Vela was staring fixedly at the priest.

'The gods,' the Haruspex said turning to stare at the temple floor, 'The gods favour peace with Rome,' he muttered.

'What! How can this be so?' Vela cried jumping to her feet. Her face had grown pale with shock.

'The gods have spoken. I have seen it in the liver,' the Haruspex muttered as he refused to look Vela in the eye.

The room once more fell silent. Then Vela turned sharply on her heel and stormed towards the exit. Her shock had been replaced with rage. She was closely followed by Marce and the slaves. As she approached, Decia stepped out into her path and brought her head close to Vela's.

'It seems our priest prefers gold over having his cock sucked,' Decia whispered in Vela's ear. 'I outbid you, bitch.'

Then before Vela could answer Decia turned and strode away. As she moved towards the sunlight and the temple doors she heard an outraged gasp. Decia smiled. Euphoria swept through her as the tension that had been building all morning was released.

'Come Luca,' she said, 'Let's go home.'

***

Decia was at home relaxing on her couch. It was late in the evening and as usual she was alone. Proculus had sent her word that he would be home late as he had state business to attend to. So she had instructed the cook to bring her dinner for one, which she was enjoying when a slave came hurrying into the atrium.

'Lady, you have a visitor,' the slave said.

Decia paused. 'A visitor at this hour? Who is it? What do they want?'

'They insist on seeing you, lady,' the slave replied.

Decia sighed and gestured for the slave to show the visitor into the atrium. A few moments later the hooded figure of a woman appeared. Decia rose as the visitor drew back her hood. It was her friend Arnthi.

'Arnthi,' Decia said with a smile as she gently touched both the woman's hands in greeting, 'How lovely to see you. Is everything all right?'

Arnthi looked flustered.

'I have just come from the temple of Saturn,' she gasped, 'There is terrible news. Someone has just murdered our Haruspex.'

Chapter Twenty-Two - The Messenger

Decia lay in bed. She was naked. The house was silent. It was the middle of the night but she could not sleep. Proculus lay on his side. He too was naked. In the darkness she glanced at him. For a while she watched the gentle movement of his chest and listened to his quiet breathing. He looked like he was sleeping but she knew he was awake. She reached out to his hand and brought it up to her naked breast. He stirred and tried to move his hand away but she pressed it firmly against her breast feeling the warmth from his hand flow into her body.

'I am not in the mood,' he muttered, 'Another time Decia, tomorrow perhaps.'

She sighed and looked up at the ceiling. 'What is the matter?' she whispered. 'Is there something on your mind, husband?'

Proculus turned onto his back. His eyes flicked open. For a while he didn't speak.

'If Scipio is beaten at Volaterrae,' he muttered, 'Our position here will be threatened. I am worried about our future. Vela came to me a few days ago. She warned me that anti-Roman sentiment is growing amongst the population. She told me that we may have to abandon our treaty with Rome if we want to stave off a new rebellion. She may have a point. She was very persuasive.'

Decia raised herself up on her elbows. 'Vela came to you,' she whispered in alarm. 'What else did she say?'

Proculus stared up at the ceiling. 'She urged me to abandon the Roman alliance. She said that Rome was going to lose and that the Samnites were going to win. There is a rumour that the Samnites have just won a great victory in the south. She told me that if I were to change sides the Etruscan League would reward us. She said the people would love me. If I were to change sides my family's popularity would go through the roof. We would be hailed as liberators.'

'She tried to bribe you,' Decia whispered, 'What was your reply?'

Proculus sighed. 'I told her that we must wait for the outcome of the battle.'

'So if Scipio were to lose,' Decia said with growing alarm, 'You would consider abandoning our allies? Husband, do you realise what kind of position that will put me in?'

Proculus nodded but said nothing.

'It would be a most foolish thing to do,' Decia snapped. 'Think it through. How can I stay here if we are at war with Rome? The people will see me as a spy. They will see you and your family as the enemy because you have a Roman wife and what are you going to do to Remus and the Roman garrison? They are not going to sit idly by whilst the city rebels. You would lose all your influence and power. We would have to leave the city. We would have to leave everything behind. Don't you see. This is what Vela wants. That woman wants to see us utterly ruined. She is manoeuvring to get Marce and the Larna into your job. You should refuse to see her again.'

Proculus turned on her and there was a sudden anger in his eyes.

'I saw my father being murdered by the mob,' he retorted. 'Three years ago.' His eyes bulged as he stared at her, 'I saw what they did to him. You were not there. You don't know the terrible things that the mob did to my family. I am not going to let the same thing happen to me.'

'But Rome restored your family to their position,' Decia snapped. 'Roman soldiers keep the peace in this town. You owe my people. If you abandon them now they will never forget or forgive you.'

Proculus remained silent.

'If we do have to abandon our alliance with Rome,' he said at last. 'I will send you away. I will send you back to your family in Rome. You will be safer there than here.'

Decia stared up at the ceiling in shock. For a while she said nothing. Then she turned and ran her fingers lightly across her husband's chest. Without a word she got up and straddled him and placed his hands on her breasts. She smiled coyly.

'Would you really do that dear,' she purred. 'Would you really neglect your wife like that?'

Proculus pushed her roughly off him.

'I told you,' he snapped irritably, 'I am not in the mood.' He swung his legs out of the bed and got up and reached for his clothes.

'If you are feeling neglected I will send a slave to satisfy your needs,' he growled.

Decia stared at her husband.

'I do not want a slave,' she cried angrily, 'I just want a husband who acts like a man. Are you a man? Are you a real man Proculus?'

Proculus strode out of the room without saying a word.

***

Decia sat in the atrium. A table full of food dishes stood before her but she had lost her appetite. Once again she was dining alone. Three days had passed since she'd had the row with her husband and she had not seen him since. He had stormed out

179

of the house and had not returned. The gods only knew where he had gone or who he was with. Decia had not gone out to look for him. She should have, she supposed, but part of her couldn't be bothered. She was tired, irritated and tense. The tense oppressive atmosphere in the house and the city seemed to be growing by the hour. Nervously she picked at her fingernails. If Proculus sent her back to Rome she would have failed. The shame and humiliation would run deep. She would have failed to help her countrymen. She would have let her father down. She would have abandoned her brave soldiers. Maybe she should go and find Proculus and beg him for forgiveness. Maybe she should purchase poison and get Vela to eat it. The thoughts came thick and fast but in her heart, she knew there was only one thing she could do, and that was to wait. She would wait to see what fortune had decided for her.

Luca suddenly appeared in the doorway to the hall. He looked excited. She glanced at him. The slave boy may not be able to speak but he could still communicate. She blinked in surprise. He was telling her that she had a visitor. He was telling her that the visitor had urgent business.

'Who is it Luca?' she asked as she rose to her feet.

The slave boy shrugged. He didn't know. He had not seen the visitor before. Decia gestured for him to show the stranger in.

She composed herself as best as she could and waited. A few moments later a young man came striding into the atrium and Decia gasped. The young man was wearing a mud splattered Palla. He looked tired and flakes of dirt clung to his forehead and cheeks. A sword hung from his belt. He dipped his head respectfully as he saw her.

'Lady Decia,' Gaius said wearily, 'I bring you news. I have come straight from the camp of Consul Scipio Barbatus with a message for you. The Consul was victorious at Volaterrae. The enemy have fled back into their cities. It was a hard fight with many casualties on both sides but Roman arms are victorious.'

The atrium fell silent. Then Decia shrieked in delight, took two steps forwards and flung her arms around Gaius.

When she released him, Gaius took a surprised step backwards. Decia was smiling from ear to ear.

'This is great news,' she cried, 'great news indeed. Thank you, thank you for coming here to tell me this.' Decia paused to study Gaius for a moment. Then she glanced at his dirty travelling cloak.

'Have some fresh clothes brought down for my guest and some water so that he may clean his face,' she said turning to Luca. Then she gestured for Gaius to sit and take some of her food. The young man sat down gratefully and tried to wipe the dirt and sweat from his face.

'I remember you,' Decia said with a sparkle in her eye. 'You were the entertainment at the feast to honour my grandfather. You told us about the fall of Bovianum. My father told me that you are my brother's companion now, his friend and client. How is Quintus? Is he well? And father and mother, are they both well?'

Gaius nodded and glanced hungrily at the food dishes. 'They were all doing well, Lady Decia, when I last saw them,' he replied.

'You may call me Decia,' she said, 'My father spoke highly of you. You must have impressed him. If my father likes you, then so shall I.'

Gaius took a piece of cheese and stuffed it into his mouth. He ate hungrily and as he did so Decia had a moment to study him. She remembered the somewhat arrogant rough mannered youth accompanied by his little sister who had come to stay with them all those months ago. She had noticed the way he'd looked at her when she had first met him. His glances had not displeased her, for there was something exciting and mysterious about him, but he'd only been a boy then she thought, a boy who afterwards would probably have pleasured himself in bed by thinking of her. The story he'd told her family that night had fascinated her.

As she watched him eat she noticed the change in him. There was a maturity about him which had not been there before. He looked older and graver than when she had first met him. The boy had gone. Gaius had become a man, a Roman warrior who knew how to handle himself. Her fingers found their way to her necklace. She had a habit of doing this when she was pleased.

'Quintus and I came north with Scipio,' Gaius said between mouthfuls. 'Your father is also with the army as a tribune. He instructed me to come and find you. He has a message for you. I have come straight from the battle.'

Decia frowned. 'My father has a message for me?'

Gaius nodded. 'He instructed me to tell you that amongst the men that we captured at Volaterrae are a couple of senior members of the Larna clan. Scipio wants them ransomed but your father has spoken with the Consul. He says that you will know what to do with this information.'

Decia brought her hand to her mouth, leaned back on her couch and turned to look away. Then suddenly a single tear appeared in her eye. All this time she thought, all this time she had believed that she was alone, that she was fighting a lonely battle, far from home, to protect her country. But she wasn't alone. Her father had sent help. Even from afar he had been watching over her. She had never told him what she was doing but somehow he'd known anyway and now he'd sent her the tools with which she could win her fight.

'I am sorry I did not mean to upset you,' Gaius mumbled.

182

She shook her head and dried her face with her hand. 'It's nothing. It is not your fault,' she sniffed. Then she composed herself and turned to face Gaius.

'Will you ride back to my father, Gaius, with a message from me,' she sniffed.

Gaius nodded.

'Tell him that his daughter will do her best. Tell him to give me some time,' she said with another sniff.

Gaius grabbed a hunk of bread and nodded as he stuffed it into his mouth. For a moment, the two of them were silent.

Then Gaius rose to his feet and picked up the pile of fresh clothes that the slave had brought him. Without a word, he pulled off his sweat stained tunic and undid his under garments. A moment later he stood before her stark naked. Decia blinked in surprise and as she caught sight of his fine physique she blushed and turned to look away. For an insane moment lust surged through her and she felt a desire to rip off her clothes and throw herself upon Gaius. Her blush deepened. She could feel her heart pounding in her chest. Then Gaius was pulling on his fresh clothes and the moment passed. He seemed oblivious to the consternation he had caused. Decia took a deep breath. However much her body wanted it, she would not be his lover she decided in that moment. Something didn't feel right. It felt incestuous and wrong.

'Decia,' Gaius was talking to her. She blinked and turned to look at him. He had finished dressing himself. There was a gentle self-confident smile on his face.

'Quintus and I have become good friends since I last saw you and your father treats me as if I were a second son,' Gaius said. For a moment, he searched for the words. 'So I was hoping that you would become like a sister to me, an older sister.' Gaius paused and stared at her carefully. 'But if that offends you, then

I will understand and I will continue to treat you like the lady that you are.'

'An older sister, yes I would like that,' Decia murmured in relief. She managed a little smile.

'Is that why you took your clothes off in front of me then?' she said boldly.

***

An angry crowd followed Decia as she made her way through the streets of Arretium. It was just before noon. The crowd of mainly young men were shouting at her, insulting her and calling her a Roman whore. Luca strode along at her side and whenever one of the men got too close, the former gang member would raise his stick and push them back. Luca had warned her that she was going to get a rough reception in the city. The news of the Roman victory at Volaterrae had ignited the passions of the unruly sections within the populace and Decia had been an easy target to pick on. Her father however had told her once that she should never show fear in public, for a mob fed on fear. So, she had declined the carriage that Luca had arranged for her and had gone out on foot instead.

Decia ignored the hostile townsfolk. She held her head high and her stride was full of purpose. The hostile youths would melt away if Remus and his soldiers were to appear. They were just a mob, a leaderless mob looking for someone upon which to vent their frustration. That morning Gaius had returned to the Consul's camp. She had been sad to see him go but he was under orders to return. Proculus, her husband had still not returned home. She had heard a rumour that he was holed up in a brothel but it was impossible to know for certain. She was certainly not going to go there to find out. A man standing on the side of the street glared at her and spat onto the paving stones. From a window above her in one of the houses she heard a woman shout her name and then curse her. She ignored them all. Her reception was not all hostile however. As she and Luca

184

strode through the street she noticed anxious faces peering at her from small workshops and doorways. The majority of the citizens of Arretium seemed fearful of what the future was going to bring. They had all witnessed the ruthlessness with which Rome had restored the Cilnii family. If there were to be another revolt the Roman response would likely be harsh in the extreme.

The Larna family were taking no chances. As Decia approached the villa she saw armed guards standing outside their front door. The hostile crowd behind her started to disperse as they caught sight of the armed men. Decia sighed. There was anger on the streets of Arretium but no appetite it seemed for bloodshed and looting. Not yet at any rate.

A slave showed her into the atrium where Marce and Vela Larna were already waiting for her. The two of them were standing beside the doorway that led out into the garden. Marce looked harassed and refused to look Decia in the eye. Vela however fixed her with a little superior smile. As no one had asked her to sit Decia remained standing.

'You have heard the news?' Decia said calmly.

'Yes,' Marce replied with a hint of irritation in his voice, 'Apparently, Scipio is victorious. Congratulations.'

'The Etruscan League does not want to make peace,' Vela snapped, 'Even if they have suffered a setback, they will continue the war. Rome cannot take our walls. They are too strong for you.'

Decia ignored her and addressed herself to Marce.

'I have received a message from Scipio. He agrees to the terms of our arrangement. He will exempt the Populonia metal works from Roman control and taxes if you can persuade the Etruscan League to offer peace talks.'

Vela glared at Decia. 'Where is the proof that Scipio agrees to this? We asked you for proof but you bring none. Why should we believe you?'

'Maybe you should go and ask Scipio yourself if you do not believe me,' Decia replied in a calm voice.

Vela looked away in disgust.

'Scipio does not have the time nor the temper to come here in person,' Decia suddenly snapped, 'Nor is he inclined to send you an official letter. I have received my instructions by courier. He arrived two days ago. The Consul is a busy man. He instructs me to tell you that if you do not agree or deliver on your promise he will simply hand your metal works to a new owner.'

Decia's eyes flashed dangerously. 'He has that power and he will use it. If you cannot deliver peace talks he will have no further use for you. You and your family will be finished. So, what is your answer?'

Marce suddenly looked nervous.

'I think she is bluffing,' Vela snapped, 'Do not let her frighten you, husband. Our people do not want peace. You know this. The Romans cannot take our cities. There is talk that the Gaul's will be coming to our aid soon. All this talk about peace just shows how desperate Rome is. The Samnites must be hurting them badly.'

Marce muttered something to himself. He looked undecided. Decia stared at him. It was time for her to play her final trump.

'The Consul has also informed me that he holds two members of your family prisoner. They were captured during the battle. Scipio has given orders for them to be executed if you do not agree to his proposal.'

Marce and Vela exchanged glances and for once Vela remained silent. Marce turned to look into the garden with a troubled expression.

'Yes,' he muttered wearily, 'I have heard of what has happened to my kin. Are they well? Are they being treated well?'

'I have no idea,' Decia replied bluntly.

For a moment Marce stared out into the garden. Then he turned on Decia and there was a sudden aggression in his posture.

'It seems that I have little choice,' he growled. 'Rome controls the countryside, Rome controls Arretium through that weak-willed idiot of a husband of yours and now they have my nephews as captives. Very well then. You win Decia. I shall go to the Etruscan League Council and argue that we should open peace talks with Rome but on one further condition.'

'And what would that be?' Decia asked.

Marce leered at her with a sudden lustful look.

'If this Peace Treaty means so much to you, then first, you will suck my cock,' he hissed. 'Then we will have a deal.'

Decia felt her face brighten. Quickly she glanced at Vela. Vela was staring at her husband with a disappointed but resigned expression. Then her arch enemy turned to look at Decia and there was no sign of surprise or discomfort. Instead Vela seemed to be relishing the imminent humiliation of her rival.

Decia looked down at the floor. Rome needed peace with the Etruscan League. Her father had said so himself. Slowly and with as much dignity as she could muster she got down on her knees. She would do this. She would do this for Rome and her country.

Chapter Twenty-Three - Brothers of the Wolf

PART 3 - February 297 BC - The City of Rome

Gaius and Quintus stood in the middle of the crowd of excited young men watching the Luperci, the brothers of the wolf, slaughter the sacrificial dog. The priests, clad only in goatskins, stood in a semi circle, their knives gleaming in the fresh morning light. In front of them beyond the stone altar, on which the dog lay dying, was the dark cave mouth where the She Wolf had suckled Romulus and Remus. The dark cave vanished into the Palatine hill. Gaius glanced round at the hundreds and hundreds of people, mainly women who lined the street. There was an atmosphere of tense excitement amongst the crowds. The feast of Lupercalia, the festival to honour the She Wolf was about to start with a vengeance. He looked down at himself and grinned. Gaius was naked. Quintus was naked. All the tense young men standing behind the priests were stark naked. In his hand he gripped the goatskin thongs. Soon when the Magister, the chief priest gave the signal the group of naked young men would surge off down the street and race around the Palatine Hill. Gaius had seen the race once before when he'd been a boy but he had never expected to be a participant. The naked young men would race each other trying to be the first to complete the lap and so be hailed and noticed by the crowd. Girls and women would line the roads, holding out their hands, palm upwards, hoping that the running men would strike them with their thongs, for a girl would be blessed with fertility if she was touched on Lupercalia.

'Look its Claudius Centho,' Quintus muttered giving Gaius a nudge with his elbow. 'The arrogant prick thinks he has already won the race.'

Gaius glanced in the direction in which Quintus was pointing and saw a young man standing on the start line. The man's white blond hair and light blue eyes contrasted sharply with the black-haired youths around him. He looked around the same age as Gaius and Quintus but he was bigger and fitter looking and his torso and leg muscles were beautifully toned. The man would be from a wealthy family Gaius thought for he looked in too good a shape to be poor. There was a sharp, confident expression on Centho's face. He sneered as he caught sight of Quintus.

'Who is he?' Gaius muttered.

Quintus shook his head in disgust. 'Centho is the son of Appius Claudius,' he murmured, 'You know, the man who built the Appian Way. They belong to one of the most powerful families in Rome. Centho and his father consider themselves to be first amongst the patrician families. They hate New men like me and my father. They fought long and hard to exclude us from the Senate. They despise us for our humble origins. They are always looking for new ways in which to humiliate us.'

Quintus's cheeks broke out in a light blush.

'But today Gaius, today I am going to beat him. I am going to beat him.'

Gaius turned to look at the priests. Quintus was a good friend but sometimes he could be rather unrealistic. There was no way he was going to beat Centho. The young patrician looked far too strong and fit. In contrast Quintus, Gaius had learned, liked to spend his days lying on the couch reading and reciting poetry or visiting the taverns and whore houses for a different kind of relaxation. Gaius stroked his dark beard as he felt a tingle of nerves in his stomach. The Luperci had finished the sacrifice. It would not be long now before the signal came. Impatiently he slapped the thongs against his thigh. Aeliana would be somewhere in the crowd lining the streets. She had promised she would come. Aeliana was Gaius's girlfriend. He'd met her just before he had been sent to join Scipio's army in Etruria. She was a sweet, quiet and hard working tavern owner's daughter. He studied the faces of the eager women lining the streets but could not see her. He sighed. The girl had recently started to put pressure on him in her own particular silent way. She was only sixteen but already impatient to get married and start a family. He would have to make his decision soon.

'I hope you manage to touch her,' Quintus said pushing his fist affectionately into Gaius's shoulder.

'I hope you beat blondy over there,' Gaius said turning to Quintus with a grin.

'I will,' Quintus said with a determined look.

Gaius nodded. Participating in the Lupercalia had been Publius's idea. Quintus's father had said that it would be good for Quintus's image and reputation if he were to be seen amongst the runners. Quintus had gone along with it in his usual reluctant but dutiful manner. Gaius sighed. Everybody could see that father and son had diverging interests. It was becoming harder and harder to hide the fact that Quintus was not going to be like his father. Gaius had tried his best to please both father and son but sometimes it had been an impossible act. His first and only attempt at trying to help Publius make a man out of his son had resulted in Quintus pouring a pitcher of wine over Gaius's head. It hadn't stopped Publius from continuing to push Quintus into following in his footsteps, to become a leader of men and to compete for political office, for the old man still dreamed of one day making his son a Consul. Quintus obeyed his father but his heart was just not in it. Quintus, it seemed was happiest when reading or writing a poem with a pitcher of wine in his hand. Father and son were not going to be reconciled. Soon, as everyone in the house knew and dreaded, one of them was going to have to accept it, back down or leave.

***

The group of naked young men surged forwards with a great, excited cry. In the rush Gaius was quickly separated from Quintus. He was in the middle of the group as he ran down the street. Up ahead he caught a glimpse of Centho. Gaius gasped in dismay. The young patrician was already well ahead of the others. The man looked like a beautiful indestructible young god as he stormed down the street. Then just as Centho disappeared around a corner Gaius caught a glimpse of a figure in pursuit. It was Quintus. He blinked in surprise. Quintus must be going flat out. He was not going to give up without a fight. Around him the crowds were cheering and yelling. A runner in front of Gaius lashed out at a woman's palms with his thongs and the girl squealed in delight, as she was touched. Gaius veered to the left side of the street. Female faces flashed past him as he ran. The women were crying out to him imploring him to strike their outstretched hands. Suddenly a girl up ahead opened her dress and flashed her breasts at him. The girl was beautiful. She smiled at him expectantly but Gaius ran on without raising his thongs. Aeliana could be anywhere in the crowd. The thought of having to explain to her why he'd chosen to bless another woman with fertility didn't really appeal.

Gaius rounded a corner and caught sight of Centho up ahead. Quintus was doing a magnificent job in keeping up with him but it wouldn't last. The young patrician was moving at a steady pace whilst Quintus seemed to be giving it his all. As Gaius stared at the two leaders Centho suddenly swerved towards a lady clad in a beautiful white Stola and lashed her hands with his thongs. It was a superb and smoothly executed movement and the crowd around the lady erupted in cheers. The woman looked pleased but before she could withdraw her hand Quintus too had struck her with his thongs. The next few moments were confused. Centho suddenly lurched towards Quintus, caught him and with a powerful shove sent him flying into the crowd of onlookers. Someone shrieked. Then bodies tumbled to the ground in a confused tangle as Quintus went crashing into the crowd. By the time Gaius caught up with him Quintus was back on his feet. Blood was welling up from a cut to his lip. Quintus looked furious.

'The fucking prick pushed me. I am going to have him,' Quintus yelled as he started off up the street.

Gaius caught up with him so that the two of them were running side-by side.

'Let him go,' Gaius gasped, 'He's not worth it. He is fitter than you. He is going to win. Don't let him under your skin.'

'He's not going to humiliate me,' Quintus hissed.

When Gaius and Quintus rounded the last corner and saw the dark entrance to the Lupercal cave it was immediately obvious who had won the race. Centho was parading up and down before the entrance holding his arm up in a victorious salute as the crowds roared and yelled. The young patrician was smiling and his naked body glistened and steamed. Gaius caught Quintus's arm and shook his head as he saw his friend's furious expression. Quintus wrenched himself free as they approached the finish line.

'Gaius, Gaius,' he suddenly heard a voice yelling out his name from the crowds. Gaius wiped the sweat from his brow and peered at the faces lining the street. Then he saw Aeliana and Cassia. The two girls were shouting and gesturing at him. Gaius swerved across the street towards them and as he approached the two girls held out their hands and smiled at him excitedly. He slapped his thongs across both of their arms and grinned wearily.

Aeliana's eyes sparkled and her body seemed to glow as he touched her. Cassia gave him a grateful look and he knew that she was happy he'd not forgotten about her. His little sister was turning into a young woman. She had grown since they'd left Sora nearly a year ago and she was now nearly as tall as Aeliana. She would be eligible to marry within the next year if he gave her his permission. Gaius came to a halt and was just about to kiss them both when behind him a high-pitched shriek of rage silenced the crowds. Gaius turned and was just in time to see Quintus charging at Centho. Then the two young men clashed and tumbled to the ground in a confused tangle of arms and legs. Gaius's face turned pale. Then he was thrusting his way through the onlookers towards the two wrestling men. By the time he'd made his way through the crowd Centho had gained the upper hand. The patrician had Quintus in an arm lock and was pummelling his face with his free fist. Quintus's face was covered in blood and one of his eyes looked badly bruised.

Gaius strode forwards and caught Centho's arm as he was about to strike Quintus again. The patrician snarled as he looked up at Gaius.

'Let him go, that's enough,' Gaius snapped.

'What's this?' Centho bellowed furiously, 'Mind your own business. He is going to get what he deserves.'

But Gaius did not let go of Centho's arm.

'I said that it is enough,' Gaius growled.

Centho was panting as he looked up at Gaius. For a moment, he said nothing. Then he sneered.

'I have seen you before,' he cried. 'You two are always together. So, what is it? Master and slave, lover boys, the two losers? You have one more chance to let go of my arm before I thump you into these paving stones, boy.'

Gaius struck Centho just under his chin with his fist. The blow sent the young patrician reeling onto his back. Gaius took a step forwards so that he was standing over Quintus. Centho looked astonished. For a moment, he lay on the ground. Then he touched his chin with his hand and looked up at Gaius.

'All right boy, you have asked for it now?' he snarled as he rose to his feet.

Gaius stood his ground as Centho came at him. Then at the last moment he twisted away and the patrician's fist struck empty air. Around them the crowd had gathered in a circle and were staring at the fight in hushed expectation. Centho lunged once more and again he missed. On the ground Quintus stirred and tried to get up but Gaius's sharp command made him stay where he was. Centho was eyeing Gaius warily now. For a few moment's the two naked men circled each other looking for an opening. Then with a bellow of rage Centho came charging in with his head held low as if intending to wrestle Gaius to the ground. Gaius waited until his opponent was nearly upon him before he lifted his right leg and kicked Centho in the side of the head. The blow knocked the patrician unconscious and he collapsed onto the stones. The crowd fell silent. Gaius limped painfully towards Quintus and helped his friend up onto his feet. Blood was streaming down Quintus's face from a deep cut above his left eye. Yet Quintus still managed to give Gaius a look of awe.

'You have made an enemy today, Gaius,' Quintus whispered as he spat some blood from his mouth, 'But I would do it all again just to see you knock him out like that. That was just fantastic. Gods that arsehole deserved it.'

Chapter Twenty-Four - A Battle of Wills

Gaius lay on the garden couch watching Cassia. It was mid-morning and the house was quiet. Quintus had shut himself away in his room to write and Crispus had accompanied Publius to the Senate House. Pytheas, Cassia's teacher, was sitting beside her on the couch. He had given her a text to read and the two of them were ploughing through it. Gaius smiled as he saw how hard Cassia was concentrating on her work. His sister had made remarkable progress in the past year. Despite his initial reluctance to be her teacher, Pytheas had been pleased with her work. The old Greek explorer had reported that Cassia was a quick learner and that she had an insatiable hunger for knowledge. Often when the lessons had finished for the day Cassia had begged him to keep going. The girl, Pytheas had concluded, understood all too well the great favour that was being bestowed on her and she was determined to make the most of it. Gaius glanced at Pytheas and suddenly he felt sorry for the man.

Gaius had not seen much of his sister in the months since he and Quintus had returned from Scipio's summer campaign in Etruria. His position as Quintus's client and companion meant that he'd had to go and do what Quintus wanted which meant frequent trips to the artists' quarter of Rome with its bawdy taverns, whorehouses, actors, prostitutes, artists, transvestites, pickpockets and thugs. Gaius was ill at ease in such surroundings but Quintus could not have been happier. He'd surrounded himself with a group of adoring artisans who provided inspiration for his writing. The artists and prostitutes were drawn to Quintus like flies to a lamp, Gaius thought sourly. He'd lost count of the days he'd spent sitting on a chair inside a squalid house listening to Quintus discoursing poetry, arguing philosophy or banging his favourite prostitute. It had been boring and sometimes uncomfortable work but his reward was that Cassia was receiving a first-class education. With such an education, she would be able to marry a man of some standing. Gaius stroked his chin thoughtfully. He would have to start making inquiries about a suitable husband within the next year. For a moment, he studied Cassia intently. A suitable husband would have to be able to handle her cheeky and stubborn personality he thought. His sister continued to surprise him. There had not been much time to talk about what had happened to them back at their old farm or what she had witnessed in the battle for Bovianum but that morning Cassia had come up to him and told him that father and mother, Marcus and Atia were happy and that they were following her life with keen interest. Somehow the girl had managed to make her peace with what had happened to her. If only he could do the same, he thought sourly.

He glanced up at the statue of Publius Decius Mus that stood in the far corner of the garden. The stern stone face glared down at everyone and everything as if demanding to know what they were doing in his garden. Sometimes Gaius felt as if the old legend, dead for forty-three years now, had never really left the house. In nearly every room there was a reminder of him. The urn containing his ashes, the black wax death mask, his old sword, the marble bust. To Gaius, during such moments, it felt as if the dead man was bent on reminding everyone of who he had been and what he had done. It was impossible to escape or forget. It was as if the dead man was demanding to be heard and noticed. Occasionally Gaius had managed to ask a few questions about Quintus's grandfather but most people were too young to have known him and even Publius had not been able to say much. But if the private memories were fading, Quintus's grandfather's public memory was not. Rome loved its hero's and a special place had been reserved for Publius Decius Mus in the people's collective memory. The man who had purposefully sacrificed his life to turn the tide of battle in Rome's favour was a revered figure. The people's reverence had in some aspects made life easier for the family but with such a reputation to uphold, it had also placed a burden on the family members. Like with everything, there were those mean spirits who were constantly comparing the deeds and actions of Quintus and Publius with their illustrious ancestor. Publius had been right

Gaius thought. Reputation was everything in Rome. The family could not afford to be compared unfavourably.

Pytheas suddenly bent forwards and retched onto the ground. For a moment, the old man remained bent over. Gaius stared at him. The Greek teacher's hands were trembling as he wiped his mouth. Then he looked up and Gaius caught his eye. Pytheas gently shook his head and a little sad smile appeared. Cassia placed a hand on the old man's shoulder to steady him. Gaius looked away. Pytheas was dying. He'd overheard the family doctor discussing the matter with Publius. The doctor had not been entirely sure but he suspected that Pytheas had contracted malaria. The Greek explorer would most likely be dead within a few months. The day upon which Publius would release him from his duties was fast approaching but Gaius had not had the courage to tell Cassia about it yet. Publius had promised to find a new teacher but Cassia seemed to have grown fond of the old Greek. She would be very upset, Gaius thought gloomily, but he would have to tell her soon.

Quirinia, Quintus's mother, suddenly appeared in the doorway to the house and as she did Gaius, Cassia and Pytheas scrambled off their couches and onto their feet. They dipped their heads respectfully as she approached. Quirinia was dressed to go out and there was a strict, cold expression on her face. For a moment, she paused and gave Cassia a critical examination. Then she caught sight of the pile of sick splattered onto the paving stones in front of Pytheas. She glanced quickly at the teacher and for a fraction of a second Gaius thought he saw a rare glimpse of emotion on her face. During all the time Gaius had spent at the family house he had never had a proper conversation with Quirinia. The mistress of the house liked to keep herself aloof from everyone apart from her husband and son. Slaves and guests were only to be spoken to when she required something from them.

Gaius blinked as Quirinia turned to him.

'I am going out,' Quirinia said, 'Gaius, I would like you to come with me.'

Without waiting for an answer, she turned and disappeared back into the house. Gaius glanced towards Cassia in surprise and in response his sister grinned and tugged at her nose. Gaius shook his head. He was not in the mood for jokes. Dutifully he followed Quirinia into the house. In the hallway, a slave was fastening a Palla, a cloak around her mistress's shoulders. Gaius picked up his sword belt, fastened it around his waist and quickly checked his sword. He was clad in a simple short-sleeved white tunic and on his feet, he was wearing a pair of iron studded army sandals. When he was done, he looked up to see Quirinia's sharp eyes examining him.

'It seems,' she said dryly,' that after your quarrel with Claudius Centho, my son has made a new enemy amongst the patrician families.'

Gaius's cheeks coloured in embarrassment but he refused to avert his eyes.

'I believe that Centho and Quintus did not like each other long before I got to know them both,' Gaius replied quietly.

'Maybe that is so,' Quirinia retorted, 'But your brute behaviour has made matters worse. One does not mock the Claudii clan and get away with it. There are going to be consequences.'

Gaius felt a spark of irritation but he maintained his composure.

'Where would you like to go?' he murmured.

Quirinia turned away from with a sharp movement. A slave opened the door and she stepped through it and out into the street.

'We are going to visit the shrine of the patrician chastity,' she announced.

198

***

The streets of Rome were filled with people, carts, horses and mules. The noise was tremendous. Quirinia set a brisk pace and Gaius followed a step behind her. From the Palatine Hill they descended some steep and narrow steps until they reached the forum. Gaius loved coming to the forum. The huge and majestic state buildings and temples were the very beating heart of Rome. It was here, enclosed on all sides by hills, that ambitious men came to make their fortunes, to compete for office and to have their names immortalised in stone. It was here in this narrow valley that the glory and greatness of Rome and her people was celebrated and honoured. It was here in the Senate House that the anxious city fathers of Rome came to debate and decide upon their country's future. Gaius had been there, half a year ago now, when the Consul Fulvius had celebrated his triumph over the Samnites and the capture of Bovianum.

Quirinia passed the small circular temple of Vesta, where the vestal virgins tended to the sacred and eternal fire and continued past the Regia, the pentagonal building where the Pontifex Maximus, the High Priest of Rome lived. Then abruptly she turned left as she reached the Sacred Way. Up ahead Gaius could see the Capitoline Hill and the great Temple of Jupiter that loomed over the forum. He sighed and smiled as he caught sight of the lonely old man sitting perched on a rock high up on the steep slope. Miniatus, the people called him, and each week, for the past fifty seven years he'd come to sit in the same place, to look down into the forum. Miniatus, it was said was the last living person who had helped hold and defend the Capitoline Hill after the Gaul's had sacked Rome ninety years ago. No one knew for sure if the legend about Miniatius was true but all agreed that the man was impossibly old. Miniatus himself had little time to answer questions for he had grown deaf many years before but he had stuck resolutely to his story that he'd been there on the Capitoline Hill during the Gallic occupation of Rome and that he had stared Brennus the Gaul in the face.

199

As Gaius drew closer he saw that the doors to the temple of the patron god of Rome were open. The temple doors were always kept open whilst Rome was officially at war. When he'd lived in Rome, before his father had settled in Sora, Gaius had never known the doors to be closed. It was, as his father had once pointed out, a reminder that the safety and security of the city and the Republic were fragile, for Rome was surrounded by enemies, some of whom were only sixty miles away, and all of whom wished for nothing more than the total eradication of the young republic.

The forum was packed. People were milling around, coming and going. Bankers stood on barrels, shaking bags of coins to attract business. Merchants were haggling with each other under the watchful eye of a statue of Mercury. Market stalls were doing a brisk trade in all kinds of delicacies and on the opposite side of the street a gaggle of people were trying to sort out a traffic accident. A trader's wagon had knocked an elderly man to the ground. Quirinia however made her way through the crowd as if the people did not exist. She held her head high and paused for nothing. Gaius kept an eye open for pickpockets, for the crowds in the forum were a notorious place for them to operate, but the gangs of ragged looking children seemed to give his mistress a wide berth. They passed along the Argiletum, the street of the booksellers, and followed the street as it curved to the left in front of the Capitoline Hill. Steep steps led upwards towards its crest. Quirinia was heading for the forum Boarium, the cattle market, Gaius thought. The cattle market was one of the oldest parts of the city. It was situated close to the city walls and the Trigemina gate that led to the bridge across the Tiber. He'd never heard of the shrine of the patrician chastity but then again it was a patrician and a women's shrine so hardly something he would have ever visited. Why she had wanted him to come with her and not a household slave was an even greater mystery.

Gaius could smell the cattle market before he saw it. When they finally came into the market a herd of cattle was being driven into a wooden enclosure. Dogs barked and the farm hands were shouting and urging their beasts on with their whips. A clutch of farmers were studying the cattle with experienced eyes. The strong bovine smell suddenly reminded Gaius of his old farm near Sora. Quirinia however did not seem to notice the cattle or the smell. She cut a straight path towards a small circular temple that stood close to the city walls. Gaius peered at the temple curiously. He had never noticed it before when he'd lived in Rome as a child. A throng of splendidly dressed women were standing outside the entrance to the shrine. Their slaves, carriages and litter bearers stood to one side waiting for their mistresses to finish their prayers. Quirinia did not pause as she strode straight towards the shrine entrance and as she did so Gaius felt a sudden tug of excitement. Something was about to happen.

As she approached, the ladies outside the shrine caught sight of Quirinia. Gaius saw their faces darken. Then a few of them stepped forwards to bar Quirinia from entering the shrine. Quirinia halted as the patrician ladies folded their arms across their chests. Gaius too halted, a step behind his mistress. The hostility on the faces of the patrician women was fierce. For a moment, no one spoke.

'Let me pass, I wish to pray at our sacred shrine,' Quirinia said quietly and calmly. She took a step forwards but the patrician women refused to move aside. Around them Gaius was suddenly conscious that everybody had fallen silent as they turned to look at the confrontation.

'This shrine belongs to us,' one of the patrician women snapped, 'You know the law. Only married patrician women are allowed to pray here.'

Quirinia fixed her eyes on the woman who had spoken. 'I am a patrician lady,' she replied in the same quiet voice, 'I was given to my husband as an unmarried girl and I am a chaste woman. So, step aside.'

But the patrician women did not move.

'You may have been born one of us,' another woman cried, 'But you married outside your class. You married a plebeian and that disqualifies you from entering our shrine. Go away. We do not want you here.'

The woman's words were followed by hissing amongst the patrician women. Gaius glanced around at the women who were staring at Quirinia. They were all hostile, belligerent and spiteful. There was not a single sympathetic woman in the crowd. Quirinia was on her own. Had she foreseen this? Idly Gaius's hand dropped down to rest on the pommel of his sword. If he had to defend his mistress, he would but surely these women would not allow it to come to that.

Quirinia raised her head proudly and defiantly and turned to look at the hostile faces around her. There was not a single shred of fear or discomfort on her face and Gaius was suddenly impressed.

'I may have married outside my class,' Quirinia's voice suddenly rose strong and powerful, 'but I am not ashamed of my husband or his deeds and achievements. My husband is a great man and I have been his faithful wife for these past twenty-two years. I have nothing to be ashamed of. My chastity is proven and equal to yours. So, I walk as one of you. Now let me pass and offer my prayer.'

But the solid line of patrician women did not budge. More hissing erupted from the crowd. Quirinia made no reply. Gaius could see that the patricians were not going to let her into the shrine.

Then as the hissing continued Quirinia turned slowly to look around her.

'Chaste women of Rome,' she said and there was a sudden mocking tone to her voice, 'If that is what you call yourself. I can name a few amongst you who are as chaste as rabbits.' She paused. 'Very well, if you bar me from my shrine I shall set up my own shrine.' Quirinia's voice suddenly rose, 'I will set up a shrine to the plebeian chastity which will compete with you for I know many plebeian women, common women you may call them, who are far better people than you can ever hope to be.'

And with that Quirinia turned abruptly on her heel and strode away. Gaius hurried after her expecting to have stones flung at him at any moment but none came. The crowd of patrician women seemed to have been silenced.

'Lady, are you all right?' Gaius said as he caught up with his mistress.

Quirinia glanced at Gaius and there was a tiny glimmer of emotion in her eyes.

'Every action has consequences, Gaius,' she snapped. 'I hope that you have learned your lesson. A few days ago, they would have allowed me to enter the shrine. What you just witnessed was revenge. Revenge for humiliating the house of Appius Claudius.'

Gaius's eyes widened. 'Lady, I am so sorry, I did not mean to put you in this position. You should tell them that the incident with Centho was all my doing and that it had nothing to do with you.'

But Quirinia shook her head resolutely as she strode on down the street.

'No,' she said firmly, 'What is done is done. You are part of our family now Gaius. No one is going to harm or humiliate my family and if they try they must deal with me.'

Chapter Twenty-Five - The Will of the Senate and the People of Rome

The Curia Hostilia, the Senate house stood upon a slight rise in the ground. As Gaius and Quintus approached along the Sacred Way, Gaius felt the familiar sense of strength that the building inspired. From its prominent place in the forum everyone could see the Curia Hostilia, the seat of government and the place where the Senate would meet to discuss and debate the future of the Republic. Gaius glanced at Quintus. His friend's left eye was still half closed and a large angry purple bruise covered his face. It was late in the afternoon and they were late because Quintus had wanted to finish his drawing of the naked prostitute. Now as they hurried along Gaius worried that they would have missed the debate.

They entered the Comitium, the large open paved space with circular steps cutting down into its centre. The Comitium was the place where the Roman people would come to listen to their elected magistrates who would speak to them from an elevated platform, the Rostra. The open space was already packed with anxious and tense citizens all of whom were waiting to hear the outcome of the Senate debate. Gaius and Quintus made their way through the crowds and mounted the broad steps that led up to the Senate House, which rose above the circular open space opposite the Rostra. The large doors were closed and guarded by armed men but as Quintus was a Senator's son he was allowed in.

Inside Gaius blinked as his eyes adjusted to the dim light. Oil lamps hung from the walls of the high and long rectangular building and in their flickering light he caught sight of three hundred or so toga clad senators sitting on two sets of benches facing each other over a narrow central space. Quintus shuffled to one side of the entrance and took his place amongst the small group of onlookers who were watching and listening to the debate. Gaius had never been inside the Senate House before and he stared at the solemn scene with eyes filled with awe.

The onlookers Quintus had told him would be mainly the sons of senators who had come to see how the Senate worked and operated. Gaius felt his heart beating with sudden excitement as he stared at the massed ranks of senators. If only Aeliana and Cassia could see him now. If only they could see him here in the very heart of the Roman state listening to the men who were going to decide his country's future. Then as his eyes drifted across the group of spectators he saw Centho and his mood soured. The young patrician was sporting a large bruise across his left cheek. He too had spotted Gaius and his lips curled into a sneer. Then contemptuously he turned to look away.

'He is such a dick,' Quintus whispered, leaning towards Gaius. 'I bet he gets his slaves to clean his arsehole with their tongues.' Quintus sniggered and despite himself a smile appeared on Gaius's face.

'Look,' Quintus said suddenly in a serious voice, 'Fabius is about to speak. This is the part everyone has been waiting for.'

Gaius blinked and peered down at the Senate floor. The previous speaker had sat down and Quintus Fabius Maximus Rullianus had risen to his feet. There was a gravity and sincerity about the old senator as he slowly made his way to the middle of the space that divided the house. Fabius was old, well past sixty and Gaius remembered the first time he'd met the man at the feast to honour Quintus's grandfather. They had not spoken of course for Fabius was of high patrician rank and descended from one of the most famous and illustrious patrician families in Rome, but Gaius had sensed a warmth and kindness in the man which he'd not noticed amongst many of the other patricians he'd observed. Quintus had told him that Fabius was one of the few men still left who adhered to the archaic Roman traditions of his forefathers. The man was old school. A tough disciplinarian, an indomitable warrior who had grown old fighting the Samnites and yet the man could be moved by simple pleasures and acts of respect and piety. In Fabius's heart and mind, Quintus had once told Gaius, Fabius was still a simple farmer defending his land and family against the raids of the highland tribes. For that after all, was the history of the Roman people, a centuries old constant struggle to defend their farms and livelihoods from the savage mountain men.

Gaius suddenly caught sight of Publius Decius Mus. Quintus's father was sitting next to Fabius's empty seat. Publius, clad in his white toga with a purple stripe, was studying Fabius calmly with an unconcerned look. As Gaius watched, Publius turned to search for a face amongst the group of onlookers and as he caught sight of Quintus, father and son exchanged a rare secret smile.

'Will Fabius accept the Consulship?' Gaius whispered turning to Quintus.

'He doesn't want it but his hand is being forced,' Quintus whispered in reply. 'The people want him to become Consul. The centuries of the people are all voting for him.'

'Why are the people so desperate to have him elected?' Gaius whispered. 'It is against the law for him to hold another Consulship so soon after his last one.'

Quintus rolled his eyes in mock exasperation. 'Because he's the best general we have got. That's why. Who else has his experience and skill in defeating the Samnites and Etruscans? The people want a proven leader as Consul for the coming year. To hell with the law. The people are worried about the war. They are worried that we are going to lose.'

Gaius scratched his chin and glanced casually at Quintus. His friend was staring at the Senate floor with mounting excitement and in that moment Gaius realised that Quintus knew something. Whatever it was Quintus was keeping it a secret. Gaius frowned. Was that why Quintus had been so unconcerned about missing the first part of the debate?

Curiously Gaius turned to look at Fabius just as the old man began to speak.

'Senators and people of Rome,' Fabius said in a grave voice, 'I hear you and see how you are voting. But I must ask you, why do you trouble me, an old man past sixty who has already clearly said that he does not want the Consulship? I am not a candidate and yet you persist in pushing me into office. Have I not served my country long enough? My physical and mental rigour is not what it used to be when I was still a younger man. Fortune has been favourable to me but I dread her wrath if she starts to believe that I am demanding more than a man's fair share of her favour. So I ask you once again, let an old man enjoy his retirement in peace. Surely there are other brave men from whom you can choose our nation's leaders?'

'We want you Fabius Rullianus!' a senator cried from the backbenches. His cry was supported by shouts and the general nodding of heads.

Fabius looked genuinely annoyed and Gaius smiled. Either Fabius was an extremely good actor or he was speaking the truth.

A hush descended upon the house as a man on the front bench stood up. The senator was tall with silver coloured hair and he had a stern arrogant face. He looked around sixty.

'That's Appius Claudius, Centho's father,' Quintus whispered as leaned towards Gaius. 'He's a most dangerous and clever man. Don't believe a word of what he says.'

'Fabius,' Claudius said in a clear and loud voice, 'I too am an old man who would like nothing more than to retreat from the world. No one here doubts your genuine desire to be left in peace and we the Senate and the people would grant you this favour, if Rome was at peace and our borders secure. Unhappily this is not the case. We are at war,' Claudius paused to look around at the assembled senators, 'It is said,' he continued, ' that our enemies and their allies are preparing to wage war on us with all their might and that they will not stop until the day they have burned our city to the ground. In such circumstances and because you are after all one of our finest soldiers you should listen to the general state of alarm amongst the people and accept your duty as a Consul of Rome.'

Then Appius Claudius abruptly sat back down in his seat.

'Why is he supporting Fabius for the Consulship?' Gaius whispered. 'I thought they didn't like each other?'

Quintus suddenly looked nervous. 'I don't know,' he shrugged.

Gaius turned to look at Publius Decius Mus. In his seat Publius shifted his weight awkwardly and turned to stare at the stone floor.

Fabius was still on his feet in the middle of the Senate House. For a moment, the old senator turned to study Appius Claudius carefully. Then he raised his hand and beckoned to a figure sitting on the front bench. A senator came up to Fabius and handed him a scroll of parchment before returning to his seat. Fabius raised the parchment high above his head and turned so that all could see it.

'Here in my hand,' Fabius suddenly thundered and there was real anger in his voice, 'I hold a copy of the law. I shall now read to you what our law says.' Fabius unrolled the parchment and began to read.

'In matters of the election of the Consuls, a man is hereby prohibited from being re-elected to the Consulship if he has held this office within the past ten years.'

Fabius lowered the parchment and glared at the Senators.

'So you see,' he growled, 'It would be against the law to elect me.'

For a moment, a ghastly silence descended upon the Senate House. Then the benches erupted in an uproar as senators rose to their feet and shouts and cries of protest filled the chamber.

'There is nothing to prevent your election,' one of the people's Tribunes yelled. 'For we will propose a measure that will exempt you from the law.'

The uproar died down a little as Fabius raised his hand for silence. The old man had begun to look weary.

'What is the point,' Fabius cried, 'of making laws when even the lawmakers are going to break them? The law must be obeyed.'

But the Senate was in no mood to listen to his objections. The cries and shouts rose once more and continued to grow in strength and volume and in response Fabius flung the parchment onto the floor in disgust.

Then Appius Claudius was back on his feet and appealing for calm. Slowly the house returned to their seats and the noise died down once more. Claudius waited until everyone was silent before turning to Fabius.

'You must accept your election, old friend,' Claudius cried. 'It is the unanimous will of the Senate and people of Rome.' Claudius paused and looked around the house and at his side Gaius suddenly felt Quintus tense up.

'I and all of us are confident,' Claudius continued, 'that with a great patrician such as yourself as one of our Consuls we shall have nothing to fear from our enemies. The people of Rome have chosen you because they want patricians, men who are descended from our great and illustrious ancestors, to lead them into battle. Now is not the time to pander to the plebeian New men who dare to call themselves equal to us.'

Claudius was interrupted by a howl of protest from a small section of the benches but the vast majority of the Senators remained silent. At his side Gaius heard Quintus gasp in dismay. Publius Decius Mus had remained silent but as Gaius looked on he raised his head and glanced carefully at Claudius.

Claudius was still speaking. 'Now is the time,' he thundered, 'for us to elect patrician Consuls. It is time for us to restore our ancient patrician rights that were lost to us so many years ago. So I propose that Quintus Aemilia Barbula be elected as Fabius's colleague and as our second Consul for this coming year.'

Then Claudius sat back down in his seat and as he did so the protests died away and all eyes turned to Fabius. The old grizzled patrician looked unhappy.

'Appius Claudius,' Fabius said slowly and wearily, 'You and I and all of us know that electing Barbula as the second Consul is also against the law. For sixty years now the two Consulships have been held and divided equally between one patrician Consul and one plebeian Consul. It is against the law to elect two patrician consuls. Must I send for the legal texts and read them to you as well?'

Fabius turned to confront Claudius but Claudius just smiled and shrugged his shoulders.

'And yet that is what most of us here want,' Claudius cried.

Fabius looked at the assembled senators. Then he turned to look at the benches behind him. For a moment, the Senate was completely silent. Then Fabius bent down and picked up the parchment that he'd thrown onto the ground. Carefully he rolled it up and tucked it away into the folds of his toga. Then he turned to the House.

'Very well,' he grumbled, 'If this is the unanimous will of the Senate and the people of Rome I will bow to your judgement and accept the Consulship for this coming year but I shall do so on one condition. You Senators must grant me one favour. I ask you to elect as my colleague for this year, my good friend and a man of proven valour. I ask you to elect Publius Decius Mus as Consul.'

Gaius gasped and glanced at Quintus. Quintus was staring at the proceedings with tense excitement and suddenly Gaius realised that his friend had known all along that Fabius was going to propose Publius as his colleague. Had all Fabius's posturing and manoeuvring which he'd just witnessed, been done solely to get Publius into a favourable position? Gaius shook his head in bewilderment.

On the benches Fabius's declaration was met with a wild outburst of joy and enthusiasm but not from everyone Gaius noticed. Claudius and a small group of senators around him remained in their seats. Claudius was staring at the stone floor with a moody expression. Then as Gaius watched, Claudius got up and strode towards the exit but as he passed Fabius he turned and said something to him before continuing on his way.

The Senate meeting was over and as the senators streamed out through the large double doors and into the daylight, Gaius and Quintus made their way to the small group of senators who had remained behind. The senators who clustered around Fabius and Publius Decius Mus seemed eager to shake their hands and congratulate them. The men were excited and happy and laughter and relief bubbled, oozed and echoed through the chamber and seat of government. Gaius and Quintus had to wait patiently before the last of the senators had departed before they could approach the two newly elected Consuls. There was a broad grin on Publius's face as he greeted his son. Gaius clasped Publius's arm in the soldiers' way and was surprised when Publius pulled him into a hug. Embarrassed Gaius took a step back but Publius did not seem to notice. He turned towards Fabius and with a grin lifted up three fingers. In response, the old patrician smiled and lifted up four fingers. Then the two men stepped forwards and hugged each other.

'My Father has now been elected Consul three times,' Quintus explained proudly as he caught sight of Gaius's puzzled look. 'And Fabius has been elected Consul four times.'

'Congratulations Sir,' Gaius dipped his head respectfully at both men.

Publius nodded. 'Come we should not delay matters,' he said. 'We have urgent and important work to do.' Mus turned to Fabius, 'Will you come to my house tomorrow? We need to plan our respective campaigns.'

Fabius nodded in agreement.

'So what did Claudius say to you when he left just now?' Publius asked turning to Fabius with a bemused smile.

'He called me a traitor,' Fabius replied.

Chapter Twenty-Six - The Republic at War

Publius's house on the Palatine Hill looked like it had been turned into a command HQ. As Gaius returned from a visit to Aeliana he had to make his way past the twenty-four lictors, the consular bodyguards, who had collected outside the front door as they waiting for their masters to finish their business inside. Once through the doorway Gaius was confronted by several armed men who despite his protestations subjected him to a thorough search. Only then was he allowed to step into the Atrium. A large rectangular table had been placed in the centre of the atrium and covering it was a big detailed map of central Italy. Small infantry and cavalry counters in different colours were spread about on the map. Publius, Fabius and seven or eight Senators clad in their distinctive white togas stood clustered around the table. Fabius was speaking in a quiet voice. Gaius noticed Crispus standing against the far wall. The big Paeligni had his hands clasped behind his back and was staring into space. Gaius glanced around and up at the landing but saw no one else. Quintus had decided to make another drawing of his naked prostitute and Publius must have given all his slaves the day off. He was just about to take the stairs to his room on the second floor when Publius caught sight of him.

'Gaius, come and join us please,' Publius said in tone that invited no refusal.

Gaius's cheeks blushed lightly as he hesitated. Then resolutely he strode across the room and came and stood beside Publius.

Fabius cleared his throat as he studied the map. Then he placed his finger on the city of Bovianum. 'So this is the general situation in the south,' Fabius said. 'Our garrisons hold what's left of Bovianum and Aufidena. We also have a strong garrison at Fregellae. The Samnites are continuing to attack us in small groups, targeting isolated positions, supply columns and such like. They refuse to stand and fight and melt away when we put up determined resistance. Further south the Campanian frontier seems quiet although the Samnites have made some isolated raids. The Campanians are confident that they can repel any serious attacks throughout the coming months although they will need our help if there is a major invasion.' Fabius paused to study the map. 'Our latest intelligence reports have identified two major Samnite armies. Both are still forming and organising themselves for the upcoming summer campaign. One is camped here in the wild country beneath Monte Miletto and the other is reported to be somewhere along the Tifernus river valley to the east. I suspect that Egnatius and Statius have divided their commands so as not to exhaust the local food supplies but we can't be sure of this.'

'How many men do they command?' one of the senators asked.

Fabius grunted and tapped his fingers on the table. 'It's hard to say but the Samnites have never had a manpower problem. Their citizens are nearly as numerous as our own. I would say that we are facing roughly the equivalent of two consular armies, forty thousand men or so.'

'Fuck,' a young senator muttered in dismay.

Fabius turned to look at the young man. 'Does that frighten you?' Fabius snapped.

The young senator blushed with embarrassment. Then he managed to compose himself and shook his head.

'We will defeat them,' Publius said with a confident smile, 'Roman courage and discipline will prove superior to their mountain valour.'

Fabius grunted in agreement and tapped the map again. 'Here on the east coast we must be careful,' he growled. 'Luceria remains loyal but most of the Apulians are restless. They fear our growing power. Although they have no love for the Samnites they may make common cause with them against us. If they do I suspect that they can bring around fifteen thousand men into the field against us. We

214

should try and avoid this at all costs.'

'How do we stop them from joining the Samnites?' a senator asked.

'We must send a consular army to keep them in check,' Publius replied as he studied the map.

Fabius took a sip of wine from his cup and wiped his mouth with his hand.

'Now here in the north,' Fabius said picking up an infantry counter, 'The Etruscans have been quiet since you, Scipio defeated them at Volaterrae last year. But our forces are too weak to take their fortified cities. Neither do we have enough men to watch each city-state in the Etrusean League. In time the Etruscans will recover, regroup and form a new army. They too are not short of men. We will have to watch the situation closely.'

'The Etruscans fought surprisingly well at Volaterrae,' Scipio Barbatus said quietly, 'I suffered heavy casualties. Fabius is right. If the Etruscan League manages to settle its internal disputes and unites under one effective leader we shall have a very serious problem on the northern frontier.'

'Then what do you propose we do, Appius?' Claudius snapped.

Fabius was studying the map. 'We should not forget the Umbrian cities,' the grizzled old warrior muttered, 'Since you Apuleius took Narnia from them two years ago they have been bent on taking revenge on us. They will want to recover Narnia and so may choose to join the fight against us.'

'It seems,' Publius said thoughtfully, 'that you are suggesting that there is a possibility that our enemies will form a grand alliance against us.'

Fabius nodded solemnly. 'Yes I think we should consider that a distinct possibility.'

215

The distinguished men around the table fell silent as the significance of what Fabius had just said sank in.

'If that were to be the case,' Publius muttered as he studied the map, 'By my count our enemies will outnumber us and our allies by three to one. Moreover, we will have to engage them on three separate fronts, the Etruscans to the north, the Umbrians and Apulians to the east and the Samnites to the south. That will stretch our forces pretty thinly.' Publius rubbed his forehead. 'So we must strike hard and we must strike fast and knock our enemies out of the war before they have a chance to unite against us. We should direct all our strength against one enemy at a time. We should move fast and go for their jugular, force them to fight and defeat them. Then we burn and ravage their towns and countryside until the population can take no more. It worked in the last war and it will work again.'

A few of the senators around the table grunted in agreement. Fabius however looked hesitant.

'Maybe that is true,' Fabius said cautiously, 'But concentrating all our forces against one enemy has risks. If we denude the other fronts of men, it may embolden our enemies and hasten their preparations for war. This is particularly the case with the Etruscans. A show of force is needed to keep them locked up in their cities. No, I think it would be better if we divided our operational areas.' Fabius glanced up at Publius and gestured at the map. 'One of us should take his army into Etruria and the other should operate against the Samnites.'

Publius looked unimpressed but he said nothing. A falling out between the two Consuls over strategy at such an early stage would not bode well for the coming campaign season.

'I agree with Fabius as regards the Etruscans,' Scipio said turning to look at Publius. 'They do fear our legions. Keeping an army in Etruria will buy us some time.'

'But it won't win the war for us,' Publius growled. 'If we divide our forces we will be unlikely to win a decisive battle. The longer we wait the stronger and bolder our enemies will become. Time is not our friend, gentlemen. Time favours our enemies. I say that we gamble everything on a two-pronged strike deep into the Samnite heartland.' Publius picked up several infantry and cavalry counters and smacked them down in the heart of Samnium. 'Here, I could advance east through Sidician territory and then turn south to ravage Apulia whilst you Fabius could march to Bovianum. Together we should be able to lure Egnatius and Statius into a battle and if they choose to hide then we can always ravage the Samnite countryside far and wide. Such a move would be welcomed by our Campanian allies.'

'He is right about the Campanians Fabius,' Fulvius said. 'Our allies cannot be left undefended and it is my opinion that the Samnites are the most dangerous and formidable of our foes.'

'Well you would say that wouldn't you,' Appius Claudius growled.

Fabius raised his finger to his mouth and bit it as he concentrated on the map. The atrium fell silent as all waited for his reply.

'I don't agree,' he said at last looking up at Publius with a sad but stubborn expression. 'We cannot denude Etruria of all our troops. A consular army should be sent to the area to keep the Etruscans in check.'

The table fell silent as the awkward difference of opinion between the two Consuls became all too clear. Gaius could sense Publius beside him growing increasingly impatient with the situation. Fabius took another sip of wine as the men around the table studied the map trying to think of some kind of compromise that would be acceptable to both consuls. Gaius glanced up at the balustrade landing and saw that Quirinia was watching the proceedings.

The silence around the table lengthened and it had just started to get uncomfortable when there was a commotion in the hallway. All eyes around the table turned to look at what was going on. Then a mud splattered and exhausted looking man still wearing his palla, his travelling cloak, hurried into the Atrium followed by two agitated armed men who it seemed had not yet finished searching him. Seeing the assembled senators and Consuls the man rushed across towards Publius, knelt on one knee and proffered up a leather satchel whilst keeping his eyes on the floor.

'Despatch Sir,' the man gasped. 'I bring a despatch from Arretium. Please Sir I was told to give it only to you. It is very urgent.'

Publius took the leather case from the despatch rider's hand.

'Arretium you say?'

'Yes Sir,' the despatch rider replied without raising his eyes.

Publius frowned as he opened the satchel and pulled out a scroll of parchment. For a moment, he stared at the wax seal. Then quickly he unrolled it and began to read and as he did so every pair of eyes in the room turned to stare at him. When he was finished, Publius handed the parchment to Fabius.

'What does it say?' Scipio said unable to stand the silence any longer.

Fabius finished reading and looked up at the men around the table. Then he glanced across at Publius and the two men exchanged a secret smile.

'The despatch has come from one of our agents,' Publius said with sudden emotion in his eyes. 'It informs us that the Etruscan League has decided to open peace talks with us. The Etruscans want to arrange a conference. They have had enough of this war.'

Fabius's smile broadened. 'Decia,' he murmured. 'This is her work isn't it? I knew that woman was worth an entire legion.'

Publius nodded silently and his face was flush with pride. Then he turned to look at the map.

'If the Etruscans are suing for peace then we should be able to concentrate all our forces against the Samnites like I suggested,' he said.

There was a general murmur of agreement around the table. Fabius tapped his fingers on the table and then he too nodded in agreement.

'It is settled then,' Fabius declared, 'both of us will invade Samnium and we will take the routes that you suggested. I will take the First and Third Legions, you will have the Second and Fourth. Have the word spread around that the men have a week to enlist before we march. They are to gather on the field of Mars. Claudius,' Fabius said turning to the silver haired figure of Appius Claudius, 'you will be in charge of the defence of Rome. Raise the equivalent of a legion and prepare the city defences. Scipio you will head up our delegation to the Etruscans. You are authorised to negotiate peace terms similar to the ones that the Etruscan League had before. If you cannot achieve this then stall them. The peace on our northern frontier must hold whilst we are away.' Fabius turned to Publius. 'Agreed?' he muttered.

'Agreed,' Publius replied. 'But there is one final matter. I have a son. I would like him to be included in your cavalry when you march south.'

'It is done,' Fabius nodded. 'Tell him to report to the field of Mars tomorrow with his horse and equipment and I will assign him to a unit.'

***

Quintus was drunk when he finally staggered into his room. He swayed on his feet and looked surprised as he caught sight of Gaius sitting on his bed. It was well past midnight and the house was fast asleep. A solitary oil lamp lit up the room.

'What are you doing here?' Quintus said slurring his words. 'Fuck off and go and lie in your own bed.'

Gaius rose to his feet and grabbed hold of both his friend's shoulders. Then he shook his head and smiled at the state that Quintus was in.

'You are a disgrace, you are an absolute disgrace,' Gaius grinned.

'I know,' Quintus said defensively, 'I know. So, what?'

Gaius sighed. 'I have stayed up to tell you that tomorrow your father has decided to send us off on campaign again. Both of us have been assigned to the cavalry with Fabius's army. We are going to be riding south to fight the Samnites.'

'Oh for fucks sake, not again,' Quintus rolled his eyes in his sockets and slurred his words. 'I have just promised that lovely prostitute that I would marry her. Well how is that going to happen when I am sitting on top of some fucking cold mountain summit. You know what?' Quintus thrust his chin forwards aggressively. 'These Samnites can go fuck themselves. Then they can fuck their cute goats and cows. Why the fuck do they have to spoil everything all the fucking time?'

Gaius grinned. 'I just wanted you to hear it from me first. Get some sleep. Tomorrow we must report to the army on the field of Mars.'

Quintus nodded wearily. Then he clasped Gaius and kissed him on his forehead.

'You are the best friend that I have ever had. Do you know that?' Quintus grinned crazily as he swayed dangerously on his feet.

Gaius shook his head in disbelief and steadied his friend. Then he pushed him towards his bed, turned and left the room.

***

The field of Mars was located just beyond the northern walls of Rome. Hemmed in by the Tiber to the west and the Quirinal hill to the east, the flat, low lying plain was the perfect place where an army could gather, train and be inspected. As Gaius and Quintus rode their horses across the wide-open space towards the simple and ancient altar to Mars, the God of War, they could see that armed men were already converging on the place from all directions and that long lines of army tents were being erected. The Consul's orders it seemed had spread rapidly and the Roman people were responding like they had done for centuries. The farmers and their sons brought their own weapons and equipment for there was no central armoury from which Rome would provide for her soldiers. A soldier was expected to provide his own weapons, armour and horses and because of this it was only the wealthiest citizens, those who could afford a horse, who formed the small cavalry units that were attached to the legions main heavy infantry force. It meant that the Roman cavalry were nearly exclusively recruited from the upper classes. Gaius and Quintus were both clad in good quality bronze pectoral armour, plumed helmets and greaves and they were carrying short spears, a small round shield and a long cavalry sword. Their horses were both young beasts trained for war. The wealth that backed up the House of Mus had ensured that the two men would not be embarrassed by a lack of good quality weapons, beasts or armour.

Quintus led the way towards the altar of Mars. There was a sour look on his face. He'd been silent all morning as the household slaves had busied themselves getting the two young knights ready for war. As they came up to the altar Quintus dismounted from his horse and strode towards the tribune who was overseeing the cavalry enlistment. The tribune took down their names and then ordered Gaius and Quintus to take the Sacramentum, the soldiers' oath of allegiance to the Senate and people of Rome.

Quintus wearily raised his right hand and repeated the Tribunes words. 'I hereby swear on my honour and that of my ancestors that I shall obey my officers and carry out their commands to the best of my ability.'

'It is the same for me,' Gaius muttered as he too raised his right hand.

They were officially soldiers again, Gaius thought. Once a man had enlisted in the army he automatically surrendered his rights and privileges as a private Roman citizen and agreed to be subjected to martial law with all its forms of severe discipline and punishment for those who broke the rules.

The tribune nodded. 'Good, report to your decurion. He's over there. After that you may return home but make sure you are back here tomorrow at dawn. The cavalry will be conducting training exercises all week.'

The tribune turned away to deal with the next group of arrivals.

Quintus shot Gaius a withering look as he turned and stomped off to report to their commanding officer. Gaius followed and then nearly bumped into Quintus. Quintus had stopped abruptly in his tracks and his face had suddenly grown pale.

'Oh fuck,' Gaius and Quintus said at exactly the same time as they recognised the decurion.

Centho turned round and examined his two newest recruits.

'Welcome to hell, gentlemen,' he sneered.

Chapter Twenty-Seven - Return to Sora

The thirty Roman cavalrymen trotted along the track in a single file. It was around noon and on their left the Liris river was flush with melting snow water. Gaius, sporting a fresh bruise on his cheek, glanced sullenly at the rider ahead of him. The squadron of horsemen had set out alone from the Roman camp at dawn and had headed south along the river valley. Gaius had known that they were heading towards Sora but the thought of seeing his old hometown again had not alleviated his sour and depressed mood. For the past few weeks his life had been utterly miserable and intolerable. Centho, his commanding officer had delighted in taking every opportunity to humiliate and punish him and Quintus. Nothing had been good enough for the young patrician. Again and again he and Quintus had ended up doing the dirtiest and least popular jobs within the cavalry troop. On a daily basis Gaius had been insulted, screamed at, spat at and struck by both hand and whip until his mind had grown numb. Quintus had suffered the same treatment and had withdrawn into himself and had not spoken a word to anyone in over a week now. Centho had been ruthless and uncaring. The remainder of the cavalry squadron had soon noticed the special treatment that Gaius and Quintus were receiving but their colleagues had offered no support or encouragement. Everyone in the troop knew that Centho was exercising a personal grudge and no one wanted to get involved.

Gaius twisted to look round at Quintus who was riding behind him. Quintus looked like he was close to breaking point. His grey face and dull eyes stared into the distance without seeing anything. It looked as if the very will to live had been knocked clean out of him. Gaius sighed wearily and turned to look at the Liris. The situation could not continue for much longer. Ever since Quintus had stopped talking Gaius had grown increasingly worried about his friend's state of mind. If Quintus did something stupid like striking back at Centho or deserting, the officer was within his rights to have Quintus executed. Maybe, Gaius thought darkly, that was what Centho wanted them to do.

Gaius looked up at the mountains to the south. The narrow river valley was heavily wooded and the colourful spring flowers were popping up everywhere. A fresh spring breeze was coming down the valley. Up ahead Gaius caught sight of Centho at the very front of the column. He'd overheard the tribune giving Centho his orders that morning. The squadron was to ride out ahead of the main army until they reached Sora where Centho was to order the Roman colonists to prepare supplies for the approaching army. The heavy infantry companies of Fabius's Consular army would reach the city by nightfall. As Gaius stared at Centho with glum resentment the decurion raised and pressed his hand to his jaw. The small movement brought a rare little smile onto Gaius's face. Serves the bastard right Gaius thought. For the past two days Centho had been suffering from a painful toothache.

Absentmindedly Gaius touched the small amulet that hung around his neck. Cassia had given it to him before he'd left. She had cut the images of her murdered family onto the bronze and had told Gaius that the amulet would protect him and that the spirits of the departed would keep him company. Before leaving he'd told her that Pytheas was dying and that he would soon stop teaching her. His sister had retorted that she already knew and then she had surprised him by firmly telling him that she liked Aeliana and that he should do the right thing and marry her. Cassia's behaviour had perplexed him and he'd gained the impression that he really didn't know his sister at all. But when the time had come to say goodbye she had reverted to her old self and had cried and nearly refused to let go of him.

Gaius gazed wearily at Centho. The patrician still had his hand firmly pressed to his jaw and as Gaius studied him an idea suddenly came to him. He straightened up and blinked. Why had he not thought of that before? Without hesitation Gaius left his position in the column and urged his horse towards Centho. As Gaius drew level Centho turned to look at him. The patrician looked annoyed and was grimacing in pain. He was just about to shout when Gaius pointed at Centho's jaw.

'Sir, I see you have tooth ache,' Gaius said quickly, 'When we reach Sora I know a good dentist who will be able to help you.'

Centho closed his mouth and stared at Gaius. Then he looked away.

'Get back to your position boy,' he growled.

But Gaius kept his horse level. 'My friend will be able to help you. He will do it for no charge. It won't take very long and we must wait at Sora anyway.'

Centho was staring straight ahead. He was in a bad mood but then the prick always was, Gaius thought. Centho grimaced. 'Is your friend any good?' he growled. 'I hear that visiting these dentists can leave a man disfigured for life.'

'He's the best,' Gaius replied quickly. 'I used to live in Sora. The whole town speaks highly of the man.'

Centho grunted and touched his jaw again.

'Very well then,' he growled. 'When we reach the colony go and fetch this dentist and bring him to me.' Centho turned and glared at Gaius, 'But if this quack leaves me disfigured and still in pain, I am going to have you, understood?'

Gaius nodded. He had no idea whether Tullus's father was any good. He'd only ever met the man once. Gaius leaned towards Centho.

'And when it's done,' he said in a quiet voice, 'You will leave me and Quintus alone. That's the deal.'

Without waiting for an answer Gaius turned his horse around and rode back to his position in the column. As he trotted down the line he expected to hear Centho's outraged bellowing voice summoning him back, but all remained quiet. Gaius winked at Quintus as he returned to his place in the line but Quintus did not seem to notice. His friend seemed shut up in his own private world of torment.

***

News of the cavalry squadron's approach had already reached the town by the time Gaius and his comrades reached the city gates and a delegation of the leading citizens was waiting for them with gifts of water, salt, bread and sour wine. Gaius glanced up at the walls of the town as Centho dismounted and conveyed his orders to the colonists. It was good to see the old place again, Gaius thought. Had it really been a year since he'd stood on those very walls defending his colony? The cavalry troop sat patiently on their horses waiting for Centho to conclude his business. Casually Gaius glanced northwards in the direction of where his father's farm had once stood. He'd expected to feel nostalgic but he didn't. It was likely he thought that someone else had taken over the land and the abandoned farm even though the land still belonged to him. The land registry office would have kept records of ownership though and Gaius wasn't worried. When he eventually returned to the place he would just have to kick the squatters off it. For the moment, however he didn't have the time to even pay the farm a visit.

'Gaius,' Centho shouted as he approached on foot leading his horse by its reins. 'Go and fetch that dentist. You have half an hour.'

Gaius nodded and dismounted and as he did so Centho refused to look him in the eye. Some of the spitefulness in the man's demeanour seemed to have vanished.

Gaius strode quickly through the city gates. The excitement of seeing his old friend Tullus, the Volscian with whom he'd stood back to back whilst defending the city walls, mingled with the dread of coming face to face with the money lender and his cronies. Would the banker have forgotten him? It was unlikely. He shrugged off his worries. Tullus's indomitable optimism was exactly what he could do with right now, after all the weeks of

226

misery he'd had to endure. He crossed the forum where the Consul Fulvius had sat and entered one of the narrow side streets. As he stared at the town folk in the street he thought he kept seeing faces of people who he recognised but on closer inspection they turned out to be strangers. He shook his head. Was he hallucinating? What was the matter with him?

He got lost in the narrow alleys of the old Volscian town and it was only by chance that he suddenly found himself before the dentist's shop. The door was open and from inside he could hear cheerful singing. Gaius grinned and stepped inside. Tullus was shaving himself with a sharp little knife. The young man had put on weight. He jumped to his feet as he caught sight of Gaius. For a moment, the two friends said nothing. Then Tullus beamed and embraced Gaius with a mighty roar.

'Good to see you again friend,' Tullus cried. 'So you are still alive. I thought that you must be dead. None of the other Soran volunteers who left with you have returned. The women were wailing in mourning for weeks. I know I shouldn't speak ill of the dead but a man has to sleep at some point, the noise was just too much.'

Tullus fell silent as he saw that there was something on Gaius's mind.

'I am still in the army,' Gaius said apologetically. 'I'm afraid that I don't have much time. The decurion wants me to return within half an hour.' Gaius grinned. 'I have got a small problem. Please tell me that your father is at home?'

Tullus sighed and looked away. 'My father died six months ago,' he muttered.

Gaius closed his eyes and raised his hand to rub the back of his head. 'Ah fuck, I am so sorry to hear that,' he murmured. He paused unsure of what to do or say. 'The thing is,' he said at last, 'I need a dentist and I need one fast. If I return to my decurion without a dentist I am fucked, truly fucked.' Gaius sighed. 'I remembered that your father was a dentist. I am sorry Tullus, are there any other dentists in Sora?'

Tullus was staring at Gaius and as he did so a smile slowly appeared on his face.

'Are you in some kind of trouble with an officer?' he said as his smile continued to grow.

Gaius nodded, glanced sideways and sighed in frustration. 'The decurion has a toothache. I promised him that I would help him.'

'There are no other dentists in the town,' Tullus replied, 'but don't worry Gaius, I will go. My father has taught me how to use all his tools. I can do it. Just wait here whilst I fetch his equipment.'

Tullus turned without waiting for an answer and disappeared into the house. A few moments later he was back holding a leather bag in his hand. He pushed past Gaius and stepped out into the street.

'So where is the prick?' Tullus grinned.

Gaius was staring at him in surprise. Then his eyes narrowed suspiciously.

'Have you ever operated on anyone's teeth before?' he inquired.

Tullus shrugged. 'No, never but maybe it's time I started. I have done nothing since the old man died. Come on; let's not keep our patient waiting. This is going to be fun.'

'Oh fuck,' Gaius muttered to himself as he rolled his eyes and hurried after his friend.

Chapter Twenty-Eight - Reconnaissance

The blackened burnt out ruins of Bovianum looked out of place amongst the beautiful rugged mountain landscape. Gaius glanced idly at the destroyed buildings and the half torn down city wall, as the cavalry patrol slowly made its way out of the Roman marching camp that had been constructed beside the ruined town. A week had passed since Fabius's army had left Sora. It was dawn and ever since Gaius and his comrades had entered Samnite territory the fresh spring mountain air seemed to have had a positive effect on him. Tullus had after a few false starts managed to wrench Centho's tooth from his mouth. Gaius had watched the operation praying to the gods that the Volscian knew what he was doing, but when it was over Centho had seemed satisfied, for since then the decurion had toned down his harsh treatment of Gaius and Quintus. A little smile appeared on Gaius's face as he remembered how Tullus had yelled in delight and triumph and had held Centho's tooth up for all to see, as if he had captured an enemy battle standard. Gaius had given Tullus the silver armband he'd looted from the Samnite dead. It would go a little way to repaying his friend for the expense he'd incurred when Gaius had first joined the army. The two friends had parted, promising to meet before another year had passed.

The thirty men in the cavalry troop passed out through the camp gates and broke into a gentle trot as Centho led them due south. The squadron had been ordered out on a reconnaissance patrol. Centho had surprised Gaius that morning by calling his troopers together and explaining his orders to them in detail. The decurion had never before bothered with telling his soldiers anything, but this time Centho seemed to want his soldiers to be involved. The short inclusive gathering had had a positive effect on the men and their mood was good. Even Quintus had started muttering to himself although he still looked miserable and unhappy. Centho had explained to them that the squadrons mission was to explore the foothills below the wild inhospitable country beneath Mount

Miletto. The senior officers in the army wanted to know where the Samnite forces were hiding.

Gaius checked his pectoral armour and adjusted his plumed bronze helmet. Then he twisted round and caught Quintus's eye, clenched his hand into a fist and gave Quintus an encouraging nod. Quintus managed a little nod in reply. As they rode away from the camp towards the rolling forested hills they passed another cavalry patrol returning from the opposite direction. Centho paused and briefly spoke with the decurion before continuing on his way. Soon they were out of sight of the camp and Gaius felt a flutter of nerves in his stomach. The patrol was in enemy territory now and every wood or dip in the ground could conceal a Samnite ambush. The troopers seemed to know it as well, for they fell silent and started to bunch together and peer more closely at their surroundings. The troop entered a wood. The forest was filled with colourful spring flowers and the undergrowth was alive with bird noises and the rustle of small creatures. Gaius glanced to his right and saw a majestic deer with large antlers watching them from a ridge. The sight of the animal reminded him of the hunting he'd done with Egnatius in the Samnite forest. Egnatius. Egnatius. Egnatius. He had not given the man much thought in recent months but now with the prospect of running into Samnite patrols and the chance of a sudden death he thought about him again. War was nothing more than a brutal, vicious struggle to survive, but there had been no reason for Egnatius to rape his mother and sister before murdering them. That had been a crime. Gaius's face hardened. *'Earn the respect of the gods and never be a coward'* his father had said. He would do that and he would stay alive and survive and Fortuna would give him Egnatius as his reward.

The patrol emerged from the forest and trotted into open fields and meadows. Close by, a solitary rundown looking farmstead stood surrounded by a clump of trees. Centho raised his hand and the cavalrymen turned towards the building. As they approached Gaius caught a glimpse of movement in the doorway to the Samnite dwelling. Centho gestured for half of the patrol to ride around the back of the farm. Then taking the remainder of his men he rode up to the front door and dismounted.

'Gaius with me,' Centho growled, 'The rest of you keep an eye open. If you see anything give me a shout.'

Then without hesitation Centho kicked the door open and vanished into the building. Gaius drew his sword and followed closely behind. Inside it took a moment for his eyes to adjust to the light. The farmhouse was small and poor and as Gaius looked around he saw there were just two rooms. He wrinkled his nose in disgust. The smell of shit was intense. Then he noticed that the floor of the second room was covered in straw. A herd of swine were grunting and rooting around in the straw. Gaius turned away and saw that Centho was staring at the huddled figure of an old woman. The woman looked terrified as she huddled trapped in the corner of her house. Centho turned to examine the woman's belongings but the house seemed to contain nothing of interest.

'Why are you so afraid of me old woman?' Centho snapped. 'Are you hiding something from us.'

The woman whimpered and Gaius suddenly felt sorry for her. No doubt they were not the first Roman patrol that she'd seen.

'Well?' Centho growled turning to look at the woman again.

There was a sudden movement behind Centho and Gaius and the two of them whirled round but it was only one of the troopers.

'Sir,' the soldier said, 'I think you had better come outside and have a look at this.'

Without a word Centho and Gaius followed the soldier out through the door and around the back of the farmstead. Gaius stopped in his tracks as he caught sight of the three crucified corpses hanging on their crosses. The bodies were bloated and

231

disfigured and the stench was awful. The troopers were staring at the bodies in silence. Centho raised his hand to his nose as he bent down to read the rough inscription that had been scratched into a stone at the base of the central cross. Then he straightened up and turned away.

'Well that explains why the woman is afraid,' he muttered with a distasteful expression, 'the sign warns anyone not to take the bodies down. Looks like one of our patrols has been here before us.'

Centho glanced at the farmstead. 'Let's go. There is nothing here,' he growled.

Gaius turned and from the corner of his eye he noticed Quintus throwing up. His friend's face seemed to have turned light green.

***

It was a few hours later, as the patrol was negotiating a steep rocky path towards the crest of a hill, when one of the troopers suddenly cried out in alarm. Startled, Gaius looked up in the direction in which the soldier was pointing. To his right a swollen mountain stream was twisting and cascading its way over the rocks into little pools and on down the hill side. The stream was making a lot of noise. On the opposite bank the bare, boulder strewn ground rose steeply towards a ridge. Gaius' eyes widened as he suddenly caught sight of mounted men staring down at the Roman patrol. They were no more than fifty yards away and they were armed with spears and shields.

'Fuck, fuck,' Centho hissed as he came charging past. Gaius had instinctively halted his horse at the sight of the armed men and the Roman column milled about in some confusion. They were vulnerable on the steep and narrow mountain track. The Samnites had caught them unprepared and Centho knew it.

'About turn,' Centho yelled, 'Back the way we came, hurry.'

Obediently Gaius started to turn his horse around. The beast seemed nervous on the rocky path but the horse managed the manoeuvre. Gaius glanced quickly up at the Samnites on the ridge. The enemy had the advantage of the high ground. The Samnites always seemed to occupy the high ground. If they had archers the Roman cavalry troop would be annihilated. Why had they not attacked yet? What were they waiting for? The Roman riders cursed and shouted nervously but at last the column had turned round. Centho led them back the way they'd come at a brisk walk. On the ridge above them the enemy horsemen had vanished from view. Gaius felt his heart thumping in his chest. What were the Samnites doing? Was there another ambush waiting for them further down the track? He glanced at Centho up ahead but the decurion's face was hidden from view.

When at last they reached flatter and more open country Gaius breathed a sigh of relief. The Samnites had not pursued them. The troopers around him were jittery and nervous. Centho too looked visibly relieved that the encounter with the Samnites had not turned into anything worse. The young officer had nearly got his entire command ambushed. The incident on the mountain track had reminded everyone of the treacherous and dangerous nature of the Samnite-mountains and the fact that the enemy knew the land much better than they did.

It was early evening and the patrol had remained amongst the rolling foothills for the rest of the day. Centho had ordered his men to refill their water skins from a stream. Ever since the encounter with the Samnites the young officer had looked tense and unsettled. Gaius was scooping water into his helmet when a flock of sheep suddenly came over the crest of the hill on the opposite side of the stream. The sheep were followed by a shepherd who was singing cheerfully to himself. The man's singing died away abruptly and he froze as he caught sight of the Roman cavalrymen beside the stream. He was armed with a single stout stick. For a moment, no one spoke or moved. Then the shepherd stumbled backwards in fright, turned and fled leaving his bleating sheep behind. Gaius rose and splashed through the stream in pursuit. The shepherd was some distance ahead but the man wasn't very fast. As Gaius came up behind him the man cast a terrified look over his shoulder. Then with a mighty lunge Gaius brought him down onto the ground.

The shepherd cried out in terror and tried to get up but Gaius had him in a firm grip.

'Stop struggling,' Gaius shouted.

The shepherd obeyed and Gaius hauled him to his feet just as Centho and a few of the troopers came up. The shepherd looked terrified and his hands and body were trembling. Centho studied him for a moment. The shepherd was old, maybe in his mid forties and he stank of sheep.

'What's the matter, why did you run?' Centho growled.

The shepherd stared at him and his lower lip started to tremble.

'Please Sir,' the man muttered in broken Latin, 'I am just a humble shepherd. Don't harm me or my flock. My sheep are all that I have.'

'Keep you company at night, do they?' one of the troopers smirked.

His words brought a smile onto the faces of the Roman soldiers who clustered around the shepherd.

'We're looking for the Samnite army,' Centho snapped, 'You are a shepherd. What do you know, what have you seen whilst roaming the land? Tell us and we will let you and your sheep live.'

Gaius felt the shepherd tense. The man glanced fearfully at the hard faced soldiers who crowded around him in an aggressive manner.

'They are not here,' he gasped. 'They marched away a few weeks ago. They have gone to besiege Luceria in the east. That's all I know.'

The troopers fell silent and Centho looked surprised.

'Luceria,' he murmured, 'That's in Apulia. The town is an ally of Rome.' He frowned.

'Are you sure that is where they were heading?' he said.

The shepherd nodded, 'That's what I heard Sir,' he murmured.

Centho was silent for a moment. Then he gestured at two of his men. 'We will take him back to our camp. The Tribunes can interrogate him further. Take him.'

'What about my sheep,' the shepherd whined in protest.

'Screw your sheep,' Centho snapped as two troopers grabbed the shepherd and hauled him away.

Centho turned to look at Gaius and stared at him for a moment. Then he nodded in appreciation. 'Well done,' he muttered as he turned away.

Chapter Twenty-Nine - The Horns of the Bull

Egnatius sat on his horse watching the clumsy and careless Roman cavalry patrol as the riders wheeled their horses around and fled back down the steep path they'd just come up. He grinned at his enemy's discomfort. His scouts had alerted him to the enemy presence long before the Romans had come into view. What fools these Romans were, Egnatius concluded. Did they really think they could enter his mountains without being ambushed? Did they not know that this was his land and that his men knew every inch of it? The Romans all looked alike in their tunics, armour and helmets, like ants from a giant colony that just kept on coming back and back. Slowly the grin faded from Egnatius's face. That was the problem though; they kept on coming back.

'Why did you let them go? We could have slaughtered them.' Titus, the commander of the Linen Legion growled in a disappointed voice.

Egnatius watched the last of the Roman riders disappear amongst the trees.

'There is more important work to be done,' he snapped as he gestured for the mixed Samnite cavalry and infantry company to resume its way.

'What can be more important than killing Romans?' Titus replied frowning.

Egnatius glanced quickly at his comrade. 'Patience Titus, you will know soon enough.'

Egnatius urged his horse on to the front of the column. His war band was only a hundred or so men strong but his warriors were all veterans and as hard as the iron in their swords. He knew everyone of them by name. All winter he and his men had roamed the mountain wilderness surviving on what they could find and hunt. They'd attacked the Romans wherever they had found them. Supply convoys had been ambushed and isolated pickets overrun. Egnatius had been merciless. Every Roman had been killed; no prisoners were taken. He wasn't interested in ransoming them. He wasn't interested in amassing gold. Egnatius had become obsessed by blood. He'd become obsessed with purifying the soil of Samnium of the cancer that was Rome. But despite his successes he'd known that he was achieving very little. The Roman occupying garrisons were still camped out on his native soil. The Roman disease still infected his beautiful mountains. The enemy were still ravaging the country far and wide and tormenting his people. So, when the days had started to grow warmer once more and the colourful mountain flowers had started to bloom he'd decided that it was time to send word to Statius, the supreme Samnite war leader and the Meddix Council.

As the company made its way along the ridge towards a vast mountain forest, Egnatius glanced up at the peak of Monte Miletto. The sybil had been right, he thought. The Meddix Council had chosen poorly when they had made Statius commander in chief. The man's strategy of scattering the Samnite army into small combat groups had achieved nothing. The Romans were still here.

It was an hour later when he spotted the deer's head nailed to a tree. The animal's antlers were fully grown and the beasts beautiful and majestic eyes stared sightlessly at the newcomers as if warning them to turn back. Egnatius raised his hand and his men came to a halt behind him. For a moment, all was quiet amongst the trees. Egnatius glanced at the forest around him.

'Do you not recognise me? I am Egnatius, Meddix of the Caraceni, companion of Alexander and tormentor of Rome,' Egnatius cried out in a loud voice.

The forest remained silent. Then suddenly all around them figures rose and appeared from out of the undergrowth and from behind trees. The men were armed with spears, swords, slings and bows and many had painted their faces and clothes green and brown so that they matched the colours of the forest. A tall man of around fifty with a beard and a baldhead stepped towards Egnatius.

'Statius,' Egnatius said sternly as he recognised the Samnite supreme war leader. 'It's a fine ambush but the Romans will never dare come this far into the wilderness.'

Statius looked like he'd aged since Egnatius had last seen him the previous summer. The man's short black beard had started to turn grey and he'd lost a lot of weight. As he came forwards, Egnatius noticed that he was limping.

'I cannot take any chances,' Statius replied wearily. 'The Meddix Council are waiting. You are the last to arrive. Follow me, we do not have much time. It's not wise to have all our leaders in one place at the same time,' he grumbled.

Egnatius gestured to his men to follow him as Statius and his green and brown warriors started to pick their way through the trees and deeper into the forest. Egnatius frowned as he studied the limping figure ahead of him. Statius seemed to have lost some of his nerve and energy. The man looked worn out.

***

The Meddix Council of Samnite leaders looked weary, dispirited and glum. They sat around an open fire in a forest clearing but no one had bothered to provide any food or drink. Egnatius sat on a large boulder playing with a Roman dagger, which he'd taken from a supply convoy he'd ambushed. Statius was explaining in some detail the operations that had been conducted in the past few months. His voice sounded tired and when at last he fell silent no one spoke. It was clear to all that the strategy that they'd agreed upon the previous summer was not working. Suddenly Egnatius looked up and glanced at the Samnite leaders.

'Where is Pontius, I miss the old man's wit?' Egnatius exclaimed with a little smile.

Statius cleared his throat. 'Pontius is dead. He died during the winter.'

'That's a shame for he would have liked to hear what I have to say,' Egnatius said as he rose to his feet and stepped into the circle and warmed his hands over the fire. Then he turned to look at the Council.

'It is time for a change,' he said suddenly in a strong clear voice, 'You all know it. You all know we cannot continue like this. Our people are losing hope. They are enduring terrible suffering and despite our valiant efforts we have achieved little.' Egnatius turned to look at the glum faces around him.

'What do you propose we do then?' Statius growled.

Egnatius looked down at his feet. 'You know what I would advise,' he said in a gentle voice, 'Only a grand alliance with the Etruscans and Umbrians will force a decisive change upon this war. With such an alliance, we could force a decisive battle and crush our enemy by sheer weight of numbers.'

'The Etruscan League is suing for peace with Rome, have you not heard?' the Meddix of Caudini snapped. 'We will find no allies amongst the Etruscans, not now at any rate.'

Egnatius nodded, 'I have heard the news but the peace negotiations will fail. Rome intends to conquer all the Etruscan cities and the Etruscans know it.'

'Even if they fail,' Statius snapped, 'The negotiations will take time and the Romans will enjoy peace in the north. It means that they can concentrate all their resources on us. Our land is being ravaged, here in the west by Fabius and in the east by Mus. Those two are picking the country clean. We have to act now.'

Egnatius turned to look at Statius. For a moment, his silent flickering eyes studied the Samnite supreme war leader. Then he turned and snapped his fingers at someone who had been standing in the shadow of the trees.

'Bring it here,' he ordered.

Titus, the young commander of the Linen Legion strode towards Egnatius and handed him a large heavy looking stained leather bag.

'Maybe for now we cannot achieve a grand alliance,' Egnatius said as he looked down at the leather bag, 'but we can do something else.' Suddenly Egnatius crouched and with his captured Roman dagger drew a straight line in the muddy forest soil. The Meddix Council leaned forwards to peer at what he was doing.

'This here is the Tifernus river valley,' Egnatius said quietly. 'You all know the valley. It cuts north and east from Bovianum towards the plains of Apulia and the eastern sea. It is the safest route for an army to take if that army wanted to march to, say, Luceria.'

'What do you mean?' Statius frowned.

Egnatius looked up from the map he was drawing in the soil. 'The city of Luceria is a staunch Roman ally,' Egnatius said with a sudden gleam in his eye. 'Now if we were to spread the news that a Samnite army was besieging the town and that the city was about to fall, Fabius may feel compelled to relieve his allies. If he decides to do so there are two routes he could take towards Luceria from his current position.' Egnatius drew another line in the mud. 'The shorter but far more dangerous route here straight across the mountains and the other, the safer but longer route here, straight down the Tifernus river valley.'

A sudden tense hush descended on the Samnite leaders as they stared at the lines Egnatius had drawn in the mud.

Egnatius looked up flush with sudden excitement.

'I wager that Fabius, being the man he is, will decide to take the safer route here through the Tifernus valley,' Egnatius said as he suddenly plunged his dagger into the mud. 'And at this point as you all know, the valley narrows and funnels into a pass. Once Fabius is in the valley he will have to go through this pass.' Egnatius turned to stare at his audience. 'It's difficult terrain,' he smiled. Then he opened the leather bag and pulled out a huge and bloodied bull's head. He placed the bull's head on the ground so that the two great horns cut across the line he'd drawn in the mud. 'It is here in this pass,' Egnatius said, 'that I propose we ambush the Romans. We should concentrate our army on the high ground and once Fabius is in the pass we will cut off both exits and annihilate him.'

The Samnite leaders stared at the bull's head and the lines in the mud in stunned silence. For a long moment, no one uttered a word.

'You propose to repeat the great victory of the Caudine Forks,' the Meddix of the Hirpini exclaimed at last.

Egnatius nodded and stared at the bull's head.

'It all depends on whether Fabius will take the bait. But I am confident that he will,' Egnatius said solemnly.

The Council fell silent once more as the Samnite leaders digested the plan. Then slowly all eyes turned to look at Statius. As supreme war leader, it was his decision on whether to adopt the plan or not. Statius was staring at the bull's horns. Then he looked up at Egnatius.

'There are many uncertainties,' he muttered. 'Will Fabius take the bait? Will he take the route we want him to take? What about the other Consul, Mus? He is operating in Apulia, won't Fabius expect him to handle any attack on Luceria?'

Egnatius smiled a little secret smile.

'Yes but it's likely that Fabius will not know for sure what his colleague is doing or where he is and we will make it very clear that Luceria is about to fall and that haste is required. Fabius will not be able to resist marching there himself.'

Statius remained silent. Then he nodded and looked up at Egnatius.

'And how do you propose we get the news of the siege of Luceria to Fabius without arousing Roman suspicions?'

Egnatius grinned. 'Some of my men will pretend to be shepherds,' he said. 'They have orders to graze their sheep close to the Roman pickets. The news should reach the Consul in that manner.'

The Council fell silent. Statius turned once more to stare at the bull's horns. Then he rose to his feet and nodded at Egnatius.

'Do it,' he snapped, 'send out your shepherds and order every war band to concentrate in the Tifernus valley. Tell them to move fast and to avoid the Romans. This whole thing now depends on speed and secrecy but with a bit of luck Fabius will never know what hit him.'

Chapter Thirty - Quintus Decius Mus has his Day

The Consul's tent had been pitched in the very centre of the camp. Two soldiers stood guard outside the entrance. It was late in the evening and numerous torches and campfires flickered in the darkness that hung over the Roman camp. Gaius and Quintus stood on either side of the Samnite shepherd grasping him by his arms. The man had been silent ever since he'd been dragged away from his sheep. Centho paced up and down in front of the guards as he waited to be given permission to enter Fabius's tent. The young officer looked anxious and impatient.

'What the fuck is taking Fabius so long?' Centho muttered. 'We have important news.'

The guards stared into space with stony vacant expressions and no one answered him. Gaius glanced at Quintus. He was happy to see that Quintus had revived somewhat since Centho had stopped picking on them. Quintus had starting speaking again for the first time in over two weeks. He'd discussed the merits of Etruscan wine over Campanian wine and Gaius had solemnly agreed that the Campanians had the edge.

A centurion suddenly appeared in the entrance to the tent and gestured for them to approach. Inside oil lamps had been fixed to the tent poles and in their reddish flickering light Gaius caught sight of Fabius. The Consul was sitting in his chair behind a table on which lay a messy pile of maps, reports and letters. A loaf of hard black bread and a half full cup of wine stood to one side. Behind the Consul's chair a tribune leaned against a tent pole. Fabius looked tired. He glanced up as Centho halted and saluted. Then he peered past the decurion at the Samnite shepherd.

'What's this? Make your report decurion?' Fabius said as a glint of interest suddenly appeared on his face.

Centho raised his eyes so that he was staring over Fabius's head.

'Decurion Centho reporting Sir,' Centho said sticking to the official way in which he'd been taught to make his reports, 'This morning I and my patrol were ordered out on a mission to discover the location of the enemy forces. I carried out my mission and found this Samnite shepherd. He has some information, which I think you should hear Sir. I believe it to be urgent Sir.'

Centho turned smartly on his heel and glared at the shepherd.

'Tell the Consul what you told us,' he snapped.

The shepherd did not respond at first but when Gaius gave him a rough shake the man started talking and once he started it became impossible to shut him up. The shepherd explained that he was a humble man, a poor man and that he knew nothing about the great armies that crossed the grazing lands of his sheep. But just recently he'd come across a Samnite war band who'd told him that Luceria was being besieged and that the town was going to fall within days. That was all he knew about the matter. As the shepherd continued to speak in his broken heavily accented Latin, Gaius noticed that Quintus was listening and studying the shepherd with sudden curiosity.

'Enough,' Fabius barked.

The tent fell silent.

'Centurion,' Fabius said, 'Have this Samnite locked up for the next three days. On the third day you are to release him.'

'Sir,' the centurion saluted. Then the officer grasped the shepherd by his shoulder and propelled him towards the tent exit. 'Come on you, move it,' the officer growled.

Fabius waited until the centurion and the Samnite had disappeared. Then he broke off a piece of the black bread and dipped it into his wine before eating it. Centho, Gaius and Quintus were silent as they waited for the Consul to finish eating. When Fabius was done he cleared his throat, studied the papers on the table and then turned to glance at the tribune behind him. The two men exchanged a thoughtful look.

'It's exactly the same story,' the tribune muttered, 'The other shepherd said exactly the same thing.'

Fabius grunted and turned to look at Centho. 'That will be all decurion, you may go,' Fabius said with a nod.

'Sir, what do you think?' Centho blurted out unable to contain himself, 'Do you believe the man's story?'

Fabius remained silent as he stared at Centho. Then he rose to his feet with a stern and unhappy expression.

'I believe that in a Roman army when an order is given it is obeyed immediately,' Fabius said in a mild voice fixing his eyes on Centho. Fabius's voice may have been mild but everyone in the room caught the dangerous and annoyed undertone in the Consul's voice.

Centho went crimson. Without a further word, he saluted and turned on his heel. Outside in the cool night air Gaius heard Centho cursing to himself as he stomped off into the darkness. Gaius grinned and turned to Quintus.

'Did you see that?' Gaius exclaimed. 'I reckon the only reason Fabius didn't have Centho flogged there and then was because his father is such an important and powerful man. Still, always good to see our officer getting a bit of shit on his face. It makes him a bit more like us.'

Quintus did not seem to be listening.

'There is something odd about that shepherd,' Quintus muttered. 'I am too tired to see it now but I am going to think about it tonight. Maybe it will   come to me in the morning.'

***

Gaius was woken by trumpets. He was on his feet in an instant. Inside his tent his comrades rose and rushed about grabbing their weapons and equipment. Gaius was fully dressed. Quickly he strapped on his armour, snatched his spear and shield and stepped outside. It was dawn and to the east the sun was a faint red ball on the horizon. The Roman army camp was a loud hive of activity as men rushed here and there. Centho came striding past, leading his horse by the bridles.

'What's going on Sir? Are we under attack?' Gaius cried.

'We're moving out,' Centho replied, 'The Consul has decided to march on Luceria. Get yourself ready.'

Gaius grunted. Then he half walked, half ran towards where the squadron had tethered their horses. As he reached his horse, a black stallion called Mars, he ran into Quintus who was already preparing his own horse. Quintus was dipping a piece of bread into a cup of sour wine. He offered Gaius a bite but Gaius shook his head.

'Looks like we're moving out,' Gaius grunted.

Quintus nodded as he offered the remainder of the wine to his horse. The beast slurped it up and Quintus patted her affectionately on her flank. There was a strange detached expression on Quintus face as if he had other things on his mind. Gaius let it go and swung himself onto the back of his horse just as the camp servants started to collapse the squadron's tents.

'Squadron, form up,' Centho cried in a loud voice.

The thirty cavalrymen in the unit urged their horses into a straight line facing their decurion. Centho waited until the last man had got himself and his beast into position.

'Right,' Centho shouted as he examined his men with a critical look, 'The army is moving out. We will be heading east to relieve our allies at Luceria. Our route will take us along the Tifernus valley. The Consul has ordered us and the other squadrons to ride ahead of the main army. We are to be Consul's eyes and ears. We are to provide warning of any Samnite traps and ambushes along the way, so keep your eyes and ears open and your fingers out of your arseholes. I will reward the first man to spot the enemy with a double ration of wine. Now move out.'

Gaius winked at Quintus as the troopers turned and started to trot after their commander.

'Looks like he is finally learning how to motivate his men,' Gaius said shaking his head. 'He will be calling us his beloved brothers next.'

Quintus however did not reply. He looked troubled as the cavalrymen trotted past the groups of heavy infantry who were milling about.

***

The rolling hills, forests and distant snow capped mountains could hide a Samnite army anywhere, Gaius thought gloomily as the squadron picked its way across a meadow towards the Tifernus river. It was as if Samnium had been created as a place where armies were to be ambushed. The encounter with the Samnites on the steep mountain path seemed to still haunt Centho too, for the decurion had kept to the flatter and more open countryside for the past few hours. Gaius glanced thoughtfully at Quintus who was riding ahead. There was something the matter with Quintus. His friend had been silent all morning but it wasn't a relapse into his earlier depression. This was something else.

The Tifernus was narrow and shallow as the lead rider reached it. The cavalry horses splashed through the water and the patrol climbed up the far bank. Up ahead Gaius could see and hear a

247

cascading mountain stream as it merged with the Tifernus. A solitary wild dog stood on the riverbank drinking. It looked up and stared at the Romans as they started to follow the river. Then without a sound it turned and ran off into the undergrowth. Gaius glanced to his left. A hundred yards or so away was a thick dark forest. For a while the patrol followed the river eastwards. Then Centho turned and started to climb towards the higher ground. The cavalrymen silently followed their commander as he vanished amongst the trees.

At noon Centho called a halt. The patrol was in the midst of a small forest clearing. They had climbed right up to the ridge of the valley but had come across nothing apart from some startled deer. Only once had they seen other humans. As they'd come out onto the ridge Gaius had seen the tiny figures of another patrol scouting the valley floor far below them. In the forest clearing the troopers eagerly dismounted and started to prepare their lunch. Centho gestured for two of his men to form a picket across the forest path they'd been following. Two more men were despatched to form another picket across the path they'd just come down. The soldiers vanished quickly into the trees.

Gaius had just finished replacing a few hobnails in his marching boots when one of the sentries came rushing into the clearing. The riders rose to their feet in alarm as the man ran up to Centho.

'There are men approaching along the forest path Sir,' the soldier gasped.

'How many?' Centho said with an alarmed look.

'It's a small party. They are carrying a litter Sir,' the soldier replied turning to look in the direction from which he'd just come. 'They will be here any minute.'

Centho took a few seconds to make his decision. Then he swung himself onto his horse and silently gestured for his troopers to disperse into the trees. Gaius and Quintus flung themselves onto their horses and trotted quickly into the shelter of the forest. A few yards in they turned their beasts around and peered intently at the spot where the path disappeared into the wood. Around them the forest seemed to have grown quiet. Gaius lifted his spear and pointed it at the clearing. Nothing moved. A minute passed and then another. Then suddenly two armed men appeared at the edge of the forest. They halted and studied the empty clearing. Gaius glanced sideway at Quintus. Quintus was staring tensely at the newcomers. By their dress and weapons Gaius could see that the men were Samnites. The Samnites seemed unhappy about something. One of them pointed at the clearing. The other man was studying the ground. Then he looked up at the trees and to Gaius it seemed as if the man was staring straight at him. For a moment, nothing happened. Then the two men started forwards into the clearing and began to stride towards the forest beyond. The men were followed by four litter bearers carrying a litter. Gaius stared at the litter trying to see who was inside but the curtains blocked his view. The rear of the party was brought up by three men, all armed.

Centho's wild cry shattered the peace. The decurion came charging out of the trees and flung his spear at one of the litter bearers. Around him the forest erupted as the Roman riders came storming into the clearing from every direction. The Samnites had no chance. The two leading men were struck by several spears before they could even draw their swords. They tumbled to the ground. Centho's spear hit the litter bearer in his back. The man cried out, staggered and then collapsed to the ground and as he did so the litter lurched sideways and then crashed to the ground and as it did so its occupant emitted a high pitched horrified shriek, that made Gaius's blood turn cold. By the time Gaius raised his spear, to fling it at his enemy, the fight was already over. All nine Samnites were dead or dying and the grass in the clearing was smeared red with blood. Centho raised his fist in triumph as the Romans dismounted to inspect their slain enemies.

Gaius turned to look at the litter. It lay on its side. Then as he took a step towards it a horrible hissing noise made him stop. Gaius drew his sword. Wrinkled bony fingers appeared scratching at the wood and slowly the curtains were pushed aside and a woman rose unsteadily to her feet. Gaius gasped in surprise. The woman looked old, impossible old. She was clad entirely in white. The woman's face contorted hideously as he caught sight of the Romans. She hissed at them. The woman seemed to have no fear at all. Gaius felt a sudden tinge of unease. All the troopers were staring at the old woman and when one of them took a few steps towards her, the bony fingers shot towards him followed by hissing and words shrieked in a language that no one understood. The man retreated nervously.

'She's a sybil, she's a witch. Don't go near her,' one of the men suddenly cried, as his face grew pale. 'She will curse you, she will put a spell on you.'

Gaius stared at the old woman. The troopers suddenly looked frightened and nervous and a few of the men had started to back away. Centho too stumbled backwards and drew his sword.

'Swords are no use,' another rider cried, 'If you touch her she will turn you into stone. Kill the bitch. Spike her heart with a spear.'

'You cannot kill her,' another man shouted, 'She is immortal. She is a creature of the gods.'

Slowly the troopers backed away from the woman. Everyone was staring at her with mesmerized fascination and dread as she continued to hiss and mutter strange words.

'Bollocks,' a voice suddenly cried.

Gaius grunted in surprise as Quintus calmly strode on past him towards the sybil. Then to everyone's horror he seized her by the neck and laughed.

'Yes, I have heard the stories lady,' he cried, 'You must be the Sybil of Cumae. You are supposed to live for a thousand years. You are supposed to get smaller with age until only your voice remains. Problem is lady; I don't believe a word of it. It's all utter bollocks, just as the existence of the gods is utter bollocks. This life is all that there is. There is no afterlife, no nothing. You are just an act. You may frighten my friends but you sure don't frighten me.'

Quintus brought his face close to that of the sybil as he grasped her by the throat.

'You see I don't believe in the gods, I don't think they exist and I don't believe in any magic spells. I think you are just a harmless old creature, so stop fucking hissing and listen to what I have to say.'

The troopers groaned in dismay and terror but the sybil fell silent as she stared at Quintus furiously.

'Luceria is not being besieged is it,' Quintus snapped, 'It's all just a trick to get us to march into an ambush, isn't it?'

The sybil hesitated and her fury seemed to vanish. Then suddenly to Gaius who was watching it seemed as if the witch had grown afraid. Her body trembled and her eyes bulged in their sockets. Quintus relaxed his grip on her throat.

'You know the will of the Samnites,' she gasped. 'How can this be so?' Then without another word she groaned and collapsed to the ground. Quintus stared at her in surprise. Then as Gaius and the others approached Quintus cautiously bent down and pressed his ear to the woman's head. It looked like the old woman was trying to tell him something. He straightened up as

Gaius reached him and stared at the old woman in bewilderment.

'I think she is dead,' Quintus muttered in confusion. 'All I did was grab her by the throat. She must have had a weak heart.' He paused. 'I think I have just killed the Sybil of Cumae,' he whispered.

One of the troopers bent down over the body and gingerly touched the woman. Then he looked up at Centho and nodded.

'Then you are cursed, you are going to die young,' one of the troopers, hissed in alarm. 'The gods will take their revenge on you for killing their favourite.'

Gaius turned to look at Quintus.

'What did she say to you?' he gasped.

Quintus looked dazed. 'She asked,' he muttered with a puzzled expression, 'for Egnatius to forgive her. She asked for his forgiveness. His father's death was her fault. That's all she said.'

Gaius frowned and turned to stare at the body of the sybil. The troopers crowded around and all were staring at the corpse with a mixture of horror and fascination.

'Well fuck me, Quintus,' Centho said at last, 'It seems that you have managed to get the enemy to reveal their battle plans. Mount up boys, we have to warn the Consul that he is marching straight into an ambush.'

'How did you know?' Gaius snapped as he stared at the body of the sybil.

Quintus blinked, as he seemed to return to himself. He gave Gaius a tense look.

'The shepherd,' he growled, 'the man was a poor actor. I should know. I have spent half my life with actors. What he was saying

252

just didn't feel right. It made me suspicious but I needed more proof. I couldn't just go to Fabius with a suspicion. He would have thrown me out on my arse.'

Chapter Thirty-One - The Pride of Samnium

Egnatius stood in his command post in the forest sharpening his sword on a stone. It was late in the morning and the sky was blue and cloudless. The clear warm weather reminded him of that day at Gaugemela, all those years ago, when he and his King had stood facing the entire, armed might of Asia. As he sharpened his sword a tiny spark sprang to life and died as quickly as it had appeared. It was a good day for battle he thought. The banner of the Linen Legion and a host of other Samnite battle standards had been pushed into the ground and around them the eager Samnite commanders had gathered. They were waiting for him to issue his orders. Egnatius did not look up from his work. His men could wait. At Gaugemela he and his comrades had realised the seriousness of their situation, when they had seen the gigantic dust clouds coming towards them, the dust raised by the hundreds of thousands of Persian soldiers that the King of kings could command. Many would have turned and run at the sight but the Macedonians had trusted in each other and they had trusted in their king, Alexander. Egnatius glanced up at the sky.

'Where is Statius, where is our commander in chief?' he said at last.

The Samnite commanders glanced at each other. Then they averted their eyes. No one it seemed wanted to be the first to answer. Egnatius looked up. Then Titus, the young commander of the Linen Legion cleared his throat.

'Statius is with his men, he is drunk.'

Egnatius ran his finger down the edge of his sword. It was sharp. He glanced down at the weapon and then sheathed it with a smooth well-practised movement.

'So our commander in chief is drunk, that's a good start,' he muttered. Egnatius glanced at his soldiers. Nearly every single senior commander in the Samnite army was watching him. They had come to him and not their commander in chief. It was a good sign. The men wanted to fight.

'Report?' Egnatius growled.

'The army are in their positions on both sides of the valley,' Titus replied, 'They know the plan. I have scouts shadowing the Romans. Fabius seems to have taken the bait. The latest news that I have is that he has entered the Tifernus valley and is marching towards us. If he has continued to come this way then I expect he will reach us in the next few hours. My scouts should confirm that shortly.'

Egnatius looked up at the sky. The ambush was going to take place late in the day.

'What about the other Consul, Mus? Why has there been no report on his movements?' he snapped.

Titus shifted his weight uneasily. 'Our scouts have lost contact with the other Consul. His last known position was in Apulia but that was days ago,' he replied.

Egnatius frowned and turned to stare at Titus. 'So you mean to say that we don't know where the Mus is at this moment?'

Titus looked uncomfortable. 'Yes,' he muttered, 'That's right. He could be anywhere right now.'

Egnatius looked annoyed. He didn't like surprises but it couldn't be helped. Just that morning he'd been wondering why the sybil had not yet arrived. He could have done with her presence for there were questions he'd wanted to ask her. She should have been waiting for him but no one had seen or heard from her or her escort. Her disappearance bothered him. It was not like her to be late. Something had happened but he didn't have the time to investigate. It would have to wait until after the battle.

He turned as he heard the noise of galloping hooves. A rider was coming up the path towards him. The man was in a hurry.

255

As Egnatius looked on, the rider slid from his horse and ran towards Titus. The two men spoke briefly. Then Titus turned to Egnatius and from the expression on the young commander's face Egnatius suddenly knew that something was wrong.

'Fabius will be here within the hour,' Titus said tightly, 'But his marching formation has changed. The Romans are advancing in a hollow square formation and there is no sign of their baggage train or civilians.'

A mutter broke out amongst the assembled Samnite commanders. Egnatius looked disappointed.

'They know about the ambush,' Titus exclaimed, 'For why else would they march in such a formation. They have come to fight. The Romans know about our plan.'

'Titus is right. We should retreat,' one of the commanders muttered.

'Retreat,' Egnatius hissed, 'We will not retreat. I am tired of running and hiding. If we retreat now we will always be running away. No, we will stand and fight. That is what I have come here to do. That is what all of us have come here to do.'

No one replied. The officers were all staring at him.

'It doesn't matter what happens to you,' Egnatius said, 'What is important is how you react to it.' He jumped up and clambered onto a large boulder from where he had a fine view of the valley below. For a moment, he studied the valley floor. 'If Fabius has come to fight then we shall not disappoint him,' he said turning to his men. 'We shall meet him in open battle and defeat him. Titus, take your men down onto the level ground. You and your Linen Legion will hold our centre. The rest of you will take your men and form up on either flank with your rear to the pass. You will hold the Roman assault and wait for my signal before attacking. You will not leave your positions until you hear my signal. This is important. Is   that clear?'

The Samnite commanders nodded and hurried forwards to pull their battle standards from the earth. As the men dispersed Egnatius turned to Titus. His young prodigy looked eager and excited.

'Titus,' Egnatius said laying a hand on the young man's shoulder, 'Instruct your men to remain on the defensive. You will occupy the high ground. Let the Romans wear themselves out against your shields. I will be right behind you. Then when the moment is right I will lead the counter attack with my fresh Caraceni. Wait for my signal, two long trumpet blasts followed by a single short one. With a bit of luck we should be able to drive the Roman centre from the field.'

Titus nodded that he had understood. Then he grasped Egnatius's arm and the two men embraced briefly.

'Let this be the day when we drive Rome from our sacred land,' Titus said solemnly.

Egnatius nodded and turned as another rider came racing up the path towards them. The man jumped from his horse and ran towards Titus. 'The Romans have come to a halt. They are deploying Sir,' the scout gasped.

'They know exactly where we are,' Egnatius said with a wry smile. The scout saluted and returned to his horse. Across the valley floor several trumpets suddenly blared at the same time and from amongst the trees and undergrowth, where they'd been hiding, Egnatius saw hundreds of Samnite warriors rise to their feet. The men looked resigned and tense.

Titus was just about to leave when an angry cry reverberated through the wood and a figure came galloping towards Egnatius. It was Statius. The commander in chief of the Samnites nearly fell from his horse as he dismounted. He staggered towards Egnatius with an angry drunken expression on his face. Egnatius studied him calmly as he approached.

'What are you doing?' Statius growled, 'What is going on? Who gave you permission to move my army down into the valley? We are supposed to be ambushing the Romans. You are revealing our positions, you fool.'

'You are drunk, I suggest that you go and sleep it off. We don't need you. I am not going to let you fuck things up for us again,' Egnatius replied contemptuously.

Statius's eyes blazed with sudden fury and he struck Egnatius with his fist. The blow sent Egnatius staggering backwards. Egnatius reached for his sword and with a single smooth movement plunged it into Statius's chest. The commander in chief gasped at the impact and his eyes bulged. Blood suddenly appeared in the corner of his mouth. He stared at Egnatius in horror. Then without another sound he collapsed to the ground. Egnatius stared at the corpse and then crouched to wipe his bloody sword on Statius's tunic. When he was done he looked up. The Samnites who had witnessed him kill Statius were staring at him in silent horror. Egnatius ignored them. He turned to Titus.

'Burn this piece of shit and tell the men that I am now officially in command,' he growled.

***

Egnatius stared in silent fascination as the line of square Roman Maniples of Hastati advanced straight towards Titus's men. The Romans looked sure of themselves and their armour and weapons glinted in the bright afternoon sunlight. From their ranks he could hear trumpets ringing out and then on the gentle breeze he caught his enemies battle chants.

'Samnium must die, Samnium must die,' the Romans chanted as they advanced.

Further back Egnatius saw the second and third line Maniples moving up behind their comrades. He grunted in contempt. The

Romans had copied the whole Manipular organisation of their army from his people. There had been a time when his enemy had fought in a single Phalanx just like the Greeks but the mountainous terrain of Samnium had demanded a more flexible organisation and the Romans had been quick to see the advantages of the Samnite battle formation. That's what Rome did, Egnatius thought with growing contempt, they invaded and conquered and took everything that had any value.

He wrenched his eyes away from the enemy and turned to look at his own army. The Samnite units had formed a line that stretched across the valley floor. They occupied the ridge of the gently sloping and open ground and to his right he could see that his flank was securely anchored against a steep forested hill, which was impossible to climb. He glanced to his left. He'd posted his cavalry on his extreme left flank. They would be most effective there amongst the open hilly ground but, as he stared at the distant men he felt a slight tug of unease. The Samnite cavalry had gone to their positions in a sullen and rebellious mood. They had after all, been Statius's men and the death of their commander had not gone down well. Egnatius bit his lip. He wasn't sure he would be able to rely on the horsemen. But there was nothing more he could do. He would have to hope that before the end, Statius's men would remember that they were Samnites and that Rome was their first and most dangerous enemy. He turned to look at his own Caraceni tribe. The warriors clustered around him and as he studied them he felt a surge of confidence. His men looked sharp and eager and in that moment he knew they were not going to let him down. Egnatius raised his arm and cried out in his native Oscan.

'For our land, for our people, for our children!' he roared.

The cry was taken up by the tens of thousands of men and it rippled along the Samnite battle line until the entire army was shouting. The noise was tremendous and startled flocks of birds rose into the sky from the trees and fled northwards. The mighty Samnite battle cry echoed off the distant hills until the men were chanting in one voice and in   one rhythm.

259

'For our land, for our people, for our children. For our land, for our people, for our children.'

A little tear appeared in Egnatius eye. The sight and sound of the Samnite army was magnificent. They were undoubtedly the finest warriors in Italy. Oh, how long had he yearned to command such fine men! The Samnite chants echoed once more. Then the army fell silent as they braced themselves to meet the enemy assault.

The Roman Maniples had not hesitated. They came on at a steady pace and as Egnatius looked on they suddenly halted when they were fifteen paces away from the Samnite front line. Egnatius frowned. Something was different about the Romans. Where were the long thrusting spears that the Hastati normally carried? For a moment, the battlefield fell silent as the two armies stared at each other. Then with a loud cry the Roman Hastati raised the spears, which they had been concealing behind their large oval shields and flung them at the Samnite line. Egnatius grunted in surprise as the volley of pilum's smashed into his men. He had never seen the Romans do that before. The pilum's, the throwing spears were Samnite weapons. The Romans must have copied them and the tactics of the massed volley. The hail of spears shredded the Samnite front line and Egnatius heard the shrieks and cries of the wounded. The noise however was quickly drowned out as the Roman Hastati drew their swords and with a loud roar charged straight at the Samnite line. The two front lines met with a horrible screaming crunch and instantly the front lines descended into a chaotic mass of shoving, screaming and stabbing men. But as quickly as contact had been made the two battle lines recoiled. Then with another loud cry the Roman Hastati charged once more into the Samnite ranks. Egnatius tensed as he stared at the battle that had broken out along the length of the valley floor. Titus's men were holding their own. The Linen Legion was doing its job. The Roman Hastati had been flung back. He sighed with relief and turned to stare towards his left flank. In the distance, he could just about see the Samnite cavalry drawn up on the crest of a small hill. The horsemen were facing the Roman cavalry squadrons and both sides seemed content to sit and watch each other. Maybe that was for the best. Egnatius grunted and turned his attention back to the infantry melee in the centre of his line. The Roman Hastati had grown wary of their opponents and the two sides suddenly seemed reluctant to close with each other. But it had not stopped the two armies from hurling missiles at each other and the shrieks of wounded and dying men echoed off the sides of the valley. Egnatius glanced beyond the Roman front line to where the patient Maniples of the Roman second and third line stood waiting to enter the battle. No, the time was not yet right for his massed charge. He would wait until Fabius had committed his main strength.

'Sir,' a young man was suddenly tugging at his arm. Egnatius turned to stare at the boy. It was one of his scouts. The young man's face was splattered with mud and streaked with sweat. He looked worried.

'What is it?' Egnatius growled with sudden foreboding.

'Sir,' the young man was panting, 'We found the sybil. She is dead and so are her escort. The men who accompanied her were killed but there are no marks or wounds on the woman. We don't know how she died. We brought her body back with us. I came here right away to tell you.'

Egnatius blinked and stared at the boy in stunned silence. Then he turned away to look at the fighting but he didn't see or hear the vicious struggling masses of men. His thoughts were far away. The sybil, his sybil was dead. How could this be? She had always been there for him, all his life. She had been his closest friend. Then he groaned quietly as everything seemed to slot into place. So, that was how the Romans must have learned about the ambush. Egnatius's face darkened. Had the sybil betrayed him? She had been one of the very few who had known all the details of his plan and no one, not even the Romans would dare to hurt a sybil on purpose. For a moment he was confused. Then he remembered her final words to him

261

before they had parted company. She had told him to seek out the other one, her other servant, the spy operating in the very heart of the Roman government. The man she had called her beautiful son. Egnatius cursed quietly and clenched his hand into a fist. She had told him to protect him at all costs for the information the spy had started to supply was becoming increasingly valuable.

Chapter Thirty-Two - The Battle of Tifernus

Gaius stared at the battle that was raging to his left. The vicious hand to hand combat between the Roman Hastati and the Samnite Linen Legion had been going on for over an hour and neither side had made any progress in dislodging their opponents. It was the same all along the line. The initial Roman assault had failed to drive the Samnites from the field and the struggle had turned into a stalemate. His horse stirred nervously underneath him and Gaius quickly patted her on her neck. Quintus and he stood drawn up in a horizontal line just behind Centho. All the troopers were staring at the battle but the order for them to join in had still not come. A couple of hundred paces away the Samnite cavalry squadrons stood watching their Roman counterparts. Neither side had moved since the battle had begun.

Centho twisted on his horse for the umpteenth time and glared back in the direction where Fabius had planted his banner. The decurion looked impatient.

'What the fuck is Fabius waiting for?' Centho growled. 'Are we going to just sit here all day? The Hastati need our help.'

No one answered him but Gaius noticed Quintus give him a tense glance followed by a little shake of his head. Gaius could feel his heart thumping in his chest. All this waiting was destroying his nerves. He had never felt so pumped up in his whole life. Centho was right; it would be better to be doing something, anything, apart from this intolerable waiting.

To their left the shrieking murderous combat continued and Gaius noticed that some of the Principes companies had begun to get sucked into the fighting. He glanced in the direction of Fabius's battle standard. If Fabius did not act soon his whole second line would become sucked into the battle. He peered intently at the distant group of horsemen. Gods! He hoped that the old warrior had a plan. The Samnites were not giving up an inch of ground, if anything the enemies confidence seemed to be rising as they threw back one Roman attack after the other.

Then suddenly a trumpet blared and after a few moments hesitation the Hastati companies closest to Gaius began to retreat. Their place in the front line was immediately filled by the Principes. Gaius stared at the manoeuvre. The Hastati companies continued to retreat passing through the third and final line of Roman Triarii before another trumpet signal brought them to a halt. Now Gaius could hear the distant shouting of the company centurions. Puzzled he stared at the scene. Then with a near perfect turn the thousand or so men began to jog away towards the rear. They vanished behind a rise in the ground. Gaius's eyes narrowed. What was Fabius up to?

'Look,' Quintus suddenly cried, 'Fabius is moving his standard. He is coming towards us.'

All eyes turned to stare towards their left and sure enough the tight knit group of officers and men that surrounded the Consul were moving. Rapidly the party of officers came towards the Roman cavalry squadrons and then Gaius suddenly recognised the Consul. Fabius had a white scarf tied around his neck. He sat bolt upright on his horse and was staring at the Samnite cavalry. The old man's presence suddenly seemed to fill the troopers with renewed confidence. Gaius glanced at Quintus and nodded encouragingly but Quintus just shook his head.

A young tribune was suddenly galloping towards the six hundred Roman cavalry troopers. Centho straightened up as the officer came up to him. The tribune looked flushed and he spoke rapidly in an excited voice.

'Decurion, when you hear the cavalry signal you are to attack the Samnite infantry to your left. Do not move until you hear the signal.'

Then the officer was off racing down the line to repeat his message to the next squadron. Centho grunted irritably and turned to look once more in the Consul's direction.

Gaius wiped the sweat from his brow and stared at the massed Samnite infantry. Had he just heard that order correctly? Was Fabius ordering his cavalry to attack a solid line of spear armed Samnite infantry on higher ground. Such a charge would be suicide. The cavalry would be slaughtered. He turned sharply and stared at the Consul's party. What the fuck did Fabius think he was doing?

Time passed and the shrieking, howling fight to their left continued unabated. Gaius felt a sudden spasm of cramp in his leg. He bit his lip. His nerves were in shreds. He wanted to scream; the waiting was becoming intolerable. Then suddenly a confused blast of trumpets echoed across the battlefield. Centho's head whipped round and his eyes widened.

'That's the signal,' he cried, 'That's our signal.'

'No, wait,' Quintus yelled, 'I am not so sure it was. Centho wait.'

But it was too late. Centho's voice reverberated down the line. 'Cavalry, charge. For Rome! For Jupiter!'

Without waiting to see what his men were doing the young patrician shouted his battle cry and charged straight at the Samnite infantry. After a moment's stunned silence the six hundred or so Roman troopers raised a mighty roar and thundered off in pursuit of the decurion. Gaius felt himself carried along in the headlong charge. A hurried trumpet blast echoed across the valley. It was the recall order but it had come too late. No one paid it any attention. The Roman cavalry charged straight at the Samnite infantry. Gaius cried out savagely as he closed with the enemy ranks. Then with a splintering crash the Roman cavalry ran straight into the Samnite spearmen. The world was suddenly filled with terrified shrieks, screaming horses and the thud and crunch as bodies

265

and beasts crashed and tumbled to the ground. A Samnite spearman loomed up and thrust his spear into Gaius's horse and the beast staggered sideways sending Gaius flying. He hit the ground and tumbled head over heels. Close by a cavalryman lay trapped under a dead horse. A Samnite sprang forwards and rammed his spear into the man's head. Gaius rose unsteadily to his feet. His helmet had been knocked off his head and he had lost his shield. All around him the Roman cavalry were locked in a fierce and unequal struggle with the Samnite infantry. Riderless horses were cantering back towards the Roman lines. Gaius cried out in pain and horror. A Samnite sprang towards him and Gaius managed to draw his sword just in time and parry the man's blow. Then another rider thrust his spear into the Samnite's back and the man collapsed.

Close by Gaius suddenly caught sight of Centho. The decurion lay on the ground. The broken shaft of a spear was sticking out of his thigh. Centho was screaming in agony. Gaius ran towards him, grabbed the decurion by his arm and began to drag him away from the shrieking murderous melee. Centho screamed again. Blood was welling up from his wound. He'd lost both his spear and sword. Gaius looked up as a rider came thundering past him. Then he heard a familiar voice and the hairs on his neck stood up. It was Quintus. His friend was screaming at the remaining Roman cavalrymen to reform. Gaius opened his mouth in amazement as he saw Quintus raise his arm and rally the few remaining Roman cavalrymen. Then with a harsh cry Quintus led his few companions in a fresh charge towards the Samnite line.

'No, Quintus, no,' Gaius screamed.

But it was too late. The Roman horsemen thundered past Gaius and the screaming Centho. Gaius turned and stared in horror as the few men crashed into the Samnite infantry. It was an utterly hopeless and futile charge. His eyes closed in despair. Centho was still screaming in agony. Gaius opened his eyes and refusing to look at the carnage behind him he bent down, gripped Centho tightly and started to drag the decurion to safety.

The Roman cavalry had been slaughtered. The shrieks and cries of agony reverberated across the slope of the hill. Gaius turned, terror struck as he stared at the massed Samnite cavalry squadrons. There was nothing left to stop them from now wheeling around the Roman flank and attacking the Roman infantry in the rear. The battle was lost. He and every other Roman was going to be massacred. His mouth worked quickly as he muttered a prayer to Jupiter. It was all over and he had better make his peace with the gods. A stupid mistake had cost Rome the battle.

Centho was still screaming in agony as Gaius dragged him back towards the Roman lines. Gaius turned to look behind him but the Samnite infantry had not immediately followed up their victory. The Samnite cavalry however, having seen the destruction of the Roman horse, had started to move forwards. Gaius turned and stared in despair in the direction of the tight knit group of officers who clustered around the Consul. Fabius, clearly visible by his white neck scarf, stood like a rock as all around him riderless horses thundered past. Gaius staggered forwards dragging Centho behind him. Then behind him he heard a trumpet blast. The trumpet was followed by a short silence before a great victorious roar swept across the battle. Gaius blinked and turned to look behind him. To the rear of the Samnite army Roman standards had suddenly appeared in the mountain pass. Then he heard the shout that came sweeping down the ranks of the Roman infantry companies.

'Mus has come, Mus has come with his army. Mus has come! The Samnites are trapped.'

Gaius stared at the scene in shock. How could this be so? The Samnites too had seen the Roman standards and for a moment their ranks milled around in confusion. Then suddenly they seem to break. Gaius collapsed to his knees as he saw the massed Samnite cavalry squadrons turn and gallop away. The infantry, seeing their cavalry desert them, followed a few moments later. Within a few moments the ordered Samnite battle line descended into chaos as the enemy officers lost control and their men started to flee. Gaius cried out. Then as the Samnites started to stream back across the hilly slopes he forced himself up onto his feet and turned back towards the carnage he'd just left behind. To his left the Roman infantry had set off in pursuit of the Samnites. The Romans were slaughtering those who could not flee or run. Gaius was oblivious to it all. He strode through the debris of battle until he found what he was looking for. Quintus lay beside a fallen horse. He'd suffered a sword blow to his arm and a spear had punctured his stomach. Gaius saw at once that he was dead. The weapons had not killed him but the fall from his horse had broken his neck. Carefully Gaius crouched down on the ground and lifted his friend's head into his lap. Tears were suddenly streaming down Gaius's face. He gripped Quintus's tunic unwilling to let go. Then he raised his head to the sky and roared with pain. He was still there cradling Quintus's head when strong arms lifted him up onto his feet.

Chapter Thirty-Three - A Father's Grief

The news that the Consul's son had fallen had spread rapidly throughout the entire Roman army. Fabius had ordered the body to be wrapped in white linen and placed in a tent on its own. A guard had been stationed outside and no one had been permitted to enter. Gaius sat outside the army tent mending the tears and holes in his tunic. It was morning. After driving the Samnites from the field the Romans had returned to the sight of the battle. It had been too late in the day to build a camp and Gaius had slept on the ground out in the open and had listened to the shrieks and cries of the wounded. It was only when it had grown light and he had been reunited with a few of the survivors of the cavalry charge, that he had learned what had happened during the battle. Fabius had sent the thousand Hastati around the back of the enemy and had been intending to use them to catch the Samnite line in a co-ordinated attack from the front and rear. When the attack had failed, it was only by sheer chance that the Romans and Samnites had both mistaken the Hastati companies for Publius's army. Publius, it turned out, was a hundred miles away on the other side of Italy.

Gaius looked up from his work as someone called out to him. It was Centho. The decurion came hobbling towards him and was leaning for support on a comrade. A blood-soaked bandage had been tied around the wound in his thigh. He grimaced as he approached and Gaius greeted him with a silent nod. For a moment Centho said nothing. Then he stretched out his arm and Gaius got to his feet and clasped it and the two of them embraced. Centho looked embarrassed. He glanced quickly at the tent that contained Quintus's body.

'Thank you Gaius,' he murmured. Centho suddenly seemed unsure of what else to say. An awkward silence followed.

'The Consul wants you to report to his tent immediately,' Centho muttered. Then he turned and hobbled away.

Gaius watched him go. Then he packed away his bone needle and thread and turned in the direction of the Consul's command post. Two soldiers stood guarding the entrance and a little way off he noticed three mounted despatch riders chatting to each other. A tribune with a nasty looking cut across his face showed Gaius into the spacious interior of the army tent. Gaius saluted as he saw Fabius sitting behind his desk. The Consul looked busy. A pile of despatches lay on the table waiting to be signed and sealed. Fabius kept him waiting and the tent remained silent as the Consul read the despatches for a final time. Then at last Fabius grunted in approval, rolled up and sealed the letters. He nodded to the tribune and the officer took the despatches and strode outside. Fabius looked up at Gaius. Then the old man rose to his feet and clasped his hands behind his back.

'I remember you,' Fabius said quietly, 'You were present in the Senate House that day when I was elected to the Consulship. I understand that you were the client and companion of Quintus Decius Mus.'

'I was his friend Sir,' Gaius replied staring straight ahead.

'Yes, his friend,' Fabius nodded. Then he sighed. 'I need someone to ride to Publius the Consul and tell him that his son is dead. I could send a despatch but I think it would be better if the Consul heard the news from you.'

Gaius nodded, 'I will go Sir, I will tell him the news.'

Fabius looked pleased. 'Good,' he murmured. He paused and the old man's grey eyes studied Gaius carefully.

'Mistakes happen during war,' Fabius exclaimed, 'I trust that you will not try and turn the Consul's son's death into an issue that will make my dear friend Publius turn against me? That would be most unfortunate.'

'I understand Sir. No one is to blame for what happened,' Gaius replied.

'Good,' Fabius said confidently, 'I am glad that I can trust you. The tribune outside will issue you with a horse and official orders. And Gaius,' Fabius said as Gaius saluted and turned to leave, 'Be sure to tell the Consul that I grieve for his loss.'

Gaius rode slowly past the hundreds of small groups of men who clustered around their campfires. The soldiers were sleeping, eating and taking stock of their situation. The mood was subdued and most of the men looked exhausted. As he picked his way across the field, Gaius suddenly heard a man scream in pain. The cry had come from close by and it was followed by a ripple of laughter. Idly he glanced in the direction from which the noise had come. Then he frowned and brought his horse to a halt. He peered at the figure at the centre of the small commotion. Surely it couldn't be. He shook his head in disbelief and turned towards a group of men sitting around the fire.

'Tullus, what the fuck are you doing here?' Gaius cried in a loud voice.

Tullus turned at the sound of his name and blinked in surprise as he saw Gaius. Behind him a soldier was on his knees punching the ground. The man was howling in pain. Tullus grinned in delight at the sight of his old friend. Then he turned to the man behind him.

'You will get that one for free,' he cried. Without waiting for an answer Tullus strode towards Gaius. A leather bag was slung over his shoulder and the Volscian was wearing a simple white tunic.

'What are you doing here?' Gaius gasped.

Tullus grinned and patted Gaius's horse on her flank.

'Well after you came to fetch me to fix that decurion's toothache, I realised that I actually liked being a dentist. So, I decided to accompany the army and offer the soldiers my services. You won't believe the demand around here for a good dentist. I have never seen so many rotten mouths before.' Tullus grew serious. 'I have made a huge amount of money Gaius,' he whispered.

Gaius shook his head in disbelief. Then he straightened up and turned to look off into the distance.

'It's a shame Tullus,' he muttered sadly, 'I am just about to leave the camp. I have orders that are going to take me to the eastern coast. I will catch up with you when I return my friend.'

'Fuck that,' Tullus growled, 'I am going with you. Just wait here whilst I get my horse. I won't be long.'

***

The Roman camp had been placed close to a little mountain stream. From the crest of the hill upon which he stood Gaius stared down at the long lines of neat white tents. The camp was enclosed by an earthen rampart upon which stood a wooden palisade. A deep V shaped ditch ran alongside the edge of the walls. From his vantage point he could see a troop of horsemen leaving the main gate. The sentries patrolling the walls raised their arms and cried a greeting to their comrades. At Gaius's side Tullus sighed in relief. Seven days had passed since the two of them had left Fabius and his army. They had reached Apulia after two day's hard ride and when Gaius had inquired from the locals where he could find the Consul and his army, the villagers had told him to follow the trail of destruction across the Apulian countryside. It had not been hard to find. Gaius and Tullus had ridden past burnt and blackened ruins of cities, villages and farms. Everywhere they had encountered death and scenes of massive destruction. They had followed the plumes of black smoke rising into the sky. Publius Decius Mus had cut a swath across the Apulian and Samnite countryside and nothing had escaped him. The Apulian and Samnites that

Gaius had come across had been terrified and panic stricken. They had told him that an Apulian army had taken the field against the Consul but that Publius had beaten it with contemptuous ease, slaughtering thousands.

Gaius glanced at Tullus and the Volscian cleared his throat.

'I will go and see if I can find some business in the camp,' Tullus said. 'I will come and find you later.'

Then the two of them urged their horses on down the hill towards the Roman camp.

The Roman sentries manning the walls eyed them suspiciously as Gaius, followed by Tullus, rode up to the gate.

'I have an urgent despatch for the Consul,' Gaius cried.

The gates were opened and Gaius and Tullus trotted into the camp. They hadn't gone far before a centurion and a party of soldiers stepped out to block their path.

'You can give the despatch to me,' the centurion said. 'I will see that the Consul gets it right away.'

But Gaius shook his head.

'Sorry Sir, I have instructions to deliver my message verbally and in person to the Consul and only to the Consul.'

The centurion's face darkened and he glared at Gaius. 'Says who?'

In response Gaius handed over the leather despatch case he'd been given. The centurion opened it, unrolled the parchment and glared again at Gaius before turning to read the document.

'All right,' he grunted at last as he lowered the letter, 'Seems in order, follow me. You are lucky. The Consul has just returned.'

Gaius followed on behind the centurion as Tullus drifted off into the camp. The Consul's tent had been pitched in the very centre of the fort. Gaius dismounted and handed his horse's reins to a camp servant who led the animal away. Two soldiers were standing guard at the entrance of the tent. Gaius was about to step inside when he caught sight of a Fetial priest. He hesitated in surprise. It was the same Fetial who had come to Sora a year ago. The priest was bent over a table upon which lay the scattered remains of a chicken. He looked up as he saw Gaius staring at him. For a moment the Fetial's clever intelligent eyes registered no emotion. Then a crooked smile appeared on his lips.

'The boy who bears the mark of the Wolf still lives, whilst all around him men are dying,' the Fetial said in a quiet yet powerful voice.

'What does Fortuna want with me?' Gaius said. 'What is it that she wants me to do Holy Father?'

The Fetial examined Gaius curiously. Then he chuckled and turned back to the chicken on the table.

'You don't know, do you?' Gaius said, 'You don't know what I should do?'

The Fetial did not reply. Gaius looked away and entered the Consul's tent.

The tent was large and similar to the one in which he had met Fabius. Publius Decius Mus was washing his face in a bowl of water. He looked up as Gaius followed by the centurion stepped forwards and saluted.

'Gaius,' Publius exclaimed, 'This is a surprise. What brings you here?'

Gaius tried to smile. 'Sir, I have come straight from the camp of Consul Fabius. The Consul has won a great victory against the

Samnites in the Tifernus valley. The enemy have been scattered far and wide.'

Publius nodded and looked pleased. 'This is good news, this is very good news,' he said. Then his voice trailed off and his face suddenly grew pale. He paused and opened his mouth and stared at Gaius. 'But Fabius did not send you here to just tell me that did he?'

Gaius felt a lump in his throat. 'No Sir,' he forced the words from his mouth. 'I have come here to tell you that Quintus, your son, has fallen in battle. Your son is dead Sir. Fabius thought it best if I brought you the news.' Gaius took a step forwards and raised his hand. 'I have brought you his ring Sir.'

The tent fell silent. Publius was staring at the ring in Gaius's hand. Then he took it and turned away so that Gaius could not see his face.

'How did he die?' Publius said at last with a tight voice.

Gaius opened his mouth to breath. 'I was there with him until the end Sir. We charged the enemy ranks. It was chaotic; many men died Sir. I was thrown from my horse...' Gaius paused and looked down at the ground. 'He died like a soldier Sir. The last time that I saw him alive, Quintus had rallied our men and was leading another charge. He followed his orders until the end. You would have been proud of him if you had been able to see him Sir.'

The tent fell silent once more. Then the Consul turned and nodded gratefully at Gaius. Publius's face looked strained.

'Centurion, leave us,' he said.

The officer saluted smartly and strode out of the tent. Publius turned and poured himself a cup of wine from the jug that stood on a table. Then he poured another and handed it to Gaius.

'To the spirits of the departed,' Publius muttered raising his cup.

The two men downed the wine in one go. Then Publius looked up at Gaius with a sad smile.

'I am glad Quintus remembered who he was before the end,' he said quietly. 'He was my son and a father must have a son Gaius.' Publius paused. Then he fixed his eyes upon Gaius and there was something hard and uncompromising in his look.

'Quintus has gone. He is not coming back and I shall be needing a new son, a son to whom I can pass on everything when my time comes, a son who I can trust to lead my family and who will honour my name.' Publius paused. 'I have no other natural sons, so I shall adopt,' Publius said gently, 'I would like that man to be you. I would like you to take my name and become my adopted son.'

Gaius's eyes widened. For a moment, he was stunned and unable to reply. This was completely unexpected.

'If you accept my offer then get down on your knees and kiss the hand of your father,' Publius said.

Gaius was staring at the Consul. Then slowly he knelt and kissed the outstretched hand.

'When I die,' Publius said quietly, 'You shall take my name, you shall promise to be known as Publius Decius Mus, like me and my father before me.'

Chapter Thirty-Four - The Devotio of Publius Decius Mus

Publius reclined on his couch in his tent and poured himself another cup of wine. It was the early hours of the morning and Gaius was dog-tired and the wine was going to his head, but his adopted father had not allowed him to get any sleep. The two of them had been talking for hours with Publius doing the talking and Gaius listening. Publius took a sip of wine and Gaius stared at him wearily. His adopted father's capacity to consume wine was very impressive and so was his capacity to talk and talk and to ignore fatigue.

'As my son you will need to know what happened to your grandfather,' Publius said, 'Do you know what happened to him, Gaius?'

'I heard that he died at the battle of Veseris during the Latin War,' Gaius replied. 'I heard that he devoted himself to the gods of the underworld in order to win the battle.'

Publius nodded solemnly and turned to stare into space. 'Yes, that's right. I was ten years old when he died. I never really knew him. He was always away and there was little time for us to talk.' Publius smiled sadly, 'That is why I am so keen to spend some time with you now. I know you are bone tired but before you may go, I want you to hear my father's story.'

'Yes Sir,' Gaius replied forcing his eyes to remain open.

'He made our family fortune,' Publius said, 'He was a gambler, like myself and his bets made us all rich and raised us up in the world. The patricians hated us of course, for we were New men, common men who had risen above their station and according to them we had no right to be competing for high office. This angered your grandfather for he felt that a man should be treated with respect once he'd lawfully managed to raise himself up in the world. Gaining the respect of the patricians became an obsession for him but nothing that he did would impress them.

277

They hated us then and they hate us now. They will always hate us.'

'Is that why he performed the Devotio?' Gaius interrupted, 'Did he sacrifice himself in order to impress the patricians?'

Publius looked across at Gaius and nodded.

'Yes, I suspect that that was part of the reason,' he murmured. Publius paused. 'The Devotio is an act of love,' he said quietly, 'Your grandfather knew this and by sacrificing his life he was showing his love for Rome and his family. By uttering the sacred words and performing the holy ritual and by riding out to die in battle he believed he was saving Rome and all of us from ruin.' Publius smiled sadly. 'He chose death so that we may live. There is no greater act of valour and love than that Gaius.'

'I think I would prefer to win the battle and live,' Gaius replied.

Publius was once more staring into space. 'All my life,' he muttered, 'I have tried to live up to the standards set by my father and so far I feel I have succeeded. I have been Consul three times, I have expanded the family's wealth and I have been victorious in battle,' Publius sighed, 'But who will remember all of this in a few hundred years, who will remember us, who will remember what we did and what we achieved? It is likely that the House of Mus will be forgotten if we fail to continue to honour our name.'

The tent fell silent.

'As my son and heir,' Publius said at last and there was a sudden sternness in his voice, 'you shall strive to live by the code set by your grandfather. You shall ensure that our family name is revered and remembered. That will be your task. That is all that I ask of you.'

'I shall try and earn the respect of the gods and not be a coward,' Gaius murmured.

Publius was silent for a moment. 'Tomorrow I want you to go north to Arretium,' he said changing the subject, 'Your sister Decia needs help. She is isolated up there and I am worried about her. The Etruscan and Umbrian countryside is lawless and swarming with bandits, so you had better take a ship and make your way north along the coast. When you get to Arretium, give Decia all the support you can. She is the reason why the Etruscans are suing for peace but I suspect she will have made some powerful and dangerous enemies.'

Gaius nodded and closed his eyes.

Chapter Thirty-Five - Scodra

The prow of the ship rose and pitched as the galley ploughed through the sea. Gaius stood beside the mast steadying himself as the vessel groaned and plunged. The choppy waves smashed into the hull of the galley sending salty spray flying across the deck and the strong western wind was trying to push them further out to sea. On his left the grey Italian coastline was just about visible. It was afternoon and they had been heading north all morning. Gaius turned to look at Tullus. The big jovial Volscian was holding on tightly to the side of the boat. He looked unamused and his face had grown paler and paler as the hours had passed. Gaius smiled. Tullus had not said a word as they had boarded the ship but it had soon become clear that the Volscian was terrified of the water.

'It's only three days sailing and we shall spend each night ashore,' Gaius shouted at Tullus, as he tried to make himself heard above the shriek of the wind and the crash of the waves.

Tullus nodded but said nothing.

Gaius turned away. To his right the Adriatic Sea stretched away to the horizon. The ship's rowers had packed away their oars and were sitting about in small groups eating, talking and resting. A blast of cold spray hit the deck and splattered across Gaius's face and he raised his hand to wipe the water away. As he did so Tullus bent forwards and vomited over the side of the galley. Gaius however did not seem to notice. His thoughts were faraway. He had a new father and a new family and one day he was going to inherit a vast fortune and a noble and proud name. It was almost too good to be true. Tullus had been speechless when Gaius had told him. Gaius bit his lip pensively as he stared out across the sea. His fortunes may have changed dramatically he thought but he had also been given a heavy burden of responsibility and a steep path to climb. How was he going to equal and outdo the deeds of his new father and grandfather? They were and had been great and victorious Consuls, they had received the best education and they had grown up knowing they were destined for greatness. What was he compared to such men? How was he going to honour the proud and noble name that he'd been given? It was going to be a daunting task. He was going to have to learn fast. Gaius ran his hand over the stubble on his chin. But he was going to try he thought with sudden determination. He was going to try and honour the great name, which had been entrusted to him. He was going to earn the respect of the gods and he was not going to be a coward.

'Sails to starboard,' a voice suddenly yelled.

Gaius turned to look in the direction that the sailor was pointing and sure enough four white sails had appeared on the horizon and were bearing down on them fast. The captain of the galley muttered something under his breath and came towards the mast. He glared up at the lookout.

'Well, who are they? he cried at the lookout who was sitting high up in the mast. The sailor took his time in replying.

'They are certainly not Roman or Italian and they are too small to be Macedonian or Greek,' the lookout shouted at last. 'No, wait,' the man yelled suddenly. He paused. 'They look like Lemboi ships, captain' he screamed.

Beside Gaius the captain's face grew pale. In horror he turned to stare at the four sails that were bearing down on his ship.

'Illyrian pirates,' the captain whispered. He ran to the edge of the galley and peered at the approaching vessels. Then he turned and screamed at his sailors.

'Pirates, they are pirates, get back to your oars and turn us towards the coast! Move, move damn you.'

The galley erupted into a frenzy of activity as the rowers rushed to deploy their oars and take up their positions. Mesmerized Gaius stared at the four ships. They were approaching rapidly in a line with their sails bulging in the wind. As they drew closer he could see that they were smaller than the Roman galley. Banks of oars were plying the sea in perfect harmony.

'Move, put your backs into it, run for the shore, damn you,' the captain screamed as his rowers pushed their oars into the sea.

Gaius turned sharply to look at the coastline to port. The Roman galley had turned and was wallowing in the waves as the rowers cursed and shouted at each other as they tried to find their rhythm. Gaius felt a sudden tug of unease. The coastline was too far away. They were never going to make it. He swung round to look at Tullus. The Volscian was staring at the pirates in amazement. His earlier seasickness seemed to have been completely forgotten.

'Tullus, can you swim?' Gaius yelled.

The Volscian turned and stared at Gaius with large eyes. Then he shook his head. and Gaius's shoulders slumped.

'What will they do to us?' Gaius said turning to the captain.

The sailor was peering anxiously at the coastline. He looked grim. 'What do you think?' he hissed. 'They will take my cargo and depending on their greediness they will either make us all slaves or knife us and throw our bodies overboard. Then they will take my ship and sell her. Fucking pirates, they are nothing but scum. I hate them.'

Gaius turned to stare at the pirate ships. They were closer now and he could clearly see the men standing on the decks. They looked heavily armed.

'We're not going to make it,' the Captain hissed in despair as he too stared at the pursuing vessels.

The rowers seemed to have realised the same thing for their efforts were becoming increasingly uncoordinated and panic stricken. Gaius's hand came to rest on the pommel of his sword.

Tullus noticed the movement and his hand also came to rest on his sword. The Volscian's nervousness and fear seemed to have vanished. He gave Gaius a little sad smile.

'Row, row, for Jupiter's sake,' the Captain screamed in desperation.

Gaius did not move. His eyes were fixed on the approaching ships. They were closing in fast and he could see now how manoeuvrable and quick these little pirate ships really were. Onboard the ships their decks bristled with armed men. Gaius's heart sank. They were not going to out run their pursuers, nor were they going to be able to hold off any boarding parties. He glanced towards the coast. It was too far away to swim to and besides Tullus couldn't swim.

'Ah fuck this,' the captain hissed as the lead pirate vessel approached rapidly. Without another word the sailor dropped his knife on the deck and leapt overboard into the green swirling sea. Gaius whirled round and was just in time to see the man's head bob up before a wave obscured his view. A few moments later the lookout also plunged into the sea with a hoarse cry.

The rowers were still at their posts but their efforts were uncoordinated and they kept staring over their shoulders. Then a loud panic stricken cry rose up from amongst the benches and in an instant all order broke down and the rowers were up on their feet and dashing to retrieve their weapons. As Gaius looked on in horror he saw several of the rowers leap overboard into the waves.

'Tullus,' Gaius screamed, 'to me, stay beside the mast and do as I say, do exactly as I say.'

Tullus leapt towards Gaius just as the lead pirate ship came shooting past along the starboard side of the Roman vessel. The prow of the Lemboi cut straight through the banks of discarded oars, splintering the wood with a terrible cracking crash. Onboard the Roman galley the oarsmen shrieked and screamed as they rushed to defend the side of the ship. As the pirate ship came level, a swarm of Illyrians, small, dark haired and heavily armed men, jumped down onto the Roman deck. The pirates punched straight through the flimsy line of oarsmen and in a moment, the deck was turned into a melee of screaming, stabbing and dying men. A man with an axe came at Gaius. Gaius ducked just in time and the weapon slammed into the mast above his head. Tullus rammed his sword into the pirate's exposed chest and kicked the dying man backwards. Around them the sound of fighting was already dying away. Gaius was panting as he stared at the bloody carnage on the deck. The oarsmen lay where they had fallen and in the sea, bodies were floating, face down, their lifeless arms and legs spread out in the water. The rowers had not stood a chance. Around the mast Gaius and Tullus seemed to be the last men left alive. The pirates had surrounded them.

'Wait,' Gaius yelled as he raised his sword, 'Wait, I am the son of a Roman Consul. If you harm me or my companion you shall invite war with Rome. I say again, I am the son of Publius Decius Mus, Consul of Rome.'

The pirates looked unimpressed but for a moment they hesitated. Then a fierce looking man with a golden torc around his neck elbowed his way to the front and stared at Gaius for a long moment.

'This here is my ring, this will prove who I am,' Gaius said slipping the ring Publius had given him from his finger. 'I am the son of Publius Decius Mus. He is not faraway and he has an army of twenty thousand men.'

The man with the golden torc glared at Gaius. He looked like he was the captain of the ship that had boarded them. Around him the pirates had started to mutter in a language that Gaius could not understand. Gaius stretched out his hand and handed his ring to the pirate captain. The man took it without saying a word and for a moment he examined it carefully. Then he looked up.

'I have heard of the Roman Consul,' the pirate captain said in heavily accented Latin. He paused to study Gaius and Gaius thought he noticed a sudden greediness in the man's eyes. 'If you are his son then your father will pay us a good ransom for your release. Now you will come with me as my hostage.'

The pirate gestured at Gaius and muttered something in his own language and his men surged forwards and Gaius and Tullus were quickly disarmed and their arms pinned and bound behind their backs.

'Where are you taking us?' Gaius snapped as he was forced down onto his knees and a hood was pulled down over his head.

'Scodra,' the pirate captain growled.

Chapter Thirty-Six – Homecoming

PART 4 - Spring 295 BC

It was morning and the small group of silent men rode their horses down the Appian Way. There were six of them and they were clad in long brown riding cloaks and were being led by a Fetial priest carrying his holy spear. As the horsemen reached the crest of a hill they saw the walls of Rome in the distance. Gaius brought his horse to a halt and stared silently at the distant city. He looked tired. A black beard covered his chin and his cheeks were hollow and grey and he looked older than his twenty-one years. The Fetial turned to look behind him and halted in the middle of the road. For a while no one spoke. Then Gaius urged his horse on and the small party resumed their journey.

'Not far now Gaius,' Tullus said softly.

Gaius did not reply. His eyes were fixed on the distant walls and the nervous twitch in his left eye had started up again. He touched the birthmark across his neck. It no longer felt strange and embarrassing for the prophecy had helped him to survive. Two years had passed since he had last seen Rome, Cassia, Aeliana and his family. It felt longer, much longer but it was just two years since he and Tullus had been captured by the Illyrian pirates. The Illyrians had taken them across the sea to their pirate lair of Scodra. The journey had been a nightmare. For most of it he'd been hooded and bound. He had been regularly beaten with sticks. cold water had been poured over him in the dead of night and the pirates had frequently held mock executions where he'd been told that he was about to die. Scodra had been an inland city and his captors had marched him through villages, where he and Tullus had been subjected to all kinds of verbal and physical abuse. The women in these pirate villages had been the worst. They had thrown stones and emptied buckets of shit over him. All had blamed him, the son of a Roman Consul, for the loss of their men. The Roman policy and habit was to have captured pirates crucified without trial.

In the walled city of Scodra he and Tullus had been thrown into separate underground dungeons. Those first six months had been truly terrible. Gaius had been kept isolated from the other prisoners in a tiny, cramped and dirty cell. There had been no natural daylight, no window, no exercise, little human contact, little food and nothing but intolerable boredom, day after day, night after night. During those long dark months of solitary confinement, Gaius had come close to utter despair. His captors had told him nothing about the ransom negotiations and he had started to fear that every day was going to be his last. The stress, uncertainty, lack of news and sense of utter helplessness had taken its toll on him and he'd developed a nervous twitch in his eye. It was Tullus who had kept him alive. Each day the Volscian had sung out loud and the sound of Tullus's rich deep voice had reminded Gaius that he was not alone. The Volscian too, had paid a price for his stubborn singing for one night the drunken guards had entered his cell and raped him. But the singing had continued and day after day Gaius had crouched by his cell door waiting to hear the soothing Volscian melody. The guards had been unable to shut Tullus up and in that small victory there had been a spark of hope.

Then one day without warning their circumstances had improved. Gaius and Tullus had been taken out of the filthy underground prison and transferred to a small house. Within the confines of the high walls that surrounded them they had been able to do what they liked. The improvement in their conditions had been matched by a change in the guards' attitudes towards them. It was from their guards that Gaius was able at last to glean the news that contact had been made with his father and that a ransom for his release had been agreed.

But as the days had turned into weeks and weeks into months nothing had happened. Gaius and Tullus remained locked up in their house. The guards had been unable to enlighten Gaius and as a whole year passed he'd grown increasingly restless and agitated. What was causing the delay? His thoughts had turned to escape but that had proved impossible. As his frustration with the delay had grown Gaius had felt the familiar sense of despair creeping back. He'd become listless and angry and irritated by the slightest, smallest things. It was during those months of mounting boredom and helplessness that he had remembered the birthmark across his neck. The prophecy was superstitious nonsense but as the days had dragged on he had started to cling to that superstition, to revel in its absurdity for it gave him the one thing he needed and craved, it represented a way out, an escape from captivity. The prophecy had given him hope.

Then the day had come when his captors had taken him and Tullus away. They had left Scodra and had headed for the coast and there, on a sandy beach, Gaius had come face to face with the Fetial priest and he and Tullus had been exchanged and handed over to the priest and a small Roman fleet.

'You father instructed me to negotiate your release,' the Fetial had said.

On the journey back to Rome Gaius had learnt the reason for the delay in getting them released.

'Whilst you were in captivity a new king ascended the throne of the Kingdom of Epirus,' the Fetial had said. 'His name is Pyrrhus and it is he who delayed the negotiations for your release.'

'Why should he do such a thing?' Gaius had asked.

'Who knows,' the Fetial had shrugged, 'The King likes to keep his motives to himself. It doesn't matter, what is important is that you are free. Your family shall meet you in front of the gates of Rome, Gaius.'

***

288

As the small party rode towards the city gates they started to pass the tombs and graves of the dead. The Fetial walked his horse up to a small white marker stone and within sight of the Capena Gate, the priest raised his holy spear and halted before the stone. Publius Decius Mus and Quirinia stood just beyond it on the side of the road. They did not move as they caught sight of the horsemen. Gaius took a deep breath and dismounted. A young woman was suddenly coming towards him and for a moment he didn't recognise who it was. Then his eyes widened. It was Cassia. His sister had grown. She had become an adult, a young woman. Her hair was done up and held in place by a silver fibula and she was wearing a beautiful Stola. Without a word she flung her arms around her brother and buried her head in his chest. Gaius gripped her tightly and when he finally released her Cassia looked up and smiled. There was a single tear in her eye.

'I knew you would return,' she whispered. 'Welcome home Gaius.'

Gaius nodded and glanced in the direction of his adopted father. Publius Decius Mus and Quirinia remained silent and did not move. They looked solemn and serious and behind them Gaius caught sight of Crispus. The big Paeligni had his arms folded across his chest. The man had not aged at all. Gaius took a step towards them but the Fetial lowered his spear and blocked his path.

'You shall not cross the sacred Pomerium of Rome until you have been purified and the harmful spirits driven from your body. You shall be born again and accept the new name that is given to you. Only then may you cross,' the Fetial snapped.

Gaius looked up at the priest in bewilderment. Without another word the Fetial dismounted and gestured for Crispus to come forwards. The slave stooped and picked up a bucket that stood on the ground beside his feet and strode towards the priest. As he set the bucket down beside the Fetial Gaius saw that it was full of blood. The Fetial picked up the bucket and bidding Gaius to stand still, the priest poured the blood out in a circle around Gaius. Then the priest took a step back and muttered a few words and, as he did so, Publius and Quirinia stepped forwards and slowly walked around Gaius until they had completed a full circle. The Fetial raised his holy spear and chanted something in a language that Gaius had never heard before. Then he looked directly at Publius.

'How do you wish to name this boy, this son of yours?'

'I name him after myself, he shall be called Publius Decius Mus,' Publius said in a loud and clear voice.

The Fetial turned to Gaius. 'It is done,' he said sternly,' You may cross the sacred Pomerium and enter Rome and greet your father and mother.'

Gaius stepped across the circle of blood and embraced his adopted father. Then he did the same with Quirinia.

'It is good to have you back,' Publius murmured with a warm smile.

Gaius nodded and felt a hand tugging at his arm. It was Cassia. She pointed in the direction of a large family vault that stood on the opposite side of the road. A young woman was standing beside the tomb.

'She has waited for you for over two years,' Cassia said. 'But she dares not approach us. She is worried that you will no longer want to marry her.'

Gaius blinked as he recognised the young woman. It was Aeliana.

***

It was the early hours of the morning and through the opening in the roof of the house Gaius could see the bright stars. He lay on a couch. Tullus had gone to sleep early and Publius had given

290

Crispus and the household slaves the night off. Now his adopted father lay across from him on his own couch. He was studying Gaius intently. Quirinia and Cassia completed his audience. Cassia was staring at him eagerly and he had noticed the calm elegant composure in the way she now spoke and moved. Gaius could still not believe that the attractive young lady watching him was his little sister. In the few moments in which they had been alone together, she had told him that Pytheas, her tutor, had died a year ago and that Publius had arranged for her to have another tutor until a husband could be found for her. Publius had decided to leave the decision of who her husband was going to be to Gaius. That Cassia was now of eligible marriage age was beyond doubt and Cassia had left Gaius in no doubt that he could not postpone his decision forever.

Quirinia had aged and there was a sadness about her that never seemed to leave. Cassia had told him that his adopted mother had mourned for Quintus for an entire year. She had worn nothing but mourning clothes during that time and had refused to attend any parties, banquets, plays or social gatherings. Her son's death had affected her badly. But she had found some solace in her shrine to the plebeian chastity, that she had founded in her small garden. Cassia had told him that the house now had a regular stream of female visitors, all of whom came to pray at the shrine.

As Gaius recounted what had happened to him he glanced at his adopted father. Publius too had aged and he looked exhausted. He'd lost weight and dark bags had formed under his eyes and his hair was turning white. He looked tense and worn out and Gaius guessed that the pressure of state affairs and the war was beginning to take its toll on his father. The Consular elections were coming up again and it was likely, the Fetial had told him, that the people would once again choose for Fabius and Mus, for the two of them were a tried and tested combination.

When at last he fell silent the house too grew quiet. Then Publius cleared his throat. 'I should never have instructed you to take that ship. I should have sent you north with a strong escort,' he muttered.

'Don't blame yourself father,' Gaius replied. 'I survived and I am here, that is all that matters.'

'I would like to thank you Gaius for what you did for Quintus,' Quirinia said quietly in her posh voice. She turned to look at the floor. 'I know he liked you and I know you were a good friend to him. It pleases me to think that you were with him at the end. His spirit rests easy, of that I am sure.' She paused and to Gaius it seemed as if she was mustering up all her courage for what was coming. Then she lifted her head and looked at him. 'I accept you as my son, even though you do not have my blood. Your spirit and loyalty make up for that. When the time comes and if it is my lot to outlive my husband, then I shall defer to you Gaius, as father of my family.'

Gaius rose from his couch and came and knelt before Quirinia. He took her hand and bowed his head and kissed her hand.

'You have shown me great kindness,' he replied. 'I shall honour you as a true Roman mother whose virtue is beyond reproach.'

Gaius rose to his feet and from the corner of his eye he caught Cassia smiling at him. Quirinia looked away and remained silent but he could see that she was pleased.

'The Fetial has told me about the course of the war,' Gaius said turning to Publius. 'He has told me that even after all our victories against the Samnites, our position has deteriorated and that we face a grave situation. Egnatius has taken a Samnite army north. He has abandoned Samnium and has joined the Etruscans in Etruria. There is talk that he is organising an alliance against us. There is talk that the armed might of three nations will soon be converging on Rome.'

292

Publius nodded wearily. 'Yes, that is so,' he muttered. 'The appearance of Egnatius and his Samnites in Etruria has filled the Etruscans with renewed hope that they can beat us. They have broken off peace negotiations. The whole of the Etruscan League now favours war, as do the Umbrian cities.'

'What about Arretium and Decia, is the city still loyal to Rome?' Gaius asked.

Publius raised his hand irritably. 'Arretium will go over to the enemy within weeks. Decia reports that the populace is increasingly restless. Appius Claudius is in Etruria with his army, but he can't be in two places at the same time and he lacks the manpower to take on both the Etruscans and Samnites.' Publius paused to rub his eyes. 'Then there is this damned spying business. The Senate suspects that there is a Samnite spy in Rome who is providing the enemy with highly secret information on our strategy and troop movements. Last year the Samnites launched a number of raids deep into Campanian territory just when both Consuls were marching towards Etruria and the Samnite frontier was denuded of men. Then just a few months ago an entire legion was ambushed near Clusium. The news is bad, relentlessly bad. It cannot go on like this.'

Publius scowled and fell silent and Gaius was suddenly shocked by his adopted father's mood. If a veteran soldier like Publius could be so pessimistic then things had to be really bad. Gaius sighed and glanced at Publius, waiting for him to speak, but Publius remained silent, his eyes turned to the floor.

'Does the Senate have an idea of who this spy may be?' Gaius said at last, 'After all there surely can't be that many people with access to the Consul's decisions.'

Publius muttered something to himself and his face darkened.

'There are several suspects and theories but we have no proof,' he snapped. 'But if you were to ask me then I would point my finger at Appius Claudius. He has been present at all our councils and his son Centho has not been seen for months. It is strange and suspicious behaviour but I have no proof.'

Gaius looked surprised. 'But Claudius is one of the Consul's for this year,' he exclaimed, 'Are you saying that the Consul is betraying his own people, his own soldiers? Why would he do such a thing?'

Publius turned to glare at Gaius. 'Who knows?' he muttered. 'Maybe the Samnites are blackmailing him or maybe he wants to see the Republic defeated, so that he can crown himself King of Rome when our enemies come marching up the Sacred Way. The prick already hates anyone who does not belong to his own class. Maybe he thinks that with Etruscan help, he can restore the privileges and power that the patrician order once enjoyed. It is a good thing that his Consulship will soon be coming to an end, it has been a disastrous year.'

Gaius shook his head in bewilderment. That a Consul could betray his own people had never crossed his mind, but if what his adopted father was saying was true then it was terrible, disastrous news.

'But such matters do not concern you,' Publius said suddenly. 'Decia needs help. She is trapped inside Arretium. The Etruscan countryside is a very dangerous place for a Roman at the moment.' Publius looked up at Gaius. 'A supply column and reinforcements are leaving Rome for Claudius's army in ten day's time. I want you to go with them until you can slip into Arretium and get Decia out of there. You are to help her get out before it's too late. You are to bring my daughter home. Is that clear?'

Gaius looked down at the floor and nodded.

'But he has only just returned, he needs to rest,' Quirinia said suddenly turning to her husband. 'Ten days is no time at all.'

'Arretium may fall by then, there is no time,' Publius snapped irritably. 'Doesn't anyone realise that Rome itself may be under siege within weeks!'

The atrium fell silent after Publius outburst.

'There is something that I need to discuss with you before I go,' Gaius said at last, 'I have a woman, her name is Aeliana and I have decided that I want to marry her. I ask you father for your permission.'

From the corner of his eye Gaius noticed that Cassia was suddenly blushing. Publius looked thoughtful.

'This woman,' he replied, 'I understand that she is a tavern owner's daughter of no particular status or wealth. What then do you hope to gain from this marriage?'

'Nothing, but she will make me happy,' Gaius replied.

Across from him Quirinia stirred and the look on her face was doubtful.

'So you do not seek to advance your career and the position of this House by marriage. You are willing to give up the influence and power that a marriage with a well-connected, high born lady can bring you? When you enter the Senate you shall need these alliances, you shall need friends.' Publius sounded bewildered and annoyed.

Gaius nodded. 'Yes. She is a good woman and she will make an excellent mother and she will honour this family. As regards to the position of this House, I shall forge my alliances and make my friends on the battlefield.'

Publius grunted and muttered something under his breath and looked away. For a moment he seemed to be thinking it through.

But it was Quirinia who decided the matter. She turned to Gaius. 'Tell her to come and visit me and I shall have a talk with the woman and see whether she is suitable,' she said in her posh voice.

Publius glanced at his wife and for a long moment he was silent. Then he shrugged.

'Let it be so then,' he murmured.

Gaius looked pleased and glanced at Cassia. His sister was glowing with excitement.

***

It was still dark outside when Gaius gently shook Tullus awake. The Volscian looked tired as Gaius sat down on the end of his bed.

'Tullus,' Gaius whispered, 'What do you think of my sister Cassia?'

Tullus scratched his cheek and blinked. 'She is all right I suppose,' he muttered.

'Good,' Gaius nodded, 'For you have ten days in which to decide whether you want to marry her.'

Chapter Thirty-Seven - Conversations

Decia stood beside the window looking out at the armed men lounging about in the street below. It was dusk and the daylight was fading fast. She was a prisoner in her own house. She sighed. Arretium was teetering on the brink of something ugly and violent, with anti-Roman sentiment running high and Proculus, her useless husband, had seen it fit to lock her up in her own home for her own safety. For her own safety she thought scornfully. She had been unable to go out for over six weeks now and it was driving her crazy. She had tried to bully the guards to let her go but they had told her that they only answered to her husband. The guards were everywhere and it had been impossible to escape. She had thought about sending a letter to her father telling him of her plight but who would deliver it? There was no one she could trust apart from Luca her faithful slave boy, but Proculus would be the first to notice his absence and besides, she needed Luca to keep her informed of what was happening in the outside world.

Decia returned to her seat beside the table. She was alone. For a moment, she stared at the jug of wine that stood on the table. The wine was poisoned. She had laced it with hemlock, which Luca had managed to bring her, intending to feed it to her husband when the moment was right. Quirinia, her mother had told her once that this was the way women, since ancient times, had got rid of husbands who had not performed. But as she stared at the poisoned wine Decia was suddenly torn by indecision. She and Proculus no longer saw eye to eye. Over the past two years they had grown apart and had started to hate each other, but did Proculus really deserve to die for that? She ran her fingers lightly around the jug. He had not touched her in over a year; he had hardly spoken to her either. The situation was becoming intolerable and she had to do something, but murder?

From downstairs in the hall she suddenly heard voices. Quickly she placed the jug of wine back in her cupboard. Then she glided towards the doorway that led out onto the corridor. The slaves had already lit the oil lamps along the walls. Her view of the atrium was obstructed by a column but she recognised Vela's voice and then that of Marce and her husband. They seemed to be in high spirits. Carefully Decia stepped out of her room and glanced down into the atrium. In the dim light she was just in time to see Marce Larna disappearing into her husband's private rooms on the opposite side of the house. The rooms had a door and as Decia looked on it was closed and an armed guard took up position in front of it. Decia's cheeks began to glow with curiosity. What was going on? She glanced down into the atrium but there was no one else about. She turned to look at the closed door and the guard. There was just one doorway into her husband's private quarters. Ever since her marriage had effectively broken down, she and Proculus had been sleeping in separate rooms. But what were Vela and Marce doing here?

Then she had an idea. Quietly she strode along the corridor until she came to the last room. She slipped inside. It was a small room and used mainly as storage space. She paused to listen but the house was quiet. Carefully she undid her stola and laid the dress on the floor. Underneath she was clad in a simple white tunica and her strophium and subligaculum undergarments. The stola would only get in the way or get caught on something. Carefully she clambered over the casks, barrels and neat rows of amphorae until she reached the small open window. The window overlooked her neighbour's garden. In the fading light she could just about see the high wall that divided the two properties. Decia had considered trying to escape this way but the distance between the wall and the house was too great. She glanced down into her neighbour's garden and was relieved to see that no one was outside. For a moment, she hesitated. What if one of the guards saw her? Shouldn't she wait until it was completely dark? But by then she may be too late. Without waiting she grasped the edge of the window and heaved herself out and up until she was crouching in the windowsill. With her free hand, she felt around for the edge of the flat roof above her. Then she found it and with a mighty effort she pulled herself up and onto the roof. She rolled onto her back and lay there for a moment as she sought to get her breath back. The climb out of the window wasn't too difficult and she had learned how to do it by spying on her slave girls. The slaves had often come up onto the roof when they wanted to have some privacy. Her girls thought she didn't know about their little secret but she did.

As quietly as she could Decia began to crawl across the flat roof until she was directly over her husband's private rooms. She paused to listen. Nothing. She looked up at the sky. The light was fading fast and she could see the moon. She took a deep breath and poked her head over the side of the roof. The window was just below her but it was too far for her to see if anyone was in the room. She paused again and her ears strained to catch any noise but all she could hear was the crickets croaking and the sound of the traffic in the street outside her house. She took another deep breath and swung her legs over the side of the roof. For a moment she hung precariously in the air as her feet struggled to find a footing. Then she was standing on the windowsill. As quickly as she could she lowered herself through the window. The room was small and dark and apart from the window the only entrance was a square hole cut into the wooden floor. She crouched on the ground trying to control her breathing. Then from below her she suddenly heard voices. She stared at the square hole in the floor a couple of yards away. As her eyes adjusted to the dim light she noticed that a ladder led down into the room below her. She inched towards the hole and then lay still. She could clearly hear the voices below her now. A man whose voice she didn't recognise was speaking in accented Latin.

'Now that we have formed our alliance,' the man was saying, 'the general plan is to lure both Mus and Fabius to our camps near the town of Sentinum in the territory of the Senonian Gaul's. Our scouts report that the new Roman Consuls are about to set out northwards from Rome with two full Consular armies. Once they arrive we shall destroy them with our vastly superior numbers. We have had to form two separate camps for such is the size of our armed might. Four nations have gathered at Sentinum and it is at Sentinum that the fate of Italy will be decided once and for all. We Samnites have already had to abandon our homeland but we have not given up the fight. Rome dares to dream of being the sole ruler of Italy but we shall wrench that destiny from her hands and scatter her people to the winds.'

'You all know the prowess and ferocity of the Gauls,' Marce interrupted. 'They have come in their tens of thousands. With such allies, we cannot lose. With such allies, we will not lose.'

Decia's eye's widened in shock. What was this? Had the Gauls decided to join the alliance that had formed against Rome? If this was true, then it was terrible news. The Gauls were a truly formidable warrior people. Decia emitted a silent groan. No Roman child was ever allowed to forget how; only ninety or so years ago Brennus had sacked and occupied Rome. The stain of that shameful day had been seared deeply into her from the day she was old enough to understand. Never, never again must such a catastrophe be allowed to happen. It was every Roman's duty to prevent it.

'How many men do we have? How many do the Consuls bring?' Vela inquired.

'We have around eighty-five thousand men,' Marce replied, 'We expect that the Romans will have around forty thousand or so.'

'Will the Gauls fight or will they trick us like they did last time?' Vela asked sharply.

'They will fight; they fear the growth of Roman power just like all of us,' the stranger replied. 'I and Marce have received their solemn assurance made before their gods and so has Nerva, the general of the Umbrians. Rome is finished. Her time has come. Once we defeat Fabius and Mus we shall march on Rome and take the city. There will be nothing left to stop us.'

'Good, good,' another man interrupted smoothly and Decia shuddered as she recognised her husband's voice. 'That brings us back to our situation here in Arretium. The time for our uprising is at hand. As we all know, anti-Roman sentiment is running very high amongst the populace and the concentration of our combined forces at Sentinum has distracted the Romans. The time has come for us to act and put our plan into action. The Roman garrison is to be massacred and once we are in control of the city, Arretium will declare for the Etruscan League and join the war against Rome.' Her husband fell silent.

Decia stared up at the dark roof in disbelief. Her husband was planning to change sides. He was planning to stab his allies in the back.

'My men have done as you have requested and have smuggled the weapons into the city. They have been distributed amongst your supporters,' the stranger said breaking the silence. 'I will stay for a couple of more days to ensure that your supporters know what they are doing, after that I will need to return to my army.'

'Then everything is in place and we are ready?' Vela inquired.

The room was silent for a moment.

'Yes, we are ready,' her husband replied, 'The Roman garrison will be celebrating a feast in three day's time. They will be relaxing and I shall make sure that their guard is down. Then Vela, when you see my signal you will order the attack. You are to massacre them all. Every one of us should be left in no doubt that if we fail it will be us who will be crucified. We shall either win or we will die, make sure your supporters know this.'

'I am leaving for Sentinum in the morning,' Marce growled, 'As the League has elected my brother to lead the Etruscan army, I feel it's my duty to be with him. It's such a shame that I won't be here to see the uprising. The Roman scum deserve what is coming to them but I must go.'

The room fell silent again.

'What about your Roman wife? Should she die too?' Vela said quietly.

Decia froze. The room remained silent for a moment. Then her husband cleared his throat.

'No, once we are in control of the city I shall keep her here,' he replied. 'She may prove to be a useful hostage. Her father is one of the Roman Consul's after all.'

'She is dangerous,' Vela hissed, 'Maybe it would be better to kill her. Since she came here she has done nothing but cause us trouble.'

'No, she stays alive,' Proculus snapped, 'I want her as a hostage. That's my decision.'

Decia rose silently to her feet and turned to the window. She had heard enough. Her mind was reeling. Rome and her people were in terrible danger. Her father and Fabius may be skilled and experienced soldiers but how could they hope to defeat such a great host of men. Rome had fought many wars before but she had never done so against the combined might of four nations at the same time. Her father and Fabius were going to be obliterated. She had to do something. She had to try and help them but what could she do? She was on her own, a captive in her own house. She clambered out of the window and heaved herself up onto the roof. The sky had turned dark and in the heaven's the stars twinkled playfully. She rolled onto her back, caught her breath and started to crawl across the roof and as she did so an idea started to grow. It was desperate, shocking and distasteful but she could think of nothing else.

She had made it back to her own room and was pulling on her stola when she heard her husband's voice calling out to her. A moment later she heard his footsteps coming down the corridor towards her. Proculus appeared in the doorway and gave her room a cursory inspection. A tall rugged and older man appeared behind him. The stranger was dressed in Etruscan civilian clothes but he looked foreign.

'I must go out,' Proculus muttered, 'I have some business to attend to. Marce and Vela are my guests tonight. Go downstairs and entertain them whilst I am away. I will be back by midnight; it might be later.'

Her husband turned to leave.

'Who is your friend?' Decia inquired staring the tall stranger in the eye. The man seemed unruffled by her sharp gaze. A little knowing smile appeared in the corner of his mouth as he examined her.

'His name is Egnatius,' Proculus snapped, 'he has come up from the south for a few days.'

Chapter Thirty-Eight - The Actress

Decia watched as her husband and the tall stranger disappeared into the hall. A moment later she heard him talking to the guards at the front door. Then his voice faded and she heard the door slam shut. She retreated to her room and leant against the wall and closed her eyes. Did she have the courage to see it through? It was a desperate idea. It was a disgusting idea but there was no time to think of an alternative. She took a deep breath and opened her eyes. She would do this. Her countrymen needed her; her father needed her. She steeled herself. There was no one else who could do this but her.

Marce and Vela were giggling together like children when Decia came downstairs. As they caught sight of her the giggling stopped abruptly and Marce rose to his feet and dipped his head respectfully. Vela glanced at her husband and then, with a little insolent shrug, she too rose to her feet and greeted her hostess. Vela was clad in a colourful dress with distinctive patterns and on her head, she was wearing a beautiful veil that drooped down over her shoulders.

Decia nodded politely at her guests and for a moment she studied Vela's clothes with sudden interest. Then she glanced at the table in the atrium, which was covered with an assortment of different food dishes.

'Bring us some more wine, after that you may leave us,' she said turning to the slave who was standing beside the table.

Vela and Marce were silent as the slave refilled their wine cups and left the jug on the table before vanishing into the kitchen.

'We have had our differences you and me, haven't we?' Decia said turning to look at Vela, 'and I suppose that you must hate and despise me. No, please hear me out,' Decia said with a little shake of her head as she lay down on the couch opposite her guests. 'My own husband keeps me a prisoner inside my own home and I and he no longer share the same bed, or meals or anything for that matter. I do not want your pity but I would like you to understand something.'

'We have nothing but the greatest respect for you Decia,' Marce said grandly. On her couch Vela smiled.

'Good,' Decia said returning the smile, 'This is difficult for me,' she paused and looked up. 'I have always tried to remain loyal to my family and to promote their interests,' she swallowed nervously. 'It was never my intention to become your enemy. It was just that my interests always seemed to diverge from yours. But now I have heard about this grand alliance, this coalition of nations who are aligned against Rome and I do not think that we shall be able to win.' Decia took a deep breath and glanced down at the floor. 'I would like to be on the winning side. What matters to me is that my family survives, that's all I care about.' She looked up at Vela. 'I want us to be friends,' Decia said quietly. 'I want us to forget about what has happened in the past.'

The atrium fell silent. Marce looked away with a bemused little smile. Vela was studying Decia closely. Then she smiled showing off a perfect line of white teeth.

'You want to be friends with us now,' Vela said in slightly mocking tone. 'Well dear, I am not so sure how I feel about that. Does Rome and your father mean so little to you now?'

'We cannot possibly win this war,' Decia said as she drained her cup of wine and slowly rose to her feet. 'I want to be on the winning side and if that means being humiliated by you, then I shall do so for the sake of my family. Life will go on after this war has ended. I don't want to spend it living as I do now.'

Decia glided across the floor and as she passed behind Marce she lightly ran her fingers over his shoulders and neck. Then she bent down so that her mouth was close to his ear.

'What must I do to become friends with you and your wife?' she whispered.

She felt his body tense. Then he turned to look up at her. For a moment, his eyes were filled with surprise.

Decia glanced at Vela and then back at Marce and as she did so Marce's eyes filled with sudden lust.

'Well you are full of surprises Decia,' he murmured. Then he kissed her and as he did so his hand stretched out to fondle her breasts. Decia broke away and looked at Vela. She was lying on her couch staring at the spectacle in silence but Decia could see that she was excited by what was happening. Without a word Decia took Marce by the hand and stretched out her other hand to Vela. After a momentary hesitation Vela rose from her couch and took her hand.

'Not here,' Decia whispered, 'Let's go to my bedroom.'

***

Decia collapsed back onto the bed as Vela's gasps and moans slowly faded away. She was naked and her body glistened with sweat. In the dim light she could hear Marce's faint panting. He lay beside her staring up at the ceiling. All three of them were stark naked. For a while they were silent.

'Gods you are a good fuck,' Marce exclaimed at last.

Decia closed her eyes and in the dim light no one saw the sudden shame that appeared on her face.

'My husband neglects me,' Decia whispered, 'sometimes I feel so lonely that I think it would be better if I were dead.'

Marce chuckled. Then Decia felt cold female fingers grasp her chin and press her into the cushion. Vela was suddenly leaning over her. In the dim light, she could just about make out the woman's face.

'If you want to die it can be arranged,' Vela said huskily.

Decia struggled to free herself but Vela rolled on top of her so that she was straddling Decia and pinning her to the bed.

'You said you want to be our friend,' Vela exclaimed, 'Prove it. Prove to me that you mean what you say.'

Decia gave up her struggle and turned her head away but Vela forced her to look up at her. There was a cruel triumphant gleam in Vela's eyes as if the woman revelled in her own power and relished seeing the humiliation of her rival.

'All right,' Decia cried, 'I am your friend. I swear it. I will prove it to you. When the Consuls leave Rome to confront the Etruscan League and your allies, they will leave Rome practically defenceless. The forces left behind to guard the city are desperately weak. The Senate is bluffing. They are gambling that no enemy army will advance on the city whilst the Consuls are away.'

At her side Marce grunted in surprise. Vela stared down at her in silence.

'If an Etruscan or Umbrian army were to evade the Consuls,' Decia muttered wearily, 'They would be able to march on Rome unopposed and take the city. The Senate has ordered that every able-bodied man be sent north with the Consuls. They are terrified by the alliance that has formed against them.'

Marce sat up and turned to look at her with sudden interest. For a moment, no one spoke. Then Decia felt Vela's grip on her chin relax. Marce grunted and muttered something to himself. Decia suddenly felt Vela's fingers stroking her cheek.

'You are a pretty little thing aren't you,' Vela whispered hoarsely, 'Now do it to me again with your tongue.'

***

Her bedroom had grown quiet when Decia opened her eyes. The room was dark for the oil lamp had gone out. Decia blinked. How long had she been here? She would have to hurry. She glanced at the dark shape on the other side of the bed. Vela too seemed to be asleep for she could feel the woman's steady regular breathing. Decia closed her eyes and then slowly sat up. The two sleeping bodies beside her didn't stir. Cautiously she slipped from the bed and turned to look at the floor where their discarded clothes lay in a great heap. Her heart was thumping in her chest as she stooped and quickly gathered the clothes into her arms. Then with a final glance at Marce and Vela she slipped out of her room and tiptoed along the corridor to her dressing room. The house was dark and silent and she guessed that the slaves had all gone to bed. Inside her dressing room she flung the clothes on the ground and as quickly as she could, slipped into her undergarments and tunica. Then she picked up Vela's multi coloured and beautifully patterned stola and pulled it over her head. The dress was slightly too big for her but it would have to do. She thrust her feet into her shoes and rummaged around amongst the clothes until she found what she was looking for. Carefully she placed Vela's veil over her head. She turned to look at herself in the mirror. Then she grasped the veil and brought it across her face so that only her eyes were showing. It looked a little odd but it would have to do. She turned for the doorway and poked her head out into the corridor. The atrium lamps had all gone out but the two lamps in the hall way were still burning.

Quickly and silently she descended the stairs and crossed the atrium. As she approached the hall she suddenly froze as she saw a figure sitting on a stool beside the front door. The figure was bent forwards with his elbows on his knees and he was holding his head in his hands as if he were asleep. Decia forced herself towards him and as she came up to the front door the figure suddenly raised his head. On seeing her, the startled man jumped to his feet. It was Luca. Decia raised her veil across her face and nodded at the door. For a moment Luca looked confused as he recognised his mistress. Then he seemed to understand for a blush spread across his cheeks. Decia gestured at the door and Luca nodded. A moment later he inserted a key into the lock and opened the door. As Decia stepped out into the cool night air Luca bowed politely. Decia had taken one step outside when three armed men moved to bar her way. They peered at her suspiciously. Luca appeared at Decia's side and gave the men his all-clear signal.

'What's this? Don't you recognise me? I am Vela. I am your master's guest,' Decia said boldly trying to imitate Vela's voice. Her attempt sounded pathetic but she was banking on the hope that the guards had only seen Vela and not heard her speak. As she strode towards the men with her veil covering her face they moved aside to let her pass. Decia felt light headed with joy and relief as she stepped out into the street and vanished into the darkness. She had done it. So far, so good. She tried to calm her breathing. There was not much time. If either Vela or Marce woke up or her husband came home, they would soon notice that she was missing. She broke into a little run. She had to hurry.

As she hurried on through the dark and deserted streets she thought again about her plan. She had no idea whether it was going to work. The chances seemed slim but if Marce kept to his schedule and left the city as he'd said he would then there was a chance that it would work. Suddenly she turned and peered into the darkness. Had that been someone following her? But in the dark street nothing moved. She shook her head in disgust at her own jitteriness and continued on her way. In the night sky a multitude of stars twinkled. Somewhere in the city she heard a man's scream. Then as she came round a corner she saw her destination. The old Etruscan barracks building loomed up in the pale moonlight. The darkness obscured the two gigantic Roman banners that hung from the walls on either side of the main gate. The Roman garrison had been billeted inside the barracks. She halted and pressed herself up against the wall of a house. The street ahead seemed deserted and quiet. She peered into the darkness trying to spot anything unusual but she saw or heard nothing. Satisfied at last she turned to look at the barracks. She had to warn the Roman commander and his men. She had to warn them about the impending uprising in the city.

She stepped away from the wall and started out towards the main barracks gate. It wasn't far now. A triumphant smile appeared on her face. She had done it. Her plan had worked. To her right she suddenly sensed movement in the darkness. A boot scoffed on a cobblestone and then a hand came out of the darkness and clamped itself around her mouth. Decia cried out in shock. A man cursed and then someone was dragging her into an alley. Decia twisted and tried to break free but the man's grip was too strong. She struggled on but it was no use. The man dragged her deeper into the alley and suddenly an oil lamp was thrust into her face. In its light, she suddenly caught sight of her attacker.

'You,' the man gasped in surprise.

With a horrified expression Decia stared into the face of the stranger who had visited her house earlier that day, the man her husband had called Egnatius. Panic stricken she slammed her knee into the man's groin. Egnatius doubled up with a deep groan of agony and the oil lamp crashed onto the ground. Close by she heard a second man cry out in alarm but his path was momentarily blocked by Egnatius's groaning body. Decia whirled round and fled back the way she had come. Behind her she heard running feet. She shot out of the alley and into the main street. From the direction of the barracks she heard running feet racing towards her. Instinctively she turned and fled back the way she had come. Behind her she heard a shout and then another. She nearly tripped over her dress. Panic gave her strength but she was never going to outrun her pursuers. Wildly she looked around for a place to hide. In the darkness she could see very little. Then she saw a faint glimmer of light off to her left. The light was coming from a house and beside the building was a dark alley. She swerved and banged into a cold hard stonewall before she found the alley entrance. Then she vanished into the darkness. It was not a moment too soon. Seconds later she heard the sound of running feet moving up

310

the street. She stumbled on down the alley slowing her pace as the sound of her pursuers faded. At last, panting and exhausted, she collapsed beside a doorway. The alley stank of piss and shit but she didn't care. Her heart was pounding in her chest and the shock of coming face to face with her husband's friend had not yet worn off. As she fought to regain her breath she tried to think about what to do. She couldn't go home and this Egnatius and his men must have been watching the Roman barracks so she couldn't go there either. She groaned and buried her head in her hands. She had nowhere to go to. Then she looked up. That was not true she thought. There was one place and one person she could try. It was a desperate act but she had no choice. The whole city would be out looking for her when daylight returned.

Chapter Thirty-Nine - Rome gathers its Strength

The field of Mars echoed to the clash and crunch of arms, boots and the shouted commands of officers as they went about drilling and training the thousands of men who'd been packed into the flat space just beyond the walls of Rome. Gaius, followed closely by Tullus, strode past the training exercises and headed towards the Consul's tent that had been erected close to the altar to Mars. It was morning and the sky was clear and blue. Gaius was clad in his armour and as he approached the tent he removed his helmet. The guards at the entrance recognised him and saluted smartly. Gaius turned and grinned at Tullus.

'Don't get into trouble, my sister won't like that. I shouldn't be long,' he said.

Tullus nodded and turned away. It had taken the Volscian nine days to decide but on the ninth day, yesterday, he had finally come to Gaius and told him that he would marry Cassia if she would have him. Gaius had laughed and told him that the decision was not up to his sister but that he was glad Tullus had agreed. The two of them had embraced briefly and cracked some jokes about brother in laws but since then Gaius had had no time to tell Cassia the news. He was hoping he would be able to have a word with her before he left for the front. The girl deserved to know who her husband was going to be.

He entered the tent. A gaggle of staff officers stood clustered around a table behind which Publius was sitting. They were all examining a large map of central Italy. Gaius saluted.

'You sent for me Sir,' he said.

Publius looked up and nodded at the men around the table. 'That will be all,' he said. The officers saluted and filed out of the tent until only Publius and Gaius remained.

'Congratulations on being elected Consul again father,' Gaius said.

Publius grunted. 'Yes, it's good to see that the Roman people have such faith in me and Fabius. We shall do our best, as usual. But the war has taken a turn for the worse now that the Gauls have weighed in against us.'

'The Gauls,' Gaius's face grew pale, 'They have declared war on us?'

Publius nodded solemnly and fixed his eyes on the floor. 'They have indeed. We are now facing the might of four nations and they have combined their armies near a town called Sentinum. Our scouts have reported that the Gauls have crossed the mountains in their tens of thousands. It's not a pretty picture. Gods forbid that we see a repeat of the disaster of the Allia. Your grandfather would never forgive me. Jupiter would have me flogged for all eternity.'

Gaius sighed. 'This is bad news,' he murmured, 'But Roman arms will triumph in the end. I am confident of that.'

'Of course they will,' Publius growled looking up and studying his adopted son. For a moment, he was silent. Then the Consul cleared his throat. 'I want you to head north into Etruria at dawn tomorrow. You are to find Appius Claudius and his army and give him this letter.' Publius retrieved the rolled up parchment bearing his official seal set in wax and handed it to Gaius. 'The letter from the senate confirms the election of myself and Fabius as the new Consuls and it orders Appius to lay down his power and return to Rome at once. His army is to remain in their camp and await my arrival.' Publius took a step towards Gaius and laid his hand on his adopted son's shoulder. 'If that prick gives you any trouble I want you to report it to me at once. Remember what I said about spies in our midst.'

Gaius dipped his head in acknowledgment.

'I am promoting you to tribune,' Publius continued, 'Tomorrow I want you to take command of the six companies of Triarii of the Third Legion. They are to act as escorts to the supply wagons that I am sending to Appius's army. In addition, you will take the Campanian horse with you. There are a thousand of them. Treat them well; they are our allies and they are an elite unit. We can't afford to lose any of those horsemen before the decisive battle. Remember, they are our allies, not citizens; so you will have to treat them with some degree of independence. You will take your men to Appius's camp and instruct them to remain there until I arrive to take command.'

'Yes Sir,' Gaius's face glowed with sudden excitement.

'You will be charge of over two thousand men. Do you think you can handle that?'

Gaius nodded. 'I can Sir,' he said quietly.

'Good,' Publius looked away, 'When you have carried out your orders you are to proceed on to Arretium. You are to get my daughter out of that shit hole and bring her back to Rome. I am sending Crispus with you to help you. Take whatever force you need in order to get it done and Gaius, if those Etruscans try to obstruct you, obliterate them.'

'What about Decia's husband? I thought he was an ally. What should I do if he objects to his wife's departure?'

'I don't give a rat's arse what that man thinks,' Publius growled. 'If we lose this coming battle then nothing is going to matter much anymore. Just get Decia out of there alive. Report back to me when you have done so.'

Gaius saluted.

Publius was muttering to himself. Then he came up to Gaius and there was a sudden feeling in the old man's face.

'When we finally do meet our enemy in battle, I will need you at my side,' Publius said. 'Make sure that you are there.'

**

Outside Gaius blinked in the bright sunlight. Then across the crowded plain he caught sight of long lines of tethered cavalry horses. He started towards them slapping the two letters he'd been given against his thigh. Moments later Tullus was at his side. The Volscian was looking at Gaius with curious excitement.

'We are to leave tomorrow,' Gaius murmured, 'He has given me command of two thousand men. I had better go and meet their commanders right away.'

Tullus grinned and Gaius could see that he was impressed. 'Well it does help when your father is the Consul,' Tullus replied. 'Did he mention whether he needed any dentists?'

Gaius shook his head and there was sudden sternness about him. He turned on Tullus and grasped his friend's shoulders.

'You have a decision to make,' Gaius said quietly, 'You can either stay here in Rome with your bride to be or you can come with me. I shall not judge you either way. This is not your war Tullus; this is not your people's war. Maybe it would be better if you didn't come with me on this one.'

Tullus grinned and looked up at the sky. 'You still don't see it do you,' he muttered. 'My fortune is bound to you and your family. It has been so since that first day when we defended the wall. I know it and the gods know it. My fortune is bound to yours Gaius so don't be stupid; ofcourse I am coming with you. You are going to be a great man one day and I am going with you on that journey.'

Gaius touched the birthmark on his neck and Tullus nodded. His friend's eyes sparkled with sudden fervour.

'All right,' Gaius growled. 'Enough, let's go and find these officers.'

***

The Campanian cavalry officers were clad in splendid armour and tunics that made Gaius feel conspicuously plain. They had formed a semi-circle around him and their hard weather beaten faces were watching him intently as he explained his orders. Their leader was a man called Calavius. He was small, wiry and nearly twice as old as Gaius and the scars along his arms and across his face testified to a life that had been devoted to war.

'Don't worry boy,' Calavius growled in accented Latin when Gaius at last fell silent, 'We will cover the column, you can count on me and my men. We are the best horsemen in all of Italy.'

Gaius turned to examine his officers. They all seemed to be veterans and most of them were much older than himself. Choosing his words carefully he spoke to them.

'We have already fought together. I was with the Consul Fulvius three years ago when the Samnites caught us in the mountain pass on our way to Bovianum. You and your men saved me and my company that day.'

A smile spread across the faces of the Campanians and they glanced at each other.

'We have heard of you too,' Calavius said suddenly as a little smile appeared on his face. 'The boy who carries the mark of the wolf on his neck. The boy destined to save Rome. Don't let it go to your head. We do not want to lose you just yet. But the men do love a good story.'

Gaius blushed with sudden embarrassment and the Campanians burst out laughing. Then Calavius slapped Gaius on his back with a good-natured grin.

***

Appius Claudius did not look pleased to see Gaius. He glared as him as Gaius saluted and proffered the letter from his adopted father. The two men stood in Appius's tent. It had taken Gaius over a week to move his slow-moving column of supply wagons up to the Roman camp deep in Etruria but he had made it without any significant difficulties or mishaps. The thrill of having his first command, even if it was only a small temporary one, had been intoxicating and he'd been forced to control himself and temper his excitement and appear calm when he was anything but calm. Only once had they sighted a roving Gallic war band but the invaders had withdrawn quickly when they had seen the size of the Roman column.

'So I have heard that your father has been elected Consul,' Appius growled as he tore apart the seal on the letter and unrolled the parchment. He read quickly and when he was finished he grunted and dropped the parchment onto the table. Then he turned and placed his hands on his hips and examined Gaius with a contemptuous look.

'I have heard about you,' Appius said. 'You are Publius's adopted son. What were you before that? A simple farmer's son from the colonies. I suppose that you now consider yourself one of us, one of the best men of Rome, but let me tell me you something, you boy, you are nothing, you owe everything to your adopted name. History is not going to remember you. Rome is not going to remember you.'

Gaius kept his eyes on the back of the tent as the ex-Consul took a step towards him and challenged him to make a reply.

'Will that be all Sir?' Gaius replied stiffly.

For a moment Appius's aggressive eyes flashed dangerously. Then abruptly he turned away. 'Centho, my son tells me that you saved his life at the battle of Tifernus,' Appius snapped. 'You wasted your time on that boy. He doesn't deserve to live, not after committing that blunder. He is a disgrace to his family.'

An awkward silent followed. Then Appius glanced at the parchment on his table and gestured for Gaius to leave. Gaius saluted, turned on his heels and left the tent. Outside he saw Tullus and Crispus spooning some hot soup into their mouths and he veered towards them.

'The man is such an arsehole,' Gaius muttered as he took Tullus's spoon from the Volscian's hand and dipped it into the pot of soup that was hanging over the campfire.

Tullus cried out in protest and tried to snatch his spoon back but Gaius pushed him away with a friendly shove.

'Your father should have the whole patrician class thrown from the Tarquin rock,' Crispus said with sudden bitterness as he stared at Appius's tent.

Gaius frowned and glanced at the slave. Crispus had been silent for most of the journey from Rome and Gaius had guessed that he was none too happy about being sent away from the comforts of the family home. But the sudden bitterness in the man's voice surprised him.

'They are not all bad. Fabius is a decent man,' Gaius replied spooning the hot soup into his mouth, 'You wouldn't throw him off the Tarpeian rock would you?'

'He has the Roman arrogance,' Crispus snapped, 'You all do. You think the world belongs to you.'

And with that the big man stomped off into the camp.

Gaius opened his mouth in surprise as he watched Crispus walk away. He was just about to call him back when Tullus nudged him and shook his head.

'What's the matter with him?' Gaius muttered.

Tullus was staring at Crispus, 'On our way here,' the Volscian said quietly, 'Crispus got into a fight with a couple of

318

Campanians. I didn't tell you about it because you seemed to have a lot on your mind. He called them slaves. He knocked one of them unconscious with a single blow. It's probably best to let him cool down. Fuck knows what is bothering him but I don't think he's ready to talk about it.'

Gaius grunted and turned to watch Crispus disappear into the camp.

Chapter Forty - Rebellion

The horsemen clattered noisily along the street in single file and as they moved deeper into the city the Etruscan civilians quickly stepped out of their path. Gaius rode at the head of the thirty Campanian riders. He'd selected them to accompany him to Arretium and he was glad he'd brought an escort for the mood inside the city was tense and hostile. He glanced at the civilians who lined the edge of the street. They stared back at him in silence, with sullen and resentful eyes and here and there he saw openly scornful faces peering at him and his men. The Etruscans did not want him here. He was a foreigner, an oppressor. Gaius fixed his eyes on the street ahead and tried to ignore the silent spectators. It was an unpleasant experience, riding through a hostile crowd. The sooner he could leave this place, the better he thought. Close by a stone clattered against the wall of a house and Gaius whirled round in the direction from which it had been thrown, but all he could see was an open window.

At last as he turned a corner he caught sight of the Roman banners draped from the walls of the old Etruscan barracks building and he sighed in relief. The gates to the barracks were closed but on the walls, he could see armed soldiers. He came to a halt beside the gates and looked up at the guards. A few moments later the gate swung open and Gaius raised his hand and ordered his men to follow him as he trotted into the central courtyard. As he dismounted he saw a centurion striding towards him. The man peered at him suspiciously.

'Who are you? I was not expecting any reinforcements,' the officer cried.

'I am here on private business,' Gaius replied as the two men saluted each other, 'Publius Decius Mus, the Consul has instructed me to find his daughter and take her back to Rome. I thought it wise though if I paid you a visit first. Are you the officer in charge of the garrison?'

'I am, my name is Remus, I am in command of Arretium,' the centurion said in a proud voice.

Gaius glanced at the soldiers who were closing the gates behind them. 'I just rode through your streets, centurion,' he said. 'Are the Etruscans normally this hostile?'

Remus muttered something under his breath and nodded. 'Some are I suppose. There is a section of the populace, mostly the poorer people who don't like us but it's never anything serious. They know better than to pick a fight with my men. We had some trouble a couple of years ago just before the battle of Volaterrae but since then it's been quiet. Proculus and the Cilnii help to maintain order and the wealthier families seem to be on our side.'

'Sounds like an ideal posting,' Gaius said.

Remus shrugged, 'The food is good and the whores are entertaining, what more could a man want?'

Gaius nodded. 'Good,' he muttered, 'I won't take up much of your time centurion. I will leave my men here with you. We should be gone by tomorrow morning. Can you see to it that my men and their beasts are fed and get a little wine? We have a long journey ahead and I need them to be rested.'

'I will get my men to bring them some food,' Remus said.

***

Gaius slid the latch across the door and peered out through the small vent. The streets outside the barracks looked normal and he saw nothing unusual. He closed the latch and turned to Tullus and Crispus who were standing behind him. Both of them had swords hanging from their belts. They were staring at him waiting for him to speak.

'It looks all right,' Gaius muttered, 'So this is the plan. The three of us will go to Decia's home. We shall ask her to come with us

321

to the barracks. The excuse will be that there is someone there to see her. Once she is with us in the barracks I will tell her the truth.' Gaius sighed, 'Let's hope that my sister doesn't object.'

'What happens if she is not at home?' Tullus said.

'Then we shall wait for her to come home. My father gave me strict instructions. He wants her out of here as soon as possible. So, let's do this as quickly as possible and then get out of this shit hole.'

Gaius turned to Crispus, 'Can I count on you, big man?'

Crispus nodded but said nothing. Since his argument with them in Appius's camp he'd hardly said a word to Gaius or Tullus. The big Paeligni seemed to have withdrawn into a world of his own.

***

It was the middle of the afternoon. Gaius strode boldly down the street towards Decia's home and as he did so he remembered the last time he had visited his sister. He had been alone on that occasion. It had been over two years since he'd last seen Decia and he was looking forward to their meeting. There was a lot to talk about but he doubted that he would get the time. He recognised her house immediately. Three armed men were standing guard outside the front door and Gaius raised his eyebrows and glanced at Tullus who shrugged. As he approached the guards turned to block his path.

'I am looking for Decia, this is the lady's house is it not?' Gaius said.

'Who wants to know?' one of the men replied.

'Just let us speak to the lady,' Gaius growled, 'or do I have to come back with the entire city garrison and force my way inside?'

The guard hesitated and then banged his fist on the door. A moment later it was opened by a slave boy.

'We are here to see Lady Decia, is she at home?' Gaius called to the boy.

The slave boy looked confused. For a moment, he stared at the visitors. Then he seemed to recognise Gaius. The boy opened his mouth and his lips moved but there was no sound. Gaius frowned and then remembered that Decia had a slave boy who'd lost his ability to talk. This must be the boy. However, before he could say another word, a finely dressed man thrust the slave aside. The man glared at Gaius from the doorway.

'My name is Proculus, I am Decia's husband. What do you want with her?' he said in an aggressive, impatient voice.

'I am her brother. I have come to visit her. May we come in to see her?'

Proculus stared at Gaius in surprise. For a moment, he said nothing. 'I don't recognise you,' he sneered. 'Decia has only one brother and he is dead. Who are you?'

Gaius took a step towards the door and raised his hand. 'Like I said I am her brother, her new brother,' he replied. 'See this ring here, this bears the mark of the House of Mus. My name is Gaius. She will know who I am.' Gaius said confidently.

Proculus looked confused. He glanced at Tullus and Crispus and then back to Gaius before taking a step forwards and peering at the ring on Gaius's outstretched fingers. Then he looked up and there was a strange gleam in his eyes.

'Decia is not at home,' he said as he stepped back into his house and slammed the door shut behind him.

Startled Gaius took a step back and glanced at Tullus. The Volscian frowned. What strange behaviour was this? The guards sniggered and moved to block the entrance to the door

Devotio: The House of Mus

before folding their arms across their chests. Defeated Gaius turned away and beckoned for Tullus and Crispus to follow him. What was going on? What kind of man welcomed his wife's family in such a manner? They had only moved half way down the street when Gaius heard someone laughing. He looked up and caught the eye of a youth who was leaning casually against the wall of a house. The young man was laughing at him.

'Say gentlemen,' the young man exclaimed as he took a step towards them, 'Are you perhaps looking for some male company to relieve you of all your anxieties? My rates are reasonable and today I have a special price.'

Quick as lightning Tullus barged into the youth and shoved him up against the wall of a house. The youth cried out in shock and pain. Tullus looked furious as he brought his head close to that of the young man.

'Do I look like a queer to you,' he cried, 'Well do I, you fucking idiot?'

Gaius took a step towards his friend and tried to restrain him. He'd forgotten that Tullus had been raped by his guards whilst being held captive in Scodra. They had never discussed it and Tullus had never brought it up.

'No,' the youth whispered suddenly, 'but you are a very good actor. Keep pushing me against the wall. Then let me go, spit on the ground and follow me as discreetly as you can. My name is Larth and I have come to help you. Now do as I say.'

Tullus stared at the young man in surprise. Gaius took a step towards them.

'What do you mean, you have come to help us?' he hissed.

'If you want to see Decia do as I say,' Larth whispered, 'They have eyes and ears everywhere. You are in danger.'

'Tullus, do as he says,' Gaius said abruptly.

Tullus's eyes smouldered angrily. Then he relaxed his grip on the youth, spat on the man's clothing and turned away with a contemptuous look.

Larth cried out in protest and hurled a few choice curses in Tullus's direction. The Volscian halted and was about to turn round and punch the youth in the face when Gaius grasped him by the shoulders and shoved him down the street.

'Keep walking, do as he says,' Gaius whispered.

Larth came storming past in disgust and turned into a side street and after a few moments hesitation Gaius, Tullus and Crispus followed him. The youth kept ahead of them as they made their way through a crowded street filled with small shops and work places. The noise was terrific and the smell overpowering but Gaius hardly noticed. As he pushed his way through the crowd he kept his eyes firmly on the young man up ahead resisting the temptation to grab him and demand an immediate explanation.

Larth slipped down an alley and as Gaius turned to follow him he noticed that they had entered the prostitute's district. The whores and punters were doing a brisk trade and the alley was filled with chatter, haggling and the noise of sexual intercourse. No one paid them any attention as they thrust past the seedy doorways and the advertising calls of the pimps. The alley grew narrower until Gaius saw that it came to a dead end. He stopped in alarm and as he did so Larth vanished into one of the seedy and rundown brothels.

'What would Decia be doing inside that place?' Tullus said glancing around. 'This is no place for a lady. That fucking pimp is trying to lure us into a trap.'

Gaius did not reply. He glanced at Crispus but the slave looked as lost as himself.

'All right,' Gaius said making up his mind, 'I will trust him. If he'd wanted to rob us he would have done so by now. Come on.'

Without waiting for an answer Gaius ducked through the doorway and disappeared into the brothel. Inside the building it was dark. A staircase led upwards. Carefully he started to climb until he emerged onto a small landing. An old woman was sitting on a chair beside the window mending a tunic with a bone needle. She didn't look up as Gaius stepped out onto the landing. Three doors led away from the landing and two of them were closed. From behind one of the doors he could hear the sound of someone having sex. Larth was leaning against the doorpost opposite him. There was a smile on the male prostitute's face.

'Decia, look who I found wandering the streets? I think he's the man you told me about,' he said turning to someone in the room.

Decia appeared in the doorway and as she caught sight of Gaius she gave a little cry of joy and rushed to embrace him.

'Gaius, Gaius, it is so good to see you,' she exclaimed as she buried her head against his chest. 'What are you doing here? How did you find me?'

Gaius chuckled as he ruffled her hair. 'Our father sent me to find you. He wants you to return to Rome. He thinks that Arretium has become too dangerous for you.' Gaius gestured towards Larth. 'Your friend here spotted us. I have come to take you home Decia.'

She broke away from the embrace and looked up at him with a sudden fierceness in her eyes.

'I am not going,' she said, 'I am not running away. I still have work to do here, important work.' She stared at Gaius and he could see that she meant every word she had just said.

326

'There is so much I would like to talk to you about,' she groaned, 'but we have no time. You have arrived in the midst of terrible danger Gaius. You must warn the Roman garrison. My husband is about to lead an uprising. I think it's going to happen tomorrow at dawn. We must warn the garrison.'

'Your husband is going to lead an uprising in the city?' Gaius looked confused. 'Why would he do such a thing?'

Decia shook her head impatiently, 'They are looking for me,' she whispered. 'The whole city is about to rise up. They hate Rome more than ever. Vela and Marce have been poisoning people's minds for months now. My husband is planning to change sides. He thinks Rome is going to lose the war. There is this foreigner, I think he is a Samnite, he is helping him organise the rebellion. His name is Egnatius, that's how my husband introduced him.'

'Egnatius,' Gaius's eyes widened, 'Egnatius is here in Arretium?'

***

Gaius hastened down the street. He had left Tullus and Crispus with Decia and he was on his own. It was too dangerous to try and get her into the Roman barracks. If what Decia had told him was true, then the rebels were keeping a close watch on the garrison. The news, which Decia had given him was stunning. Not only was Arretium about to rise up in rebellion but the commander of the Samnite army was himself somewhere in the city. If he could capture Egnatius it would have a dramatic effect on the war. If only he could capture him. It was late in the afternoon. He looked up at the sky. Decia had told him that she thought the uprising was scheduled to start at dawn. He glanced around him at the people going about their daily business. They didn't look concerned, tense or frightened. As he reached the corner leading to the barracks he paused. If Egnatius was indeed watching would he recognise him after all these years? He glanced across the fifty paces that separated him from the barracks gate. All seemed normal. Boldly he moved out into the open and strode straight towards the closed gates. Nothing happened. He reached the gate and banged on the wood. A moment later the gate creaked open and he slipped inside.

Remus, the centurion stared at Gaius in horror. The two of them faced each other in the officers' private quarters.

'You want me to do what?' he exclaimed.

Gaius took a deep breath. The nervous twitch in his left eye had reappeared as he had explained his plan to the Roman commander of Arretium.

'I want you,' Gaius repeated patiently, 'right now, to send your soldiers to arrest all the leading citizens of this city. We do not have the time to find out who is in on the plot and who isn't. Arrest them all and bring them here. We must do this quickly. If they resist, your men should kill them. If they are not at home then take their family as hostages. Bring them all here and then spread the word that if there is any civil disobedience all the hostages will die.'

'But all the leading citizens in this city?' Remus protested. 'Some of them are my friends.'

'Friends,' Gaius cried slamming his fist on the table, 'If they were truly your friends then they would have warned you about this uprising long ago. The Samnite commander has even managed to slip into your city. Wake up!'

Remus looked away in sudden shame. Then he cleared his throat and collected himself.

'All right,' he muttered. 'Proculus is in his quarters just down the corridor from here. I will have him arrested at once,' he muttered, 'But I only have five hundred men and thirty three of them are either sick or on leave. If your plan doesn't work and the uprising takes place then I am going to be hard pressed to defend these walls even counting your Campanians.'

'We are not going to abandon Arretium,' Gaius snapped. 'Send half your men out into the city and get the remainder up on the walls. This old fort seems sturdy enough. It will withstand the attack by a mob.'

***

Gaius stood on the wall beside the gate staring out into the town. It was dusk. Remus's snatch squads had moved out into the city and he could hear them at work. Screams and yells had started to erupt from the wealthier neighbourhoods. As he stared down at the street below he saw the first groups of soldiers returning, dragging their unwilling hostages with them. Gaius did not move from his position as dusk turned to darkness and the snatch squads continued to return with their human cargos. As the darkness deepened his confidence grew. The rebels had to be in disarray for there had been no attempt to interfere and confront Remus's men. What a bunch of cowards he thought. Then at last Remus came to find him. In the torchlight Gaius could see that the centurion looked tired but excited.

'We got most of them,' Remus said as he saluted, 'Proculus is none too happy but I told him that you will explain it all to him. My men killed three and I have one wounded. A few managed to escape. I have ordered my men to withdraw into the barracks.'

'What about Egnatius? Did you find him?'

Remus shook his head. 'I don't think so, you can check the hostages yourself but there are not many amongst them whom I don't recognise. You have nearly all the nobles of this city down there in the courtyard. They are none too happy either. They certainly aren't going to be inviting me to their dinner parties again.'

'Well done centurion,' Gaius said. 'I will speak with this Proculus later. There is one final task. My sister and my friends are holed up in a brothel. Can you get some men down there to bring them back here? It is important. My sister is the daughter of Publius Decius Mus. She must not fall into the hands of the enemy. That would be most unfortunate.'

Remus nodded, 'I will send out a party right away.' He turned to look out into the city. In the darkness, the town seemed ominously quiet.

'Will it be enough do you think?' Remus asked.

Gaius shrugged. 'I suspect that we will know the answer to that by the morning.'

It was half an hour later when he heard the clink and clatter of the soldiers' armour and boots on the cobble stones and saw the procession of torches coming down the street towards the barracks. After verifying the password, the gates were opened and the Romans entered the barracks. Gaius turned to look at the latest arrivals and smiled as he caught sight of Tullus and Decia. He left his post on the walls and climbed down the ladder to greet them. But as he strode towards them he noticed that something was wrong. Tullus looked agitated.

'Gaius,' he cried as he caught sight of him, 'It's Crispus, he has gone. He has disappeared.'

Chapter Forty-One - Death Sentence

Startled Egnatius rose to his feet and stared in the direction of the hall. The loud urgent knocking on the front door continued. He glanced at Vela who had also risen to her feet. His hostess looked anxious.

'Lady,' a slave said as he came hurrying into the atrium, 'There is a man outside who is demanding to speak with your guest. He claims that it is urgent. Shall I let him in?'

'He wants to speak with me? Who is it?' Egnatius said frowning.

The slave did not reply. He was staring at his mistress waiting for her to reply. Vela glanced at Egnatius.

'Are you expecting anyone?' she murmured.

Egnatius shook his head. 'No one, apart from a very few people, knows that I am here.'

Vela turned to her slave. 'Is he alone?' she snapped.

The slave nodded.

'Let him in,' she ordered.

The two of them waited in silence as the slave vanished into the hallway. A few moments later a big man appeared. He was covered in sweat and his chest was heaving as if he had been running.

Egnatius eyes bulged as he recognised the man.

'You,' he gasped, 'What are you doing here?'

Crispus glanced at Vela and then back towards Egnatius. Then he wiped his forehead with the back of his hand.

'I have come to warn you both,' he said, 'I know where Decia is hiding. I have seen her. She knows about your plans. She has sent her brother to warn the Romans about your uprising. You are all in danger.'

For a moment Egnatius stared at Crispus in stunned silence. Beside him Vela's face had turned pale.

'I ordered you to stay in Rome,' Egnatius said at last as he managed to master his surprise, 'You were supposed to report on the deliberations and decisions of the Senate and the Consuls. That was your task. You were our spy in Rome. What are you doing here? I don't need you here.'

Crispus looked annoyed. 'That was my intention,' he growled, 'But Publius ordered me to accompany his son. I had no choice. I had to go with him. But you need to listen to me now. You need to act fast. If you are planning an uprising, then you need to attack the Romans right now for they will soon know what you are up to. Send some of your men to capture Decia. I know where she is hiding.'

'How did that bitch come to know about our plans?' Vela interrupted with unmistakeable venom in her voice. 'Someone must have talked. Someone has betrayed us.'

'No one betrayed you,' Crispus snapped turning on her with a contemptuous sneer, 'She overheard you discussing your plans. You were careless, you took no precautions, that's what's got you into this mess.'

Vela's eyes narrowed at the unexpected rebuke and she opened her mouth to respond but Egnatius cut her off before she could speak. His face darkened and he glared at Crispus.

'Do you mean Decia, Proculus's wife? The daughter of Publius Decius Mus?'

Crispus nodded.

Egnatius looked away as he remembered his first encounter with Decia in Proculus's house. He had sensed then that the woman was dangerous. There had been intelligence and determination in those dark eyes of hers and she'd had the courage to kick him in the balls as well. He grunted as he suddenly realised what she had been doing that night so close to the Roman barracks. Then he forced her image from his mind and looked up.

'I am here on my own, I have no body of trained soldiers with me,' he said. 'Our supporters look to Proculus for their orders.' He turned towards Vela. 'Can we get a message to Proculus, can we move up the hour of the attack?'

Vela opened her mouth, closed it and opened it again. There was a sudden indecision in her eyes.

'Marce has already left to join the Etruscan army at Sentinum,' she replied, 'and Proculus is inside the Roman barracks. He was going to open the gates for us.' Her shoulders slumped in sudden defeat and she groaned. 'There is no way we could get a message to him in time. He is trapped.'

The atrium fell silent. Egnatius looked down at the floor, his mind torn by terrible indecision.

'They also know that you are inside the city,' Crispus said. 'They will be specifically looking for you Sir.' Crispus paused and his eyes gleamed with sudden fervour as he studied the Samnite commander. 'You are the last hope of all the mountain people,' Crispus said. 'You need to get out of here and return to your army. The coming battle is going to decide all our peoples' fates once and for all. I can help you Sir.'

After a moment's hesitation Egnatius nodded. 'Yes you are right. I need to get out of the city. It was stupid of me to come in person.'

The noise of someone slamming on the front door suddenly reverberated through the house.

'Open up in there, open up!' a voice cried in Latin.

A slave came running into the atrium. He looked alarmed.

'Romans, mistress, there are Roman soldiers outside the door and in the street,' he cried.

Vela gasped in dismay. Then she turned to Egnatius.

'Quick get out into the garden and climb over the back wall. There is an alley, follow it to the left and it will lead you to the city gate. I will stay here and delay them. Go!' she gasped.

Without a word Egnatius and Crispus turned and ran out into the garden. They halted before the high wall that surrounded the property. Egnatius looked up at it and groaned. It was too high to climb up. He turned to look back at the house as he heard a thud and a splintering crash followed by Vela's furious protests. Then Crispus was shouting at him and he turned to look at the spy. Crispus was crouching and had cupped his hands. He gestured for Egnatius to place his foot in his cupped hands and Egnatius understood. He took a deep breath, ran towards Crispus and with a mighty shove the spy sent him flying up onto the wall. Desperately Egnatius scrambled to get a grip. Then he heaved himself over the top and dropped down into the alley behind the wall. For a moment, he struggled to regain his breath. Then with a grunt Cripus's head and hands appeared on the top of the wall and after a brief struggle the spy rolled himself over the barrier and dropped down into the alley beside Egnatius.

'Thank you,' Egnatius panted. Crispus acknowledged him silently and the slave was just about to start off down the alley when Egnatius caught him by the shoulder.

'Once I am safely out of the city,' Egnatius said with sudden bitterness, 'I want you to remain here and kill Decia. Publius Decius Mus is my enemy. I want you to kill his daughter. The time has come for the Consul to personally pay for all the destruction he has inflicted on my people.'

Crispus looked at Egnatius in silence. Then he nodded.

'I know her well,' he muttered, 'I have known her since she was a little girl. I will see it done Sir.

Chapter Forty-Two - The Fate of the Crushed

The hostages sat in a circle on the ground in the courtyard of the barracks. It was dawn and Decia paused to study them from the doorway. The men and women had been hooded; their hands bound behind their backs and their feet clamped in slavers chains. Some had pissed themselves and were sitting in their own urine. At first they had protested, complained and struggled but as the night had worn on their cries and struggles had faded and ceased until exhaustion and hopelessness had finally silenced them. Now as Decia looked on they looked bedraggled and defeated. Decia rubbed her tired eyes. She knew all the hostages. The ruling class of Arretium had always attended each other's parties and banquets. Her time in Arretium was ending. She would not be able to stay here, not after what had happened. Not after the role she had played in crushing the uprising. She would have to return to Rome and her family. But she had performed her duty to Rome she thought and the realisation pleased her. She had done her bit.

She stepped into the courtyard and strode towards the hostages. The Roman guards watched her as she walked up to one of the captives. Decia paused before the figure, then bent down and grasped the woman by her chin and forced her to look up at her. With her other hand, she pulled the hood from the woman's head. Vela blinked. She looked exhausted, confused and frightened. Then as she recognised Decia she started to hiss. Decia slapped her hard across the face and Vela cried out. The hissing stopped.

'You have lost,' Decia said quietly as she looked down at her arch enemy,'but I will give you this one chance to redeem yourself. Kiss my hand and on the gods above and below, swear loyalty to Rome and the Roman people, now and forever.'

Vela stared up at Decia with large blood shot eyes. Her cheeks burned red. For a moment, the two women held each other's gaze in a fierce battle of wills. Then noisily Vela cleared her throat and spat at Decia.

'Go fuck yourself bitch,' she hissed.

Decia straightened up and wiped the spit from her face. Then she turned to the Roman guards.

'Take her to the prison cell,' she said.

Two soldiers grasped Vela by her arms and led her towards a door in the barracks building. Decia followed on behind. They entered a dark corridor lit up by a line of oil lamps and strode down it passing several storerooms. At the end of the corridor the soldiers paused before an iron barred door that led to the barracks prison cell. One of the Romans fumbled for the keys. Then he inserted the key into the lock and the metal door swung open. The cell was dark, cold and small. With a rough shove the soldier pushed Vela into the small cell. She stumbled and tripped and fell to the ground. Decia followed her in. She turned to the soldiers.

'Leave us,' she ordered.

When the soldiers had gone Decia turned to look at Vela. She stood in a corner of the cell glaring at Decia in silent bitterness. Her hands were still tied behind her back. Decia sighed.

'Marce is not amongst the prisoners,' Decia said quietly, 'Where is your husband Vela? Where has he gone?'

'Somewhere where you will not find him,' Vela sneered. 'He has left the city and has gone to join his brother who leads our army. You are too late. He is beyond your grasp.'

Decia nodded and looked down at the floor.

'I am glad to hear it,' she replied. She paused. 'Do you know the reason why I seduced you and your husband that night? Well let me tell you,' she said taking a step towards Vela, 'The whole point of that seduction was to get your husband to believe that the defences of Rome were weak and that an Etruscan army would have a chance in taking the city whilst the Consuls were busy fighting the Samnites and Gauls. If the Etruscan army now marches away it should give my father a chance to force a battle at Sentinum without being hopelessly outnumbered. My plan may work or it may not, only time will tell, but in our association Vela, I have outwitted you for the last time. You thought you had me in your power but you were wrong. It is you who has been duped.'

Vela was staring at Decia with growing horror.

'You and your associates were plotting an uprising in this city,' Decia continued, 'You were plotting to massacre the Roman garrison. The punishment for this is death. You will never leave these walls alive. They are going to crucify you.'

Decia slipped her hand into the folds of her Stola and when she withdrew her hand she was holding a knife. She stepped towards Vela, spun her around and cut the rope that bound the woman's hands. Then she turned for the door and as she passed out of the cell she dropped the knife on the floor. She closed the metal bar door and locked it. Vela was staring at the discarded knife. The hatred on her face had been replaced with shock.

'I will come back in an hour,' Decia said quietly, 'You have until then.'

***

As Decia stepped out into the bright sunlit courtyard she saw Gaius coming towards her. She smiled and he replied with a grin.

'There you are, I have been looking for you,' he said as he gently took her arm and guided her towards the officers' quarters.

'Has there been any reaction in the town?' Decia inquired as the two of them walked across the sandy exercise terrain.

Gaius shook his head. 'No nothing. A few shops remain closed but others have opened and there are a few people about. I have asked Remus to send a few patrols into the city to gage the mood but I think that we can assume that the uprising is crushed before it could take place.' Gaius paused and turned to her. 'And that is thanks to you Decia,' he said proudly.

Decia smiled. Gaius could be very charming when he wanted to be she thought. Her father had done well to adopt him. Ever since Quintus had died and Gaius had gone missing the family had been in turmoil. On her rare visits to Rome she had seen the stress that the loss of two sons had caused her father and so when after two year's news had finally arrived that Gaius had been freed and was returning to Rome she had been overjoyed. Her family needed a male heir. It was imperative but there had been another secret reason for her joy. For Gaius's return had relieved the growing pressure on her to produce a son with her husband. For she could not bear the thought of having a son with Proculus.

'There is no news about Egnatius,' Gaius continued as they reached the door leading into the officers' quarters. 'The city gates are closed and under our control but I suspect that he may have managed to slip out of the city by now. We don't have the manpower to search the entire town I'm afraid.'

'That's a shame,' Decia replied. She glanced at the door leading to the officers' quarters. 'What are we doing here?' she asked.

Gaius shrugged. 'Remus is confident that he has matters under control but we still need to speak with your husband. He has been confined to his quarters. Are you willing to see him?'

Decia nodded. 'Yes, I have a few things that I would like to say to him.'

A soldier was standing guard outside the door to the Zilach's private chambers. He saluted and stepped aside as Gaius and Decia unlocked the door and stepped into the room beyond.

Proculus was sitting on a chair staring at them. As he caught sight of Decia his face grew pale. Then with a cry he got down on his knees and bowed his head.

'Decia, I am so sorry,' he whined. 'I never intended to hurt you. I was tricked into this. They tricked me into agreeing to go along with their plan. It's all Vela and Marce's fault. It was their idea.'

'Shut up and listen,' Gaius growled as he grasped Proculus by his neck and forced him back up onto his chair. The chief magistrate of Arretium suddenly looked terrified. His eyes darted from Gaius to Decia and back and his body was trembling with fear.

'Please, please, I don't want to die,' he shrieked.

Decia struck him across the face with the flat of her hand and the blow stunned her husband into silence.

'Remus and I have agreed to let you live for now,' Gaius said quietly as he fixed his eyes on Proculus. 'Arretium still needs a government and unfortunately for now you and your family are the only people capable of running this place. So you will return to your duties as Zilach of this city and you will order the people to obey the laws. You will also send hostages from your own family to Rome. Then when this war is over the Senate will have to pronounce its verdict. If matters remain calm in Arretium then I shall advise my father to be lenient, but were you to revive dissatisfaction and hostility to Rome then rest assured that Rome will sack the entire city and transport it's peoples to a disease-ridden swamp. Make sure that the people of this city know the severity with which any further trouble will be punished.'

Proculus rubbed his cheek, looked up at Gaius and nodded.

'Thank you, thank you,' he muttered. 'I will obey the will of Rome.'

Decia noticed that Gaius was glancing at her. She took a step forwards and gazed down at her husband.

'You have failed me as a husband and as a man,' she said. 'So here is what you are going to do. You are going to write to my father and tell him that you are divorcing me. You are going explain why and you are going to amend your will so that when you die you will bequeath the city of Arretium to the Roman Republic.'

Proculus was staring at Decia open mouthed. Then at last he looked away and nodded again.

'I will do as you ask,' he stammered.

Decia brought her face close to his. 'Goodbye Proculus,' she said. 'And for the sake of this city, I do hope that your descendants grow some balls.'

***

Decia looked up as Gaius tapped her on her shoulder. She could see that there was something else on his mind. For a moment, he hesitated. The two of them stood in the exercise terrain not far from the main gate.

'Our father has instructed me to bring you home,' Gaius said at last. 'He is the Consul and I cannot disobey him. You need to come with me Decia. You have done as much as you can in this place but the time to leave has arrived. I have an escort and I can take you as far as your father's camp at Clusium. From there you can travel to Rome with one of our supply columns.'

Decia smiled and ran her fingers affectionately down Gaius's unshaven cheek. He was right she thought. She had done everything that she could. She turned to look at the circle of bound and chained hostages.

341

'I wish I could have been a soldier like you Gaius,' she said. 'I loved Quintus and I still do but you were the son that my father always wanted to have.'

Gaius smiled. 'I am sure that you are the daughter that he always wanted to have.'

Decia nodded and for a moment her thoughts were faraway. 'I have heard,' she said at last, 'about the armies of Samnites, Gauls, Umbrians and Etruscans that are gathering at Sentinum. They say that the enemy will massively outnumber us. Do you think, Gaius that there is any hope that we shall win?'

Gaius's smile faded away, 'There is always hope,' he muttered, 'Numbers do not decide battles.'

'But they do help,' Decia retorted, 'And when the enemy outnumbers us by such a huge margin it becomes difficult to believe how we can win.'

Gaius shrugged, 'Don't dwell on it, it will do you no good. A soldier obeys orders and does his best. That's all he can do. Your father and Fabius are experienced men, they will lead us to victory, outnumbered or not.'

Decia looked up at Gaius and smiled as she felt a sudden warm glow. There was something in her brother's voice that was calming and soothing and from which she could draw strength.

'Maybe the enemy numbers will not be so bad as we think,' she said hopefully. She turned away. 'All right, I will come with you. I just need to return to my house to collect a few personal belongings. I also have a slave boy; his name is Luca. He has served me faithfully and I am not going to leave him behind. Give me a few hours and I will be back and ready to go.'

Gaius looked doubtful and for a moment he hesitated.

'All right but on condition that some of Remus's soldiers escort you,' he replied. 'The city is   still a dangerous place.'

Decia nodded and was about to say something else when she spotted Remus, the centurion hurrying towards them. The man looked alarmed.

'Gaius,' the centurion cried out as he caught sight of him. 'One of the hostages has been found dead in the prison block. It's the woman, Vela, Marce's wife. She cut her own throat.'

Chapter Forty-Three - The Unknown Soldier

The house looked deserted as Decia stepped into the hallway. The door had been kicked down by one of Remus's snatch squads and it hung awkwardly on its hinges. Pieces of shattered pottery and splinters of wood covered the mosaic floor of the hall. Decia peered towards the atrium but she couldn't see anyone. The slaves must have fled after yesterday's disturbances.

'Luca, Luca, are you here?' she cried.

She glanced at the Roman soldiers who had escorted her through the city. They were at her command Gaius had told her. The city had been quiet and cowed and she'd had no trouble in reaching her home. From inside the house she heard a sudden noise. Then a figure appeared in the doorway to the atrium.

'Crispus,' Decia said in a surprised voice, 'What are you doing here? What happened to you yesterday? You just disappeared.'

The slave was staring at her strangely. Then he bowed and glanced warily at the soldiers in the street.

'I am sorry mistress,' he muttered, 'I have something to confess but I would prefer to do it in private. Will you send the soldiers away? Your father sent me to find you. You will be safe with me.'

For a moment Decia hesitated. Then she turned to the men behind her.

'It's all right, you may go, he is my slave,' she said.

The soldiers turned away and Decia stepped into the hallway. Her sandals crunched on the broken shards of pottery as she followed Crispus into the atrium. Then she gasped at the sight that met her eyes. The space was completely empty save for a few discarded vases. She turned to look around her. Someone had urinated against the wall. The house must have been looted during the night. She looked up at the rooms on the second floor and groaned. If the looters had been able to take everything from the atrium they would certainly have taken all her personal belongings too. She turned towards Crispus.

'So tell me, why did you disappear like that, without a word of explanation or even a goodbye? That was most unsatisfactory behaviour. You should remember who you are.'

Crispus looked down at the ground and Decia felt a sudden stir of unease. There was something odd about his behaviour that she couldn't place. It almost looked like he was guilty about something.

'Mistress, I must confess,' he muttered avoiding her gaze, 'when you told us how badly your husband had been treating you, I came here with the intention of killing him.'

Decia blinked in surprise. 'You wanted to kill Proculus?' she said.

'Yes,' Crispus nodded, 'But when I got here the house was empty, the door was open and the place had been ransacked. But I found your boy Luca. He's upstairs in your bedroom. He was wounded trying to prevent the looters from taking everything. I have tried my best to patch him up mistress but he is in a bad way.'

'Luca,' Decia exclaimed in alarm, 'He's here, he's wounded?'

Crispus nodded.

Without a word Decia started up the stairs. Luca was wounded. How bad could it be? The boy needed help. She climbed the stairs and emerged onto the landing. Crispus followed her up the stairs. The house was silent. She strode quickly across the landing and froze at the doorway to her bedroom. Luca lay spread eagled on the bed in a large pool of blood. Someone

345

had cut his throat and his sightless eyes were staring up at the ceiling. He was dead. Decia gasped in horror. Then a hand clamped itself around her mouth and Crispus shoved her into the bedroom. Decia squealed and tried to resist but the slave was too strong. Expertly he twisted her round and drove his knee straight into her stomach. With a deep groan, she doubled up in agony and collapsed to the floor. Calmly Crispus grabbed hold of the table and upended it before the door blocking the only entrance to the room. Then he knelt beside her, produced a knife and pressed it against her throat.

'I knew you would come back for your slave boy,' Crispus whispered. 'You are so predictable Decia. Now be a good girl and keep your mouth shut. If you scream or cry for help I will slit your throat like I did with your young friend.'

Crispus smiled. 'Just nod your head if you have understood me,' he whispered in her ear.

Decia groaned in pain and managed to do as he'd asked. Crispus withdrew the knife and as he did so Decia looked up at him in horror. What was Crispus doing? She had known him for years.

'You were once my brother's closest friend,' she wheezed. 'He treated you with every respect. He trusted you. We all did. Why are you doing this?'

Crispus was smiling. Gently he stroked her face and pushed her hair back from her eyes and as he did so Decia felt a sudden chill run through her body. There was a crazy smile on Crispus's face, a smile that seemed to tell her that the man didn't care anymore whether he lived or died.

'All this time,' Crispus murmured, 'No one suspected that I was spying on Rome. Your father was such a gullible fool Decia. He provided me with such a perfect position. He never sent me away when the great men of Rome came to his house to discuss strategy. He never forbade me from listening in on all the conversations he had. He never hid his official letters from me and because he trusted me; so did the others. Oh yes, no one noticed me, no one noticed me standing beside the wall staring off into the distance, waiting to obey my master. You all thought I was just a statue, a man without a brain, a slave who didn't exist.' Crispus's eyes bulged. 'But I do exist Decia, I am alive and my mountain people need me. Your father forgot that. He forgot where I came from. He never realised that I was sold to him on purpose. He never suspected that the old lady who planted me in your household was his mortal enemy.'

Decia closed her eyes and willed the pain in her stomach to go away. Then she opened her eyes.

'Then this has nothing to do with freedom,' she hissed, 'My father trusted you. Quintus adored you. I can understand hatred Crispus but what kind of twisted sick mind spends half his life pretending to be friends with people he knows he is betraying. Was it worth it in the end?'

Crispus's fingers closed around her throat but he didn't squeeze.

'Careful Decia,' he grunted, 'careful now my little princess.' He paused. 'But you still don't see it do you? Oh how long have I waited to tell you this.' Crispus's eyes sparkled feverishly. 'I was never a slave. Once I lived in Corfinium,' he murmured running his fingers over her cheeks, 'I was an orphan living off other people's discarded rubbish and then one day my mistress came and found me. She took me in and taught me to fight and provided me with everything I wanted and so when the time came for me to start doing her bidding, I did it enthusiastically. I happily pretended to be a slave and I gladly started to spy on your father. I have been doing so for over thirteen years. I wonder what Publius would have to say about that?' Crispus chuckled. 'Oh think of the shame that your father would feel Decia; the shame of having harboured a Samnite spy in his own family for all these years. It would finish of your family for good. They would never survive the disgrace and everything your father and his father had built up, over such a long period of time, would be undone.'

Decia choked as she felt his fingers tighten around her windpipe. Then he relaxed his grip.

'What are you going to do with me?' she whispered.

Once again Crispus ran his fingers across her cheek. She turned away but he forced her to look at him.

'I haven't made up my mind yet,' he muttered.

Decia wrenched her eyes away and stared at Luca's motionless body on the bed.

'I never liked you,' she hissed, 'and now I know why. Your obsession with cleanliness and orderliness, it's not natural, you are sick, you are sick in the mind Crispus.'

Crispus slapped her hard across her face and the pain made her cry out. A bead of sweat rolled down his forehead and he was panting.

'That's not my only obsession,' he whispered, 'I have watched you grow up. I have watched you become a woman and not a day has gone by when I have not had the same thoughts about you. I can't help it Decia. I have dreamed about you every night and it's always the same dream. You come to me dressed as a Vestal Virgin; you are one of the untouchable and chaste priestesses of Rome. You take your clothes off before me and then I fuck you. But you see its not you that I am screwing, I am fucking the very purity of Rome, I am fucking your gods and if I can release my seed into you I will be able to arrest the destiny of Rome itself.' Crispus was staring at her with large eyes. 'It's the truth Decia, when we fuck, Rome is going to fall. So that is what we are going to do.'

Decia was looking at him in horror. The room fell silent. Then she turned away.

'You are mad,' she said nervously, 'You have gone mad.'

Crispus chuckled. 'I always knew it was going to happen one day. I knew that if I was patient I would be rewarded.'

Decia did not reply. Her thoughts seemed distant. Then she turned to him and there was something cold and unemotional in her eyes.

'What can I do?' she said shrugging, 'Let's get this over with. But first let's drink, will you take a drink with me Crispus?'

He was watching her closely and for a moment he hesitated. Then he nodded.

She rose to her feet and turned to the cupboard from which she took the jug of wine. Crispus watched her carefully as she placed the wine on a chair and poured a generous quantity of the red liquid into two cups. She handed him a cup and took the other. Then she raised her cup in salute.

'To my father and to Rome, may their greatness never diminish,' she said quietly.

Crispus raised his cup to his lips. Then he stopped.

'You drink first,' he said with sudden suspicion in his voice.

Decia hesitated and looked down at her cup. For a moment, she did nothing. Then calmly she looked Crispus straight in the eye and took a sip from her cup.

Crispus watched her. He grinned and downed his cup in one go. A little trickle of wine escaped from his mouth and meandered down his chin. He turned and rummaged around in his bag and then flung a set of clothes onto the floor in front of Decia.

'Here,' he said, 'I managed to get one of the vestals to lend me her clothes. Put them on.'

But Decia shook her head. She stood quite still and her face was calm and composed.

'No Crispus,' she said quietly, 'You no longer have any power over me. You are going to die soon, just like I am going to die. It's all over for us now.'

Crispus turned to stare at her. His eyes narrowed. For a moment, he looked confused. Then confusion turned to alarm.

'What have you done bitch?' he hissed.

'I have poisoned you,' Decia replied calmly taking a step towards him. 'You are going to be dead soon. Are you afraid of death Crispus? Shall I tell you how you are going to die?' Decia stared at him with sudden contempt, 'First you shall lose all feeling in your legs, then the poison will take out your groin and stomach and then finally it will stop you breathing and you will suffocate.' She laughed and her contempt was palpable. 'And all this time you will be perfectly aware of what is happening to you. You are going to watch death as it slowly takes you away. You are going to struggle and scream but it's not going to do you any good.'

Crispus's eyes bulged in sudden terror.

'The wine,' he gasped, 'but you drank it also, you drank the wine. I saw you.'

Decia nodded. 'You were going to kill me anyway,' she said quietly, 'I do not fear death Crispus and I shall gladly go to the next world for I have done my duty to Rome. I am my father's daughter.' She paused and a single tear trickled down her cheek. 'No one will ever really know what I have done,' she murmured. 'I shall become one of the countless soldiers who did their duty but whose name and deeds are unknown. But you Crispus,' she said and her face hardened, 'You shall be remembered as the man who never lived, who never had the courage to be his true self. You shall go to the next world not knowing what you are.'

Crispus was staring at her with growing horror. Then with a high-pitched scream he launched himself at her. The force of his impact sent them crashing against the wall. Decia felt a jarring pain. She cried out. The two of them slithered to the floor and Crispus's hands closed around her throat. He was yelling and screaming like a man possessed. Decia spluttered as his fingers began to squeeze. It was becoming harder to breath and she felt her cheeks starting to burn. Wildly her hands grasped and pulled at his tunic but he was far too strong for her. Then her fingers brushed across the handle of his knife. Desperately she yanked it from his belt and with her remaining strength drove it straight into his side. Crispus gasped with sudden pain and his grip on her throat weakened. Decia yanked the knife free and plunged it once more into his body. Crispus groaned. Frantically she tried to pull his fingers away from her throat. She could feel blood pouring onto her leg. Crispus moaned and tried to throttle her again but his strength was fading fast. She managed to pull his hands off her throat. For a moment, she lay there gasping and panting as she sucked great mouthfuls of air into her lungs. Crispus lay half on top of her. He was groaning. Decia pushed him off her and he rolled onto his back. Slowly she got up, retrieved the knife and looked down at the slave. Crispus was staring up at the ceiling. He was muttering something to himself.

She crouched down beside him and pressed the knife into his throat.

'Do it,' he whispered closing his eyes, 'finish me; end it quickly, please!'

Decia took a deep breath and with a single quick movement slit his throat. Then she rose to her feet, dropped the knife and stared down at the corpse. All of a sudden she felt tired, very tired. She stumbled towards the doorway and pushed the table out of the way. Her legs felt heavy and strange and she seemed to have difficulty in walking. She made it out into the corridor and steadied herself against the balustrade. She couldn't feel her legs any more; it was as if they didn't exist. She took another step and collapsed onto the floor.

'Father,' she whispered stretching out her fingers, 'father.'

Chapter Forty-Four - The Council of War

Gaius had never seen such a large Roman camp. He strode along the long lines of white tents heading for the very centre of the fort where the two Consuls had pitched their standards. It was morning and he was clad in his engraved bronze cuirass armour over which he was wearing a red mantle. On his head was a fine Attic helmet that had once belonged to Quintus. In the camp the Roman soldiers were going about their daily routine. He caught the smell of freshly baked bread and heard the noise of whinnying horses, soldiers' curses and shouted commands. Two full strength Consular armies had been billeted in the same camp and the forty thousand or so men formed one of the largest armies that the Republic had ever fielded. Gaius sighed. It was an impressive sight but everyone knew that their enemies outnumbered them more than two to one. He paused and turned to look in the general direction of the enemy camps. The small town of Sentinum lay in between them on the low ground. Four miles separated the two sides but so far the Etruscan, Umbrian, Samnite and Gallic alliance had been reluctant to come out and fight. Gaius grunted. Maybe there was some hope in that little fact, maybe the enemy were not as formidable as everyone thought they were.

Tullus handed him a piece of freshly made bread and Gaius stuffed it into his mouth. The Volscian had slung his small round cavalry shield over his back and was wearing a bronze breastplate, greaves along his left leg and a plumed helmet. He was armed with a long cavalry sword and a short throwing spear with sharpened points at both ends. After they had left Arretium, Gaius had given him the opportunity to go home but Tullus had once again refused. The two of them had been through too much together Tullus had said. He would never be able to look Cassia in the eye knowing he'd allowed her brother to go to war without someone to watch his back.

Gaius strode on through the camp. Roman morale seemed low and here and there, as he passed by, he heard the men grumbling and muttering beside their campfires. They seemed uneasy and depressed about the huge difference in numbers. Gaius glanced at Tullus who raised his eyebrows in a silent reply. It wasn't the only thing that was weighing on Gaius's mind. Decia's death had been a heavy blow. He'd ordered her body to be taken to the Roman barracks and there, when he had been alone with her at last, he had lost his composure and had wept. The doctor who had examined her had told him that she'd suffocated, most likely from being poisoned. From interrogating Vela's household slaves, he'd learned that Egnatius had stayed in her house and that a man fitting Crispus's description had arrived shortly before Remus's men had come to arrest Vela. That the slave had come to kill Decia seemed beyond doubt. He'd ordered Crispus's body to be burned and his ashes scattered into a river so that the man would never find a final resting place. He would never know what had possessed Crispus to do what he'd done.

With a heavy heart he'd set out for the Consul's camp to tell Publius that his daughter was dead and that he'd failed in his mission. He had hated being once more the bearer of bad news. Publius had taken it badly. He had dismissed Gaius without a word and had shut himself away in his tent for a whole day. Gaius had not seen or heard from him since that day, a week ago now, but that morning the Consul had sent a messenger summoning Gaius to a Council of War.

'Gaius, is that really you,' a faintly familiar sounding voice suddenly cried out. Gaius stopped in his tracks and peered at the soldier who had called out. The centurion was sitting around a campfire eating porridge from a wooden bowl. Then he rose to his feet and removed his helmet and Gaius grunted in surprise. The big man came towards him. It was Verrens, his old company centurion. The man looked much older than when Gaius had last seen him.

'Remember me,' Verrens said stretching out his arm, 'How long has it been boy, two, three years?'

Gaius clasped the man's arm   and grinned.

354

'More than two,' he replied. 'It's good to see you alive, Verrens. Are you still in charge of the tenth company of the Fifth?'

Verrens nodded. Then he froze. 'Fuck me,' the centurion said with a startled voice as he suddenly recognised Gaius's uniform, 'They have turned you into a military tribune.'

Gaius nodded as Verrens saluted smartly.

'I am a tribune of the Fifth Legion now,' he said, 'although it is not my turn to be in command of the Legion for another few months.'

Verrens was eying him cautiously. 'So you heeded my advice. You made friends with that young patrician whose life you saved. I forgot his name.'

'I did. His family adopted me as their son. My father is Publius, the Consul.'

Verrens raised his eyebrows in surprise and Gaius could see that the officer was impressed.

'So it is I, who will be taking orders from you now then,' Verrens said, 'well Sir, just make sure that you remember everything that I taught you.'

Gaius examined Verrens coolly.

'Tell your men, Verrens, that they should not fear the enemy numbers. Tell them that the fewer there are of us, the greater the share of honour.'

Then Gaius was striding away.

***

'Wait for me here,' Gaius said to Tullus as they approached Fabius's tent. A long row of battle standards had been thrust into the ground on either side of the entrance and Gaius recognised the four legionary standards of the Wolf, the Boar, the Horse and the Minotaur. Gaius slipped past the guards and into the tent. Inside it was crowded with officers and he had to push his way to the front. A circular table had been placed in the centre of the tent and Publius together with his senior officers was standing around it. There was no sign of Fabius. Gaius made his way around the table until he was standing behind his adopted father. Publius looked like he had aged in just a few weeks. His cheeks were hollow and there were dark bags underneath his eyes. He looked like he had not slept in days. He turned, glared at Gaius and beckoned to him.

'I am giving you command of the Latin cavalry squadrons,' he said tersely. 'When we form up for battle you will take your men and position yourself on my left flank. I am giving the same command to another tribune. You will have to share and alternate your command on a daily basis.' Publius fixed his eye on Gaius and there was something hard and unflinching in the Consul's eyes. 'We shall see who of you two will be the best commander.'

Gaius saluted. 'Yes Sir,' he replied quietly.

'How is the morale of the men, what are they saying out there?' Publius growled looking away.

'Morale is low Sir,' Gaius said, 'They are worried about the enemy numbers.'

The Consul grunted and stared morosely at the table that was covered with a large map upon which the positions of the three camps were clearly marked.

'Well the men had better remember that they are Romans and they had better remember the name of the Consul who leads them,' he snapped.

A cry made everyone look up and a moment later the officers nearest to the tent entrance stiffened and saluted. Fabius made

356

his way slowly through the crowd until he stood before the table. The two Consuls briefly acknowledged each other and then Fabius turned to look at the officers crowding around the table. His old wrinkled face looked calm and composed.

'Good news gentlemen,' he said without a hint of a smile, 'My scouts have just reported that the Etruscan and Umbrian armies have abandoned their camp and are marching away.'

An incredulous muttering swept through the tent. Gaius glanced at his adopted father. Publius had turned to look down at the table. His hands were gripping the wooden table edge.

'Could it be a trick?' Publius replied. 'Could they be circling round to attack us in our rear?'

Fabius seemed to weigh the suggestion for a moment. Then he cleared his throat.

'I don't think so,' he replied. 'A few Etruscan deserters have come in and they have told us that their general believes that the road to Rome is wide open. It looks like the Etruscans and Umbrians have decided to march on Rome. They must think that we will have our hands full with the Samnites and Gaul's.'

Publius scratched his unshaven chin. 'So much for unity amongst allies,' he said contemptuously. Then he turned to study the map. For a moment, the tent was silent with tense excited expectation. Then Publius continued.

'It should take the Etruscans and Umbrians a week before they realise that the roads south are blocked by the forces of Propraetors Fulvius and Megellus. Maybe we should order the Propraetors to advance and pillage the Etruscan and Umbrian countryside. Get them to destroy everything in their path. That should keep the Etruscans and Umbrians busy, long enough for us to force a battle against the Samnites and Gaul's.'

Publius looked up at Fabius and as he did so all eyes in the room turned to the grizzled sixty-five-year-old warrior. Fabius was looking at the map. Slowly he nodded in agreement.

'Send orders to Fulvius and Megellus,' he said turning to his staff officers, 'that they are to make contact with the Etruscans and Umbrians but that they are not to engage the enemy. I repeat, they are not to engage the enemy. All they need to do is hold the enemy in the south and prevent them, for as long as possible, from coming back north to support their allies.'

The officers in the tent muttered in loud approval and Gaius could sense a sudden change in the mood. The unexpected departure of the Etruscan and Umbrian armies had provided a glimmer of hope.

Fabius too seemed to sense the change for a faint smile appeared on his lips.

'If they continue to move away,' he said looking Publius in the eye, 'then by tomorrow the Etruscans and Umbrians will be too far away to take part in the battle. We should take this opportunity and force the Samnites and Gauls into action right away.'

Publius raised his finger to his mouth and bit it hard showing his teeth. He seemed to be considering the idea. Then he looked up and nodded.

'Let's kill them,' he growled, 'Let's show them who they are up against.'

His words were met with a loud outburst of shouts and cheers as the officers stamped their feet on the ground in approval. Gaius glanced around him. The tension and anxiety amongst the officers had been far greater than he had suspected.

Fabius tapped the map and as he did so the noise died away.

'I reckon that even without their allies,' the veteran commander said, 'the Samnites and Gauls will still command around 50,000 men against our 40,000. They will still outnumber us and as you all know, out of all our enemies, it is the Samnites and the Gauls who are by far our most fiercesome and dangerous opponents. We all know the Gauls, we know what they can do.' Fabius paused and looked around the table at the eager faces and to Gaius, the Consul suddenly had the determination and outrage of a man defending his farm from cattle raiders, 'But let me make this clear gentlemen,' Fabius said. 'There is going to be no repeat of the Allia. We will stand our ground here and we shall be victorious, for this battle is going to decide the long struggle for Italy, this battle is going to decide the fate of our country and our people. Tell your men this, tell them that when they are facing the enemy, that they are to remember the names of those Romans and Latins who have died for Rome. Tell them that on this day, at this battle, we are going to honour them, we are going to honour the spirits of the departed.'

As Fabius fell silent so did the tent. Then slowly at first the officers started to call out.

'Rullianus, Rullianus, Rullianus!'

The cry grew louder and louder until everyone was shouting and stamping their feet.

***

Gaius accompanied his adopted father back to his tent. A few staff officers followed behind them and from the corner of his eye Gaius caught sight of Tullus sharing some porridge with a group of soldiers around a campfire. Publius was looking at the ground and Gaius had the faint impression that the Consul was a little jealous of the ovation his colleague had received. The soldiers guarding the entrance to Publius's tent snapped out a salute as the Consul strode past. Inside Publius splashed some water over his face and rubbed his eyes. Then he turned to Gaius.

'This is a cruel world we live in,' he muttered darkly, 'First the gods take my son, then Crispus betrays me and now my daughter is taken from me. What else is there left to live for but a man's service to Rome.' Publius scratched at his chin and muttered something to himself. 'And sometimes I wonder whether they will not demand that too.'

Gaius remained silent. His adopted father did not look happy. Decia's loss was clearly still very much on his mind.

'Tomorrow we shall take our positions on the left of the line,' Publius said changing the subject, 'the Fifth and the Sixth will be in the centre with the Latin Legions on either side of them. The Latin cavalry will be on the extreme left flank.'

Publius turned to his second in command, the Pontifex Maximus who was standing watching him quietly. 'Livius, when we enter the battle you shall stay with me at all times,' Publius said. 'You will not leave my side. Make sure that the men are rested and well fed tonight for tomorrow I want them up and in formation by dawn and find me a replacement prefect who is capable of commanding a Latin Legion. One of the prefects has been taken ill.'

Livius dipped his head in acknowledgement and was just about to leave when Gaius intervened.

'Sir, I know a man who could fill that position,' he said. 'His name is Verrens, he's a Centurion in the Fifth, a good man. He has never held such a command before but he will be able to handle it, I know him Sir.'

Publius eyed Gaius carefully. 'That name sounds familiar,' he murmured, 'He was your old company centurion was he not?'

Gaius nodded.

'Fine, do it, have the man come to my tent at once,' Publius said. 'That will be all.'

Outside and on his own at last Gaius took a deep breath. The Consul had given him command of 1800 Latin cavalrymen, half of the combined army's cavalry force. It was a huge responsibility and even though he was going to have share command from day to day he felt weak in his knees. Gaius took another deep breath and steadied himself. Idly he raised his fingers and touched the red brown birthmark on his neck. Had the time come? Was the prophecy actually going to come true or was it, as he had always suspected, nothing more than superstition.

Chapter Forty-Five - Sentinum

The noise of thousands of marching men reverberated through the wooded hills. Gaius sat on his horse staring across the open fields at the distant tree line where, half a mile away, he could just about see the Gallic infantry moving up to form their battle line. The enemy were singing. It was early morning and the sun shone brightly in a clear blue sky. He sensed that it was going to be a hot day. Behind him the Latin cavalry squadrons were forming up in a long line that stretched away into the trees to his left. The jangle of their equipment and the nervous snorting and whinnying of the horses was interspersed by the hurried shouted orders of the decurions. Gaius calmed his breathing. It was his day to command the cavalry. Two days had passed since the Council of War, two days in which the Consuls had done everything they could to force the enemy to fight but the Samnites and Gauls had seemed reluctant to come out of their fortified camp. But now as he studied the enemy it seemed that there had been a change of heart. The Gauls looked like they had come to fight. Gaius turned to look at his small staff. Apart from Tullus he had two trumpeteers, a couple of mounted messengers and his second in command, the young tribune with whom he shared his cavalry command on a day-to-day basis. The tribune was holding the battle standard of the Latin Cavalry.

'You,' Gaius said turning to one of his messengers, 'ride down the line and make sure that the men know that accepting a challenge to single combat from the enemy is strictly forbidden. Any man who disobeys this order shall be executed. Those are the Consul's orders.'

Without a word the young man turned his horse and rode away. Gaius watched him go. Then he turned to look across the open fields at the enemy. The Gallic infantry to his right was forming up in a densely packed phalanx bristling with spears and overlapping shields. As they advanced he could see that they were tall, big and brawny men with horned helmets and long blunt looking swords. They looked stronger and bigger than the

Romans. Most of the Gauls were clad in rough animal hides and were wearing long colourful trousers. Some had painted their faces and others were stark naked. As they halted along the edge of the field Gaius could clearly hear their voices as they lustfully sang their songs of triumph. Behind him the Latin cavalry squadrons remained silent.

'Sir, look, there they are,' his second in command said pointing off to the left. Gaius turned and saw a long line of Gallic cavalry emerging from the treeline. The Gauls urged their horses into the gently sloping fields and halted. Gaius studied them intently. Until today he had never seen a Gaul up close before. The Gallic horse had the same task as he had, namely to protect their armies flank. As he stared at the enemy he noticed the white human skulls dangling across some of the horses' breasts. Others had fixed human skulls onto the end of their spears. Catching sight of the Romans the Gauls roared and raised their spears in the air. Gaius grunted. These riders knew what they were doing. They looked like veterans. They must be the men who had destroyed a Roman legion near Clusium earlier in the year.

'All squadrons are in position Sir,' a decurion cried as he came galloping up to Gaius and his small staff.

Gaius acknowledged the officer and turned to look to his right where the gently rolling countryside opened up into fields. The thousands of Roman and Latin infantrymen of Publius's army stood drawn up ready for battle in their Triplex Acies formation. Their oval shields rested against their legs. The three lines of Maniples stretched away until they vanished from view over a hill a mile away. The sun glinted and reflected off the men's armour and shields and in the rearmost line the Triarii, carrying their long hastae thrusting spears, had knelt on one knee as was their custom. Here and there a Maniple was still moving into position but the bulk of the legions were already facing the enemy. Verrens would be in there somewhere Gaius thought. Last night the centurion had come to find him and thank him for his promotion and for once Verrens had seemed truly lost for words.

The mournful blaring of a Carnyx shattered the relative calm. It was followed by another and then another. Gaius's horse snorted nervously at the sound of the Gallic war trumpets. The noise of the Gallic songs drifted across the fields but the Roman and Latin ranks remained silent. Gaius turned to stare at the enemy. So, the Gauls were to face his adopted father. That must mean that Fabius was facing the Samnites. He glanced again to his right, hoping somehow to get a glimpse of the whole battle line but the hills obstructed his view. He would have to rely on messengers and trumpet signals if he wanted to know what was happening to Fabius's army. He glanced at Tullus and his friend gave him a tense little smile. Having the Volscian beside him suddenly seemed to give Gaius fresh courage. Tullus would watch his back.

A breeze started to pick up and Gaius felt the cool air on his cheek. What was his father planning to do? Publius had not revealed his strategy to him. He had no idea how the Consul intended to defeat the Gauls. All he could do was wait and carry out his orders when they came.

'Have any of you fought against Gauls before?' Gaius said turning to his staff.

'I have Sir,' one of the trumpeteers replied, 'I was with Fabius when we crossed the Ciminian forest. They are big powerful men and at their fiercest and most dangerous at the start but if you stand up to them they will soon tire. They cannot handle fighting in the heat and their weapons are heavy but of wretched quality.'

Gaius nodded. To his right the last Roman Maniples had taken up their positions and across the fields the Gauls had at last fallen silent. The two armies did not move and the tens of thousands of heavily armed men on both sides could do nothing but stare at each other. Time passed and still no orders came and no one moved. Gaius could see the Gallic cavalry massed ahead of him. Their horses looked tense and nervous. Then he blinked in surprise. To his left a hind had appeared. The animal was running for its life for it was being chased by a mountain wolf. The hind bounded into the fields that separated the two armies and then, as if suddenly becoming aware of the thousands of men, it veered sharply towards the Gallic line whilst the wolf peeled off towards the Roman Maniples. Mesmerized Gaius stared at the strange unexpected sight. The hind seeing no way through the solid Gallic line swerved and bounded along the front desperately seeking an avenue of escape. Then a Gaul ran forwards and with one well-placed throw he brought the animal down with his spear. A great roar of approval rose from the Gallic ranks. On the Roman side the wolf had streaked through the gaps between the Maniples and Gaius quickly lost sight of the beast.

'This is how flight and bloodshed will go,' Gaius said turning to his staff, 'You see the beast sacred to Diana lying dead, while here the wolf of Mars is the winner, unhurt and untouched, to remind us of the race of Mars and of our founder!'

The men who heard him growled in approval. The noise had hardly died down when trumpets rang out all along the Roman line. To their right the Roman and Latin Hastati lifted their shields from the ground and started to advance on the enemy. The rhythmic thud of the Roman spears banging upon their shields sent flocks of birds fleeing from the distant forests.

Gaius stared at the advancing Maniples. The order for the cavalry to attack had not come. To his right the Roman and Latin Hastati companies closed with the Gauls. Then when they were ten yards apart the Romans flung their spears at the enemy, drew their swords and with a loud cry, they charged. The two lines met in a crunch of screaming, stabbing men that recoiled and met again in a frenzy of stabbing, slashing, blocking and shoving. Shrieks and screams erupted all along the line but it was immediately clear that the Gauls were not giving an inch. Gaius calmed his breathing. What was his father trying to do? Surely he didn't expect to force the Gauls from the field with the very first attack? Another trumpet rang out and Gaius gasped as he saw the Roman second line Maniples, the Principes lift their shields from the ground and advance in support of their colleagues. Publius was throwing everything he had at the Gauls.

In front of him the Gallic cavalry stirred restlessly. The masses of wild looking Celtic horsemen were eying their opponents warily as the infantry battle began to intensify. Gaius bit his lip. He wasn't going to repeat the mistake that Centho had made at Tifernus. He had to wait until he heard the order. Time passed and to his right the shrieking bloody infantry battle had begun increasingly to look like a stalemate. The Gauls were packed too closely together and had formed an impenetrable shield wall, which repulsed one Roman assault after the other. Gaius could see that the Princeps companies were already heavily engaged. Only the Triarii, resting on one knee had not yet moved forwards.

A sudden trumpet blast made his heart leap. He recognised that signal.

'That was the order for us to attack Sir,' one of the trumpeteers said hastily. Gaius did not answer. He turned to his staff.

'Sound the order to advance,' Gaius snapped, 'We will walk. Then on my command we charge.'

The trumpeteer raised his tuba to his mouth and the noise from the trumpet blared out across the fields. Gaius gripped his spear and urged his horse forwards and behind him he heard the youthful cavalry squadrons start to follow. Slowly the Latin cavalry began to close the distance with their Gallic opponents. The Roman horsemen remained silent but from the Gallic lines a great roar rose as the enemy horsemen moved forwards to meet the Roman attack. The distance between the two forces closed rapidly. Then Gaius shouted at his trumpeteer and a moment later the signal to charge reverberated across the fields. With a loud cry the Latin horsemen urged their horses into a gallop straight at the Gaul's. Gaius heard himself shouting as he charged forwards. A big Gaul, naked from the waist up came charging towards him and Gaius flung his spear straight into the man's exposed chest. The weapon struck the Gaul and knocked him clean off his horse and his body disappeared in the melee of charging horsemen. Gaius ripped his long cavalry sword from its scabbard as he narrowly avoided crashing headlong into an enemy rider. All around him the two surging cavalry forces met in a confused tangle of screaming men and beasts. A horse collapsed next to Gaius flinging its rider to the ground. Men were screaming in agony and terror. A Gaul swung his heavy long sword at Gaius and he caught the blow on his small round shield.

'Drive them back, drive them back,' Gaius roared.

A giant of a man wielding a spear came at Gaius with a roar but before he could throw his weapon Tullus impaled him with his spear and the warrior slid off his horse. Wildly Gaius stared around him. The shock of the Latin cavalry charge was driving the Gauls back towards their own lines. He gasped. They were winning. They were driving these northern savages back. All around him the youthful Latin nobles were gaining the upper hand. Gaius turned to look at the Gallic lines. The gaps left by the cavalry were being filled up with a line of spearman. Was the enemy trying to lure him onto a line of spearpoints? He growled in irritation.

'Retreat and reform the line, reform the line,' he screamed. A few moments later he heard his trumpeteer ringing out his signal. The Gallic cavalry too was retreating towards their own men. Gaius wheeled his horse round and rode back towards his own lines. The long line of Latin cavalry had heard the order and most obeyed but here and there tangled knots of fighting continued.

'Sound the order again,' Gaius yelled at his trumpeteer. Once more the trumpet rang out. The decurions were screaming at their men as they moved as fast as they could to get them back into some kind of formation. Gaius wiped the sweat from his forehead and stared at the fields littered with the dead and wounded. Riderless horses were cantering away in every direction.

'Tribune, what is this, why did you give the order to retreat?' an angry voice suddenly boomed.

Gaius turned and looked shocked as he saw Publius, the Consul riding towards him followed by his staff and lictors.

'The enemy were trying to lure my men onto their spearpoints,' he cried, 'We would have been massacred if we had charged into those spearmen Sir.'

Publius sneered and stared at the Gallic cavalry across the fields.

'I ordered you to attack and that is what you will do Gaius,' Publius shouted. 'Order your men to attack again and this time rout them.'

Irritably Gaius twisted round to stare at the Gallic lines. Then he turned back to his adopted father and with a resigned look he nodded.

'Trumpeteer, sound the order to advance,' he cried.

Gaius gave his father a hard look as he turned his horse to face the enemy. Then as the trumpet rang out he cried out and joined the surging mass of Latin horsemen as they advanced out into the fields. The Gauls had seen the movement and were once again advancing to meet the Roman attack.

'Charge!' Gaius screamed as they closed with the enemy and a moment later the thunder of hooves seemed to shake the very earth. Gaius glanced sideways and in the briefest of seconds he caught a glimpse of Publius. The Consul had joined the attack. His adopted father caught his eye and Gaius thought he saw a sudden smile of pride on the man's face. Then his attention was wrenched back towards the enemy. The two cavalry lines met in a screaming thud and in a split moment riders were impaled on spears or toppled from their horses. Gaius's horse rose on two legs and kicked at another horse. Gaius clung on as the beast righted itself. Beside him one of his trumpeteers screamed as a Gallic sword cut the man's arm off in a single blow. Gaius jabbed at a Gaul with his sword but his attack was blocked by the man's shield.

'Drive them back, for the love of Jupiter and Diana, drive them back,' he roared. A Gallic horseman tried to get at Gaius but his path was blocked by Tullus, who parried the man's attack with his shield. A Carnyx bellowed in defiance. Gaius stared around him. The Gallic cavalry were once more being driven back. His young Latin nobles were gaining the upper hand.

'Kill them, drive them back,' he roared. Another Gaul with a huge moustache and clad in black leather armour tried to get at him but one of the Consul's lictors stabbed the man in the back and with a shriek the Gaul tumbled from his horse. Slowly the Gallic cavalry started to give way. Then within a few moments the gradual retreat turned into a rout as the enemy horse fled back towards their own lines. The Latin cavalry surged after them crying out in triumph. Gaius galloped across the field as the first of his men ploughed into the Gallic infantry formations. The air was rent with screams and shrieks as men and beasts tumbled to the ground. Gaius bit his lip furiously. This was madness. His men were never going to force those spearmen from their position. Not with a frontal attack, but it was too late now. A Gallic spearman roared and jumped forwards and plunged his spear into the horse of one of the riders ahead of him and both man and beast crashed to the ground. Here and there the Latin nobles had managed to force a way through but Gaius could see that if was not going to be enough to rout the enemy infantry. The cavalrymen suddenly looked horribly isolated and vulnerable. Wildly Gaius searched for his father but he couldn't see the Consul anywhere.

Up ahead and all along the line wild confusion reigned as the Latin cavalry attempted to overrun the Gallic positions. Then to his left Gaius caught sight of a something that made him groan in horror. A line of Gallic chariots was bearing down on his flank. The fiercesome chariots with their unfamiliar noise and spear-armed occupants crashed into the Roman line and kept on coming. Shrieks of terror and panic broke out amongst the Latin cavalry. Gaius opened his mouth and closed it again. He had never seen such vehicles before and their unexpected assault was causing havoc amongst his men.

'Sound the retreat, we must reform' he screamed at his trumpeteer but there was no answer from the mass of struggling yelling men around him. 'Fuck,' Gaius roared as he saw the inevitable start to happen. The Latin cavalry unable to break the Gallic infantry line in front of them and unable to meet the Gallic chariots had started to break and flee towards their own lines. The panic rapidly spread along the entire line and with a roar of frustration Gaius turned and joined them. He had to restore order and reform the line but the disorder amongst his men seemed to great and he'd lost his signallers. From the Gallic ranks a great triumphant roar rose as the closely packed infantry set off in pursuit of the fleeing Roman cavalry. Gaius screamed at his men but no one was listening to him. As he retreated he saw that the chariots had started to drive his fleeing men into the ranks of the Roman infantry companies. Gaius groaned as he saw the chaos his panic-stricken men were causing amongst the infantry. Gallic chariots were trampling over anyone in their path, cutting swathes through the densely packed infantry and his own horsemen were scattering and disordering the Maniples. Here and there a company standard had started to retreat.

'Where are you fleeing to?' a voice was screaming amongst the chaos. 'Do you think you will be safe if you run away? Come back and fight you cowards!'

Gaius blinked as he recognised Publius's voice. The Consul and a few of his lictors were vainly trying to rally the Latin cavalry.

Gaius spurred his horse towards the group. Publius saw him coming and there was a sudden fierce glow in the Consul's eyes. Then he undid his red mantle and flung it to the ground. Gaius swore in shock as underneath his cloak he saw that his father had been wearing a purple edged toga in the Gabine manner, which allowed for free movement of his arms. As he looked on Publius tore off his helmet and veiled his head before turning to Marcus Livius, the Pontifex Maximus, the High Priest of Rome who was at his side.

'I cannot lose this battle. The time has come old friend,' Publius cried, 'The time has come for me to offer the legions of the enemy and myself as victims to the gods of the underworld. It is my turn to honour the destiny of my house. Speak the sacred prayer, quickly before they are upon us and all is lost.'

Livius was breathing heavily and he was bleeding from a cut to his face. He hesitated briefly but it was clear to Gaius that the priest had been prepared for this moment. Then Livius raised his voice and began to speak and Publius repeated his words and as the ritualistic prayer tumbled from his mouth Gaius felt his body grow cold. His father was preparing himself, Publius was preparing to devote himself like his father had done before him. The Consul was about to sacrifice himself in battle in order to save his army. For a moment Gaius wanted to cry out, to prevent what was happening but something held him back. His father had been preparing for this day for some time he suddenly realised.

Livius finished speaking and smiled at Publius with sudden fierce emotion.

Publius turned to stare at the Gallic infantry and chariots, which were rapidly approaching and forcing everything before them into wild panic fuelled flight.

'I shall drive before me,' the Consul muttered darkly, 'dread and defeat, slaughter and bloodshed, the wrath of the gods above and below and I shall pollute with a deadly curse the standards and arms of the enemy so that the place where I shall perish, shall be the place where the enemy will meet their destruction.'

'Father,' Gaius groaned.

Publius turned to look at Gaius and there was a sudden gentle smile on his face.

"I am sorry, I should have listened to you,' Publius said. 'I am proud of you Gaius. You should know that always. Honour me.'

Then before Gaius could say another word Publius raised his spear in the air and charged straight towards the advancing Gauls. Gaius cried out but his cry was lost in the terrible din of battle. The Consuls mad charge however did not go unnoticed by the fleeing Latin cavalry and here and there men cried out as Publius charged through their ranks towards the enemy. Gaius caught a last glimpse of his adopted father as he thundered straight towards a Gallic spear band. Then his view was obstructed by the retreating Latin riders.

There was no time to dwell on what had just happened. All around him the remnants of his squadrons were fleeing for their lives. Gaius felt a hot flush spreading across his cheeks. He turned on the Pontifex Maximus.

'Tell the men,' he yelled, 'Tell them that their Consul, my father, has devoted himself and the enemy army to the gods of the underworld. Tell them that we cannot now lose the battle. Tell them to reform and stop running.'

Livius was breathing rapidly. He looked at Gaius with large eyes. Then he nodded. Gaius urged his horse forwards and galloped off into the midst of his retreating men. A rider was suddenly at his side. It was Tullus. The Volscian was bleeding from a cut across his arm. There was a grim look on his face.

'Reform, reform,' Gaius screamed at the fleeing horsemen, 'Rome has won the day, the Gauls belong to mother earth and the gods of the underworld. The Consul is carrying them off into the underworld.'

Here and there a rider slowed and turned to stare at him. Then a decurion was repeating the orders. Gaius slowed his horse and turned to stare at the enemy. Around him more and more fleeing men were slowing and turning to face the advancing Gauls. The news of the Consul's devotion was spreading rapidly and with it the Romans seemed to have gained renewed hope and self-belief. Gaius was breathing rapidly. His men were far too disordered to renew their attack but maybe, just maybe they would be able to bring the enemy advance to a halt and restore the line. That was the best he could hope for now.

Across the fields the Gauls seemed to have run out of energy. The Gallic infantry that had routed the Latin cavalry seemed to have stopped advancing and some of the Gauls were throwing their spears without purpose or aim. Others appeared stupified unable to fight or flee. The enemy too must have learned of the Consul's devotio. Gaius glanced to his left and right. The harsh cries of the surviving decurions were audible as they cursed and screamed at their men to turn and face the enemy. As Gaius stared to his right where the infantry battle was still raging a blood smeared and wounded horseman galloped towards him. The man saluted. Blood was pouring down his face from a head wound. It was his trumpeteer. A few moments later his second in command still holding his standard came racing towards him.

'Sir,'the bloodied trumpeteer gasped, 'What are your orders?'

'The men should reform and hold their position,' Gaius snapped. 'We are going to hold them here. I am done with retreating.'

The signaller nodded and his trumpet rang out across the battlefield.

Gaius took the standard from his fellow tribune's hands and started towards the Gauls. Around him the remnants of the Latin cavalry started to move with him. They looked pitifully few in numbers. The Gallic chariots and cavalry however looked equally depleted and as the Romans started to restore their line they showed no appetite for continuing their attacks.

Gaius was shouting at his men when far off to his right beyond the hills that blocked his view he heard the great roar of thousands of men. All the men around him heard it and for a moment all eyes turned to look in the direction from which the noise had come. Something had happened in the battle between Fabius and the Samnites but it was impossible to know what. To his right the Triarii of the four Roman and Latin legions had joined the battle. The army that had belonged to Publius had committed all its reserves but the Gallic line was holding.

The minutes passed and as they did the din of the hand-to-hand combat to his right did not cease. The infantry companies of Publius's army must have taken frightful losses Gaius thought but the men were holding. The bloody stalemate had turned into an endurance contest.

'Gaius,' Tullus suddenly cried out, 'look, look over there.'

The Volscian was pointing towards the rear of the Gallic line. Then Gaius saw what he was looking at. Streaking across the open fields were hundreds and hundreds of horsemen. Gaius stirred in disbelief. Then he recognised the Standard that one of the riders was carrying and he opened his mouth.

'They are Campanians, that is the Campanian horse.'

The Gauls too had seen the sudden threat posed to their rear but they were too late. The Campanian horsemen came crashing into the rear of the struggling infantry formations and in a few moment's everything turned to chaos. Attacked from the front and from behind, the Gauls broke en masse but there was nowhere to run to. As the desperate enemy scattered Gaius heard a trumpet ringing out and saw company after company of Roman infantry appearing in the Gallic rear. The riders around him were shouting for joy at the sight. Fabius must have routed the Samnites and sent his men to attack the Gauls in the rear. The desperate Gallic infantry were fleeing for their lives now but they were caught between two lines of infantry. The battle was about to become a massacre. In front of him the Gallic cavalry, seeing the fate of their comrades turned and started to gallop away. It was the moment Gaius had been waiting for.

'After them,' he roared, 'kill them, kill them all.'

The cavalry troopers needed no trumpet signal to tell them what to do. They surged forwards shouting and yelling and set off in pursuit of the fleeing enemy. Gaius held on to his standard and galloped towards the Campanian battle standard. Around him the horsemen were cutting the fleeing enemy infantry down as they ran. The shrieks and screams of terrified men could be heard across the battlefield.

Gaius pulled up close to the tight knot of riders who clustered around Calavius their commander. The aged warrior squinted as he saw Gaius.

'Where are the Samnites?' Gaius cried.

'We routed them,' Calavius growled proudly, 'They are fleeing back to their camp. Fabius is pursuing them. He sent us to help you. Is it true that the Consul is dead?'

Gaius nodded. Then he raised his standard high in the air and galloped off after his men. Behind him the screaming frenzied massacre of the Gauls began to intensify as Fabius's Roman infantry companies closed the circle that had formed around the remaining tightly packed Gallic formations, which had refused to flee.

Gaius could see that his men were never going to catch up with the Gallic cavalry. The enemy were riding for their lives. They were going to get away. Well let them he thought. They could do no more harm.

375

'To the Samnite camp,' he bellowed, 'To the Samnite camp. Follow me, follow your standard.'

***

Egnatius stood with his back against the earth rampart of his own fort. The Romans had trapped him against the wall of his own camp. All was lost; his men had broken and were fleeing for their lives. The crushing disappointment made him blush. Death was not far away now but he didn't fear it. He had lived his whole life surrounded by death. Around him the thousands of desperate Samnites were thronging the entrance to their camp but the gates were too narrow to let them all in at once. The warriors were terrified and panic stricken. Fabius's Legions were hacking his men to pieces as they milled about in confusion. All order and thoughts of resistance seemed to have ceased. As he stared at the bloody carnage Egnatius saw groups of Samnites trying to surrender only to be killed where they stood. That decided it he thought, the Romans were not taking any prisoners. They would not take him alive. He would die like he had always imagined he would, with a sword in his hand. That had always been his fate, ever since as an eighteen-year-old he'd crossed the Hellespont with his King, Alexander.

A small group of Samnites were still valiantly fighting to protect their standard but their numbers were dwindling rapidly as the Romans hurled volley after volley of spears at them. The screams and shrieks of terrified men filled the afternoon. Close by a spear smacked into the rampart and beside him a man groaned and fell to his knees with a spear sticking out of his chest. Egnatius stared at his enemy who were cutting their way towards him and the bitterness of defeat suddenly threatened to overwhelm him. That had been the story of his life, he had failed in everything he'd ever done and this battle was no exception.

'Egnatius, Egnatius,' the cries suddenly rose from the Roman ranks. The enemy had recognised him; they had finally spotted him. It would not be long now before they reached him.

376

'Egnatius,' the Romans shouted. 'Egnatius.'

The enemy soldiers suddenly seemed desperate to be the first to reach him. In front of him the last of the Samnites tried to defend their general as best as they could but the men were cut down one by one, their bodies tumbling into the V shaped ditch that ran alongside the ramparts. The ditch was already filled with corpses. Egnatius looked up at the sky and muttered a short prayer. Then above the din and roar of the bloodbath around him he heard another voice screaming his name. He stared at the advancing Romans and his eyes fixed on a young man on horseback. Egnatius grunted in disbelief. It was Gaius, the young Roman whose life he'd spared all those years ago. The young man was pointing his spear at him and was yelling something but Egnatius could not hear what. For a moment, he caught Gaius's eye. Then Egnatius smiled. Maybe not everything he'd done in his life was destined to end in failure and as the realisation came to him he sensed the bitterness that had lain on him for so long lift and vanish. The boy had made it. The boy had survived. He took a step forwards and raised his sword and cried out.

'Long live ancient Samnium, Long live the Lords of the Mountains.'

With a wild triumphant yell a Roman soldier thrust his spear into Egnatius and the Samnite leader fell to the ground.

***

It was dusk and the cries of the wounded could still be heard in the cool evening air. The battle was over. Gaius and Tullus picked their way across the fields where they had fought only a few hours before. The dead and the slain horses littered the ground as far as the eye could see and a bloody gore of human entrails, hacked off limbs, decapitated heads and discarded weapons, helmets, shields and battle standards lay scattered amongst the thousands of corpses. Tullus was limping from a wound to his leg around which he'd tied a linen cloth. The two of them were silent as they searched for the body of the Consul. At last Gaius sighed and straightened up. It was no use. The heaps of dead Gallic infantry, many of whom had died and fallen on top of each other, were just too numerous and the light was fading. He would try again tomorrow. Across the battlefield he could see groups of Roman and Latin soldiers looting the dead. He gestured for Tullus to follow him and the two of them slowly picked their way back towards the Roman camp. As they approached the camp Gaius could see and smell smoke rising from a huge fire where Fabius had ordered the bodies of the enemy to be burnt lest the corpses led to disease spreading amongst the living. The enemy had been decisively beaten and although the numbers were still being calculated the latest estimate was that twenty-five thousand must have died whilst thousands more had been taken prisoner inside the Samnite camp. As they strode into the camp Gaius thought again about Egnatius. By the time he'd managed to reach him the Roman soldiers had so badly mutilated and disfigured the Samnite general that Gaius had hardly recognised him. He would never know, Gaius had realised, what had possessed his former friend to murder and rape his family but the man had got what he deserved. Gaius sighed wearily. It was time to move on and let the past rest where it belonged he thought. Men could do both evil and good. There was no longer anything to be gained from dwelling on the past. Justice had done its work in the end.

***

The wagon carrying the corpse of Publius Decius Mus rolled and jolted. Gaius accompanied by Tullus strode alongside it holding onto the cart with one hand. It was noon. Fabius had sent a search party to look for the body of the Consul and eventually they had found it underneath a heap of dead Gaul's. A white linen shroud had been placed over the body. As the horses and wagon rolled into the Roman camp Gaius blinked in surprise. A line of fully armed Roman soldiers stood on either side of the gate. Their shields had been placed on the ground and were resting against their feet. At the end, he caught sight of Fabius, clad in his splendid armour and surrounded by a

378

crowd of officers. The Consul was waiting for him to approach. As the wagon entered the camp a centurion bellowed an order and the Roman honour guard saluted smartly. The decurion leading the wagon halted before Fabius and his staff. For a moment, all was silent. Then the old grizzled Consul stepped towards Gaius. There was a humble look on his face.

'Your father was my friend,' he said quietly laying a hand on Gaius's shoulder, 'He was a great man and his loss will be greatly mourned by all of us. I shall give him a funeral with all the honour that he deserves.'

Gaius dipped his head respectfully and nodded his thanks and gratitude. Then Fabius beckoned to someone within the group of assembled officers. The Fetial priest, the same man who Gaius had seen all those years ago in Sora, peeled back the death shroud that lay over the corpse and quickly pulled the rings from the dead Consul's fingers. Then he walked towards Gaius and bowed.

'Here are your father's rings,' the Fetial said gracefully, 'I greet you as the new father of the House of Mus. You are the head of your family now and so you shall do away with your old name and adopt a new one. From now on you shall be known as Publius Decius Mus, after your father's will.'

Gaius felt his cheeks burning. He took the rings from the priest's hands and slipped them onto his fingers. They fitted perfectly.

'I accept my new name,' he said quietly.

The Fetial was studying him closely. Gaius touched the birthmark along his neck.

'I did not save Rome yesterday. I nearly lost the battle for us, Holy Father,' he said, 'The prophecy that you spoke of is just superstition, nothing more.'

The Fetial's expression did not change. 'No,' he said shaking his head, 'Your destiny is still to come.'

Authors notes

The early and mid-Roman Republic has always fascinated me for it was a time when Rome could very well have been erased from history. This was the period of Rome's finest hour when her rustic and civic virtues were at their best. This was also the Roman heroic age when consuls and generals would still engage in single combat. Gaul's, Samnites, Etruscans, Greeks and Carthaginians, all tried to conquer Rome and all failed. To my mind the early and mid-Republican period was the age of Rome's true greatness for the resources of Rome were far more limited than during the Imperial age. The mid-Republic was the time when Rome was defended by a true citizen army whose training, equipment and leadership were far below those of the later professional army but whose spirit, traditions and values, the Mos Maiorum or ancestral customs, would be looked upon by later generations of Romans with great fondness, nostalgia and pride.

In the House of Mus, I have tried to stick as closely as possible to the known history that has been passed down to us by the ancient writers. Livy tells us that at Sentinum the Etruscan and Umbrian armies did indeed march away before the battle. In Arretium, the Cilnii family did really exist and one of their descendants was Gaius Cilnius Maecenas who was to become a close advisor to Augustus. Gellius Egnatius also existed and according to Livy he died at Sentinum, although everything else that I have written about him is fictitious. Livy also tells us in great detail about the devotion of both Publius Decius Mus and his son who bore the same name. Some historians have disputed that these events actually happened and it is of course impossible to know for sure what happened but the stories persist and on balance I have chosen to believe Livy.

Quintus Fabius Maximus Rullianus was the great grandfather of that Fabius who rallied Rome after the great disaster of Cannae.

Devotio: The House of Mus

Printed in Great Britain
by Amazon